HEARTBREAKER HERO

Center Point
Large Print

Also by Susan Page Davis and available from Center Point Large Print:

The Priority Unit
Fort Point
Found Art

This Large Print Book carries the Seal of Approval of N.A.V.H.

HEARTBREAKER HERO:
Eddie's Story

MAINE JUSTICE
• BOOK 4 •

SUSAN PAGE DAVIS

CENTER POINT LARGE PRINT
THORNDIKE, MAINE

This Center Point Large Print edition
is published in the year 2018
by arrangement with the author.

The text of this Large Print edition is unabridged.
In other aspects, this book may vary
from the original edition.
Printed in the United States of America
on permanent paper.
Set in 16-point Times New Roman type.

ISBN: 978-1-68324-852-1

Library of Congress Cataloging-in-Publication Data

Names: Davis, Susan Page, author.
Title: Heartbreaker hero: Eddie's story / Susan Page Davis.
Description: Center Point Large Print edition. | Thorndike, Maine :
    Center Point Large Print, 2018. | Series: Maine justice ; Book 4
Identifiers: LCCN 2018013096 | ISBN 9781683248521
    (hardcover : alk. paper)
Subjects: LCSH: Large type books. | GSAFD: Mystery fiction.
Classification: LCC PS3604.A976 H429 2018 | DDC 813/.6—dc23
LC record available at https://lccn.loc.gov/2018013096

Chapter 1

Saturday, December 25

Leeanne opened the closet and pulled out her parka. Eddie had hopes that the two of them would actually get out the door ahead of the rest of Leeanne's family. As she put on her jacket, his friend Harvey, who was Leeanne's brother-in-law, walked briskly into the kitchen.

"Ed, hold up," Harvey called. "We've got an urgent case."

"Now?" Eddie looked at Leeanne and back at Harvey. "We were leaving."

"Sorry. This one's critical."

"On Christmas?" Leeanne asked.

"Yup." Harvey paused to kiss his wife, Jennifer.

"Don't they have someone on call for this?" she asked.

"We're it."

Eddie sighed and put down Leeanne's suitcase. Sisters Leeanne and Jennifer and their entire large family, including Grandpa Wainthrop, had planned on driving from Portland up to the farmhouse in Skowhegan to spend Christmas Day together. That plan seemed to be on hold, at least for Eddie and Harvey.

Jennifer followed Harvey into the entry. "I'm staying, too," she said.

"You can go with your folks," Harvey told her.

"Nope. We're not going that far from you." Jennifer rubbed her stomach.

Crestfallen, Leeanne unzipped her jacket.

"I'm sorry," Eddie said.

Leeanne shrugged. "You can't help it."

"Got your gear?" Harvey asked Eddie.

"In my truck."

"Good. You drive."

Marilyn Wainthrop came bustling in with an overnight bag and a pillow. She smiled at her daughters. "I think that's the last of it."

Jennifer said, "Mom, Harvey and I can't go. He and Eddie just got called in on a new case."

"Oh, no! How long will it take?"

Eddie tried to smile. "We never know with these things, Mrs. Wainthrop." Harvey was his supervisor, and he'd taken the call, but he hadn't said what kind of case it was. Eddie figured it had to be a homicide, or the department wouldn't sabotage their Christmas like that.

"Well, you come up with us, Jennifer. The guys can follow when they're finished."

"Mom, they probably won't finish today. I'm staying, so I'll be here when Harvey comes home."

"But I wanted so much to get the whole

family together for Christmas! We missed it at Thanksgiving."

"I'm sorry." Jennifer sounded determined. "We were together yesterday for Jeff's wedding, and you got pictures of all six of us kids in the same room at the same time."

Her father came in from the garage and looked at them. "What else needs to go in the van?"

Jennifer broke the news, and her father was noticeably disappointed.

"Look, why don't you all just stay here another day?" Jennifer asked. "We can all be together for Christmas that way."

"But the ham is in Skowhegan, and the gifts are all up there," Marilyn wailed.

While they talked, Harvey prodded Eddie toward the door. Eddie threw Leeanne an apologetic smile. As they went out, Jennifer was saying, "So? What's really important is that the whole family is here. We can come up with something for dinner, and . . ."

As soon as he'd buckled his seatbelt in the truck, Eddie said, "Where to?"

"Fifteen-oh-seven Bingley Lane."

Eddie reached for the ignition and stopped. "We're going to Mike's house?"

"Yeah," Harvey said grimly. "I didn't want to discuss it in front of everyone."

"Oh, man. What's going on?" Eddie asked.

"I'm not sure. Mike said, *'Harvey, it's me. Get*

7

yourself over here fast. My granddaughter just found a d.b. in the back yard.'"

Eddie's jaw dropped. "There's a dead guy in Mike's yard?"

"Just drive, Eddie. Those were his exact words. I don't know any details."

Eddie lowered his snowplow, and they roared out onto the street. Probably Harvey's neighbors would complain about the ridge of snow he left from the driveway halfway across Van Cleeve, but Eddie wasn't going to stop and clean it up. And all he'd been worried about was how to escape without having Leeanne's two younger brothers hitch a ride with them on the drive to George and Marilyn's house in Skowhegan.

He put his strobe light on and drove as fast as he safely could to the police chief's house. Snow had fallen most of the night in southern Maine. Bingley Lane had been plowed sometime in the wee hours, but the pavement now had a couple of inches of snow on it again. The thick cover on the ground muffled sounds, and they glided almost silently toward Mike's place with blue lights flashing.

The police chief's house looked like a greeting card, with snow on the roof and smoke coming out the chimney. Holiday lights strung along the eaves glowed faintly through a layer of powdery snow, and a wreath with a big plaid bow hung on the door.

Someone was wielding a snow blower in the driveway, so Eddie parked at the curb. He grabbed his kit from behind the seat and walked toward the house with Harvey. The guy blowing snow waved and kept working. He looked thirtyish, but Eddie didn't recognize him.

The garage was closed, and a minivan sat outside it, covered with snow about four inches deep. The flakes had stopped falling, but the storm had sure done a job during the night.

Mike came out of the house and walked toward them as he pulled on a parka. When he reached them, the snow blower was far enough down the driveway to let them hear each other over the engine.

"Hi. Thanks for getting here so quick." He nodded at Eddie, showing no surprise that he'd arrived with Harvey. "It's out back. I checked him to make sure he was dead, but I haven't let anyone go out there since."

"What happened?" Harvey asked.

"I don't know." Mike grimaced. "Why today, of all days? Debbie and her family are here, and the rest of the kids are on their way today to spend Christmas with us."

Harvey nodded toward the guy operating the snow blower. "Is that Debbie's husband?"

"Yeah. The kids wanted to go out and play in the snow first thing this morning, so she had them rig up and told them to stay in the back yard. I was just getting coffee, and Kelly comes running in the back door screaming her head off. *'Grandpa! Grandpa! There's a man lying in the snow, and he looks funny!'*"

"What'd you do?" Harvey asked.

"Ran out there and checked him, of course. No pulse, and he's got a layer of snow over him. His coat's red and black. I think she noticed the red first."

"Did you recognize him?"

Mike shook his head. "Couldn't see his face, and I didn't want to disturb the scene."

"Did you call it in?"

He hesitated. "I wanted you as first responder. After I called you, I waited five minutes and then called Com. They're calling the M.E. and sending out a couple of patrolmen. All of Legere's detectives are off today. He said he could call Ron in, but I told him not to."

"Okay," Harvey said. "So, nobody's seen the body but you."

"That's right. Well, me and Kelly and Mickey. I'll stay in the house and wait for you boys to do your thing. I told Debbie and Sharon to keep everyone inside. Elliott offered to blow the driveway so vehicles could get in and out." Mike swore. "How can a guy freeze to death right outside my window and I don't know it?"

"You think he froze to death?" Eddie asked.

10

Mike shrugged. "I guess I'm hoping. I didn't see any obvious wounds."

"We'll take a look," Harvey said.

"Yeah. Go right through that gate." Mike pointed to the opening in the fence that enclosed his back yard.

Harvey laid a hand on the chief's shoulder. "You done good, Mike. Go get another cup of coffee. I'll see you in a few minutes."

"Right." Mike's facial muscles were strained, and he looked every day of his fifty-five years. "I'm so glad you were available, Harv. Thanks."

Harvey nodded and headed for the fence, and Eddie followed. The recent tracks were obvious in the snow. The two children had gone out the back door from the Brownings' kitchen and meandered about, scooping up a little snow here and there. A small scoop shovel and a plastic igloo brick mold lay abandoned ten feet from the door, and a yard to the side, two snow angels completed the Norman Rockwell view.

Mike's tracks cut straight through the children's trail. The smaller footprints stopped a few yards before his, then turned back in a beeline for the house.

Harvey had zeroed in on the body near the fence at the back of the lot. He stood a yard from it, just looking, when Eddie reached his side.

"He hasn't been here all night."

Eddie nodded. Only a half inch or so of snow

11

shrouded the man's form. He had on gloves, the red-and-black jacket Mike had described, dark pants, and pac boots. The hood was flipped up and covered most of his head, which was turned to the side, away from the detectives. From what Eddie could see, he was at least thirty, no older than forty, hadn't shaved in a couple of days, and had fallen in his tracks.

Eddie looked at the fence. It was a nice, textured wooden one that people like Mike bought for privacy. Along the top, the snow tapered into a ridge at least three inches high, but a short distance away, there was a stretch about a yard long with much less snow.

"Look at the top of the fence, Harvey. That's where he climbed over."

Harvey looked. "Possibly. Get pictures now."

Eddie dug out his phone and moved along the fence, taking photos of the undisturbed part and the place he figured the man had crossed the barrier. He looked down at the ground below it. Depressions in the snow had been layered over with new fluff, but not completely filled.

Harvey put on sterile gloves and was searching the man's pockets when Eddie got back to him.

"No I.D." Harvey's phone rang, and he stood to take the call.

"Yeah? Okay, Brad. Thanks." He put the phone away and gave Eddie a sour look. "It's going to be another half hour before the M.E. gets here. Let's see if there's anything under him."

"You sure?"

"Yeah, let's do it."

Eddie crouched to help him lift the body partway, and Harvey patted the ground underneath. He froze for an instant then slowly pulled his hand out. In his grasp was a Smith & Wesson pistol.

"What do you know." Eddie eased the body back into its original position.

"I still don't see any blood," Harvey noted, examining the gun. Eddie took out an evidence bag, and Harvey dropped the pistol inside. "Careful. It's loaded."

A commotion at the gate drew their attention. Mike was talking to two uniformed officers.

"Go tell them not to come in here yet," Harvey said. "I don't want to mess up the snow." Though the flakes had stopped falling, evidence could be lurking beneath the white stuff.

"Do you want them to check with neighbors?"

"Yeah," Harvey said, "And see if someone can get us a metal detector."

Eddie went over to the gate, following his own tracks back as much as possible.

"Hi," he said to patrol officers Elaine Bard and Aaron O'Heir. "The captain says don't come in yet. We need some canvassing done to see if the neighbors saw or heard anything early this morning, say after four o'clock." He was reckoning on the snow that still fell when he cranked out of bed at six. He looked to Mike. "And we could use a metal detector."

"I can get you one," Mike said. "Can you tell me anything yet?"

Eddie nodded. "There was a pistol underneath the body."

"GSW?"

"Not that we can see." A fatal gunshot wound was usually pretty obvious, but this guy was wearing winter clothes, so they couldn't be sure. "It's a Smith & Wesson semi-automatic. And he's got no I.D. on him. They'll have to take prints at the morgue."

"After he thaws out." Mike's eyes narrowed.

"He might not have been there that long," Eddie told him. "There's not much snow on him."

"I noticed that."

Eddie nodded. "And there's a spot on the fence where he might have climbed over. What's behind the fence?"

"A ravine where a stream runs through when there's runoff, then more people's fences."

"So, a greenway in between residential streets?"

Mike shook his head. "Nothing that fancy. Just a gap between the lots, where they preserved the stream. I think it was an inconvenience back when this neighborhood was built."

14

"Okay."

"Do you want us to check the other side of the fence?" Elaine asked.

"I'll probably do that while you chat up the neighbors," Eddie said. He wanted to know for certain they hadn't missed anything, and if someone else took the responsibility, he'd wonder. He was getting as meticulous as Harvey.

He pointed to the fence at the back of the yard. "That's where we speculate he may have entered the yard."

Elaine and Aaron craned their necks, looking through the gate and toward the far fence line.

"Oh, yeah, I see the part with less snow," Aaron said.

"It's about all we've got to start with." Eddie looked at Mike. "Chief, the M.E. won't be here for a while."

"Great. That's what you get on a holiday." Mike sighed. "I'll see if Sharon and Debbie can get the kids out of here for a couple of hours. Is the Maine Mall open today?"

"I don't think so," Elaine said.

"Okay, maybe they can go to the park," Mike said. "But Tommy and Mike Junior and their families will be pulling in soon."

"Just keep them out of the back yard," Eddie said. "I don't see why you can't go ahead with your family dinner."

He walked carefully across the yard, back to

where Harvey was standing, staring down at the body. Sometimes he worked that way, just looking and thinking. Harvey's attention span for thinking was a lot longer than Eddie's. He could sit perfectly still for fifteen or twenty minutes, until Eddie wanted to poke him to make sure he was still breathing. Then all of a sudden, he would stand up and go into high gear with a fully formed plan. It didn't seem natural.

"Find anything else?" Eddie asked.

"Not much in his pockets. Who'd we get?"

Eddie knew he meant the support officers. "O'Heir and Bard."

Harvey grunted. "I'm glad Elaine's okay." She'd been shot a few months earlier and had taken some time off.

"She looks fine," Eddie said. "I sent them out to canvass, and Mike's trying to get a metal detector. What else can we do now?"

"Look at the snow."

Eddie looked. All of it was white.

They stood there, and after a while Eddie looked back at the low spot under the fence, beneath the place where he thought the dead guy had crossed it. The sun was shining now, and that would make the snowpack settle and compact by afternoon. He squinted against the glare.

"Okay, so we're pretty sure he climbed into the yard there." He nodded toward the spot with less snow on top of the boards and the depressions

16

beneath it that could be where the man landed and took a few steps.

"Yeah, that's pretty certain," Harvey said. "I haven't been able to spot any other footprints in the snow except the kids' and ours."

"You think he was alone?"

"Yes."

"So how did he die?" Eddie asked.

"The M.E. can help us out with that." Harvey looked at him. "Why would a man with a gun come into the police chief's back yard alone on a snowy night?"

Eddie shook his head. "That's assuming he knew it was the chief's house. Maybe it was a shortcut, and he was just passing through."

"Chasing someone? Or running away?"

"Maybe." Eddie glanced at the fence. "Guess I need to get around to the other side."

"That's right. And don't climb over."

Mike told Eddie where he could get into the strip between the houses, and he walked down the street half a block to access it. The sidewalk hadn't been cleared, but several people had waded through the snow there. Eddie sighed and plunged off the walkway into virgin snow.

There was no stream at the moment, but a crease in the land showed where it would have been. He tried to be careful, but that was hard in four inches of loose snow. He took his time searching the ravine and the thin woods on each side. A half hour later he was satisfied, but his toes were going numb.

He walked halfway up Mike's block behind the houses and out between two of them where the fences didn't touch. A squad car, a hearse, and two other vehicles were parked at the curb in front of Mike's house, besides Eddie's truck. He went past them and into the back yard.

Harvey stood near the body talking to the medical examiner, and two men stood by with a stretcher, looking none too happy. Their breath made little clouds of vapor, and one of them stamped his feet. Called out to move a body on Christmas Day. Eddie totally sympathized with those guys and their winter of discontent, as Shakespeare would say. His feet were cold, too, and the woman he loved was pining for him. These guys no doubt had stories of their own.

Harvey looked up as he approached. Eddie recognized Dr. McIntyre, one of the M.E.'s who lived in the Portland area. He nodded to Eddie.

"What have you got?" Harvey asked.

"It looks like he went to the fence alone. I could see dimples in the snow where he'd walked, and I followed them back as far as I could. I think he came into the strip behind the fence higher up, off the sidewalk. But as near as I can tell, nobody was with him or following him. I took a few pictures, but . . ." Eddie shook his head.

"Okay," Harvey said.

The dead man lay on his back now, and the snow all around him was disturbed.

"Have you examined the body, Dr. McIntyre?" Eddie asked.

"Yes, and my preliminary findings were few. No obvious cause of death. I'd say he's been dead four or five hours. Until I get him to my table, I can't tell you much more."

"Okay, I guess you might as well take him," Harvey said. "Please call me right away if you find anything unusual."

"Understood." Dr. McIntyre motioned his men to take the body away.

After they'd loaded him and headed for the gate, Harvey said, "That man did not die of natural causes. I won't believe that."

If Harvey wouldn't, Eddie wouldn't either, although it would have made their day so much easier. "Then I guess we'd better get back to work."

Mike's sons, Tommy and Mike Junior, had arrived with their families, and they wanted an update after the hearse left. Mike was restless, but he knew he should keep out of it, unlike Harvey, who was right in the middle of the investigation when someone got shot at his house. That had cost him, and everyone in the unit had learned from it.

The family's biggest headache was keeping the

kids distracted. Mike Junior had a twelve-year-old daughter, and the two children who had found the body were Debbie's. Tommy was twenty-five and married, but had no kids yet.

The metal detector arrived, courtesy of day sergeant Brad Lyons, and Harvey and Eddie made a thorough search of the area where the body was found and all along the fence. For nothing, as it turned out, except to be sure they hadn't missed something. O'Heir and Bard reported that none of the neighbors had seen any prowlers or noticed anything unusual the night before or that morning. Harvey sent them back to the station and told them he'd call if they were needed again.

They went to the back door, stomped the snow off their boots, and knocked. Mike opened it.

"I don't think we can do much more here," Harvey said.

Mike nodded. "You boys might as well go home. You probably won't get anything out of the M.E. until Monday."

"Maybe not," Harvey said.

Mike sighed. "It's the darnedest thing."

"I agree." Harvey looked over his shoulder at the back yard. "Nothing pops out at me as to why he was out there, let alone why he died out there."

"Okay. You boys did what you could, and I appreciate it."

"Mike," Harvey said. "You know we'll get to the bottom of this."

Mike smiled. "Of course you will."

"I'll stay in town in case something breaks on this."

"Sorry to ask that of you." Mike frowned, but Eddie knew he wouldn't tell them to go ahead and run off to Skowhegan. His family's space had been violated, and he wanted his best detectives close by.

"Call me anytime," Harvey said.

"I will."

In the truck, Eddie turned the heater on full blast. "What's the plan for the rest of the weekend?"

Harvey sighed. "We really can't do anything until we get an I.D., but we definitely need to stay in town."

"Right. Maybe his prints are on that gun," Eddie said. "We could run them through IAFIS." It was a computerized—or "automated"—fingerprint identification system.

"Yeah, maybe," Harvey said. "If we could get one good print."

Eddie knew that was anything but a lead pipe cinch. The gun had fallen in the snow beneath the body. "It's worth a try."

"Okay. We need to be at the dinner table, though, or Jennifer and her mother will be very disappointed. Let's take the evidence to the station and go back after dinner. I'm game if you are." He looked at Eddie with his eyebrows arched.

"Sure." Eddie started the engine. "Maybe I should go to my folks' and make my mother's day. I'd rather go to your house, though."

"She doesn't even know you're still in Portland," Harvey said.

"Yeah, but . . ." Eddie tried to forget the phone conversation he'd had with his mother early that morning. She was upset about him not being with his own family on Christmas, but that was only the top item on her long list of complaints.

"Call her later and ask if you can take Leeanne over for dessert," Harvey suggested.

"Maybe." Eddie scowled, thinking about the dead man. "This whole thing at Mike's is ridiculous. Who would dare to climb into the chief's yard and die?"

Harvey gave him a mirthless smile. "I don't think he planned it that way, Eddie."

"I know. So, what *was* he planning?"

Chapter 2

Leeanne folded the green linen napkins meticulously into geometric shapes. They were supposed to stand up and look like a bishop's crown, but even with printed instructions she'd found online, it took her four tries to get one right.

Jennifer, meanwhile, fussed with the centerpiece, a big bowl of pinecones and Christmas ornaments, while their sister Abby and their mom held sway in the kitchen.

"How disappointed do you think Mom is?" Leeanne asked.

"On a scale of one to ten, maybe a seven." The entire Wainthrop clan had gathered in Portland the day before for their older brother Jeff's wedding, which had gone beautifully. Jeff and his bride were now off on their honeymoon at an unknown destination. It was their mother who had persuaded them all to move the celebration an hour and a half to the north for Christmas dinner at the family home. She had been planning the festivities for weeks. Jennifer smiled. "She's feeling a lot better since I opened the freezer this morning and gave her carte blanche for the rest of their visit."

"Personally, I never understood why she likes

cooking so much," Leeanne said. "Do you really think Harvey and Eddie will get home for dinner?"

"It's possible." Jennifer stood back to survey the table they'd set up in the dining room. "Looks good. Want some help with those?"

The house phone rang, and she hurried into the kitchen to grab it. She returned a minute later, smiling. "They're both coming. They'll be here in fifteen minutes."

The day suddenly looked a whole lot brighter. Already Leeanne could see that her fledgling relationship with Eddie would be at the mercy of his unpredictable schedule. She accepted her sister's help with the napkins, and they had just finished folding them when Harvey breezed in with Eddie close behind.

"Hi," her mother called out. "Are you boys hungry?"

"Starved," Eddie said.

Harvey sought out Jennifer. "Hey, gorgeous." He kissed her.

"Do you have to go back?" Jennifer asked.

"Eddie and I might run to the office later for a little while. Other than that, it depends on if the medical examiner calls, and I doubt he'll forgo his Christmas dinner to do an autopsy." He looked at the vacant spot where the kitchen table usually sat.

"It's in the dining room, of all places," Jennifer

said. They'd never used the dining room to eat in, but had turned it into a shared study. "It was the one place we could seat everyone at once, so we put two tables in there."

"Maybe we need a dining room after all?" Harvey asked.

"I hope not, because then we'd need a study."

Abby walked past them carrying a large bowl of mashed potatoes. "So it was a homicide."

"Had to be that or terrorists to get these two out on a holiday," Jennifer said.

Meanwhile, Leeanne had just stood there, watching Eddie. He smiled at her, and she felt self-conscious. Eddie was devastatingly hand-some. He had to be smart, or he wouldn't hold down a detective's job in the police department's hotshot unit. And his personality—that was what made her heart flip every time he entered a room. She knew he was popular. Everywhere he went, he had friends or made new ones. People flocked to talk to him. His nature was the opposite of her own cautious reserve. How could a guy like him like her?

"How'd your morning go?" he asked.

"Good. I'm surprised you got back so early." It was nearly one o'clock, but still.

Eddie's smile broadened. "I guess we were lucky today. We ran out of clues to investigate."

"How will you solve the case, if you don't have any clues?"

"The autopsy will tell us a lot. Once we have an I.D., we'll get some info."

"You don't know who the victim is?" Leeanne frowned. "Does that happen a lot?"

"Usually they have some I.D. on them, or someone nearby knows who they are. This guy was all alone, from the look of things."

Her mom headed for the dining room carrying a platter of fried chicken pieces.

"Leeanne, would you please call the others? We're ready to sit down. And Eddie, you can wash up in the hall bath."

"Thanks, Mrs. Wainthrop." Eddie winked at Leeanne and headed off to hang up his coat and wash.

Leeanne stepped into the living room. Her father, Grandpa, and her younger brothers were watching a football game. "Time to eat."

It was a squeeze, getting them all around the one long table made of two pushed together, but her mother insisted they all eat at the same table for Christmas dinner. Leeanne had made place cards for all of them: Grandpa, George and Marilyn, Harvey, Eddie, and the five Wainthrop siblings: Jennifer, Abby, Leeanne, Travis, and Randy. Only Jeff was missing, but he had the best of reasons for that. She settled in between Eddie and Randy.

Lacking a ham or a turkey, they had raided Jennifer's stockpile for entrees and come up with oven-fried chicken, stuffed pork chops, and baked salmon filets.

Harvey looked over the spread. "I guess we've got something for everyone."

"That's right," her mom said. "There's no excuse for anyone to go hungry." She had made breadsticks, and they'd found several frozen vegetables. Dessert would be no problem—they had a third of Jeff and Beth's wedding cake left from last night's reception.

Harvey asked the blessing, and they all began to eat and talk. Laughter filled the conversation, along with speculation about how the honeymooners were doing.

"I hope they're having a blast, wherever they are," Abby said.

"Jeff said they needed passports," Randy said. "Would they be there already?" Trust their youngest brother to do the math, even when it included time zones.

"Depends on where they were headed, I guess," Harvey said.

Leeanne hoped Jeff and Beth would have the time of their lives. Jeff had surprised them all by falling so hard and fast for Beth Bradley, Jennifer's former roommate.

"I thought the wedding went off pretty well," Abby said.

"Yeah," Eddie said. "Without a hitch. Well, except Jeff and Beth getting hitched."

"Wasn't it lovely?" Marilyn brought the coffeepot over and topped off his coffee. "Beth was just beautiful."

Things had moved quickly on a lot of fronts this year. Jennifer had met Harvey and married him, and Abby and Jeff had both moved to Portland to work. Abby was living with Jennifer and Harvey temporarily and holding down a nursing job at Maine Medical Center, while Jeff had landed a spot on the Portland Fire Department. Jeff's wedding was the latest stir to the mix.

Odd, how the family had regrouped. Leeanne supposed Abby would be next to settle down. She'd had several dates since she came to the city, and she had two somewhat regular male admirers at the moment.

When he tasted the chicken, Eddie smiled at Leeanne. "Did you help make this?"

"Yeah, we girls all acted as Mom's sous chefs."

"That's nice. It's very good."

"Thanks."

"I'm feeling a little guilty," Eddie confessed in a whisper. "I probably could have made it to my folks' without being too late, but I'd rather be here."

"Should you call them?" Leeanne asked.

"Maybe later. Hey, you want some broccoli?" He held the serving dish up for her.

"Thanks." She took some and noticed he hadn't put any on his own plate. "You want some?"

28

"I try never to eat broccoli," he whispered, sober as a judge. Then he smiled, as if they had a really important secret, and she almost laughed out loud. Eddie was older than her by almost eight years, and sometimes he seemed very mature. At other moments, he acted like an overgrown kid.

"I hate oysters myself," she said.

"Good thing Jennifer didn't have any of those in her freezer."

He had the most gorgeous brown eyes. Her stomach fluttered as she remembered the last time he had kissed her. He'd driven up to Skowhegan to spend a day with her, and they'd gone out to dinner and a play at Lakewood Theater in Madison. Before he took her home, they'd stopped for milkshakes, and he'd kissed her thoroughly.

That was a kiss she would remember for the rest of her life. It was so different from the few kisses she'd shared with boys before. The kiss of a man who knew what he wanted—but not in a bad way. She'd never for an instant felt he was trying to seduce her. That moment was a life changer for Leeanne.

He's kissed a million other girls, she told herself. Did they all feel this way? She hoped not. But how could they help it?

Jennifer had warned her last summer that Eddie had been considered wild when he was younger, and that he'd dated a lot. But her older sister and

Harvey both admitted Eddie had changed over the last six months. He trusted in Christ now—he'd become a believer even before Leeanne had. And Harvey had said that now Eddie was trying to do things right. He loved Eddie like a younger brother, that was obvious. So what was there to be afraid of?

When the meal was over, there was talk of singing Christmas carols and playing table games, something Jennifer and Harvey loved. It sounded very cozy and fun to Eddie. He wished his own family would get along so well when they were all together.

But Harvey said, "Eddie and I need to run over to the station for a couple hours."

Jennifer's smile drooped. "Do you have to?"

"We need to check a few things, but unless something major turns up, we'll be back by five o'clock."

"Okay."

She looked tired. Her mom and sisters were helping her, but Eddie had the impression—largely from things Harvey said—that pregnant women needed extra rest. Eddie was still getting used to the idea of Jennifer having a baby, and he wasn't sure he wanted to know too many details. Harvey would be a great dad, though.

Leeanne walked with him to the hallway, where he'd left his jacket.

"I guess we'll see you later," she said.

Eddie smiled at her. "*A bientôt, mon amie.*"

She frowned for a moment, then her face cleared. "See you soon?"

"Very good." Harvey was coming toward them. Eddie gave her hand a quick squeeze.

"Leeanne, make sure Jennifer's not on her feet all afternoon, huh?" Harvey said.

"Sure. I'll make her have a nap."

Eddie went out to his truck with Harvey and drove over to the station. The snow was already melted to about half of what it had been. Hardly anyone was in the foyer of the station, and Sergeant Dan Miles was on the desk.

"You got the short straw, eh?" Harvey asked him.

"Yeah, but I get New Year's Eve off."

Harvey told him what they wanted to do, and Dan logged the dead man's effects out of the evidence locker and opened the lab for them.

Eddie had been lifting fingerprints for years, so he went right to work on that with the dead man's pistol. The only other things Harvey had taken off the body were a few coins and an inhaler. Harvey sat down at a work station with the inhaler.

"There's no prescription label, is there?" Eddie asked.

"No. I'm pretty sure they come in a box."

They worked in silence for several minutes. Eddie was extra careful as he took the clip out

31

of the pistol and emptied the chamber, so he wouldn't blot out any possible fingerprints. There were tools on hand to help him do that.

"I've got a partial on the inhaler," Harvey said.

"How good is it?"

"Not very. You got anything?"

"Hold on." Eddie was still dusting the clip.

Harvey came over to stand beside him.

"Want some?" Eddie asked.

"Sure."

Eddie used the tweezers to push several shells Harvey's way.

A print appeared in the powder Eddie had dusted onto the clip. "Abracadabra."

Harvey leaned in close. "Looks good."

Half an hour later, they had three usable prints off the clip and a couple of the shells inside. Harvey was light years more advanced in computer stuff than Eddie, so he set up the samples on the IAFIS program while Eddie did a routine check on the gun's serial number. He didn't find any concealed weapon permits or records connecting that gun to past crimes.

Harvey leaned back in his chair, watching the computer screen without really seeing it.

"Nothing on the serial number," Eddie said. "What are you thinking?"

He shook his head, but Eddie knew better. Harvey was never not thinking.

"It could take hours," Eddie reminded him.

"Yeah, but I set it to run local prints first."

"Coffee?"

"Yeah, thanks."

Since no one was working in the lab that day except the two of them, there wasn't any coffee in the pot. Eddie went out and got some from the machine in the patrol officers' duty room. He took the two Styrofoam cups back, but when he got to the lab, Harvey was on his feet, putting the shells back in the evidence bag.

"We're done," he said.

"No joke? You got a hit?"

"His name is Kyle Quinlan. He lives in the West End."

Harvey went to one of the computers and logged in, while Eddie closed down the IAFIS program, put everything away, and added information to the tag for the evidence room.

Harvey was printing something when he finished. Eddie walked over to the lab's printer and caught the sheet it kicked out. He deliberately didn't read it on his way back.

"Here you go."

"Thanks." Harvey logged out of the computer and took the paper. "He's thirty-one."

"That's awfully young to die on Christmas."

"Or any other day." Harvey frowned at the paper. "He graduated from Portland High, but I couldn't find that he went on to college."

"A lot of kids don't."

"Yeah."

"Does he have a record?" Eddie asked.

"Unfortunately, yes, hence the fingerprint match. Drugs, small time, and a couple of traffic violations."

"OUI's?"

"Two."

Eddie gritted his teeth. Two impaired driving arrests would pretty much guarantee a suspended license for several years. That would be hard on a guy Quinlan's age.

"Did you find the next of kin?"

"Yeah. He's divorced, so I guess we go to his parents. But I want to see Mike first."

Eddie nodded. "Maybe we should ask Dan on the way out if he's had any missing persons reports."

"It's awfully early," Harvey said. "He just died this morning."

"True. But people worry, you know, on the holidays."

"Yeah."

"What about searching his house?" Eddie asked.

"I put in a warrant request, but we're not likely to get one today."

"Okay, let's go see the chief."

Eddie picked up the coffee cups and handed Harvey one. They stopped at the desk, but Dan said it was pretty quiet. A couple of cars had

34

crashed in North Deering, and there were a lot of fender benders earlier in the day. Two break-ins and a domestic dispute had been reported, but patrol officers were taking care of them.

Eddie drove to Mike's house. Debbie, Sharon, and Mike Junior's wife, Julie, were out in the front yard having a snowball fight with the kids.

"Mike's inside," Sharon called.

"Thanks," Harvey said.

Eddie stooped and made a snowball and lobbed it at her granddaughter, Lexie.

"Hey, you!" The twelve-year-old was hopping mad, or at least she wanted Eddie to think she was. She scrambled for a snowball, and Eddie ran inside after Harvey. Tommy had opened the door.

"Yo, Eddie," he said.

"Hi, Tommy." Eddie had only met Mike's younger son a couple of times, but Tommy was everybody's friend. He took them into the living room, where Mike, Elliott, and Mike Junior were watching a football game. They all looked glutted, but Mike had a can of Moxie in his hand, and his boys were drinking Bud.

"Hey, guys." The chief passed the remote to Mike Junior and lumbered up out of his chair. "Come on in here so we don't disturb the game." He took them into the dining room. "What have you got, Harv?"

"We've I.D.'d the corpse. He's local."

"Oh?" Mike's eyebrows arched. "Anyone I know? I didn't get a good look at his face."

"Maybe. Kyle Quinlan."

Mike went still as the statue of Henry Wadsworth Longfellow downtown. After the space of a breath, he said, "That numbskull."

Chapter 3

"So, you do know him," Harvey said.

Mike walked over to the doorway and yelled, "Hey, Michael, come in here a sec."

Mike Junior sauntered into the dining room.

"Who's winning?" Mike asked.

"Still the Pats."

"You remember Kyle Quinlan?"

"Sure. What about him?" Mike Junior looked at his father's face, then looked at Harvey and Eddie. "Oh, no. You don't mean—Really? Come on, Dad, no."

Mike sighed, shaking his head. "I'm afraid so." He swung around to look at the detectives. "Is this a visual I.D.?"

"Fingerprints on the ammo," Harvey said.

"Ammo?" Mike Junior zeroed in on it. "There was a gun? What are we talking about, Dad?"

"Yes, there was a gun under him," Mike said.

Junior's jaw dropped. "Tell me Kelly and Mickey didn't touch it."

"They didn't touch anything," Mike said. "They came straight to me."

Mike Junior walked over to the table, pulled out a chair, and plunked down into it, looking dazed. After a few seconds, he looked up at his father. "So, do you know what happened?"

"Not yet."

"Was he shot?" Mike Junior looked at Harvey.

"We don't think so," Harvey said. "Was this young man a friend of yours, Michael?"

"Yes—well, no—I mean, he was my friend's kid brother." He rubbed his eyes and then looked up. "Jordy Quinlan. Jordan. We were good friends in high school. Ran track together."

"Do you keep in touch with Jordan?"

"Not much. I see him once in a blue moon, when I come home. In fact, I was thinking of giving him a call and seeing if he would be around tomorrow." Michael swore and pounded the table. "That kid was always a knucklehead. What did he do?"

"We don't know," Harvey said.

"But you'll find out." Mike looked at his son. "Michael, these two guys are the best of the best." That made Eddie feel pretty good, but he tried to look appropriately sober for the occasion. Mike put a hand on Mike Junior's shoulder. "Do you want to go over to the Quinlans' with me?"

Harvey cleared his throat. "I was planning to see the family."

"Of course," Mike said. "You'll have to, officially. I thought Mikey and I might go as friends. But you're in charge of this. If you want to get the official stuff out of the way first, fine." He met Harvey's gaze. "Unless you want me to break it to them?"

"You know his parents personally?" Harvey asked.

"Sure. Lonnie and I went to all the boys' track meets. Jordan was over here half the time, and Michael was at their house the other half. I didn't know Kyle so well. He was two or three years younger—between Michael and my Tommy. But he was always into mischief, I remember that."

"Yeah, he was an idiot," Mike Junior said. "But he was still Jordan's brother. I'll go with you, Dad." He stood up.

Harvey looked at Eddie. "Maybe you should go on over to my house. I could ride over to the Quinlans' with Mike, and he could drop me off at home later."

"Sure," Mike said. "We could go together and only bother them once. You don't mind, do you Eddie?"

Not mind getting out of telling a couple their son was dead? He was happy to let Mike and Harvey handle it.

"That's fine. I'll see you later, Harvey."

"He did most of the work in the lab," Harvey said to Mike.

"Thanks, Eddie." Mike looked into his eyes. "If you want to go along—"

"No, I'm good, Chief." Eddie took a step toward the door.

Tommy appeared and looked in at them. "What's going on, Dad?"

39

Mike sighed. "Come on in, son."

Eddie left. On the way to Van Cleeve Lane, he remembered the possibility of taking Leeanne to his folks'. He wanted very much to introduce her to them. Maybe seeing Mike with his sons had made him a little wistful for his family. He'd ask her what she thought. Maybe she wasn't ready. Harvey and Jennifer were like part of his family now, but Jennifer's large clan could be daunting. Eddie didn't want to scare Leeanne off with his own tribe.

Leeanne met Eddie at the door. Harvey wasn't with him.

"Everything okay?" she asked.

"Yeah." Eddie reached for her hand. She almost pulled away, knowing her mother and brothers would stare at them. She was a private person, and they weren't used to watching her act romantic. But Eddie was different from anyone she'd dated before.

They walked into the kitchen holding hands. Jennifer, Abby, and their mom were making dough for pizza and a salad for supper.

"Hey, Eddie," Jennifer said. "Where's Harvey?"

"He's with Mike. I think it's okay to tell you we identified the body."

"Anyone you know?" Jennifer asked.

Eddie shook his head. "No, but he's local, and the Brownings know the guy's family. Harvey

40

went to their house with the chief. I doubt he'll be more than an hour."

Jennifer nodded somberly as she chopped cucumbers into a big bowl of greens. "That's one part of the job Harvey hates, but lately he's been trying to see it as a way he can minister to the victims' families."

Leeanne looked hesitantly to Jennifer. "We could sit down and pray for them."

"I think Harvey would appreciate that." Jennifer put the bowl in the refrigerator and led Leeanne and Eddie into the sunroom. Nobody prayed very long, but they all asked for strength for Harvey and Mike. Eddie prayed for Mike Junior, too. It seemed he had taken the news hard. Jennifer was almost eloquent in praying for the young man's parents, even though she didn't know their names.

When they were done, Eddie smiled at her. "Thanks. That made me feel part of the family. You know, God's family."

Jennifer returned his smile. "Isn't it a great family to be part of?"

"Yeah."

She patted Leeanne's shoulder and went back to the kitchen.

"You pray with Harvey and Jeff, don't you?" Leeanne asked, looking into his soft brown eyes.

"Yeah, on our running mornings. I feel like I've got brothers, and it's great. I only ever had sisters. But this seemed bigger. I mean, people praying for other people, and then those people pray for even more people, and on and on."

"It's a pretty big family," Leeanne said.

"Yeah."

"So, I guess you guys won't be coming to Skowhegan at all."

"Probably not soon," Eddie said.

"Do you think you'll have to work tomorrow?"

"We might." He cocked his head toward one shoulder. "I was thinking of going over to my folks' house for a few minutes after supper. Would you like to go with me?"

Leeanne fought back the panic that ambushed her. "Sure, I guess. I'd better help Jennifer with the meal now."

"Okay," Eddie said. "You go ahead. I'll go do the man cave thing with your dad and Grandpa."

Leeanne laughed. Eddie seemed as comfortable joining the football crowd as he had praying together. He never seemed nervous. Was it because he was older? Leeanne was already nervous about meeting his parents, and they hadn't even left the house yet. She wished she had half his confidence.

When Harvey returned, he looked tired and sad. Jennifer hugged him and put her hand up to his cheek.

"You okay?"

"Yeah." Harvey kissed her. "Supper about ready?"

"Yes, it is."

They gathered for pizza and salad. There were rumors of pie to be served later. As soon as everyone had eaten and the dishwasher was loaded, Jennifer shooed them all into the living room so the family could open what gifts they had there. Eddie slipped into the study and pulled out his phone. No more procrastinating.

"Pop, it's me. You guys having a good Christmas?"

"Yes. Your sisters are here, where they should be."

Eddie ignored that little jab. "Have a big dinner?"

"Of course. How about you?"

"Well, I'm still in Portland, Pop. Harvey and I got called in for a new case, and we're not going to Skowhegan."

"So why aren't you over here? You still working?"

"No, I thought I'd come for a few minutes. And bring Leeanne. That is, if you don't mind."

"Mind? Mind? We finally get to meet this girl?" Eddie knew the hand his dad wasn't holding the phone with was in the air. "*Viens*! We'll wait on the presents."

"Oh, you don't have to."

43

"Your grandmother is here, and your nieces and nephews. Come on!"

"*J'y serai*," Eddie told him; I'll be there.

He went into the living room. Leeanne had her gift, a blue wool jacket, and was thanking Harvey and Jennifer with a priceless smile.

"Ready?" Eddie asked. She nodded and stood up.

Leeanne was a little overwhelmed by the Thibodeaus. Eddie's sisters, Élise and Monique, looked her over critically. Élise, whom Eddie told her to call Lisa, seemed to come to a decision and kissed her on the cheek, and Monique followed suit. Their mother's embrace nearly smothered her.

"Finally, we meet Leeanne. What a little girl!"

"Okay, Maman," Eddie said. "You're embarrassing her."

"I'm fine." Leeanne gulped. She wasn't that short. She turned to meet his father. He and Eddie's brothers-in-law were less effusive. The kids—five between the two sisters—were noisy, but seemed happy. Most of them slowed down enough to say hi to Leeanne, some exuberantly, but four-year-old Josette, Élise and Ansel's oldest, made a shy little curtsy, which won Leeanne's heart.

Eddie's grandmère had not left her place on the

couch, and he took Leeanne's hand and led her over there.

"*Joyeux Noel, Mémé.*" Eddie kissed her wrinkled cheek. "This is Leeanne."

Mémé looked directly into her eyes and said, "*Alors, comme elle est belle, Edouard.*" Leeanne understood that and blushed a little. Mémé looked sharply at her and said, "*Tu parles français?*"

"*Un peu,*" said Leeanne. She'd had two years of French in high school, but she'd forgotten much of it.

"That's good!" Eddie's mother said. "Most of the French girls don't speak French nowadays." She looked pointedly at her elder daughter, Monique.

"Monique and Wyatt insist on speaking only English in their home," Eddie explained.

Leeanne's French soon reached its limits, and Monique said, "Hey everyone, let's be polite to our guest and speak English."

Eddie's father frowned at Monique. "There's nothing wrong with a little taste of the heritage. You should make those kids bilingual."

"Like you?" Monique asked with a touch of bitterness. "We all know how they punished you if you spoke French in school. You've told us the story a million times."

"They don't have that law anymore," Mr. Thibodeau said with an apologetic glance at Leeanne.

"That's right," Lisa put in. "Nowadays it's chic to speak more than one language in the home."

"Well, our kids are going to be Anglophones." Monique turned away with a scowl.

Leeanne looked hesitantly at Eddie's father. "I haven't heard the story, Mr. Thibodeau. They punished you if you spoke French?"

He waved a hand through the air. "It's an old law, to force all the immigrants to learn English. They made it when our families came down from Canada eighty or a hundred years ago to work in the mills. Maybe it was a good thing, who knows? Teachers weren't allowed to teach in French unless it was a foreign language class."

"It was hard," Mémé said. "The children would come home so confused."

"Yeah," Eddie's father said. "If I had a dollar for every time I had to write, 'I will not speak French at school,' I'd be a rich man."

"They made you write lines?" Leeanne glanced at Eddie, and he nodded.

"One hundred times every time you opened your mouth and French came out," his father said.

"Wow. I'm sorry that happened to you." Leeanne felt the injustice of it. She hadn't seen much prejudice in Skowhegan, but then, Mr. Thibodeau was probably thirty or forty years older than she was. Attitudes changed with the times. She turned to Eddie. "Did they do that to you and your sisters?"

"No. They did away with it before we hit school. Besides, we mostly spoke English by the time we started school."

"But we were still encouraged to speak English only in the classroom," Monique said. "I don't want to set my kids back a generation."

"Hey, enough about the Dark Ages," her mother said. "It's getting late. Let's do the gifts while Eddie's here."

They all sat down in the living room, where the Christmas tree twinkled in a corner. Eddie looked questioningly at Leeanne as they began the gift ceremony, and she smiled to reassure him that she would not be embarrassed. Eddie had told her on the way over that he took his presents over to his parents' house a few days before and left them with his mother. Nothing big, just tokens.

Mémé opened her package from her grandson and cried over the hairbrush and the new picture of Eddie. He leaned close to Leeanne's ear and whispered, "She always cries when I give her anything."

His parents had given him his gifts early because he wasn't supposed to be there that day, but they opened theirs from Eddie. His mother liked the sweater, Leeanne could tell.

His father was harder to read. Eddie watched

anxiously as he opened the box on a new GPS unit.

"That's for your truck," Eddie said.

"Oh."

Leeanne thought Mr. Thibodeau liked it, but she wasn't sure. Maybe he was one of those men who was hard to buy for. He worked in construction, she knew. He probably had all the tools he'd ever need. A GPS seemed a stroke of genius, but Eddie didn't seem certain.

The kids got noisy as they opened their gifts, mostly toys, and tried them out. Eddie gave his sisters scarves, with the gift receipts included. Leeanne wasn't sure if Eddie had meant that as a thoughtful gesture, or if he knew they'd return whatever he got them. He'd chosen rechargeable flashlights for Wyatt and Ansel, which she thought made a lot of sense.

Somewhere in there, Mémé cornered Eddie and questioned him extensively in French. Leeanne couldn't understand most of what they said, except that Eddie seemed to be explaining who she was, and her connection to Harvey.

"I'll tell you everything later," he whispered to Leeanne.

They ate cake and drank coffee, and finally Eddie excused himself and Leeanne in two languages, and they went out to his truck.

"I hope that wasn't too bad," he said, buckling up.

"No, no, it was very . . . interesting."

Eddie laughed. "Yup. That's my family, all right. Interesting. Or is it *intéressant*?" He turned the engine on but didn't put the truck in gear.

Leeanne frowned. "I didn't mean it in a bad way. Do you think they could ever . . . like me?"

"Of course. What's not to like? The question is, could you ever like them?"

She smiled. "I think your family is very lovable. It would just take some getting used to. I didn't realize your home would be so different."

"Different how?"

"Oh, the language mostly, I guess. You seem so . . ."

"Anglicized?" he asked.

She shrugged, not sure how to explain how out of place she had felt.

Eddie said, "Most of the French Mainers are no different from their Anglo-Saxon neighbors. By the third generation the accent is gone, and usually the language is, too. But when the old ones live in the home, that keeps it going, I guess."

"Your grandmother lives here?"

"She always did until last spring. She's in a retirement home now. If she hadn't lived here when we kids were little, we probably wouldn't speak a word of French."

Leeanne nodded. "It's your heritage, like your dad said."

"I suppose so. My grandfather came down

49

from Quebec to work in the mills. He brought my Mémé, and they never went back."

"I like her a lot," said Leeanne. "What happened to your grandfather?"

"Fell off a ladder at work thirty years ago. I never knew him."

He was watching her closely, and Leeanne wondered what he saw. Her pulse careened, and she gave him a soft smile. Was he going to kiss her? After his trip to Skowhegan in November, she hadn't seen him again for six weeks. Phone calls and e-mails had helped them deepen their acquaintance, but they'd lost some ground.

Eddie looked at the house, and she followed his gaze. Monique's oldest boy, David, was standing up on the couch in the living room, staring out the window at them. Eddie moved the gearshift to DRIVE and pulled into the street.

On the way back to Harvey's, he seemed lost in thought. Finally he said, "You know, I got you a present."

"You did?" She smiled. "I got you one, too. It's at Jennifer's."

"Well, yours is in here. Would it be okay if I stopped for a minute to give it to you?"

"I guess so."

He pulled into an empty parking lot, leaving the engine running so they'd stay warm, and leaned over and opened the glove box. He took out a small package and a flashlight.

"Here." He gave her the box and turned on the flashlight, so she could see to open it without turning on the dome light.

She felt a little breathless. Books, candy, and flowers, her mother used to tell her. Nothing too personal until you're engaged—but this box was too small for those. Eddie had probably given other girls personal things before, but she didn't want to know it if he had. She looked up into his eyes. He was watching her anxiously.

He held the flashlight for her, and she untied the ribbon and carefully removed the silver paper. She lifted the lid.

"It's beautiful." She held up a small cross, less than an inch long, on a gold chain. "What's it made of?" She held it closer to the light.

"Jade."

"Oh, Eddie." Her stomach lurched a little. "Thank you. Very much." She lowered the necklace back into the box and put the cover back on it, and tucked the box into her pocket.

Eddie leaned over and put the flashlight away and shut the glove compartment. When he sat up, he lifted his arm over her head and brought it down on her shoulders. Her nerves went into overdrive. He put his left hand up to her cheek. She hesitated, then met him halfway. His kiss was gentle, but purposeful. She slid her hands up around his neck and settled into his warm embrace.

They sat there for a few seconds after the kiss ended, with Eddie's forehead against her temple. She could feel his breathing, and he smelled terrific.

"You're welcome," he whispered at last.

She laughed a little, glad it didn't come out as a giggle. She could see his magical smile by the light from the streetlamps. He squeezed her gently and let her go, then he put the truck into gear and drove to Harvey and Jennifer's house.

Chapter 4

When they got back to the Larson house, the tables had been moved out of the study, and Leeanne's brothers, Travis and Randy, were in there playing computer games. Marilyn nagged at them to go to bed.

"I'm almost done with this level," Travis said, and he kept playing.

George went to the doorway between the kitchen and the study. "You boys quit giving your mother a hard time and get on up to bed!" They reluctantly started shutting the computers down.

"Hi," Marilyn said, as Eddie and Leeanne walked by.

"Hi, Mom," said Leeanne.

"Did you have a good time?"

"Yes, very nice."

They walked into the sunroom, where Abby and Grandpa Wainthrop were playing Scrabble.

"Hey, guys," said Abby.

Grandpa looked up. "You missed the pie."

Leeanne smiled. "It's okay. We had *gâteau*."

"What's that?" Grandpa asked.

"Cake," Abby told him.

"Oh. How do you spell it? Maybe I can make that word with my letters." He started rearranging the tiles on his Scrabble rack.

"We're playing in English, Grandpa," Abby said, "but if you have all those letters, you can spell *gate*."

Eddie guided Leeanne on into the living room, and finally they found Harvey and Jennifer. At some point in the evening, Harvey had changed into jeans and a Harvard T-shirt, and Jennifer was giving him a back rub on the couch. Eddie couldn't even think about the possibility of Leeanne giving him a back rub yet. Yes, marriage definitely had some perks.

"Hi, Eddie," Harvey said lazily. Sometimes Harvey seemed almost hyperactive, especially at work, but Jennifer had a narcotic effect on him.

Leeanne said, "I'm going up and get that thing. I'll be right back."

Eddie nodded, and she went off upstairs.

"How did it go?" asked Jennifer.

Eddie sat down in an armchair. "Well, my parents are not the most tactful people. I think it went pretty well, considering."

"Were they rude to Leeanne?" Harvey asked.

"No, but they weren't exactly comfortable with her yet."

"It will happen in time," Harvey said. "Your folks have always treated me well."

"Sure, they like you." It was true. Eddie's father looked up to Harvey. Maman thought he was a real gentleman, which he was, and Mémé absolutely adored him. She got all coy whenever

Harvey was around and told him that if she ever got arrested she hoped he'd be the one to take her fingerprints so she could hold his hand. Stupid stuff like that.

"You know, Maman has been after me for years to find a nice girl and settle down," he said.

"All mothers do that if their kids get to a certain age without marrying," Jennifer said. "My mom used to ask Jeff all the time when he was going to find himself a wife."

"So you'd think she'd be happy, now that I've found someone I really like, wouldn't you?"

"One might think so," Harvey said cautiously.

"Yeah. She treated Leeanne okay, but I could tell she was thinking, 'No, no, Edouard Jean, not this girl. Find a nice, Catholic, French girl and settle down.' She didn't have to say it out loud. And Monique wasn't much better, even though she thinks she's above the French culture."

"Give them time," Harvey said.

Leeanne came back, and she had a small, rectangular package in her hand. She stood uncertainly before Eddie. The jade cross was hanging around her neck, out over the neck of her red shirt.

Harvey sat up, looking at the package. "Is that Eddie's present?"

"Yes," Leeanne said, blushing. "He gave me this." She bent toward him and Jennifer, holding out the cross.

55

"Oh, nice," said Jennifer.

"Pretty classy." Harvey looked at Eddie with eyebrows raised and an approving nod.

Travis and Randy came in from the study and went stomping up the stairs.

"Goodnight, guys," Harvey said loudly.

They stopped halfway up and looked back.

"Goodnight, Harvey," said Randy.

"Goodnight," said Travis. They went on up, and George strolled in and sat down.

"Maybe you'd like to use my computer for a minute," Harvey said.

Leeanne blinked at him. "Huh?"

But Eddie understood him. "Sure. Come on in here, Leeanne." He stood up and grabbed her hand and took her into the now-empty study.

Harvey and Jennifer's computers and a file cabinet were in there, and tons of bookshelves. Jennifer kept a poster of Harvey on the wall near her desk. He had his old gun drawn, pointing up, and was wearing his Kevlar vest. Eddie smiled every time he saw it, but Harvey found it annoying.

Everyone who saw it said he looked tough or something. Jennifer loved it because the vest had saved his life. Besides which, it was a pretty good picture of him. He wore his most serious look, like he was about to arrest somebody, but would use the Beretta if necessary. Sort of a grim look, but Eddie thought it meant security to Jennifer.

He pulled out Jennifer's desk chair for Leeanne and wheeled Harvey's chair over close and sat down.

She smiled and held out the package. "Here. It's . . . well, I hope it's okay."

Eddie tried to untie the green ribbon, but his fingers were clumsy, so he worked it over a corner of the box and pulled it off, still tied. He tore the paper off slowly. Inside the box was what looked like a leather bracelet, but he could tell it was some technological thing. He looked up at her.

Her forehead was all wrinkly. "It's a fitness band. I thought you might like it when you go running with Jeff and Harvey. It will tell you how many steps you take, and your heartbeat, and all kinds of other things."

"Cool." Eddie sounded stupid to himself. Harvey was right; he needed to increase his vocabulary. He smiled at Leeanne. "I like it a lot. Thanks."

"Really?"

"Yeah. Tony Winfield, my new work partner, has one."

"Does he run?" she asked.

"I don't know. He lifts weights, I think." Anyway, Tony could help him figure out the gadget, and it would give Eddie something to ask about when they were out on some boring surveillance duty.

Leeanne smiled a little, and Eddie wished he could kiss her again, but people were moving around in the kitchen. Leeanne was pretty reserved, and she'd probably die if anyone walked in when he was kissing her.

"So, what do you want to do now?" he asked.

"Let's see what everyone else is up to."

Eddie was a little disappointed. She didn't seem to have gotten to the stage where she wanted to spend every possible second alone with him. But she let him hold her hand as they went back into the living room, and they sat down together on the raised hearth. The fire had burned down to coals by then.

The Scrabble game was over, and Grandpa Wainthrop and George were in there with Harvey and Jennifer.

Grandpa said to Harvey, "So, did you catch the murderer?"

"Not yet," said Harvey. "Kind of a funny case."

"Funny ha-ha, or funny peculiar?" asked Grandpa.

"Peculiar. We don't know for sure that it *was* a murder. But I can't really talk about it." Harvey would talk about it with Jennifer when they were alone, though. He told her everything, but she would never betray a confidence. Maybe someday, Eddie would have that kind of relationship with Leeanne.

"Do you know what Abby got from Greg?" George asked.

"What?" asked Harvey.

George shook his head. "A special delivery truck brought it here today. A dozen roses and an iPod full of romantic music."

"Oh, Dad, a lot of it's classical," said Jennifer.

"Doesn't matter," he said. "It's too expensive. She should send it back."

"What did Peter give her?" Harvey asked.

"A stuffed tiger and a picture of him and the boys," said Jennifer. "He gave it to her last night after the wedding."

"A tiger?" Grandpa said. "What does that mean?"

"Their first date was to the circus," Jennifer explained. "Abby really liked the tigers."

Abby and Marilyn came in through the sunroom doorway.

"Are you talking about me?" asked Abby. She sat down on the arm of the couch by Jennifer, and her mother took the rocking chair.

They sat and talked for a while, and about ten-thirty, George, Marilyn, and Grandpa headed up the stairs. "I should go to bed, too," said Abby. "I'm the one who has to work tomorrow." She said goodnight to all of them and went on up. That left just Harvey, Jennifer, Leeanne and Eddie.

"You want me to leave?" Eddie asked Harvey.

"No. You want *me* to leave?" Harvey looked serious for a second, then started laughing. He squeezed Jennifer. "Just get out of here before midnight, okay? We need to check in at the office in the morning."

"You guys are going to make it to church, aren't you?" asked Jennifer.

"I hope so," Harvey said.

Eddie shifted in his seat. "I was thinking I'd go out to my truck and bring in your presents."

Christmas presents had always been a funny thing between him and Harvey.

A cryptic expression came over Harvey's face. "Sure, Eddie, go ahead. I've got yours right here, too. You skipped out on us earlier."

Eddie got up and went out into the cold night, reflecting on the changes in their relationship. They'd been work partners for over five years. The first Christmas he'd known Harvey, they hadn't been together long. Soon after Eddie went into the Priority Unit, they'd discovered they lived only four blocks from each other and had started carpooling to work. They spent eight hours or more together every day, but they still weren't exactly close by Christmas. Harvey got exasperated with him at times, and Eddie wanted to please him, but he wasn't sure if it was worth the effort.

That first year, Harvey had showed up at Eddie's apartment on Christmas Eve with a six-pack of beer. He'd never been to the apartment before. Eddie thought it was kind of strange. Harvey wasn't his boss exactly, but he was Eddie's senior, and he was responsible for him at work. Eddie had felt he was maintaining a distance on purpose.

But that night, he came with a melancholy air. Eddie wondered if his old partner Chris used to invite Harvey over on Christmas Eve, to spend the evening with his family. Chris had been shot a few years earlier, and between that and his divorce, Harvey had plenty to make him depressed during the holidays. Christmas Day he would go to his sister's house, like Eddie went to his parents', but that night he was definitely at loose ends.

Eddie took him in and split the beer with him and tried to cheer him up a little. Harvey never quite loosened up, but when he left an hour or two later, something had changed between them.

After that, once in a while he'd come over. Eddie could tell when he was really down, and if it was on the weekend, sometimes they'd drink together.

In the spring, Eddie started running as soon as the temperature went above freezing, and he asked Harvey if he wanted to run with him. That was the real beginning of friendship. Monday, Wednesday, and Friday, rain or shine, they went out to run. Half the time they'd eat breakfast together.

The first time Eddie went to Harvey's place for breakfast, he got a shock. Harvey hardly had any furniture.

"How long have you lived here?" He tried to sound casual.

"Fifteen years."

Eddie couldn't believe it. There was no place to sit in the kitchen, and they ate standing up or went into the living room, where Harvey had three chairs and some bookshelves. It was a long time before Harvey told him about his past, and by then he had Eddie's absolute loyalty, and furniture didn't matter.

The second Christmas Eve, he came again. This time it was imported German beer. Eddie had halfway thought he might come, and he had cookies his mother had made ready. Eddie sipped slowly at his drink, and when Harvey reached for his second one, he saw that Eddie had only drunk a third of the bottle.

"What's the matter?"

"Nothing, only I have to drive later," Eddie said.

"You got a date?"

"Yeah."

"When?"

"Eleven o'clock."

Harvey took the cap off his bottle and took a

long drink. "Why do you want to go out with a girl like that?"

"Like what?"

"A cocktail waitress."

"Well—" He was right. She could have been a nurse or a mill worker, getting off at eleven, but she wasn't. Eddie shrugged.

"You gonna stay sober all night?" Harvey asked, "because all I need is a call saying you've crashed and I've got to break in another new partner."

Eddie wasn't helping him throw off his depression that night, but then, Harvey wasn't helping him any, either. He left soon, walking home in the crisp night. His mood put a damper on Eddie's, and Lori, the waitress, was less than enthusiastic when he wouldn't keep up with her drinking. She told Eddie to relax and take a cab home, but he couldn't get past two beers.

When he took her home, she hung around his neck. "Come on in, Eddie."

He said, "No, I guess not. You'd better sleep it off."

He drove himself home very carefully and showed up basically sober at his mother's the next day for dinner.

By the third Christmas, he and Harvey were good friends. Harvey still yelled at him once in a while, when Eddie did something stupid, like let a drug dealer whack him with a wrench when he should have seen it coming. Eddie credited Harvey with saving his life that time. He'd gotten mad earlier, when Eddie got his flashlight out and the batteries were dead, but that didn't stop him from laying out a guy that was about to kill Eddie.

Since then, Eddie had gotten a little smarter, and he no longer scheduled any dates on Christmas Eve. When Harvey dropped him off after work, he said, "Coming over later?"

"Sure," Harvey replied, and drove off in his beat-up old green Ford.

At seven-thirty, he was at the door. No beer this time, but he brought Eddie a rechargeable flashlight. "Keep it in your truck," he said.

"Thanks, Harv." Eddie handed him a high capacity flash drive.

"What's this?"

"Your Christmas present."

He looked at it and said, "Thanks, Eddie. I use a lot of those."

Eddie had beer in the refrigerator, and they had a few.

By the fourth Christmas, they were best friends. Eddie had a lot of respect for Harvey. Finally, he felt Harvey saw him as an equal, not an impetuous kid.

When Harvey hadn't shown up by nine o'clock, Eddie stuffed the box of ammo he'd bought him in his pocket and walked over to his apartment house.

He knocked on the door and waited. Maybe he wasn't there, after all. Maybe he'd gone early to his sister's, without saying so. Eddie knocked again and had started to turn away when the door opened.

Harvey was bleary-eyed. "Hey, Ed."

"Hi. I was . . . worried about you."

"Come on in."

Harvey walked ahead of him into the living room and sat down. Eddie sat down, too, trying not to count the beer bottles.

"You okay, Harv?"

He shook his head and stared at the ceiling.

"I'm not usually this sloshed," he said after a while.

"No, you're not." It struck Eddie that ammunition wasn't the best present for a depressed person.

"Don't know how I'll drive to Hillsboro tomorrow." Harvey sighed. "Shoulda quit and come over to your house."

"How about some coffee?"

"Sure."

Eddie went out to the kitchen and microwaved a cup of water, then stirred instant coffee into it.

"Shouldn't let it get to me." Harvey took a sip, made a face, and took another sip. "It just hits me once in a while, really hard."

Eddie figured he was talking about his ex-wife, Carrie. Harvey had told him some by then. Enough to make Eddie be really careful who he hooked up with.

After two cups of coffee, Harvey went to his room and brought Eddie a book on reloading.

"Pretty funny," Eddie said and brought out the box of ammo. "Of course, you want to be sober when you use that."

"Natch."

The fifth year, Harvey had come at eight o'clock, carrying a six-pack of Pepsi.

"Thought we'd better not have a repeat of last year," he said apologetically.

"Great." Eddie got out the cookies, and they sat and talked. Eddie told him stories about his cousins, and Harvey got to laughing after a while.

Eddie knew him pretty well by then, all of his deepest hurts. He knew Harvey despaired of ever having a family, and that if he thought about that too much he'd go to pieces. He was a man who rarely lost control, but that would do it—thinking about Carrie, and the baby that hadn't made it, and how he was probably going to be alone for the rest of his life.

Eddie had tried to fix him up with women once or twice, thinking he was doing his friend a favor, but Harvey didn't seem to want to try. Eddie got him as far as picking up a couple of girls at Clark's one Friday night, but when it was time to make the move and leave with them, Harvey pulled him aside.

"I just can't do this, Ed." He had a wounded look.

Eddie almost argued but decided it wasn't going to take. He apologized to the girls, told them his buddy wasn't up to a night on the town, and took Harvey home.

So that fifth year, they exchanged presents like normal people. Harvey gave him a nice necktie to wear to court, and he got Harvey a new regulation shoulder holster. He'd seen that the strap on the one Harvey had worn all his detective days was torn nearly through. They drank Pepsi and talked about a stubborn case they had then, and when Harvey got up to leave, Eddie was sorry to see him go.

Now another Christmas had rolled around. Their traditional Christmas Eve rendezvous had been scratched off the schedule by Jeff's wedding, and Eddie had felt unsettled, knowing Harvey's present was still in his truck. He got it and Jennifer's, and one for the two of them, and went back into the house.

Leeanne still sat by the hearth, talking to Jennifer, her left hand fiddling with the jade cross. Her dark hair framed her face, and Eddie felt the pure sweetness of her. Feelings of unworthiness threatened him, and he thought he knew a little bit of how Harvey felt toward Jennifer.

Jennifer sat on the couch with Harvey, her head resting trustingly against his shoulder. He kept his arm around her and smiled at Eddie when he came in with the packages. Was he thinking of Christmases past, the way Eddie was?

He sat down in a chair near Harvey, wishing it was his own house and that he and Leeanne were the happy married couple.

The changes he'd seen in Harvey in the past year were astounding. Last summer, he'd laughed when Eddie said he was a different man, but it was true. He'd fallen in love, he'd beaten his depression, and he'd given up alcohol. The big catalyst was God. From the day he met Jesus Christ, everything changed. He looked the same, only happier. He was Eddie's same best friend, only better. And he'd shown Eddie how to change, too.

Eddie held out the package to him. It was flat and heavy. Harvey looked at it speculatively. To Jennifer, Eddie passed a lighter one.

"Go ahead," Harvey told her.

She opened it and pulled out a blue maternity T-shirt with the words, "Le bébé d'Harvey" on the front. Eddie'd had it printed at the mall. Jennifer was usually pretty conservative. Harvey was, too, but he was so proud of Jennifer, he wanted everyone to know about the baby. Eddie had guessed wearing it in French would make it discreet enough for Jennifer.

She laughed and held it up so Leeanne could see. "Awesome, Eddie! Thanks. I love it."

Harvey grinned. "Pretty cute, Ed." He started in on his wrapping paper. The gift was an old metal advertising sign, with Ted Williams holding a baseball bat and saying, "Make mine Moxie."

"All right," said Harvey. He was into antiques in a minor way, and he liked stuff with local ties. Eddie had seen the sign at a flea market in September and known he wouldn't find anything better if he waited.

"Hang it in the study, by your desk," said Jennifer. She and Eddie were both too young to remember Ted Williams in his heyday, or even the Nissen bread commercials he made when he was older, but Eddie's father loved the guy and had told stories about him.

"This one is really for the baby." Eddie passed Harvey a box about a foot long and eight inches deep.

Abby had clued him in that Jennifer wanted to decorate the nursery with a Noah's ark theme. At the mall, he'd seen a soft sculpture set—the ark that you could open and put the animals inside. Two elephants, two bear cubs, two zebras, two kangaroos, and two fluffy sheep. They were soft and cuddly, perfect for little hands.

"This is wonderful, Eddie." Jennifer picked up one of the sheep and stroked it.

"It's great, Ed," Harvey said. "Thank you." He and Jennifer set the ark up on the coffee table, and it looked better than Eddie remembered. He was glad he'd gotten it.

Jennifer smiled. "It will be perfect in the nursery."

Leeanne had come close when Harvey opened the box, and she helped arrange the animals going into the ark.

"You know, I thought everyone would be disappointed that we couldn't go home this morning," she said, "but I think this has been my best Christmas ever."

"Me too," Jennifer said. "Our first real Christmas."

Eddie hadn't thought about it, but she was right. For all four of them, it was the first time they'd really known its meaning. He slid his arm around Leeanne, and she smiled at him.

"Okay, Ed, you ready for yours?" Harvey asked.

He handed Eddie a small box, and he opened it, not knowing what to expect. Inside, folded in tissue paper, were two tickets. The ice show at the Civic Center, for New Year's Eve. Harvey and Jennifer were watching him, smiling.

"You guys didn't have plans for next Friday night, did you?" Harvey asked.

Eddie held them out to Leeanne. "Will you go?"

"What is it?" She looked close and squealed. "Of course I will!"

"You'll have to stay here this week, I guess," Jennifer told her.

Leeanne jumped up and hugged her, then Harvey. Eddie wished she'd transfer a little of that energy his way.

"Do George and Marilyn know about this?" he asked.

Harvey said, "Not yet, but I think I can fix it. We're always happy to have Leeanne visit, and she has a couple more weeks of vacation before school starts again."

"Let's have some of that leftover wedding cake," said Jennifer. "We have to get rid of it." She and Leeanne got up and went to the kitchen, laying plans on the way for the coming week.

Eddie said, "Thanks, Harv. This is the best present ever. Not just the tickets, I mean, but, well, you know."

"Better than a six-pack?" he asked.

"Much." Eddie laughed. "God has been pretty good to us both this year."

"We were pathetic, weren't we?" His eyes were looking back at the past.

"Yeah." Eddie thought about it for a second. "I guess I was wrong. This isn't the best present. The best present of all is what God's done for us. We *are* different people, aren't we?"

Harvey put his hand on Eddie's shoulder and

71

steered him toward the kitchen and wedding cake and two gorgeous, sober women. Eddie couldn't help drawing the contrast to the night he'd hauled him to Clark's and tried to convince him they were having a good time.

Chapter 5

Sunday, December 26

On Sunday morning, Harvey arrived at Eddie's apartment building to pick him up at seven-thirty. It felt like an ordinary work day.

"Can we search Kyle Quinlan's house today?" he asked.

"Not yet."

A stack of crime scene photos waited on Harvey's desk—prints of the ones Eddie had taken. He'd left his SIM card in the photo lab, so they could make high-resolution prints. Bard and O'Heir had filed electronic reports, and Harvey sat down and started reading while Eddie studied the pictures.

At last Harvey sat back in his chair. "Doesn't add up."

"Maybe it will after we have the autopsy report," Eddie said.

"Maybe."

Harvey was clearly frustrated. Because of the weekend and the holidays, it could be days or even weeks before they got results from the medical examiner. After all, the next weekend would be another holiday blowout. If Harvey could have done one little thing to push them toward solving the case at that moment, he would have.

"I guess we'd better go to church and let the people do their jobs when they come back to work tomorrow," he said.

Eddie slipped into the singles Sunday school class five minutes late. Leeanne and Abby were sitting together. Charlie Emery was sitting beside Abby, but Leeanne had put her purse on the chair next to her, and when Eddie walked quietly toward her, she moved it and smiled up at him.

Harvey had gone into the adult class in the auditorium to find Jennifer. When Sunday school was over, Eddie, Abby, and Leeanne went out there to join them, and Charlie Emery tagged along, keeping Abby talking. He just didn't get it yet. She'd turned him down for dates, but he kept coming back.

The Larsons' pew was full. George and Marilyn Wainthrop sat beside Jennifer, and next to Harvey were Mike and Sharon Browning.

Mike, the police chief, didn't claim to be a Christian, but his wife certainly was, and Mike had started coming to church with her a few months earlier to humor Sharon, or at least that was the vibe he gave off at the time. Eddie was starting to think he was taking the Bible seriously now.

Travis and Randy came from the teen class and squeezed in next to George, so Eddie took

Leeanne into a pew farther back, next to Rick and Ruthann Bradley. Jeff Wainthrop's bride, Beth, was Rick's sister.

"Have you heard from the honeymooners?" Ruthann asked Leeanne.

"No, not a word," she replied.

Ruthann smiled. "Beth called us last night."

"Where are they?" Eddie asked.

"In Hawaii."

"Wow," said Leeanne. "They really kept it a secret."

Eddie leaned forward and said, "I thought they needed passports."

Ruthann made a face. "I think that was a bit of misinformation Jeff put out."

Leeanne asked, "How are they doing?"

"Sounded like they're having a great time. They hadn't been there long when she called, but she wanted us to know they got there all right."

The pianist started playing, and everyone quit talking. Eddie looked around and saw that Abby had managed to get unstuck from Charlie and was seated in the row with Peter Hobart, between his two young boys.

Watching Leeanne's face, Eddie reached for her hand. She smiled a little, so he kept it. She had on the same dress she had worn to Jeff's wedding, and the jade cross lay against the front. Her hair was loose and curled a little at the ends. She smelled a little like strawberries. Eddie had to force himself to pay attention to Pastor Rowland.

After church, Harvey invited Peter Hobart and his sons to have dinner at their house. He and Jennifer were always inviting people over on Sunday. All of the Wainthrops were still there, so they didn't invite many extras this week.

When they got to the house, Jennifer and her mom were on turbo in the kitchen. Leeanne went to lend a hand, and Eddie helped Harvey move the tables and chairs around.

Jennifer was pretty laid back about company. She believed in paper plates. She kept the meal simple, so her parents could eat quickly and get on the road.

After lunch, the women organized a cleanup crew. Eddie offered to help, but they chased him out, so he escaped with the other men into the living room. Harvey launched a conversation with his father-in-law and Peter, and Eddie gathered he was buying Jennifer a new car for her birthday, which was coming up in mid-January. He got up and wandered into the study.

"Hey, Travis, my man."

"Yo, Eddie."

Eddie sat down in Jennifer's swivel chair. "How's school going?"

Travis rolled his eyes. "It's lame."

"Okay. You've only got a few months left, right? I think you said you're going to UMO in the fall?"

"Yup." He had some kind of castle game open and mostly ignored the intrusion, but Eddie didn't take it personally. He was the same way at Travis's age, only his family couldn't afford a home computer then. Harvey's house had half a dozen of them, since they were one of his and Jennifer's favorite things.

George came to the doorway. "So, Eddie, I kind of expected the death to be on the news this morning, but I didn't hear anything about it."

"That's because of the holiday," Eddie said. "Normally reporters would have gotten to the scene a couple of minutes behind the medical examiner, but everybody was in Christmas mode. Besides, I think Mike tried to keep it quiet."

"He can do that?"

"Not completely, but yeah. There are ways."

George pulled up a chair and asked about the shooting range where Eddie and Harvey went to practice. They'd had to qualify in November with new Heckler & Koch .45s, and he was interested in that.

Harvey came to the doorway and beckoned to Eddie. He got up and followed him to the sunroom. The kids were getting noisy, so Harvey took him into his and Jennifer's bedroom. It was really nice, about three times as big as the bedroom in his old apartment. Eddie had only been in there once, when he helped move some furniture for them.

The former homeowner's wife had used a wheelchair, and the room had been added to the house to accommodate her. It had a handicapped-accessible bathroom and a huge walk-in closet, and the windows came low and overlooked the big back yard. The sleigh bed Eddie had helped Harvey pick out was in there, and the usual dressers, nightstands, and bookcases. Eddie liked to read, but Harvey and Jennifer were fanatics. They had bookshelves everywhere in their house.

"Mr. Quinlan called me," Harvey said. "His son Jordan is over there right now, and he asked if we wanted to talk to him."

"Jordan being the one who was Mike Junior's buddy?"

"That's right."

Eddie nodded. "Couldn't hurt."

"Okay, I'd better stick around until Jennifer's folks go. I think they're pulling out as soon as Marilyn decides she's done in the kitchen."

"What about Leeanne?" Eddie asked. "Can she stay?"

"George is fine with it. I told Leeanne, and she can break it to her mother."

"You don't think Mrs. Wainthrop will mind, do you?"

"Not really, although she's still disappointed that she couldn't get the whole clan up to their house this weekend."

Half an hour later, the Wainthrops drove out without Leeanne. Peter had already left.

"Ready?" Harvey asked.

"Yeah, let's go." Eddie glanced at Leeanne.

"Are you coming back later?" she asked.

"Jennifer's probably tired." Eddie looked tentatively at Harvey.

"She's exhausted, if you want the truth, what with the wedding and all the company."

Eddie nodded. "Well, I'll come back with Harvey, but I should probably go see my folks tonight." He thought it was about time Jennifer didn't have to feed everyone. Abby would go to work at the hospital, but Harvey and Leeanne could look out for themselves.

Leeanne nodded. "Okay. I'll see you later."

Harvey's Explorer was in the driveway, and they took it. "You can hang around here tonight if you want to," Harvey said.

"Thanks. I don't want to wear out my welcome, and besides, like you said, Jennifer deserves some rest. I'll clear out before supper."

"Okay."

The side roads were slushy. Worst case scenario, it would freeze again that night and leave a frozen mess in the roadways.

In ten minutes, they were at the Quinlans' house. Eddie was glad for a chance to talk to Kyle's family without Mike and his son there. Sometimes people opened up more to strangers.

Harvey introduced him to Mr. and Mrs. Quinlan. They were Mike's age—graying, looking forward to retirement, but probably a power couple twenty years ago. They took the detectives into their living room, where Jordan waited. They all looked puffy-eyed and ready to start bawling again any second.

"I'm sorry about your brother," Eddie told Jordan.

Jordan shook hands with him. "Thanks. He was . . . he did a lot of stupid things, you know? But he was still my brother."

"Do you know any more now than you did last night, Captain Larson?" his mother asked.

Harvey shook his head. "Not really. We know the gun hadn't been fired recently, and it carried a full load."

"Kyle never had a gun," Mr. Quinlan said.

"Yes, he did, Dad," Jordan said, and his parents stared at him.

His father frowned. "First I heard about it. A handgun, I mean."

"He's had it a while," Jordan insisted.

"How long?" Eddie asked.

"Five or six years, at least."

"Whatever for?" Mrs. Quinlan asked.

"I don't know," Jordan said. "That was just Kyle. He was always into stuff. When he was in junior high, he thought it was cool to smoke, so he started smoking. Later he had to have a motorbike. Are you really surprised he had a gun?"

"There's no permit on it," Harvey said. "I assume he bought it in a private sale or at a gun show."

"Probably," Jordan said.

"And you have no idea why he wanted it?"

"No. But I don't even know that the one you found is the one he showed me a few years back. For all I know, he's got a dozen of them."

Harvey nodded. "True. It could be a different weapon."

"Why would he go to the chief's house?" Eddie asked.

"No idea."

Harvey said, "You and Mike Browning Junior were very good friends."

Jordan ran a hand through his dark hair. "Yeah. Mike's a good guy. And his parents are the best." He glanced at his mother. "Next to mine, of course. They let me go over there anytime I wanted. The Brownings fed me half the time, and they put up with Mike's and my shenanigans. If I didn't have these two, I'd wish they were my parents."

"So, you knew their house well," Harvey said.

Jordan nodded. "I was in and out of there constantly. I knew every smudge on the wallpaper."

"How about Kyle?" Eddie asked.

"No, he didn't go there much. He ran with

different friends. I think he liked Debbie Browning for a while, but I don't think he ever actually took her out. She was probably smart and said no."

"So, your brother was a bad actor in high school?" Eddie asked, softening it with a smile. He wished the parents weren't hovering.

Jordan shrugged. "Everybody knew he was a cut-up."

Mr. Quinlan said apologetically, "He got in some trouble."

Jordan barked a laugh. "The only reason his class didn't vote him most likely to be arrested was that he'd already been arrested."

"He had a couple of OUI's," Eddie said.

"Yeah, and he started on pot in high school."

Eddie nodded, remembering the drug incidents on Kyle's record.

"You don't think he died because of drugs, do you?" Mr. Quinlan asked. "Maybe he was just taking a shortcut, crossing the Brownings' yard to the next street."

"Carrying a loaded weapon," Eddie said.

The Quinlans all looked at him, and he felt guilty for making the grieving family feel worse.

"We'll know more when the tox screens are finished," Harvey said. "Jordan, is there anything else you can tell us that might help? For instance, who did Kyle hang around with lately?"

"I don't know. I've lived in Berwick for five years

or so. I really don't know who he chums with."

"Girlfriends?" Harvey pressed.

Jordan shook his head. "The last time I talked to him more than five minutes—and that may have been in September—there was a girl named Misty."

"We met her," his mother said. "I wasn't very impressed with her."

"Was he still seeing her?" Harvey asked.

"I think so. Maybe." Jordan didn't meet his eyes, and Eddie thought there was something more there—something he wasn't telling.

"Do you know her last name?" Harvey looked from Mrs. Quinlan to her husband.

"Carver, Carter, something like that," Mr. Quinlan said.

Jordan raised his chin. "Carney."

Mr. Quinlan's brow cleared. "That was it."

Eddie wrote it in his notebook.

"Anyone else you can think of that he might have been close to?" Harvey asked.

Jordan shook his head. "I don't think he was working, was he, Dad?"

"No. I told the captain yesterday, he'd had a job at one of the commercial wharves, but he quit. I don't know how he thought he could pay the rent."

Eddie had some ideas about that, but he didn't volunteer them.

"Okay, we'll see if we can get hold of Misty Carney." Harvey held out one of his cards to Jordan. "In the meantime, if you think of anything else, please don't hesitate to call me."

Jordan took the card and nodded.

Mr. Quinlan walked with them to the door. "The funeral's on Wednesday."

"Even if the body hasn't been released?" Harvey asked.

"Yes. A memorial. My wife doesn't want to put it off."

"I doubt we'll have all the answers by then," Harvey said.

"But you'll keep us posted?"

"Sure. Call my cell phone if you want to, sir. If I've got anything I can share, I will." Over the last six months, Eddie had seen Harvey do that—give his personal number to victims and their families. Not just anyone—not reporters, but people with real needs who might feel they had no one else to turn to for the truth about their case. He never used to give out his private number, but since he became a Christian, he seemed to be taking down some walls.

While he drove home, Eddie asked, "Do you think Jordan was telling you everything?"

"No. You picked up on that?"

"I thought he was a little cautious, even though he told us his brother wasn't perfect. You want me to look up this girl today?"

"Let it ride until tomorrow. We're supposed to be off duty."

They got to the house around three o'clock. Abby's car was gone, since it was time for her to start her shift at the hospital. Jennifer and Leeanne were cuddled up with afghans in the living room, watching *It's a Wonderful Life*. Jennifer hit the pause button when the men walked in.

"How'd it go?"

"All right." Harvey joined her on the sofa.

"Did anyone get their wings lately?" Eddie asked. Jennifer threw a package bow at him, and Leeanne laughed. Eddie walked over to her chair. "How about a walk? I can tell you how that ends."

"I've seen it before. Oh." She realized he was joking and laughed.

"We'll be over at the park," he told Harvey.

It was warmer out than it had been that morning, and Eddie didn't bother to put on his gloves. They went out onto the sidewalk, and he took Leeanne's hand.

"So, your mom didn't mind about you staying down this week?" he asked.

"She's okay with it. Harvey said he and Jennifer will take me home next Sunday."

"Great. This is really great." Eddie looked over to see if she thought it was great, too, but he couldn't read her expression. "So, can I see you every night?"

She laughed. "Are you trying to emulate Harvey?" He was famous in the family for the rush he'd given Jennifer when he met her.

"Harvey is my mentor," Eddie said seriously. She laughed again. Eddie was glad she was catching on to his teasing. "So, I really should go home this evening, but tomorrow night?"

She glanced at him, then looked down. "I'm not sure. Maybe I should ask Harvey and Jennifer. They might have something planned."

"I'll take you someplace," he said. "You want to go out to eat?"

She hesitated. "Let me talk to Jennifer, okay?"

"Okay, sure." She seemed evasive, which wasn't like her. Eddie didn't want to make her uneasy. They walked on. After a minute, he said, "Listen, I just want to spend time with you. If you don't want me to hang around while you're visiting, I won't."

"It's not *that*." She blushed, and he decided he'd better leave it alone.

They headed for the little park at the end of the street. Some kids were building a snow fort.

"Let's make a snowman," Eddie said. They pulled their gloves from their pockets, and soon Leeanne was laughing and rolling a stomach for the snowman. A couple of kids came over to help them, and they made a pretty good statue. The kids brought sticks for his arms and rocks for his eyes and mouth.

On the way home, Eddie took off his soggy gloves and reached for her hand again. Her gloves were all wet, and she took them off and stuck them in her pockets and let him hang on.

"Your hands are freezing." He rubbed her fingers. About halfway back to the house, he said, "Leeanne, I really like you."

She looked at him, then away. "I like you, too."

"Is there anybody else?"

"No." They walked on. When they were almost to the driveway she said, "What about you? Are you seeing anybody down here?"

"No." He hadn't looked at another girl since late October, when he and Harvey had stayed at the Wainthrops' house during a couple of days of training at the Police Academy. That's when Eddie had decided Leeanne was the one he wanted to concentrate on. He'd been up to Skowhegan a couple of times since, and he'd started thinking Leeanne was it for him, for life. Now he realized Harvey had been wise when he'd warned him to take it slowly. Eddie was ready to commit, but he was getting mixed signals from Leeanne.

"So, you want to go to the ice show." Eddie wasn't asking, just making sure.

"I love ice skating," she said. "I'm not very good at it, but I love to watch people who are."

"Good. We'll have fun." He watched her from the corner of his eye, but she didn't look at him. They were almost back to the house. "Everything okay?"

She stopped in the driveway and turned to face him. "Jennifer told me last summer that you . . . had a girlfriend," she said.

So that was it. She'd heard about Sarah. "Not really," Eddie said. "There was somebody, but . . . well, she's not a Christian. I stopped seeing her. It never got really serious." He watched her anxiously, searching for clues to her thought train.

"It's not important," she said, but he could see that to her it *was* important.

"Could we walk around the block?" Eddie asked. "Because I think we need to talk some more."

She opened her mouth, then closed it and looked away. She didn't start walking.

"What else did Jennifer say?" Eddie couldn't imagine her sister saying anything disloyal. He and Jennifer were staunch friends. But something was definitely simmering.

"Nothing much, but Abby said you have this reputation."

Oh, Abby. Eddie didn't say it out loud, but he thought plenty. Should he defend himself? It was true, he'd been a real jackass. For too long. But what did Abby know?

Leeanne finally looked up at him, so he said, "Okay."

"Women she works with talk about you."

That wasn't good.

Chapter 6

Eddie's brain zoomed through the women he'd dated, trying to home in on nurses, like the IAFIS program trying to find a match for a fingerprint from a catalog of thousands. He hadn't dated many nurses.

"Do you want to tell me about it?" he asked.

Leeanne sighed. "I'm not the jealous type, really, but . . ."

Yeah, right. "But what?" Eddie was sweating inside his jacket, but he tried to stay calm. Being nervous with a woman was unusual for him. Leeanne was different from any other girl he'd ever dated, in a good way, but that and the fact that she was Jennifer's sister kept him cautious.

"I think one of them might have dated you in high school," she said.

Eddie sighed and watched a plow truck coming down the street. "I wasn't very smart in high school. And I'm not just talking about grades." He did some more mental tabulating. From the shadowy recesses of his gray matter, a couple of names bounced out. "Are we talking about Denise Rancourt?"

"I don't know her name. But she told Abby you went from girl to girl all the time, and you never went steady with anyone, but you dated just about every girl in your class and the next lower class and broke about a thousand hearts."

Eddie stared at her. She seemed to think that was a very serious charge.

"Okaaaay. Anything else?"

"Well, there was another nurse who said she met you when your sister had a baby and you came to the hospital to visit her. And she went out with you that night."

"Yeah?"

"Yeah. You just chatted her up and asked her out."

"I probably did. I don't remember."

"She, uh . . . said you're a really good kisser."

"Oh, great." Maybe this was one of those conversations it was better not to have, because if she meant the maternity nurse he'd dated after David was born, this could get really messy. He was a beat cop then, and partying hard on the weekends. He was pretty sure it went beyond kissing.

He lifted her chin a little, and she looked into his eyes.

"Listen, Leeanne, I did date a lot of girls. I used to be proud of that. I'm not anymore. I think I probably hurt a lot of people, even though I tried to be nice and not do anything really, really . . . Okay, I did some bad stuff."

He was getting in too deep. He couldn't deny too many things, because he'd done most of them. And he couldn't say what he'd done was right. At the time, he thought it was great, and he was extra cool. He'd had his pick of the single women who worked at the police station, the diner, and a couple of bars he frequented. He could have made time with some of the married ones, too, but that was one line he drew for himself early on. At least he did one thing right.

He gave himself a mental kick in the pants. That was the best thing he could think of that he'd ever done—not dating married women? That was pretty disgusting.

He stepped back. "Maybe we need to think about this."

"How do you mean?"

Her eyes were all shiny, like she might cry, and Eddie hated himself. He wished he could take a Mr. Clean eraser and wipe away all his past relationships, from Madison Smith in sixth grade to Sarah, especially the ones that went too far. But there were so many, it would take a whole bucket of erasers. And there were no relationship erasers.

He sighed and shoved his hands in his pockets. His soggy gloves weren't comforting.

"Why don't you think some more about how you feel? Because it's true I wasn't an angel. If you don't want to go out with me, I could understand that, but it's better for you to decide now."

Her bottom lip quivered. "What if I do want to?"

Relief hit him. He said earnestly, "Then I want you to know, absolutely, that I will be good to you. I won't do anything disrespectful. I want to do things the right way now, which means I want to obey God."

She nodded soberly, and that encouraged him to elaborate a little.

"If you date me, I promise I won't look at another girl again, and I won't be too . . . forward." It seemed like an old-fashioned way to put it, but it also seemed like a word she would understand the way he meant it. "If you ever tell me to back off, I will. And if you want to know anything about my past, I will tell you, but you have to be really sure you want to ask. Because I regret a lot of stuff, and I don't think it helps to hash it over. It's like scratching a sunburn with steel wool."

Harvey had told him once that discretion was the better part of valor, and now Eddie believed it was also the better part of romance.

Tears spilled over and ran down Leeanne's cheeks. "I'm sorry."

"Don't say that." He grabbed her hands. "You have nothing to be sorry about. Look, you're the kind of woman I want. But I'm the kind of guy you should keep clear of. Looking back, I'm not surprised Jennifer and Abby warned you about me. Did you know Harvey told me last summer not to start anything with you?"

"No." Her eyes were huge and teary.

"That was before. He doesn't feel that way now. But it's true I had a lot of girlfriends. But I only got involved if they knew what they were getting into. Does that make sense to you?"

She nodded slowly, but he wasn't sure. He also wasn't sure he wanted to be more explicit about it.

"Abby said you brought a girl here on a date a couple of months ago." Her voice caught.

"That's true. It was a girl from the church. Rachel Trueworthy. We went to the circus with Harvey and Jennifer. It was fun. She's a very nice person, and you'd probably like her. But I didn't kiss her, and I didn't fall in love with her. And I haven't asked her out again, because I decided I liked you better than any of the other girls I've met—women, I mean—" He stopped and shook his head. At the police station, they came down hard on guys who called the female officers and dispatchers "girls." It was too much to process right now. "Come on, let's go in."

She walked with him in silence. Harvey was watching the end of the movie with Jennifer.

"Hi," he said when they went in.

Leeanne mumbled "Hi," and went over to the stairs and out of sight.

Harvey sat up straight, and Jennifer hit the mute button.

"What's up, Ed?" Harvey asked.

"Nothing." Eddie stretched. "Maybe I ought to go home."

Harvey got up and steered him into the sun-room.

"Something wrong?"

Eddie eyed him thoughtfully. "Leeanne seems to be concerned about my past love life."

Harvey was silent for a moment, then he said, "Well, you've dated a ton of women. More than most guys have. Me, for instance."

Eddie knew Harvey hadn't been a slouch in his college days, but he said, "You were socially challenged."

"True. But you—"

"What?"

Harvey raised one hand, as if in apology for saying it. "You practically invented flirting, Eddie."

That hit hard. "I'm a friendly person."

"Yes, you are. Especially with women."

"But I'm a gentleman."

His eyebrows went up. "Sometimes you were a little wild."

"Not anymore."

"No, I'm very happy with the way you're turning out." He put his hand on Eddie's shoulder. "You're growing up, Eddie. On January first, you'll be the senior detective in the Priority Unit. I'll be putting a lot of responsibility on you."

"And you don't have any reservations about me dating Leeanne anymore, right?"

"Right. Just take it slow. You haven't been too aggressive, have you?" He looked a little anxious.

"I don't think so."

"You don't sound sure. Maybe you'd better back off a little."

Eddie sighed. "You set it up so she'll be here all week, then you tell me to back off."

"Only if she needs you to. You've got to go by her feelings, Eddie, not yours."

"Oh, have you got a Wainthrop Woman Emotion Meter in your pocket?"

He smiled. "Jenny mostly gives me a reading loud and clear. She's not the kind that keeps you guessing."

"Well, Leeanne's got me tied up in knots. And I blame Blabby Abby for that."

"Abby?" Harvey frowned.

"Apparently she's been talking about me at work with a couple of women I used to date."

"Oh, boy. I'm guessing that's not good."

"Worse than that. At least, with one of them. The other one I take it was from high school, and I don't think she would hold anything against me."

"Are you sure? High school girls can be brutal."

Eddie sighed. "Yeah. Well, I never—" He looked at Harvey and groaned. "No decent woman is ever going to want to date me, let alone marry me."

"That's not true."

"Yeah? What happened to everyone loving the dangerous bad boy?"

"It works when you *are* the dangerous bad boy. But you've reformed, and you're in a rough spot. You don't want to play with the bad girls anymore, and the good girls are still leery."

"They won't have anything to do with me."

"Not true. I happen to know you've been out with several very nice young women with high standards over the last few months. Look, you're upset. Stay and have some coffee with me. We'll sort this out."

"I promised my mother I'd eat over there tonight."

"Okay." Harvey peered at him closely. "You sure you're all right?"

"Yeah, thanks. I'm better than I was. Do you think I'm too old for her?"

"The older you both get, the less that will matter." Harvey eyed him for a moment. "Aside from the fact that she's beautiful and she's a lovely person, what attracted you to Leeanne?"

Eddie blinked at him. "Seriously?"

"Yes. Why Leeanne, and not someone else?"

Eddie could tell this was an important question, so he gave it his full attention. "I like the way she thinks. And she cares about the same things I do. Oh, not writing and goats and stuff, but . . .

well, she wants to get the truth out. I think that's why she's studying journalism, because she thinks it's important that the people writing the news are careful and truthful. And you know she'll do her work well. And she cares about people."

"Okay."

"There's probably more stuff," Eddie said.

"That's a good start. Do you want us to talk to Leeanne?"

"Only if she wants to."

"All right."

"I'm not sure if I'll make it to church tonight. Are we running in the morning?"

Harvey walked over and checked the indoor-outdoor thermometer on the bookcase. "The temp's dropping. Meet me at the track."

Eddie drove to his parents' house and tried to settle his mind before he went inside. Walking through their door would mean a different kind of turmoil. He pulled in a deep breath and got out of the truck.

"Well, look who's here," Pop said, as if he hadn't seen Eddie in years.

"About time." Maman came over and kissed him.

His sisters and their families were there again, and the meal was noisy. Ansel and Lisa had been watching the news, and Ansel turned the TV down but not off. Mémé pumped Eddie for more information about his *petite amie,* as she referred to Leeanne. He didn't wax very eloquent. If he and Leeanne quit dating, Mémé would still ask about her for a year.

Ansel called, "Hey, Eddie?"

"What?" Ansel nodded at the TV. A reporter was just closing out a statement.

Eddie said, "I missed it."

"The police chief," Ansel said. "They found a dead body in his back yard."

"How about that?"

Everybody stared at the TV.

"Did you know about that?" his father asked.

"I mighta heard something."

They let it go, and Eddie was surprised but relieved. He wondered who had told the press. Probably Ryan Toothaker found out. He was a smart, ambitious reporter for the *Press Herald*, and he came to the station just about every day to read the police log. He'd probably gone in that morning just for drill and got a bonus. Once news got out, it was everywhere. Poor Mike. He'd probably have to field a million calls tonight.

Maman had made tourtière, a sort of pork pie, which was one of Eddie's favorites. He ate a lot and turned down several offers of beer. Everyone else except the kids and Lisa were drinking. She was pregnant again. Mémé had a glass of wine. Eddie had told them all he'd quit drinking, but they refused to accept his explanations. He'd gotten to where he just said no thanks. This would probably go on for the rest of his life.

They sat around talking after supper was over, and his pop lit a cigarette.

"Put that out," Monique said. "Lisa's pregnant."

His father swore and went outside to smoke.

"You shouldn't throw a man out of his own house," Maman said.

"Oh, what are you going to do, make Lisa leave?" Monique was scowly, and her husband, Wyatt, was staying out of her way. He played with the kids, with their Christmas toys. Lisa's husband, Ansel, turned the TV up again and kept putting back the beer.

Eddie wasn't enjoying himself, but he tried to stay calm and talk to everybody. Pop came back inside complaining about the cold and reeking of smoke.

"So what are you working on now, Pop?" Eddie asked. Winter was a slow time in that climate for construction workers.

"We're drywalling a new wing on a bank downtown."

"Terrific." Eddie knew he hated working with sheetrock.

His father opened the refrigerator. "You want a beer?"

"No thanks, Pop."

He frowned and stared into the fridge. "What happened to all the beer?"

"It's probably all gone," Maman said.

Lisa made a furious face at Ansel. Pop swore.

"Paul, *ne jure pas*," Mémé said. Like telling Pop not to swear would do any good.

"I will if I want to."

"Paul, don't speak to your mother that way," Maman said.

Pop's face was going purple.

"So, Edouard, did you go to the Christmas Mass?" Mémé asked.

Eddie hesitated. There wasn't a right answer, so he'd better just face it head-on. "Uh, no, Mémé, I didn't."

His grandmother shook her head. "You missed the Christmas Mass?"

His mother turned her scowl on him. "Not even going to Mass on Christmas Day. I don't understand it."

"I told you I had to work yesterday."

"But if you hadn't worked, you'd have gone to Leeanne's parents' house. Do they go to Christmas Mass?"

"No, but we all went to church this morning."

His mother shook her head. "My son. Father Claude asked about you, and I didn't know what to say."

It was tough being the oldest, and the only boy. His family had expectations.

"You haven't been to confession for six months, Eddie." That was another familiar line coming from his mother.

"You just don't understand, Maman. I confess different now."

"Oh, I know, I know. You pray to God without the saints, and you confess without the priest. You told me."

His father glared at him. "You shouldn't upset your mother. Going to church one time out of the year wouldn't kill you."

Pop ought to know, Eddie thought. Christmas and Easter were about it, so far as his father was concerned.

His grandmother said, "Hush, now. I'll light another candle for you, Edouard Jean Thibodeau."

Eddie stood up. "I've got to get going. Great meal, Maman."

"What? You're leaving?" she asked as if in shock. "You've only been here an hour. I thought you were spending the evening with us."

"Two hours, almost, and I'm going to church. That's what you wanted, right? You can even come with me."

"To that Protestant church?" Her lip curled.

Lisa said, "Leave him alone, Maman. He goes to church more now than he ever did before. That should make you happy."

That surprised Eddie, and he whispered, "Thanks."

Lisa nodded, as though that was what sisters did for you.

"What's it like?" Mémé asked. "Do they have a shrine for the Virgin?"

"No, Mémé."

His grandmother shook her head.

Regret stabbed Eddie, and he sat down beside her.

"I'm not going there to upset you, Mémé."

"Then why *do* you go there?"

"Because I think it's right. But that doesn't mean I don't love you all."

Mémé just smiled sadly.

His mother put a plate with an éclair in his hand, and Eddie stayed another two minutes to eat it. Pop found a warm six-pack in the cellarway, took one, and shoved the rest into the fridge after a dark glance at Ansel.

Eddie was a little late to the service, but there was a spot for him beside Leeanne. He still couldn't get a meter reading on her. Eddie had no idea what she was thinking or feeling. She was very quiet, and her face was serious. He didn't try to hold her hand during church. He kept shooting up prayers in his head, asking God to not let him blow it again.

Afterward, he asked Harvey and Jennifer if they wanted to go out for a milkshake. He wasn't at all hungry. It was just a social thing.

"Why don't you and Leeanne go?" suggested Jennifer.

He looked at Leeanne.

She shrugged a little and smiled. "Okay."

While Leeanne put on her jacket, Harvey pulled him aside. "Drive carefully, and don't come back until you've talked this reputation thing out. And remember, Eddie, don't ever leave a woman crying."

"Is there a rule like that for women, too?"

"Yes, they're not allowed to ever leave a man bewildered."

"I hope someone told Leeanne that," Eddie said.

She walked out into the parking lot with him, and he opened the truck door. He drove carefully and tried to decide how to approach the topic in question.

"Look, I meant what I said earlier. I really like you, and there isn't anybody else in the picture." He turned in at the Burger King.

She smiled a little. "That's good, Eddie. I'm glad. I wasn't trying to pry into your private life."

The funny thing was, he didn't care if she did want to know about his private life. His present private life, anyway. He wanted very much to share the present and the future with her.

He parked the truck, and they went inside and ordered. When they were sitting across from each other with their milkshakes, he asked, "So, is there anything else we need to talk about?"

She looked embarrassed. "No, I—it was just that, after we went to Fort Point, Jennifer told me—I guess that was a long time ago."

"It sure was." Five or six months. It seemed years. "Look, I'm sure Jennifer was trying to be a good big sister then, but I really think she'd give you a different message now."

Leeanne looked up at him. Blue eyes, dark chestnut hair, a smooth, white forehead. Her cheekbones were high like Jennifer's.

"I talked to her after you left today," she said. "Her and Harvey. You're right. I was wrong to pull up what she said last summer and try to make it fit with what Abby said this weekend."

"Yeah, well . . ." Eddie considered slamming Abby, but decided that wouldn't help his cause. "Let's try to forget all that, okay?"

"Yeah. I'm sorry I made a major case out of it." Leeanne fiddled with her straw. "I'm not very good at relationships."

"I'm still learning, too, even though I used to think I was an expert." Eddie reached over and took her hand. "Let's give this one some time."

She nodded, with a gaze that told him it would be worth the painful moments.

He took her back to Harvey's. The lights were on in the breezeway and the kitchen, but the rest of the house was dark. Eddie unlocked the door for Leeanne.

"Looks like everyone's turned in. I'll call you tomorrow, if that's okay."

"I'd like that." She put her hand up to his face for a second and then went inside.

Chapter 7

Monday, December 27

Leeanne's phone alarm rang at quarter to six Monday. She scrambled into her sweatpants and T-shirt and went downstairs. Harvey was just emerging from his bedroom, with Jennifer not far behind. They were out the door by six. The university had an indoor track, and the police department had an agreement with the school that allowed officers to use it in off hours. Harvey and Eddie went there to run in the coldest weather.

Leeanne and Harvey were stretching when Eddie arrived. Jennifer sat in the bleachers working on a cross stitch sampler—Noah's ark, for the baby's room. She was wearing the shirt Eddie gave her.

"Hey," Eddie said. "Family day here?"

"What can I tell you?" said Harvey. "She wanted to run."

Leeanne just smiled and kept warming up. Eddie was wearing cutoff sweats and a T-shirt, and he looked pretty good. He dropped his jacket and did a few stretches, and they started out. Harvey and Eddie seemed to know several other men who were running—probably more cops.

Leeanne did six laps and dropped off. She had

run in high school and still kept up a hit-or-miss routine in summer, but she hadn't done much running since the weather turned cold. She sat down next to Jennifer and watched Eddie.

"Did you guys talk last night?" Jennifer asked.

"A little. I think it's okay."

"Eddie will treat you right. I'm banking on it."

"I guess I made more out of his past than I should have." Leeanne sighed.

"It's something you should consider and then pack away." Jennifer smiled and clipped her threads. "Because he really has changed, but there will always be people who won't believe that."

Leeanne watched Eddie as he rounded the far turn on the track. "I don't think I'm the right woman for Eddie. He deserves someone more mature."

"You're getting there."

"Am I? Because I don't think he'll put up with the drama very long. I'm surprised he still wants to take me out on New Year's Eve." Leeanne glanced at her sister. "Of course, he's committed now. I don't suppose he'd break our date for the ice show, even if he wanted to. Because *he's* mature."

"Because he's a gentleman," Jennifer said. "And because he genuinely likes you and wants to be with you that night."

"Do you really think so?" Leeanne pulled

her knees up and folded her arms around them.

"I do." Jennifer patted her back. "He's not pressuring you, is he?"

"No. He's very patient. Most guys probably would have called it quits by now." Tears stung her eyes. "Oh, Jennifer, why is dating so hard?"

"I don't have a good answer for that."

"But you met Harvey, and it was wonderful."

"Not immediately. We went through some angst." Jennifer took a new skein of embroidery floss from her tote bag and cut off a length. "I think part of your problem is that Eddie's a superhero in your mind. He's this dashing, successful detective. You don't know if you can live up to that and be his equal."

Leeanne thought that over. Harvey jogged past, and she waved. "It's not just that. Sometimes I think, how could he even like me? He's dated all these other women, and I'm sure some of them were beautiful and smart. That's what I can't live up to. He has no reason to pick me."

Jennifer stuck her needle in the Aida cloth and laid down her embroidery frame. "You stop that, right now. Honey, you're beautiful. You're smart. And beyond that, Eddie sees something in you that none of those other women had."

"What?" Leeanne wasn't ready to accept her sister's evaluation, but she wanted to hear it anyway.

Jennifer pulled in a big breath. "He's struggling,

just like you are. You're both new believers. You have that in common, and you both want to do what's right. But you're not always sure what that is. Eddie sees your commitment, your desire, your passion. And I'm pretty sure he also sees how kind and loving you are."

Leeanne shook her head. "I don't know."

"You don't have to live up to the women he used to date. If they were his ideal, he would have stuck with one of them. Ever think about that?"

"I guess not. I hope you're right."

Harvey stopped running and walked to cool off. When Eddie caught up with him, he slowed, too.

"Guess they're done," Jennifer said to Leeanne. "Can you carry this bag?"

Eddie left the track and drove home, showered and changed, then beat it for the police station. All the time, he was thinking about Leeanne and how cute she looked in her running clothes. Maybe he should just leave her alone for a year or two, until she had a little more life experience. Or not. She might find someone else and slip out of his reach. He didn't want to lose her. He wished she wasn't quite so serious, but at the same time, he'd hate to see her lose her air of innocence.

As expected, there was no report yet from the medical examiner's office. Harvey called them anyway and was told to be patient. It wasn't like they had nothing to do. Harvey handed out other assignments and detailed Eddie to locate Misty Carney.

In ten minutes, he'd found her on social media. By paying close attention to her posts, he gathered she had a job at a big box store. Eddie called in a few favors from old acquaintances, and by nine-thirty, he'd located her employer, one of the big chains that had three stores within the city limits, in different neighborhoods, and one in most Maine towns of any size. He called the one in Rosemont, then the one in Deering Center, and he hit pay dirt.

Her supervisor, Matt, was cagey about giving out information on an employee, which was good. Eddie told him he was absolutely right to be careful, and to please call the police station and ask for him. Once they got past that hurdle, Eddie had a great conversation with Matt.

In return for Misty's schedule, Eddie answered his questions about the police department's hiring. He told Matt they'd hold a new class at the Academy along about April, and he should put his name in for testing. Eddie knew nothing about him, but he was smart enough to work his way into a management position at the store, so he figured Matt would at least have a chance at getting into the pool of hiring candidates. They'd posted dates for the written entry level exam, and Eddie told him where to look online.

After their conversation, he made a note of the contact. In the detective business, contacts were solid gold, and Eddie knew he could count on Matt if he ever needed information about anything connected to the store chain.

He went to Harvey's desk. The captain was deep into something online, but he hit a few keys and looked up at Eddie.

"I found Misty. She goes in to work at eleven." Eddie told him where.

"Deering. Does she live there?"

"Nope, her current address is closer to home. In fact, it's so close to Kyle Quinlan's home, you might mistake one for the other."

Harvey's eyes went wide, like blue Frisbees. "She was living with Kyle?"

"So it appears. Either that, or he let her put down his address on her job application."

"Let me call the judge's chambers," Harvey said. "We should have had that warrant before this. I'll see if we can pick it up and go over there."

They could, and they did. In less than half an hour, they had the warrant and were parking in front of Kyle's apartment.

A young woman with dark, straight hair and lots of eye makeup opened the door. She had a lipstick in her hand, but she hadn't used it yet. Her black pants and red blouse looked like presentable clothes for a chain store clerk.

"Misty Carney?" Harvey asked.

"Yes."

He and Eddie showed their badges for the usual introductions.

"We need to ask you a few questions about Kyle," Harvey said.

"He's not here."

"When did you last see him?"

She blinked up at him. "Friday night, I think."

"You didn't spend Christmas together?" Harvey asked.

"I went to Saco to spend the weekend with my sister and her family. I assumed Kyle went to his parents' house. Why? Is he in trouble again?"

"May we come in?" Harvey asked.

"Well, uh . . ." She looked over her shoulder. "I was getting ready to go to work."

Eddie held out the warrant, and Harvey took it. "We have a warrant to search the premises."

Her shoulders drooped, and she stepped back. "Okay. Can I finish getting ready?"

"Why don't you just sit down here while I look around the kitchen?" Harvey asked.

She pulled out a chair at the small table. Harvey nodded to Eddie, and Eddie slipped into the next room.

He left the living room for last. He figured the most interesting stuff would be in the bedroom. Pot stash; bongs; other drug paraphernalia. On top of the bureau was a cell phone, and he wondered if it was Kyle's. He dropped it into an evidence bag and pocketed it. Kyle hadn't carried any I.D. on his last jaunt, and there was his wallet, just sitting there. Eddie opened it to be sure. Driver's license, debit card, a picture of Misty, and eleven bucks.

In the bathroom he found some oxycodone—in a sandwich bag, not a prescription bottle, and more in a pill bottle with another person's name on it. Also enough of Misty's makeup to stock a cosmetic counter, along with a few miscellaneous prescriptions that were legal, and over-the-counter meds.

The living room included a drawer full of bills and correspondence. Eddie flipped through them. Kyle and Misty shared a phone plan. The Internet service bill was in her name, but the rent was in his. Eddie picked up a laptop and went into the kitchen.

Harvey was just closing the refrigerator.

"Ms. Carney, do you have your phone on you?" Eddie asked.

Glassy-eyed, she pulled it out of her pants pocket.

"Thank you. And where is Kyle's phone?"

"In the bedroom. I thought it was weird he didn't take it with him. He must have forgotten it."

Eddie looked at Harvey and nodded. Harvey handed him a bag, and he looked into it. Oh, good. More pot and a dozen or so nickel bags.

"Ms. Carney, you'll have to come with us down to the police station," Harvey said.

"What? No. I have to be to work in forty minutes."

"I'll call your supervisor and explain," Eddie said. Matt wouldn't like it, but since he aspired to a career in law enforcement, he would understand.

"But—why? I haven't done anything."

"Drugs," Harvey said.

"What? Those aren't mine. They must be Kyle's."

They always said the stash wasn't theirs. Always. And they expected the cops to believe them and let them go.

"Is this your computer or Kyle's?" Eddie asked.

"Mine."

"Does Kyle have one?"

"No, he used mine or went to the library." She said "used," past tense, but Eddie didn't mention it.

"Do you have any flash drives in the apartment?" She scowled and walked past him into the living room and took one out of a bowl on top of the TV set.

"Any more?" Eddie asked as she dropped it into his hand.

She hesitated, then picked up her purse and opened it. She held out a hot pink one. "You'd better not wreck that. It's got all my pictures on it."

"I won't wreck it." He bagged it with the other one.

Harvey had asked for a backup unit to do a more thorough search of the apartment. A knock came at the door, and he let in Sarah Benoit and Ray Oliver. He gave them quiet instructions.

Ray said, "So, this is where the dead guy—"

Harvey held up a hand. "Let's just keep quiet, okay?"

"Yeah," Ray said.

Eddie was watching Misty. She lowered her eyelids and didn't meet his gaze. She knew about Kyle, all right. But how? Eddie had checked with Harvey Sunday night, and been assured the reporters hadn't put a name to the body Mike had found. They would certainly have to question Misty further.

"Look, I don't want to lose my job," she said.

"I'll call Matt right now."

Her eyes flickered, but she didn't comment about Eddie being on a first-name basis with her supervisor.

Sarah and Ray walked past him. Sarah shot a glance Eddie's way, and he pretty much ignored her. This wasn't the time or the place to chat—and there might never be one.

He stepped away and called Matt. Meanwhile, Harvey searched Misty's purse in her full view. By the time Eddie had advised Matt that Ms.

Carney would not be at work today, she was in official custody and wearing handcuffs. Another marked unit pulled up, and Harvey had the officers take her to the station.

Ray came out of the bedroom. "Hey, Captain, I'm sorry. I thought the woman knew he was dead."

"She did," Eddie said.

Harvey raised his eyebrows. "You sure?"

"Yeah, she did. You booking her?"

"We probably have enough. I'm pretty sure that's cocaine I found in the refrigerator." Harvey looked at Ray. "You and Sarah check every food package in the kitchen. I know it's a pain, but—"

"No probs." Ray held up a sandwich bag with a hundred or so pills in it. "You can add this to your evidence. It was taped underneath a dresser drawer."

It was lunchtime when they got back to the station. Harvey called Jennifer while Eddie tagged the evidence bags they'd brought in. When Harvey hung up, he said, "Lunch at the diner? Jennifer and Leeanne are out shopping, so we'll have some food in the house again."

"Sure," Eddie said. "You guys fed a lot of people last weekend."

They went to the little café down the street. The restaurant put tables outside in warm weather, but in winter their service was limited to inside tables or takeout. The place was jammed with cops that day. Jimmy Cook and Nate Miller, from the Priority Unit, had a booth, and Eddie and Harvey squeezed in with them and two uniformed officers.

"Did you have any luck running down Kyle's friends?" Harvey asked. He had sent Nate and Jimmy to Kyle's neighborhood that morning to talk to neighbors and try to scare up some of his buddies.

"A little," Nate said. "We got a couple of names of guys he hung out with, but we also found a neighbor who saw him leaving his building Saturday morning."

"What time?" Harvey asked.

"Early. It was still dark, but he was sure it was Kyle. Saw him under the security light in the parking lot at the apartment building."

"Was Kyle driving?"

"Nope. Walked off down the street."

"What was the neighbor doing up at all hours?" Eddie asked.

"He said he gets up at five every morning. He's a lab tech at the hospital and has to be in by seven o'clock."

"Good work, Nate," Harvey said. "Put the witness's contact data in your report."

"Will do."

The waitress came over to their booth carrying her order pad.

"Hi, Eddie! What'll you have?"

"Hi, Crystal. Cheeseburger and fries, please."

"You got it." She patted Eddie on the shoulder, and Harvey gave him the look he used to give Eddie when he flirted with witnesses.

"What'll it be today, Captain?" Crystal said, smiling at Harvey.

"A BLT and coffee. Thanks."

"Coming right up."

She walked away, and Eddie made himself not look at her legs below her miniskirt. Harvey was still watching him. Keeping his promises to Leeanne wouldn't be simple. Maybe it wasn't a bad thing to have a watchdog to remind you when you got out of line.

They shot the breeze with Nate and Jimmy. The other two cops left, and Crystal brought their sandwiches. Eddie's plate was heaped up with french fries, about three times as many as normal, and she set a bottle of ketchup beside it.

"What are you up to these days, Eddie?" she asked as she put Harvey's plate on the table.

"Uh, well, we're pretty busy at work."

"Yeah?" She actually winked at him before turning to Nate and Jimmy. "How about you boys? Can I get you anything else?"

Eddie wondered why she could call these grown men boys and get away with it, while if they called women her age girls they got walloped.

"I'm good," Nate said.

"Yeah, me too," Jimmy told her.

"Okay." She picked up their empty plates and looked at Eddie again. "If you need anything, just whistle." She sashayed off.

"Hey, Eddie," Jimmy said with a laugh. "Looks like you're special."

"Yeah." Nate filched one of his fries.

"Don't tell me you used to date her, too," Harvey said with a resigned air.

"Eight months ago. Almost a year. She's B.C."

Nate frowned.

"Before Coastal," Eddie said. He tended to measure everything these days by before and after the espionage case at Coastal Technology the previous year, where Harvey met Jennifer. Of course, dating Crystal was before Christ, too, but Eddie wouldn't joke about that.

Jimmy smiled. "She's still got it bad for you."

"Well, I haven't got it for her." Crystal was cute, but she had no class whatsoever. "I only took her out once, for crying out loud."

Nate and Jimmy headed back to the office, and Eddie picked up the top bread from his cheeseburger and studied the pickles inside.

"Why do you do that?" Harvey asked.

"I got a cricket once."

Harvey shook his head and took a bite from his BLT without inspecting its innards. They ate in silence for a couple of minutes.

"So, you and Leeanne are good now?" Harvey asked.

"I don't know." Eddie scowled. "I wish Abby had kept her nose out of it."

Harvey grunted as he chewed.

"Things were going all right until she butted in," Eddie said. "Then Leeanne remembered that you and Jennifer hadn't thought it was a good idea at first."

"That was last summer. You were seeing Sarah then."

"Yeah, but that's history." Eddie dunked a fry in ketchup. "She knows about Sarah."

"It came up last night when she was talking to me and Jennifer. I told her you broke it off with Sarah when you got saved."

"Good. And you know I'm not looking around anymore."

"Are you sure, Ed? Because I'd hate to see Leeanne get hurt."

Eddie gave his question serious contemplation for about ten seconds, then nodded. "It might take longer and be harder than I thought, but I really want her, Harvey. For life."

Harvey smiled, finally. "She already likes you."

"Well, that's something. But she's not completely open with me yet. I don't know what's missing."

"Trust," he said.

"Yeah. I guess I don't exactly inspire that in young women."

"You have to prove yourself trustworthy, and that can take time."

When Crystal brought their checks, Eddie made sure he didn't flirt or check out her legs.

They went back to the station. Harvey's desk phone rang as they entered the unit's office. He went to pick it up, and Eddie drifted to his own desk, focusing his mind on the case again. He was sure Jordan Quinlan hadn't told them all he knew.

"Ray and Sarah are back," Harvey called. "They're coming up here."

The four of them sat down in the interview room.

"Get anything else?" Harvey asked.

"A couple hundred bucks, but nothing resembling drug money," Sarah said.

Ray nodded. "I think you found most of it, Captain. I found some joints in a canister.

"Okay, thanks."

"You got anything else for us?" Sarah looked hopeful.

"Sorry," Harvey said. "Not today."

"I guess we pull traffic duty this afternoon, then." Ray stood up. "Thanks for an interesting morning, Captain."

Sarah sent a bleak look Eddie's way and followed Ray to the elevator.

Chapter 8

A patrolman brought Misty to the Priority Unit, where Harvey and Eddie spent half an hour with her in their interview room. She gave them her phone and computer passwords, but she became belligerent as soon as Harvey suggested she'd known Kyle was dead. He kept at her, and she broke down in tears, howling, "Can't I get a lawyer?"

Harvey sent her downstairs and told Brad Lyons, the sergeant, to let him know when her court-appointed lawyer had been there.

He took a phone call and stopped by Eddie's desk afterward to tell him he was headed upstairs. That meant the chief's office. Mike summoned Harvey frequently or came down one flight to confer with him in Priority.

Funny, in the five years Eddie had been in the unit under Mike, he'd never been upstairs to the chief's office. But since July, when Mike became chief and Harvey took over the unit, he'd been up there maybe a dozen times. It used to be really scary. When a man was called to the chief's office, it was as if a school child was sent to the principal. Not anymore. Now when Harvey went upstairs, Eddie figured either they were getting a new case, or he and Mike were just drinking coffee and having a gabfest.

Tony and Arnie came in from lunch. After Friday, Eddie would work with Tony. He was a little apprehensive about it. Taking on a new partner after you've worked closely with someone for a long time could lead to tension. In Eddie's case, he'd worked with Harvey for five years. Even since Harvey's promotion, Eddie spent more time with him than any of the other detectives. He was determined to make things work with Tony.

Their unit was the smallest one in the police department. Five men worked under Harvey: Tony, Nate, Jimmy, Arnie and Eddie, but Arnie was retiring the last day of the year, which would be Friday. Arnie was Mike's old partner, and his experience counted for a lot. Harvey and Eddie had never worked in Priority without Arnie. The unit would be very young on average after Arnie left, and Eddie would have the most experience as a detective, even though Nate and Jimmy were a little older than him.

Jimmy and Tony had only been with the unit about six weeks, and they were still getting used to each other. Jimmy and Nate had been partners before, as patrol officers. They stuck together like glue, so Eddie hadn't had a chance to get to know Jimmy well. But he was a good cop. Eddie had partnered with Nate for a few weeks before Jimmy came on board. It would all work out, he told himself.

Harvey came back from Mike's office and nodded his way. "Bring the men over here, Eddie. We've got to pick up another case."

When they had gathered around his desk, Harvey opened a folder. "Arnie, I'm sending you and Tony over to the USM campus. They're on vacation, but the bursar went into his office this morning to get something and found there'd been a break-in."

"Sounds like a routine case for Ron's squad," Arnie said.

"The office was trashed, and there's a large amount of blood on the floor," Harvey said.

Arnie nodded. "Okay, boss."

"I'll get you some techs." Harvey looked at Arnie. "Do you want Miller and Cook, too?"

"Let me see what's what, and I'll call you if I need them."

"Okay, I'll trust your judgment on that."

Tony always acted like a little spaniel, eager to please his master. He'd followed Arnie around for the last month, soaking up everything he could get from him. Eddie figured Tony was going to be a great detective someday—and not in the distant future. He was very intelligent, and he never quit unless Harvey or Arnie ordered him to. He might run circles around Eddie when they started working together, but Eddie wasn't going to chase him.

Harvey turned to Eddie. "I've got to keep you

on this Quinlan thing. Check with the techs and see if they've dumped Kyle's phone yet. And get the records for his and Misty's both."

"I asked for them this morning," Eddie said. "They'll send them electronically, but nothing yet."

"Keep on it. I'll tackle Misty's laptop."

Eddie nodded.

"Nate, Jimmy, I've got a few people who knew Kyle Quinlan that I'd like you to track down and interview. I'd also like you to find out who Misty's closest friends were."

"She's pretty active on Facebook and Instagram," Eddie said.

"I can look into that, boss," Nate offered.

"Good. Jimmy, you take the names we got from Oliver and Benoit."

"Right."

They worked all afternoon, but they didn't make a lot of progress. Everyone they depended on for evidence—mainly the medical examiner and the lab techs—was taking his time. Harvey didn't find much useful on the laptop. About two-thirty Arnie called for more manpower, and Harvey sent Nate and Jimmy over to the campus. He and Eddie stayed on their phones and computers, inching along, adding tiny bits of information to the file on Kyle Quinlan.

At five o'clock, Eddie finished his reports for the day feeling unproductive.

"Are you coming over for supper, Eddie?" Harvey asked.

"Am I supposed to?"

"Yeah, come on. Unless you want to avoid Leeanne."

Eddie hadn't called her all day, and he'd meant to. After Harvey had said she was shopping with Jennifer that morning, he'd let it slide.

"She might not want me there."

"Give her a call."

Eddie hesitated. He didn't take rejection well, and he supposed that was because he wasn't used to it. He walked into the breakroom and called her. "Hey, it's me. How are you doing?"

"I'm okay."

"Well, uh, Harvey invited me to supper, but I wasn't sure you'd want me there."

"I do," she said.

Eddie's face pulled into a grin. "I'll be there."

He and Harvey both had their vehicles at the station. Eddie stopped on the way and bought flowers for Jennifer and Leeanne. They greeted him with huge smiles and exclaimed over the flowers. Jennifer looked a little tired.

"Is Abby at work?" Eddie asked.

"Yes," said Jennifer. "Make yourself at home, Eddie. Harvey's changing his clothes."

Eddie hung up his coat and walked into the kitchen. Leeanne took a dish from the oven while Jennifer arranged the flowers in two vases.

"These are really beautiful, Eddie," she said.

He shrugged. "My mother always liked flowers in the wintertime."

Leeanne smiled at him. "It's a sure way to cheer things up." The table was already set, and she brought over a casserole and set it on a trivet.

Jennifer set one vase toward the back of the table, out of their way, and the other over on the sideboard. "Harvey says Arnie's retiring on Friday."

"Yeah. We're having a party for him Friday afternoon."

Harvey walked in while Eddie was talking. He said, "Mike's secretary, Judith, is organizing it."

"Really?" Eddie said. "I thought Paula was." Paula was their unit secretary, and she was usually upbeat. He couldn't imagine the sour-faced Judith planning a party.

"Paula's helping her," Harvey said. "We're having it upstairs."

"No kidding." Eddie shook his head. Another first. A party in the chief's office.

"They figured they could keep it a surprise if they held it up there." Harvey held Jennifer's chair for her. "I'd better call Pete Bearse and tell him to come." Pete was Arnie's old partner, who had left the unit in July to join a law practice.

After supper they talked for a while. Leeanne seemed almost back to the camaraderie she'd enjoyed with Eddie before Abby spilled the

126

hospital conversation to her, but by eight o'clock, he started to feel he should leave. Jennifer looked tired, and Harvey was drooping a little, too.

Eddie squeezed Leeanne's hand. "I'd better get going. I'll see you tomorrow, Harv."

"Good night, Ed. I'll meet with you first thing."

Leeanne got up and walked toward the entry with him. Eddie glanced back and saw Harvey standing behind Jennifer's chair, massaging her shoulders. He bent down and kissed her neck. Yup, time to leave.

"Anything happening around here tomorrow night?" Eddie wasn't sure whether to just ask Leeanne to go out.

"Well, Harvey and Jennifer are supposed to start Lamaze classes tomorrow, if he gets off work in time."

Eddie didn't know what to say to that. He was not fluent in the topic of childbirth. "What about you? You want to do something?"

She hesitated, and he thought he'd said something wrong. Why was it that Leeanne could make him feel clumsy and inept, like no other woman ever had? But when she looked up, under those long dark lashes, she was smiling.

"I'd like to. What did you have in mind?"

Eddie had checked the *Press Herald* just in case. "There's a brass quintet at a church downtown, or an opera at the Gold Top theater, or a juggler and a magician at the Sollit."

"Juggler, huh?"

"Yup. And a magician. Supposed to be really good."

"Let's do that."

He smiled and got his coat out of the closet. He glanced toward the kitchen again. Harvey and Jennifer were walking toward the sunroom together with their arms around each other.

"Those two." Eddie nodded toward them.

Leeanne turned around and watched them. Harvey stopped in the middle of the sunroom and turned around, but he wasn't looking at them, he was looking at the wall in there, and Eddie figured he was focused on the painting of Jennifer when she was six years old. Then he kissed her.

"They're always like that," Leeanne said. Eddie couldn't tell if it bothered her or not.

"True love," he said.

"I guess so." She was solemn. She stepped back a little, and he took that to mean he should keep his distance. He zipped up his coat and said goodnight.

Eddie was determined to find a break somewhere in the case on Tuesday. Arnie and Tony had found out where the blood at the university office came from—the guy who broke in smashed the glass in the door and cut himself badly in the process. They were chasing leads and hopeful of catching him. Harvey took Jimmy and Nate to the courthouse with him for Misty's arraignment, just to give them a little more court experience.

Eddie went through the previous day's reports and zeroed in on one of the names Nate and Jimmy had come up with, supposedly one of Kyle's friends. He decided to take a little drive and see if he could catch up with Trevor Brady.

He found Brady rotating tires on a Mazda at a service garage on Brighton Avenue. When Eddie pulled out his badge, Brady got that panicky look, like he might run, and laid down the wrench he'd been holding, which was a slight relief to Eddie.

"Take it easy. I just want to talk to you about Kyle Quinlan. Do you know what he was up to Friday night?"

"No idea," Trevor said. "I heard yesterday morning he was dead, and then a couple of cops came around asking about him."

"Yeah. Tell me, who did he work for?"

"Uh . . . the Commercial Wharf?"

"Nah, he quit that job. I'm talking about drugs. Who was he running for?"

"Man, I don't know."

"Sure you do," Eddie said.

"Look, Kyle was messed up. Did he O.D.?"

"Who did he work for?"

Brady's forehead wrinkled, like he was actually trying to think. "He said something about some guy called Mel, but I don't think it was his boss."

"Mel? Mel what?"

"I don't know, man." Brady looked over his shoulder. "Look, I gotta keep working, okay?"

"Do you know anyone else Kyle hung around with?" Eddie asked.

"No one I can think of. Look, he had a good job, right? Why ditch that? I told you, he was messed up."

"You want us to find out what happened to him, don't you?"

"Yeah, sure."

Eddie put a business card in his hand. "Call me if you think of something, okay?"

What a bust. He went back to the station.

It was like that all day. Finally, he wrote up his report for the day, spell checked it, and e-mailed it to Tony, who had been helping Arnie with the university break-in. Tony never got complaints on his reports.

"Hey, Winfield? Got time to edit something?"

"What, a book?" Tony asked.

"No. My report. It's short."

Tony laughed then opened the file and scrolled through it. He shook his head.

"What?" Eddie asked.

"Hold on." Tony clicked a few keys, read some more, clicked some more. "Back atcha, Shakespeare."

"What kind of crack is that?"

Tony grinned. "I usually charge fifty bucks an hour for proofreading."

"Yeah, right—so why aren't you working for the newspaper?"

"They don't pay that much."

Eddie opened the file he'd attached. It looked just like his report. He slowed down and read it carefully, trying to figure out what Tony had done. He could tell one sentence was rearranged, but other than that, he didn't have a clue.

"Okay, Perry White, what did you do?"

"Who's that?"

"Man, didn't you ever read Superman comics? Great Caesar's Ghost!"

Tony said, "A little before my time."

That made Eddie feel as old as Harvey. "Hey, they're still making Superman movies. Super Girl, too. Where you been?"

"Third star to the left and straight on to Krypton."

"Ha, ha. Thanks." Eddie almost called him Wonder Boy, which was what Harvey had dubbed Tony the previous summer, but it suddenly hit him that it might offend Tony. So far they were getting along pretty good, razzing each other a little bit. In Eddie's mind, letting Tony see his atrocious punctuation skills was worth having him fix the report. "No, really, I want to know what you fixed," he said. "I aspire to educate myself, and you can help."

131

"You left out a word in the part about the tire guy, and I put in a couple of commas and fixed a run-on sentence."

"Okay." Eddie scowled at the screen but still couldn't tell where he'd done it. "Good job, Winfield."

Tony chuckled. "Thanks."

Eddie could just see it. Someday, Tony would be in the chief's office, and he would still be down here writing reports for Tony to read and correct. Maybe a brush-up class in grammar was in order. He e-mailed the report to Harvey and walked over to his desk.

"Quitting time, Harvey."

"Mm-hmm." Harvey had his nose in a case folder and didn't look up.

"You've got a class with Jennifer tonight."

That got his attention. He glanced at the corner of his computer screen. "Yikes, you're right! I'd better get moving."

He started shutting down his computer files.

"Where's the captain off to?" Tony asked when Eddie walked past his desk.

"Baby lessons."

Tony's face scrunched up.

"Lamaze class," Eddie translated, feeling very mature and in-the-know. He went to the locker room for his jacket. He had just time to grab a bite and a shower before picking Leeanne up for their date.

Leeanne helped Harvey carry things out to Jennifer's car. Harvey took two pillows, and Leeanne brought a folded blanket. Eddie drove in just as they were stashing them in the back seat. He got out of his truck and ambled up to the garage.

"You guys are sleeping at the hospital tonight?" he asked.

Harvey shook his head. "No, Ed. Jennifer needs to learn breathing and relaxation technique. Everybody sits on the floor, and you need pillows."

Eddie looked at the bedding, then at him. "Okay," he said doubtfully.

Leeanne smiled at him. "How are things?"

"Great. You ready to go?"

"I think so."

Jennifer came out of the house. She had on her winter jacket, but it wasn't zipped, and Leeanne wondered if she'd need another one before the baby was born. She'd always been thin, but she was starting to look plumper now. Eddie took one glance at her middle and looked away.

"Hi, Eddie," Jennifer said. "You and Leeanne have fun tonight."

"Yeah, you, too." Eddie looked at Leeanne and shrugged, as if he didn't know what else to say.

"Oh, I'm sure we will." Jennifer looked happy,

and Harvey smiled and opened her car door for her.

They drove out, and Eddie stepped closer to Leeanne. "So, you ready to see the juggler?"

"Yeah, I can't wait." She closed the garage door and walked with him to his truck.

"This baby stuff is kind of weird." Eddie put the truck in gear.

"How do you mean?" Leeanne asked.

"Well, Jennifer is . . . well, she's changing."

"Of course she is."

He shook his head, frowning. "I mean, I thought I knew her pretty well, but now it's like she's different every time I see her."

"Hormones," Leeanne said. "She's still her same self."

"I guess."

"I think all women must go through some big changes, physically and emotionally, when they have a baby."

Eddie seemed to think about that. "What about Harvey, though?"

"Yeah, new dads, too. I think Harvey's a little more compulsive now. He wants to be sure everything is safe for the baby and that Jennifer's comfortable. He treats her like royalty."

"That's nothing new," Eddie said. "But I think you're right. Becoming parents has a profound effect on people."

She nodded, liking this thoughtful side of Eddie.

He looked over at her suddenly and winked. "Can you juggle?"

She laughed. "I've never tried. Can you?"

"I don't know. But I told Tony we were going to the show, and he tried to juggle three cans of soda. He dropped one, and it broke open and squirted Pepsi all over the breakroom."

Leeanne laughed. "What did Harvey say?"

"He doesn't know. We cleaned it up before he found out about it."

They arrived at the theater, and Eddie parked the truck then came around to open her door. She let him help her down, and he held her hand as they walked into the theater. The room was set up like a small club, and they sat at a table and ordered soft drinks.

The juggler kept them riveted, tossing top hats and metal rings. He juggled five balls at once, and never dropped any.

Leeanne hoped the magician in the second act would saw somebody in half, but he didn't. He did make a woman disappear in a puff of purple smoke.

"How did he do that?" she asked as they applauded.

"I don't know," Eddie said. "He's pretty good."

"My dad used to pull quarters out of our ears, but this guy is great."

Eddie squeezed her hand, smiling as the lights focused for the next trick. Leeanne sighed. If only their time together was always this care-free.

The magician's big finale was stuffing a rubber chicken into his hat and pulling out half a dozen live doves that flew out over the audience. Not Houdini, but it was fun.

Eddie helped her on with her coat and kept his arm snugly around her as they walked out to the truck. He drove back to Van Cleeve Lane. Harvey and Jennifer were home, and the living room lights were blazing. Eddie gave her a hand down from the truck seat.

"Thanks." Once she was on solid if frozen ground, she looked up at him and smiled. "I had a really good time."

"Me, too."

They went inside. Jennifer had a big bowl of popcorn ready and a pan of hot cocoa made the old-fashioned way.

"So, how revolting was your class?" Eddie asked Harvey, after Leeanne had told him and Jennifer about the magician.

"Well, we did see a movie of a birth that was a little nauseating," Harvey said.

"You surprise me. I thought you were totally into this baby thing."

"Our baby. Not everybody else's."

"How bad was it?" Eddie persisted.

"One guy passed out."

"Not you, I take it."

Harvey shook his head. "Jennifer told me she'd never forgive me if I did."

Leeanne frowned at him. "It couldn't have been worse than some of the car wrecks you've been to."

"That's different," Harvey said.

Jennifer refilled their mugs of hot chocolate. "The class was really interesting. We're learning different breathing patterns for when I have contractions."

"Contractions?" Eddie said. "This is a euphemism for labor pains?"

Jennifer grimaced at him. "Childbirth doesn't have to be painful."

"I don't know. Sounds like a scam to me. How much are you paying this Lamaze teacher?"

Harvey said, "It's supposed to be true, Eddie. Discomfort, not pain. The special breathing will help her not to think about it. But if she needs medication, she can get it."

"Oh, if it's not painful, why would anyone need to have standby medication?"

"Well, Jennifer will be fine." Harvey smiled at her. "She has a very high threshold of pain."

"So it *is* painful?" Eddie asked.

Harvey sighed.

Jennifer rolled her eyes. "Ask me in three months or so, Eddie, and I'll tell you in detail."

"No thanks."

Chapter 9

Wednesday, December 29

The next morning, Eddie ran with Harvey at the track. Leeanne and Jennifer stayed home.

"When's Jeff getting back?" Eddie asked. He was happy for Jeff, but he missed him.

"Not until this weekend. He texted me. They're soaking up sun in Oahu."

After they ran, they went to Harvey's house for breakfast. Leeanne was flipping French toast, and the talk ran mostly to the Wainthrop family, since Marilyn had called the night before and updated her daughters on everybody's business. Abby ate with them, and she kept looking at Eddie oddly. He tried to listen to what Jennifer said, but he felt like Abby was giving him the evil eye or something.

As he was leaving to go get ready for work, she followed him into the entry.

"Okay, Eddie, spill."

"What?" he asked.

"You've been glaring daggers at me ever since you walked in the door."

"I thought you were the one."

"What did I do?" Abby asked.

"You mean you don't know?"

"No. I thought we were friends."

"Ha," Eddie said. "That was before you started talking about me behind my back."

She scowled. "I haven't the slightest idea what you mean."

"I mean you yakking with your friends at the hospital about how many girls I went out with in high school."

"Oh, that."

"Yeah, that."

She looked over her shoulder, grabbed his wrist, and yanked him out into the breezeway, closing the door behind them.

"I didn't say a word. Not one single word."

"Sure."

"I didn't," she said primly. "I just listened."

"And then you told Leeanne."

"Oh." Her face morphed into what might be taken for regret. Contrition, Harvey would say. "I figured she should know. And I didn't tell her the worst bits."

Eddie felt like she'd punched him. "What were the worst bits?"

"I don't think we should discuss it."

"Why not? You discussed it with half the nurses in Portland."

"You exaggerate."

"And you gossip."

They glared at each other. It hit Eddie suddenly that Harvey would not be having this conversation, at least not in this tone. He swallowed hard.

"Hey, I'm sorry. I shouldn't have come down on you like that."

Abby blew out a breath, and it made a little cloud of mist between them. "Yes, you should have. You're right. I might not have added to the talk, but I didn't tell them to stop."

He cocked his head to one side. "I'm curious. This topic just came up in ordinary, everyday conversation?"

"Yes. Well, no. They were talking about their favorite dates ever, and I told about the circus, and they started talking about fancy parties and things, so I said a detective had taken me to a classy art meeting, and it was lots of fun because he was looking for clues in a case he was working on. I figured it was okay, because you'd solved the case."

Eddie shrugged. "I guess so."

"Okay, I admit, I was trying to impress them."

"Oh yeah? Impress them with me?"

"Yes, and when I said your name, everyone's ears pricked up, and what do you know? Two of them said they had also dated you. Once. The general consensus was that you don't date girls more than once."

"That's not true."

"Well, maybe these two just didn't hold your interest. But anyway, it got juicier and juicier. A

140

third woman said her niece dated you and cried buckets when you broke it off."

"Nurses," Eddie said with some bitterness.

"Not *all* nurses. One of them is a tray girl. She brings the patients' meals up from the kitchen on a cart. She said she went out with you in high school."

"Are we talking about Denise Rancourt?"

"No, her name's Sissy Williams. That's her married name. I don't know what her maiden name was."

It was enough to ring a bell. "Oh, Sissy. Well, I'm glad she got married. Does she seem happy?"

"Yeah, I guess. But she almost swooned when I said 'Eddie Thibodeau.' I think you were 'the one that got away' for her. And Delaney Marshall."

"Delaney." That was the nurse's name. He'd forgotten it. That was definitely a short-term relationship. "So, they don't hate me?"

"No. I think they've been looking for another guy who measures up ever since you broke up with them."

"Hold it." Eddie held up both hands. "If you date a guy once and he asks you out again and you say no, is that breaking up with him?"

"No. Are you saying they asked you out?"

"No, I'm just saying I probably didn't ask for a second date. Big deal."

"Okay." Abby hugged herself, shivering. "But apparently you did get around. A lot."

"Yeah. So?"

She looked away, and he knew Delaney had talked about more than him not calling her again.

"Look, Abby, I was a jerk. I'm sorry. I wish I could undo a lot of stuff, but I can't. And I'm sorry I called you Blabby Abby."

Her forehead puckered. "When did you call me that?"

"Doesn't matter, it was wrong. Forgive me?"

"Of course."

"Good. Because I want to stay friends with you. I realize you were just trying to protect Leeanne."

"She's my baby sister."

"I know. I want to protect her, too. And I . . ." He didn't finish.

"Are you totally done doing that stuff?"

"Yeah. I'm waiting for marriage now."

She nodded. "What if Leeanne breaks up with you?"

"Then I will be the one who's heartbroken, but I won't fall off the wagon. I promise."

"I'll hold you to it."

He smiled and nodded. "Get inside. You're freezing."

"I've got one more thing to say."

Eddie waited for the hammer blow.

Abby looked deep into his eyes. "I did tell them you were the perfect gentleman on our one date. They seemed—uh—surprised."

He opened his mouth and then closed it.

"In fact, Delaney said something like, 'Didn't he try to get you in the sack?' and I can assure you, I said, 'Absolutely not. The Eddie Thibodeau I know would never do such a thing.' She said, 'Maybe there are two Eddie Thibodeaus.'" And then our break time was up, and that was that."

He pulled in a painful breath. "Please tell me you didn't tell that last part to Leeanne."

"I didn't."

"Thank you." He still felt like Hulk Hogan had punched him in the solar plexus.

"No problem." She swung around and reached for the doorknob.

"Abby?"

"Yeah?"

"I will never treat your sister that way."

"I know. And I'm sorry I didn't shut them up sooner. Friends?"

"Yeah, friends."

She held out one little finger. He laughed and linked his pinky with hers.

Abby winked. "BFF, Eddie. Have fun at work."

He spent half the morning trying to run down the Mel he'd heard about from Trevor Brady. Even with Tony at his side while canvassing, trying to come up with clever ideas, Eddie couldn't get wind of Mel.

When they got back to the Priority Unit's office, Harvey called out, "Hey, you two, the preliminary autopsy report's in on Kyle Quinlan."

He'd emailed copies to all of them, and they sat down to read it. Then they got together to hash it over.

"So. Cocaine and sleeping pills," Harvey said.

"Not a good mix." Arnie shook his head.

"It stopped his heart, or slowed it down enough for the cold to finish him off." Harvey sighed.

"I don't get it," Tony said.

Harvey frowned at him. "What don't you get?"

"Why would anyone take enough sleeping pills to kill himself and then go out at the crack of dawn with a gun? Was the gun just insurance, in case the pills didn't work, or what?"

"More likely the coke came first," Nate said. "I'm guessing he wasn't thinking straight."

Eddie thought about Kyle's last hours. "He got over the fence at Mike's house. Was he just off his rocker, or did he intend to climb that particular fence?"

"And how did he do it with all those sleeping pills inside him?" Jimmy asked.

"How much was it?" Eddie looked at the report again.

"About three times the normal dose," Harvey said. "Suicides usually take the whole bottle."

Eddie looked up sharply. Was Harvey thinking of Carrie, his first wife, who chose sleeping pills? This case could be a real downer for his friend.

"Would the amount he took stop his heart?" Tony asked.

Harvey hesitated. "I'm not sure. Maybe I'll give Dr. Turner a call and ask him."

"I mean, Kyle was supposedly healthy, right?" Tony said.

"He had bruises on his torso," Nate noted.

"That might have been from a fall or something," Jimmy said.

"Or a car accident, or a beating," Arnie added.

"One broken carpal," Nate read from the report. "That's a finger bone, right?"

"Right," Tony said. "So, aside from the fight, if that's what it was, and the drugs, he was as healthy as a horse."

"A drugged, beat-up horse," Arnie mused.

"We'll know more when the full autopsy's done. Those toxin levels are preliminary." Harvey looked at Eddie. "Did you get anything this morning?"

"No. I'm looking for a guy Kyle supposedly worked with in the drug business, name of Mel. We couldn't get anything solid in the neighborhood or at the wharf where he used to work. I'm going to check the drug arrests."

"Use Jennifer's program," Harvey said. "It can sort out stuff like that really fast. Search for drug collars in the last year within the city, and the name Mel or Melvin."

"Got it." Jennifer was almost as smart as her

145

husband—well, maybe smarter—and the police department had recently bought software she designed that cut the unit's search times in half and notified them of any updates remotely related to their open cases.

Eddie found two Melvins with drug arrests, but he ruled them out. One had died in June. The other had moved to the state pen.

He kept at it, racking his brain. He decided not to ask Tony for ideas, though the thought nagged at him that he probably should. He stubbornly wanted to prove that he wasn't the stupid one in the unit, but that was ridiculous. All of these guys were smart.

Arnie took Tony out on a jaunt to the fire marshal's office for another case, and Harvey gave Nate and Jimmy other assignments, but Eddie kept looking for Mel.

Mike came in around three o'clock. He always wore a suit these days, but he looked awfully somber. It wasn't until he started talking to Harvey that Eddie realized he'd just come from Kyle Quinlan's funeral. Eddie caught snatches of conversation that gave him the impression the service was pretty grim. Mike left, and he kept working.

It was almost the end of the shift when something promising showed up. He walked over to Harvey's desk.

"Got a minute?"

"Yeah. What is it?"

"Mel. Some women are called that, right?"

Harvey blinked. "I suppose so."

"I found a Melanie Tucker. She's had two arrests this year, one for driving under the influence, but not alcohol, and the other for intent to distribute cocaine."

Harvey swiveled his chair back and forth a couple of times, thinking. "Yeah, that sounds right. Look into it tomorrow. Oh, and your report yesterday was good, Eddie. I didn't see any mistakes."

"Thanks." Tony was still out of the office. Eddie would be on his own today. Wasn't there some sort of built-in grammar checker on the computer? If he wanted to get to church tonight and sit beside Leeanne at the Bible study, he'd better get busy.

He called Leeanne Thursday morning before he went to the office. She'd been friendly at church the evening before, but they hadn't had much time to talk.

"Is it too early?" he asked.

"No, we're all up except Abby," Leeanne said.

"I wondered if I could see you tonight. You'll only be here a few more days. Is it okay?"

"I'm not sure. Abby has today off. Jennifer might want to do something together."

He was disappointed, but family came first.

"Let me know if you're free. We've got tomorrow night, anyway."

"Yeah. I can't wait to see the Olympic skaters," she said.

He smiled at the eagerness in her voice. "I'll pick you up early. You want to eat out first?"

"You're spending a lot of money on me this week."

"Nah. Besides, you'll be gone soon. I want to spend all the time with you I can."

"Thanks. That's sweet."

"Have you ever thought about moving down here?"

"I couldn't do that."

"Sure you could." Eddie didn't know why he hadn't suggested it earlier. "You could finish school at USM. I've heard Harvey say you could live with them."

"They have Abby already. Besides, I don't know if my parents would like it."

He let it go. Some people would have said that, at almost twenty-one, she should do whatever she wanted, get out on her own. But they were a close family.

Eddie knew what it was like to try to keep from upsetting the people you loved. He'd been twenty-three when he finally made the break, moving into an apartment two streets over from his folks. Not halfway across the country, just out of the house. And he'd successfully overcome the guilt his mother had tried to load him down with. Now his independence was the normal thing, but it had taken some determination. For a quiet young woman like Leeanne, it would be harder.

But he knew he'd be burning up the road to Skowhegan that winter. One way or another, he was going to see her.

Melanie Tucker was elusive, but Eddie knew she couldn't be too far away. Her driver's license had been suspended. With Nate and Jimmy, he hit her duplex and several other haunts where he thought they might find her, with no success. They went back to the office. Harvey, Arnie, and Tony were all out on other business.

Paula called Eddie over to her desk and handed him a message slip.

"Zoe from the lab called. She has some news on the phones you gave her."

"Great. Thanks."

He left Nate and Jimmy trying to profile the woman whose name was on the oxycodone prescription bottle from Kyle's apartment and went down to the lab. Zoe smiled when he walked through the door.

"Detective Thibodeau! Just the man I was hoping to see."

Eddie smiled back. He liked Zoe. She was an Asian woman of about forty, and always nice, but not flirty.

"I have good news for you," she said.

"I could use some."

She walked over to a workbench and picked up a cell phone. "We were able to access Kyle Quinlan's contacts and texts. You can read the texts now and compare his contacts with the record of his calls."

"Awesome." He'd served a warrant for the call record on Tuesday, and—shock—it had come in overnight.

He spent the next two hours on it. Kyle had about thirty texts in the last couple of weeks, most of them brief, most of them to and from Misty. Eddie worked on those to and from other numbers and identified his brother Jordan and one of his friends.

There were two texts from numbers he hadn't yet identified. One said, "Hey, Kyle, u still o me 40." A debt? The other one said simply, "It's a go." What was that about? It had come into his phone Friday morning. Eddie tried to track the phone it came from, but got nowhere. He decided it was a burner phone, and therefore a very suspicious text.

He started on the call records. The last call was made Friday evening, to Misty. Shortly before that was a call to the burner phone. Before it, there were none for several hours, and those from earlier in the day and on Thursday seemed routine— Misty, his friend, Misty, his dad, Misty. There was one call around four a.m. Saturday. Eddie circled it. The number was Jordan Quinlan's.

He had Misty's phone, too, and she had grudgingly given them her password. Eddie had gone through it once already, and nothing struck him as vital to the case, but he hadn't had the call records then.

He gave her call list the same treatment he had Kyle's, checking off the times they phoned each other. When they'd questioned her, she'd identified most of her contacts for the detectives—Kyle, the store, her sister, various friends. Eddie matched most of the calls with them now and checked them off.

One call early Friday evening wasn't to anyone in her contact file but seemed familiar. Eddie pulled up Kyle's list and stopped cold.

He double checked the number and spun his chair around. Harvey had gone to Stroudwater on a case of his own, and he wasn't back. Eddie called his cell.

"Yeah, Ed?"

"Are you coming back soon?"

"Yeah, I'm nearly there now. What have you got?"

"Where's Misty Carney?"

"She made bail yesterday. Do you need to talk to her again?"

"Harvey, the last person she called Friday was Kyle's brother, Jordan."

Chapter 10

When Harvey got back to the station, Tony was with him. Eddie waited for him in the garage with a folder containing all the phone records. Harvey got out of his SUV and told Tony to try to get a lead on that burner phone. They probably couldn't learn who had sent the text to Kyle, but with help from the phone company, they might be able to tell where the phone was located when the message was sent.

"Climb in," Harvey said.

Eddie got in and buckled up. "So, Misty or Jordan first?"

"Jordan, I think. He should be at work. We'll catch him off guard."

Jordan Quinlan lived in Berwick, about twenty miles away, but he worked as a team leader at a medical equipment company in Riverton, barely within Portland's city limits. Harvey set his GPS and drove right to it.

Harvey asked the receptionist if Jordan had a private office. She said he didn't but offered to call him out to the lobby.

A minute later, Jordan came through a door to one side looking curious. His gaze landed on the detectives, and he stopped for a moment then came toward them.

"Captain Larson. Is there news about Kyle?"

"We're following up on a lead," Harvey said. "Is there someplace we could talk?"

"Uh, sure." Jordan turned to the receptionist. "We'll be in the conference room, if anyone needs me."

He led them down a hallway and turned in to a room with a long table and a dozen chairs around it. He closed the door, and they all sat down. Eddie slid the folder across to Harvey.

Harvey opened it and glanced at the first page, then closed it.

"Jordan, we've found something I thought was a little odd about Friday night."

"Oh?" Jordan shot a glance Eddie's way, dismissed him as small potatoes, and concentrated on Harvey. "Like what?"

"You said you haven't had much contact with Kyle over the last few years."

"Well, some. I mean, I see him once in a while. I just haven't spent a lot of time with him."

"I see. Do you e-mail or text each other?"

"Hardly ever."

"How about phone calls?"

He shook his head. "Now and then, like if we're going to meet up at Dad's or something."

"What about Misty?"

Jordan's eyes narrowed. "I don't know what you mean."

"Misty called your phone Friday. What was that about?"

"I don't remember." He looked off down the room.

"Because I didn't think you knew Misty," Harvey said. "On Sunday, you sounded as though you thought she might be history, as far as Kyle was concerned."

"I only ever met her once," Jordan said. "I wasn't sure . . ."

"That she was still living with your brother?" Harvey asked.

Jordan's eyes snapped to his. "Oh. All right, I guess so. I didn't realize . . ."

"Didn't you? You've never been to their apartment, then?"

Jordan looked very uncomfortable and didn't answer.

"When was the last time you spoke to her?" Harvey asked. He waited about twenty seconds before adding, "I know she called you Friday around six o'clock."

Jordan let out a deep sigh. His shoulders slumped, and he stared at his hands. "She was worried about Kyle."

"Why?"

Jordan shook his head.

"Had she called you before?" Harvey asked.

"No, never. I swear."

"So, why that night?"

Slowly, Jordan lifted his chin. "She thought Kyle was in over his head. She hoped I could help him."

"What was he into?"

Again, the silence and evasive eyes.

"We know about the drugs," Harvey said. "Help us out here, Jordan. What did Misty want from you?"

"She wanted me to talk some sense into him."

"That's a start. What was it all about?"

"Look, I tried to talk to him, but he wouldn't listen to me."

"Did you phone him?" Harvey opened the folder and flipped over a couple of pages, scanning the printouts. "Misty's call to you only lasted a couple of minutes. You didn't talk to him on her phone, did you?"

Jordan shook his head. "I went over there."

"You didn't mention that when we talked at your father's house."

He nodded a few times, like a bobble-head doll. "I didn't want to get Mom and Dad more upset than they were. This has been really hard for them. For us all."

"I'm sure. So tell me about when you went to the apartment Friday night. Were they both there?"

"Yeah." Jordan folded his hands on the table and looked all around the room. Finally he said, "Look, he was in trouble, but he was my brother, okay? I had to go."

"I'd have gone," Harvey said, as though that was only reasonable. "What were you trying to talk sense to him about?"

Jordan blew out a breath. "I guess I might need a lawyer."

"Then I guess you need to come with us to the station."

Kyle looked at Harvey for a long moment. "Can I call my dad?"

"Later." Harvey stood. "Who do you need to tell that you're leaving for the day?"

Jordan did a double take then said, "My boss. Are you sure I have to leave work?"

"Unless you tell me everything right now," Harvey said, "and I can't guarantee it then. It depends on what you tell me."

Another pause during which Jordan squeezed his hands together and cracked his knuckles. "Okay, Kyle was running drugs for this guy."

Harvey sat back down. "What guy?"

"Al Something—Alfred, I think."

Harvey's gaze met Eddie's, and he nodded. They knew of a powerful drug dealer in the West End who had built himself quite a drug empire in the city. Only trouble was, they'd put him in jail several years earlier.

Eddie slid out his notebook and wrote down "Al or Alfred."

"What kind of drugs?" Harvey asked.

"I don't know. Whatever was going. Coke

maybe, or meth. Something new, too. Kyle mentioned something I'd never heard of."

"And?"

"He owed this Al guy big time. Somebody held Kyle up and stole a bundle of his drug cash. He was supposed to give most of it to Al, but he lost it all, and they beat him up pretty bad."

"When was this?" Harvey asked.

"A couple weeks ago."

Eddie hadn't seen any bruises on Kyle's face, but the M.E. found contusions on his torso.

"But Misty didn't call you until Friday," Harvey said.

"No. I didn't know anything about it until then. Well, I knew Kyle was dealing. That's one reason I stayed away from him."

"You're not into that?"

"No. I never did drugs, and I told Kyle he was stupid to start, but he never listened to me. I don't know why Misty thought he would now."

"So, what did she want you to do, exactly?"

Jordan grabbed a handful of his hair and tugged on it. "She wanted me to stop him from going out that night."

Harvey waited.

"He was going to do a favor for this Al guy, and Misty was scared he'd get himself killed."

"What sort of favor?"

"She didn't tell me at first. I went over there,

157

and Kyle was mad that I'd come. He threw a punch at me, and I clocked him."

Again, no bruises, Eddie thought. He wrote more notes.

Harvey frowned. "Jordan, I think you do need to come to the station with us. If you're in the clear about this, you'll be free to go later today, but this is something we need to have on tape."

Kyle looked from Harvey to Eddie and back. "I *do* need a lawyer."

"If you want one. I'm not arresting you, but we need your cooperation."

Jordan breathed in and out a couple of times. "I'll come if you let me tell my boss and call my dad first."

Harvey didn't usually bargain, but after a couple of seconds, during which Eddie assumed his brain was in turbo drive, he said, "Let's go tell your boss."

"You're coming with me?"

"Yes, I am."

Jordan sighed and pushed up out of his chair.

"Eddie," Harvey said, "while Jordan and I do this, would you please set some inquiries in motion?"

"Sure, Captain." Eddie knew exactly what he wanted. They left the room, and he called the Priority Unit office.

A few seconds later, Tony said in his ear, perky as ever, "Yeah, Eddie? What's up, man?"

"Can you do a quick check for us on a drug dealer named Alfred Hawkins? We put him away four or five years ago. I want to know if he's still in the state prison, or if he's out. Somebody named Al is doing his type of trade here again."

"Got it. Call ya back, buddy."

Eddie called dispatch and asked Charlie Doran if Harvey had called for a marked unit at their location.

"No, you want me to send one?"

"Yeah, we need transport for a witness." Eddie went outside and waited for Harvey. He hoped he wasn't planning to let Jordan drive his own vehicle. That was a good way to let a witness take a detour. Personally, Eddie would have had the cuffs on him by now, but Harvey seemed to be taking it easy on Jordan. Eddie wondered if it was because of Mike's friendship with Jordan's parents.

A few minutes later, Harvey and Jordan came out. Jordan had put on a gray parka.

"I called for a unit," Eddie told Harvey.

He blinked. "Okay."

Eddie shrugged. "I can cancel it."

"No, that's fine. Jordan, we'll have you ride in with a couple of officers, and they can bring you back here when we're done."

Jordan looked very unhappy, but he didn't make a fuss. A couple of minutes later, Sarah and Ray rolled up. Harvey gave them instructions, and they put Jordan in their car and left. Harvey and Eddie got into the Explorer.

"Why didn't you arrest him?" Eddie asked.

"I'm not sure he did anything wrong, except lie to us on Sunday. And he just buried his brother yesterday."

This new, softer side of Harvey still surprised Eddie, but it seemed to happen more and more frequently. Maybe Leeanne was right, and it had to do with the baby. Or maybe it was all because Harvey had straightened his life out with God, and he empathized more now with people in trouble.

Harvey pulled out into the street. "You getting along okay with Sarah?"

"Yeah, why?"

"I haven't seen you say one word to her, yesterday or today."

Eddie shrugged. "I haven't seen much of her lately." He'd wondered if they were avoiding each other by unspoken agreement.

After a few seconds, Harvey said, "You're not still thinking about her, are you?"

"Just that it's too bad it went the way it did. I liked her."

Harvey nodded. "She asked me a few days ago how you were doing."

"She did?" Eddie wished she hadn't. He couldn't think about Sarah now. He didn't want to, really. But he didn't want her to be thinking of him, either. Did she feel hurt? He didn't think he had treated her badly, but after he'd been saved, he'd tried to tell her about Christ. She wasn't interested, and Eddie had ended the relationship. Maybe she thought he had other reasons.

"She wasn't bitter or anything," Harvey said.

"Good. So, what's the plan with Jordan?"

"I told Ray to take him up to our interview room."

"Did you let him call his father?"

"Yeah. It sounded like Mr. Quinlan will have a lawyer at the station soon, and I want to finish my chat with Jordan before he gets there."

When they got to the office, Sarah was sitting at Eddie's desk. She jumped up when they came out of the stairway.

Eddie looked over at her and nodded. "Sarah."

"Hey," she said and refocused on Harvey. "He's in your interview room with Ray."

"Thanks, Sarah," Harvey said. "You want some coffee?"

"No, thanks."

Paula walked over to Eddie. "Tony asked me to tell you he's working on it, and he should have some intel for you soon. He stepped out for a minute to check on something."

"Great. Thanks."

Harvey took off his jacket, threw it into his chair, and poured himself half a cup of coffee. He took two sips while Eddie took off his coat, then left the mug on his desk. "Okay, let's do this."

Sarah watched Eddie with big, somber brown eyes. He didn't know what to say, so he said, "See ya," and felt stupid. He followed Harvey into the interview room.

"Thanks, Oliver," Harvey said. "I think that's it for now."

"Anytime, Captain." Ray nodded at Eddie and left.

Harvey turned on the tape recorder, and Eddie went to the corner and started the video recorder. After the formalities, Harvey sat down across from Jordan, and Eddie took up a post standing next to the door.

"All right, Jordan," Harvey said. "Let's resume our conversation that we started at your workplace. You told me that you went to your brother Kyle's house Friday evening, after his girlfriend called you, and that she asked you to help her talk some sense into him."

"That's right."

Harvey repeated almost word-for-word what Jordan had said earlier about his fisticuffs with Kyle and that he'd run drugs for someone named Al.

Jordan nodded.

"Please respond verbally," Harvey said.

"Yeah, that's what I said."

"All right, why was your brother so angry with you?"

"He was furious with Misty for calling me, and mad at me for interfering."

"How were you interfering?"

"I went over there because Misty didn't want him to go out that night, and I was trying to convince him to stay home. But he wouldn't listen."

"So, where did he plan to go?" Harvey asked.

Jordan hesitated and then met his gaze. "To Mike Browning's house."

It shouldn't have surprised Eddie, but it did. Up to that point, he hadn't quite believed that Kyle was heading for Mike's house packing a gun. Harvey had insisted on continuing the questioning here so that he had Jordan on tape when he revealed Kyle's plan.

"Now, by that you mean the police chief, Michael Browning?" Harvey asked.

Jordan nodded, then said, "Yeah."

"Why was he planning to go there?"

Jordan let out a big sigh. "This Al guy said that was the only way Kyle could repay the debt he owed him—to off Chief Browning."

Chapter 11

Harvey sat there a couple of seconds, then said, "So, your brother, Kyle Quinlan, planned to kill Michael Browning as a means of writing off a debt to his drug supplier."

Jordan looked down. "Yeah."

"Why did the dealer want to kill Browning?"

"An old grudge, I guess."

"How much did your brother owe this man?"

"Misty said about eighty grand. He was going to deliver it to Al before, but he'd been attacked and robbed. Since he didn't have the money, this Al guy said he'd forgive the debt if he killed the chief."

"And you were supposed to talk Kyle out of it."

Jordan's eyes sparked. "Well, yeah. Mike Browning is a family friend. I wasn't going to let Kyle waltz over there and shoot him."

"How were you going to stop him?"

"I didn't know. I mean, it was such a shock. Misty was crying and telling me I had to do something. Kyle told me to leave him alone. I think he was high, and I wasn't sure at first he was serious about doing it."

"What did you do?"

"Nothing. Kyle said he needed some sleep, and

he went in the bedroom and slammed the door."

"So, he wasn't going to do it right away?" Harvey asked.

"No. He said he'd sleep until midnight or so, and then he'd go."

"And you just dropped it?" Harvey frowned.

"No, I knew we had to stop him."

Harvey waited. Eddie leaned back against the wall and folded his arms.

"Misty wanted me to do something to make him stay asleep."

Harvey eyed him closely. "What kind of something?"

"She was wild. She wanted me to, like, hit him over the head or overdose him with cocaine or something. She wasn't thinking straight. I wasn't about to do something that could hurt him permanently." Jordan took a deep breath and looked past Harvey, at the one-way glass.

"But you did *something*," Harvey said.

"I had to. I couldn't just let him—" Jordan rested his head in his hands.

Harvey said, "Did it never occur to you to tell Chief Browning what Kyle planned to do?"

"Yeah, it did. I suggested that very thing, but Misty said no way."

"Why?"

Jordan winced. "She was scared a bunch of cops would ambush Kyle and take him out."

That wasn't so far-fetched, in light of several

incidents that had recently happened in other cities.

"Besides," Jordan said, "Misty's pregnant."

That little detail had escaped the detectives. She was hiding it better than Jennifer.

Harvey said, "So . . ."

"So, she didn't want her kid to have no father."

But that was exactly what had happened. They were all silent for a moment.

"I see," Harvey said. "Did you come up with a plan?"

"Sleeping pills," Jordan said. "Misty and I talked about our options, and we decided that was best. It would keep him down long enough for us to figure something out."

Eddie's mind zipped to the autopsy prelim. Kyle had ingested a triple dose of sleeping pills Friday night.

Harvey asked, "And how would you protect him from Al's thugs when he didn't deliver?"

"We didn't get that far," Jordan said. "We figured we'd stop him from doing the—the thing he said he'd do, and then we'd find a way to fix it with—" He broke off and shook his head.

"Wasn't Kyle already asleep after you'd talked this over?" Harvey asked.

"Yeah. But I thought Misty could get him to take them when he woke up, and it would put him out again. She said she'd try it. She had a bottle in the cupboard."

Eddie remembered seeing them when he'd searched the bathroom—over-the-counter sleeping tablets. They were perfectly legal, so he hadn't confiscated them. Ray Oliver had bagged them with the rest of the medicine cabinet's contents, but Eddie still hadn't considered them important until the tox screen came in.

"Did you give him the pills?" Harvey asked.

"No. I didn't stick around. Misty said she'd try to get him to take them. The next thing I know, she's calling me at 4 a.m."

The early morning call to Jordan, Eddie thought. Misty had used Kyle's phone.

Jordan went on, "She said Kyle took three pills she'd told him were headache tablets, but that didn't seem to slow him down. He'd loaded his gun and left."

"What did you do?" Harvey asked.

"First, I had to calm my wife down. Kay had heard my side of the conversation, and she was very upset. She'd already suspected something was up when I went over to Kyle's earlier, because I never went over there, and I had made it a point not to get to know Misty very well."

"Why was that?"

"She was a druggie, too. I didn't want them coming around our kids." Jordan swore and dropped his head into his hands again. "We didn't want to kill him! In fact, we were trying hard *not* to kill him."

167

A tap on the door alerted Eddie, and he opened it a crack. Tony.

"Quinlan's lawyer is here."

Eddie told Harvey, and he stood up and came to the door.

The attorney, Ned Baxter, was one of the better criminal lawyers in the city, and therefore one of the most expensive. Eddie was glad Jordan's father had the money to hire him, because he felt sorry for the guy.

Harvey told Baxter he was going to put Jordan in custody and charge him with conspiracy and manslaughter.

The lawyer took exception to that, but Harvey said, "Listen to his story, Mr. Baxter. The deceased man's girlfriend, Misty Carney, made bail yesterday on a lesser charge, but we'll bring her in again for this."

While he continued talking with Ned Baxter, Tony motioned Eddie aside.

"I found out that the man you asked about, Alfred Hawkins, was released the end of November. He went to a halfway house, but they said he's gone elsewhere now."

"Where?" Eddie asked.

"I'm not sure yet, but I got his parole officer's info." Tony handed him a sheet from his notebook.

"Okay, I know this guy. I think he'll be straight with us. You want to call him?"

But at that moment, Harvey called out, "Tony, Jimmy, Nate, you three go with Arnie and round up Ms. Carney again. Eddie, I need you."

The other men headed for the locker room for body armor. Eddie doubted Misty would have a gun, but then, you never knew.

Baxter had gone in to talk to Jordan.

Harvey put his hand on Eddie's shoulder. "I've got to go up and tell Mike about this in person."

"Of course. What do you want me to do?"

"I need you here to handle Baxter."

"You don't think Arnie would be better at it?"

"Focus, Eddie. Arnie will be out of here tomorrow. I'm letting him make one last collar, but we've got to get along without him. That means you boys need to find some finesse to deal with sensitive situations. I picked you to lead on this case, and I want you to deal with Mr. Baxter."

"Okay." Eddie recalled that Ned Baxter was Senator David Murphy's lawyer when they'd arrested him for murder. That was big stuff.

"You'll be fine," Harvey said, "but I need to get with Mike ASAP. No doubt he'll be taking some calls about this before the sun is down."

"I haven't seen him at all today," Eddie said.

"He's here. He's breaking in the new deputy chief."

"Okay. I've got this."

"Right." Harvey went out the door.

Eddie sent up a prayer for Mike. Yesterday he'd attended the funeral of a friend's son. Today he not only had to get acquainted with his new second-in-command, he had to learn that he was the target of an assassination plot, and that his son's friend was being arrested in connection with his brother's death.

Eddie's head spun. Arnie and the guys would get Misty, but they really needed to bring in Alfred Hawkins. *If* he was the dealer Kyle had been in debt to.

Eddie ended up not seeing Leeanne Thursday night. Misty Carney was in custody by six o'clock, and Nate and Jimmy did some legwork, confirming that Kyle Quinlan had been one of Hawkins's runners, but Hawkins eluded them. He had given a new address to his parole officer. Harvey and Eddie went there with their whole crew, but Hawkins wasn't around. The word was, he'd stayed there a couple of nights and decamped.

Harvey sent the other guys home. He and Eddie followed up on a couple of rumors, but they found no trace of Hawkins.

"Think he's left town?" Eddie asked.

"Oh, he's still here," Harvey said. "I think we should set up a protective unit at Mike's house."

"I guess that makes sense, but he'll hate it."

"He'll hate it worse if Hawkins sends someone

170

else to kill him and the new guy doesn't accidentally overdose himself."

Harvey called the night sergeant and arranged for an unmarked car to watch the chief's house that night. Then he did the hard part—he called Mike to break the news to him. Eddie could hear Mike ranting and cussing. Harvey winced and held the phone a couple of inches from his ear.

When he could get a word in edgewise, he said, "Mike, I know you don't like it, but this is not an ideal world. It's just until we bring Hawkins in. I want you and Sharon to get a good night's sleep without wondering who's creeping around in the bushes outside."

At last Mike calmed down. The chief agreed to the home surveillance overnight and an escort to the station in the morning.

They finally called it a day around ten o'clock and went home. Eddie called Leeanne, and they talked for a half hour. Everything seemed good, and he started to believe they were past the rough patch. He was sorry he hadn't seen her. She would leave on Sunday. Three days.

Ten minutes after Eddie got to the office Friday morning, Mike came off the elevator and walked over to Harvey's desk.

"You guys ready for an early prayer meeting?"

Eddie stared at him. Harvey leaned back in his chair and looked up at Mike.

"You want to pray with us?"

"I figured you wouldn't mind, and I'm taking a lot of stress right now."

Harvey stood up. "Eddie."

"I'm with you." The three of them went into the interview room.

"How close are you to finding Hawkins?" Mike asked, pacing the limited floor space.

"Not very," Harvey said. "I'm sorry, Mike. He's in the wind."

Harvey and Eddie sat down, and Mike continued to pace.

"I had to tell Sharon everything, and I called Mikey last night. He was pretty upset when he heard you'd arrested Jordy."

Mike was calling the "boys" by their childhood nicknames. Harvey seemed to take it in stride.

"I'm sorry, but we had to. You know that."

"Yeah, I do. Jordy knew about the hit on me, and he didn't tell me. Man, oh man. I taught that kid to tie flies."

"Is Sharon okay?" Harvey asked.

Mike came over and sat down at the end of the table. "You know Sharon. She's good. Always practical. Told me to delegate to Jack Stewart until this thing shakes down. She suggested a weekend in the Bahamas, but I nixed that."

"The Bahamas sounds pretty good to me," Eddie said.

Mike shook his head. "I can't skip town because some thug is mad at me."

"I looked at the reports from when we arrested him," Harvey said. "He should have stayed in longer."

"Good behavior, I guess." Mike grimaced. "Although I wouldn't have thought Alfred Hawkins was capable of that."

"It's part of that prison overcrowding flap," Harvey said. "They're trying to free up beds."

"More like they're trying to keep the press quiet about the burgeoning inmate numbers." Mike ran a hand through his hair. "I still can't believe that kid was going to kill me. On Christmas."

"Not very considerate," Harvey said.

"Ha! Debbie and Elliott and the kids were there, not to mention Sharon. What was he going to do, sneak into our bedroom and plug me? Sharon would have torn him to shreds or died trying."

Harvey put his hand on Mike's arm. "Take it easy, Mike. Do you still want to pray?"

Mike exhaled. "Yeah. That's supposed to help, right?"

Eddie closed his eyes, and Harvey started praying. He thanked God first for protecting Mike and his family. Then he prayed for the Quinlan family, for comfort and peace. Then he asked God to help the police find the people responsible and to not let anyone else get hurt.

Mike stirred, and Eddie peeked. He was getting

out his handkerchief. When Harvey said amen, he sniffed.

"You remember what Reverend Rowland talked about Sunday?"

Harvey's eyebrows pulled together. "You mean about dying to self?"

"Yeah. Giving up your rights."

Eddie remembered it too. Pastor Rowland was doing a sermon series on Matthew 5. Jesus talked about loving your enemies, not just your neighbors.

"See, I don't get that," Mike said. "Our main purpose in life is to protect people's rights. But he was talking like rights don't matter."

Harvey nodded, his blue eyes sober. "Not other people's rights, Mike. We're supposed to stand up for them. But we're not supposed to demand our own rights. For Jesus. I don't need equal treatment. I just need to do what I can for other people. That's what the job is, right?"

"Lonnie and Rita Quinlan are shattered." Mike swiped away a tear with his handkerchief. "And Jordy! He sat there all stony-faced during the memorial service, and all that time, he knew. He knew about the sleeping pills and the whole thing. He knew his numbskull brother was going to murder me, and he just sat there like a stump. And I'm supposed to turn the other cheek? What does that mean? Give him another chance to kill me?"

"Easy, Mike. Jordan never intended to kill you."

"Well, he sure didn't do much to prevent it. Give his moron brother sleeping pills? Come on! How about a little heads-up to his buddy's pop, huh?"

"I know," Harvey said.

"So, what am I supposed to do in this case?"

Harvey closed his eyes for a moment and then opened them. "I don't know, but I suspect Jesus would forgive Jordan and show some love to Mr. and Mrs. Quinlan."

Mike drummed his fingers on the table for a few seconds. "Okay. I can do that. Maybe. Lonnie and Rita, yes, but Jordy will be harder."

Harvey smiled. "One thing at a time."

"Yeah." Mike's shoulders relaxed a little. "What about Hawkins? Am I supposed to protect his right to kill me?"

"Absolutely not. You should let us protect you. We'll get him, but it may take some time. You owe it to Sharon—not to mention the entire city of Portland—to stay safe, Mike. May I suggest you wear body armor whenever you leave the building?"

"Crap."

Eddie stifled a laugh.

"Maybe you should reconsider the vacation," Harvey said.

"No way. I don't hide from scum like him."

Mike frowned. "What about you? Doesn't he hate you, too? Why is he fixated on me?"

"You made the arrest, remember? You led the investigation. You handled the court testimony. He sat there in the courtroom glaring at you while you told the judge all the wonderful things he'd done to hook our community's kids on drugs."

"Including Kyle," Mike said. "Yeah. I remember. The dirt bag."

Eddie remembered too. He could picture Al Hawkins in his jail jumpsuit, with hatred flashing from his steely eyes.

"I'll organize the protective detail," Harvey said.

"Okay." Mike pressed his lips together for a moment. "This prayer thing."

"It's not a magic potion, Mike. And it's not just prayer."

"Yeah. Sharon says if I believe in Jesus and I get myself killed, she'll be sad, but she'll know I'm safe in heaven."

"That's true," Harvey said. "I'm sure it would be a great comfort to her. The flip side is, if you don't believe Jesus died for you and you get yourself killed, she'll never see you again."

Mike met his gaze. "I . . ." He looked away.

Harvey sat there for a few seconds, and Eddie just kept his mouth shut, but inside he was praying for Mike.

"You know, God's never going to leave you alone," Harvey said.

Mike nodded about six times, gritting his teeth. "Okay. I can believe in Jesus."

"For you? Or for Sharon?" Harvey asked.

"For me. She already believes for both of us, but she says it's not enough."

"It's not."

"Okay. But tell me about the resurrection part again, because I don't get that. It's too hocus-pocus."

Harvey looked over at Eddie. "Could you please get me a Bible?"

"Sure." Eddie got up and went out into the office. The other men were all working at their computers, probably wondering what they were up to. Then he saw Lonnie Quinlan sitting in the visitor chair by Harvey's desk. Eddie looked over at Paula, and she gave him a tiny shrug.

Quinlan stood up. "Detective Thibodeau, is Captain Larson available? I tried to see Chief Browning, but his secretary told me he was out."

"The captain's in conference right now," Eddie said. "May I help you?"

"I want my son released in my custody."

Eddie didn't have the power to do that, and neither did Harvey.

"Can you wait just one second?" he asked.

Quinlan frowned and sat down again. Eddie

177

got his Bible from his desk and took it to the interview room. Harvey and Mike were deep in a discussion about dead people, ghosts, and yes, the resurrection.

Eddie handed Harvey the Bible. "Mr. Quinlan's outside."

"You can handle him."

"He wants Jordy released."

"Tell him to talk to the lawyer, who can talk to the D.A."

Eddie nodded.

"Maybe I should speak to him," Mike said.

"You stay out of it," Harvey told him. "One of his sons tried to kill you, and the other one could have warned you but didn't. You keep your distance. You could make a big mess of the legal issues in this case."

Mike sighed. "Yeah, you're right."

"He doesn't know you're in here, Chief," Eddie said. "I'll tell him to go to Mr. Baxter."

"Good." Harvey met his gaze. "And get moving on Hawkins again."

Eddie went out to Harvey's corner. Mr. Quinlan jumped up.

"I'm sorry," Eddie told him. "The captain says you'll need to let your son's attorney handle this for you, through the district attorney's office. It's out of our hands."

His whole frame slumped. "All right. Thank you."

As soon as the elevator doors closed, the other men crowded around Eddie.

"What's going on with the chief?" Jimmy asked.

"We're setting up a personal guard for him whenever he's not in the building, and a protective unit at his house at night until we catch Hawkins."

"That sounds good," Arnie said. "Want me to set up the schedule?"

"Can we do the bodyguard duty ourselves?" Tony asked. "Because I volunteer, if we can."

"Better wait and ask Harvey about that. He and Mike are talking personal stuff now. And our number one task today is finding Hawkins."

"What about that Mel Tucker woman?" Jimmy said.

"Yeah, do you still want her?" Nate asked. "Because we've got a lead from an informant on where we might find her."

Eddie wanted to ask Harvey, but Harvey wanted him to show leadership, so he made a decision. "Bring her in if you can. She supposedly works for Hawkins. Push her for any info she can give us on him."

"Got it."

Nate was halfway to the stairs, and Eddie yelled, "Flak vests, guys!"

Nate and Jimmy U-turned for the locker room.

Tony and Arnie still stood there.

"So, the kid might have a lead on Hawkins," Arnie said with a nod toward Tony.

Eddie raised his eyebrows in Tony's direction.

"It may be significant," Tony said. "EMTs responded to a cocaine overdose last night. They took the victim to the hospital. I caught their report on Jennifer's program. It was a bad batch. I was thinking maybe we could trace it back, so I called the EMT who filed the report. He says the other people at the party might be able to tell us where the coke came from."

"They never tell you that," Eddie said. "We'd arrest their dealer, and they'd lose their supply."

"But the O.D. victim died," Tony said. "I figure the girls at the party will be really upset today. They might be willing to talk."

Eddie thought about it. Tony and Arnie together should be able to charm anything in a skirt.

"Okay, go. But call in with a progress report before noon."

Tony grinned. "Got it. Thanks, Eddie."

The office was empty, except for Eddie and Paula. She got up and walked over to him, smiling. Paula was about forty-five, sweet, and motherly. She had three teenagers, and Eddie thought those kids were very lucky.

"Good job, Eddie. Turn around so I can pat you on the back."

He laughed. "Thanks. I'll feel better when we get this guy who's after the chief."

"We all will. Meanwhile, I don't say this much in order to avoid sexist stereotyping, but may I get you a cup of coffee and a doughnut?"

"I'd love it. Thanks." Eddie went over to his desk and pulled up everything they had on Alfred Hawkins.

Chapter 12

Friday, December 31

About twenty minutes after Paula brought Eddie coffee and a chocolate doughnut with sprinkles, Harvey and Mike came out of the interview room.

"Eddie, my man." Mike walked over to him grinning. Eddie thought he might shake hands, but instead, Mike pulled him into a bear hug, tousled his hair, and said, "Thanks, kid."

He let go, and Eddie eyed him cautiously. "For what?"

"For changing."

Puzzled, Eddie looked at Harvey. He just smiled, as though he understood perfectly.

"I've been watching you," Mike said. "Leopards can't change their spots. Did you know that's in the Bible?"

"No."

"It is. Sharon showed it to me. She said if Eddie Thibodeau can quit chasing women and follow Jesus, will you admit God is real?"

Eddie wasn't sure how to take that.

Harvey said, "You know, Mike, a lot of the time those women were chasing Eddie."

"Yeah," Eddie said. Seemed like he'd gotten

a totally bad rap since he started behaving himself—worse than before.

"Well anyhow, I see it, and I believe it. There's hope for you, Eddie, and that means there's hope for me." Mike slapped Harvey on the back. "Later, Harv."

He walked toward the stairway, and when he passed Paula's desk, he grinned at her. "You look especially great today, Paula."

"Thanks, Chief."

Eddie looked at Harvey as the door closed. "So?"

"He believes. He understands, and he believes."

"Even the resurrection? Because I agree, that's a tough one."

"Even that."

"Fantastic."

"He was serious about watching you. Watching both of us. I almost ruined it when I had that go-round with Jennifer about her old boyfriend."

"Wow," Eddie said. "He mentioned that?"

"Yeah. He said if I was going to act like an idiot once in a while, I cleaned up well afterward."

Eddie laughed. "Sharon's going to love this."

"I wish I could see her face when he tells her," Harvey said.

"Maybe it will make it easier for her to swallow the protective detail."

"Right. We've got to set that up."

"Arnie said he'll make a schedule," Eddie

said, "but since he went out, maybe you should set it up for tonight. We all want to volunteer for watchdogging Mike."

"I think you can make better use of your time cracking the case. Let the uniforms handle it."

He was right, as usual. Eddie told him what leads their men were following.

"Good," Harvey said. "You keep close tabs on them and follow up on anything they need."

At noon, Mike called Harvey, apparently upset because he'd asked Sharon to meet him for lunch and two beat cops insisted on escorting him to the restaurant. Eddie only heard Harvey's part of it, but it was enough.

"Forget about them," Harvey said into the phone. "This is your special time with Sharon." And a bit later, "No, Mike, do not buy them lunch. Just let them do their job. They'll eat later. No, the city's not paying for their lunch at the floating restaurant." Finally, Harvey said a bit testily, "Mike, go back to the table and tell Sharon all the things you want to tell her, and ignore the officers. Thank you." Harvey hung up, shaking his head.

"You want to go to the diner?" Eddie asked.

"Let's take turns today. You go first. I'll stay in case something breaks."

Nothing broke. They both got lunch. All afternoon, Arnie or Nate would call in and ask for intel on some two-bit felon or other. Eddie

184

would pull up the rap sheet and tell them where they might be likely to find the crooks.

Arnie's retirement party was scheduled for four-thirty. At four o'clock, Harvey called all the guys back to the station. When Nate and Jimmy came in, they went with Eddie and Harvey up to the chief's office. Arnie and Tony came in last. Paula was under orders to tell Arnie that Mike wanted him to go up to his office for a minute to finalize the surveillance schedule. She and Tony were to follow him up there.

Arnie was surprised when he saw all of them, plus Mike and the new deputy chief, Jack Stewart. Mike's secretary, Judith, had ordered a fancy cake, and the outer office was hung with balloons and streamers.

"Man, you know how to keep things on the q.t.," Arnie said to Mike.

"Comes with the job," Mike said.

Arnie swung around to look at Harvey. "Yeah, well, you shouldn't have called us in from the case, but thanks, Captain."

Harvey just shrugged.

Pete Bearse, Arnie's old partner, was there. He'd left about six months earlier to join a law practice. Mike introduced all of them to the new deputy chief. Jack Stewart looked about forty-five or fifty, a little shorter and heavier than Mike. He wore steel-framed glasses and had short, light hair. He seemed personable and chatted a few minutes with each of the men during the festivities. Ron Legere and his detective squad came in about quarter to five.

They all ate cake and drank soft drinks or coffee and told Arnie how much they'd miss him. Mike presented him with a nice .30-06, for which the men had all donated.

"I just wish we could have caught Hawkins on my last day," Arnie said.

Harvey nodded. "You and me both. I'll be glad when we put him back where he belongs."

The party wound down a little after five, and most of the guys left. Mike and Arnie and Pete Bearse were hashing over old times.

"I guess I'll head out," Eddie said to Harvey.

"New Year's Eve. Big date tonight," Harvey said.

"Well, yeah." Eddie smiled. "Thanks again for the tickets."

"Have fun. I think I'll stay a few more minutes and catch up with Pete."

Leeanne was ready long before Eddie arrived. Abby was off that night, and she and Jennifer planned to stay in and watch *To Kill a Mockingbird* for the umpteenth time and enjoy a low-key evening with Harvey. It hadn't taken long for Leeanne to learn that when Harvey was not at work, he liked peace and quiet, preferably at home with Jennifer.

Eddie, on the other hand, liked a little excitement, and she was looking forward to their evening together. He arrived shortly before six o'clock, not long after Harvey came home. Eddie looked like he'd just blow-dried his dark hair, and he wore a clean cotton shirt with his dark jeans and down jacket, and his eyes glittered.

"Hey." He bent to kiss her cheek. "You look nice."

"Thanks." She was glad she'd taken care to choose her outfit—black leggings and a long, glittery top she'd borrowed from Jennifer.

He put a small stuffed sheep in her hands.

"What's this?" she asked.

Eddie shrugged. "My cousin's kid was selling stuff to raise money for a school trip. She didn't have any goats, so I got the closest thing."

Leeanne laughed. "I like it. It's really soft."

"I guess Harvey's home," Eddie said.

"Yeah, you want to see him?" Leeanne took him into the living room. Harvey was sitting on the couch with Jennifer, and Abby was curled up in a recliner with an afghan.

"Hi, Eddie," Jennifer said. Harvey gave him a nod.

"Hi." Eddie looked at Abby and pretended to be shocked. "What? You don't have a date tonight?"

She made a face at him. "Rude, rude, rude, French Boy."

"Jeff and Beth are supposed to come home tonight," Leeanne said.

"Oh, wow. Are they coming here?" Eddie asked.

Jennifer smiled. "We hope they will."

"Go on, get out of here," Harvey said. "If they show up, we'll try to keep them around until you get home."

Leeanne stashed the toy sheep on the edge of the stairs, and they went out.

"You two have fun," Jennifer called after them.

Eddie drove to a seafood restaurant. Just from the lighting and decorations, Leeanne figured it was expensive.

"Do you eat here a lot?" she asked after the hostess had seated them.

Eddie shook his head. "I've never been here, but Tony Winfield says it's good, and it's not far from the Civic Center."

Leeanne browsed the menu and tried to ignore the prices. She didn't want him spending a week's pay on dinner.

The waiter had given Eddie the wine list, but he laid it aside.

"What do you want to drink?" he asked her.

"Uh, water, I guess."

"Aw, live a little. Have root beer."

She laughed. "Okay."

"I'll have the same," Eddie said gravely. The waiter left without comment.

"So, you want the surf and turf?" Eddie asked her.

"Oh, no, I can't eat that much."

"Get a steak, then."

She couldn't figure out if he was trying to impress her, or just to reassure her that he could pay for it.

"I was thinking maybe the scallops?"

"Yeah, okay," Eddie said. "I'm having a steak."

She nodded, glad he seemed happy.

The waiter brought their root beer in frosted mugs. Eddie took a sip and looked up at the waiter. "*Très bien.*"

"I'll tell the sommelier," the waiter said without batting an eyelash.

Leeanne swallowed a giggle. Eddie winked at her and reached across the table for her hand.

"I wanted tonight to be special."

"It is." Looking into his beautiful dark eyes made her shiver in anticipation. A hundred years ago, a woman would have swooned over those eyes.

"Did I tell you that you look great?" he asked.

"Yeah, you did, but thanks. So do you."

She wasn't sure how long they could sit there, smiling at each other, but the waiter came back with their salads.

"So, tell me about this ethics class you're taking," he said.

"Oh, it's Ethics and Libel."

"As it pertains to newspapers, right?"

"And broadcast journalism." She was surprised he wanted to talk about that, but Eddie seemed to take a sincere interest in the topic, especially where it concerned protecting people's privacy. Eddie believed that criminals gave up their right to privacy when they broke the law. The two of them discussed it at length, but didn't settle anything.

"Tell me what you learn about that sometime, okay?" he asked as he picked up the bill.

"Yeah, I'd be glad to. I really don't know much yet, but I'm eager to get started on the class—even more so now. I've always thought truthful reporting was important, but I hadn't considered the privacy angle much."

When they left the restaurant, the temperature had fallen and a few snowflakes fluttered down. The street was filled with vehicles, much worse than when they left home.

"Glad I'm not on traffic duty tonight," Eddie said.

"New Year's Eve is pretty bad, huh?"

"Yeah, the only night that's worse is Halloween."

The ice show enthralled Leeanne. Eddie told her he'd never been to one live, either, and he seemed to enjoy it as much as she did. He hardly let go of Leeanne's hand for two and a half hours, except to clap.

When they came out of the Civic Center, she felt dreamy and content. Maybe things could work for her and Eddie after all. She hoped so.

The snow was falling harder.

"I wouldn't mind if we didn't get any more snow this winter," Eddie said when he got into the truck beside her.

"I know. I used to love it when I was a kid, but now it's a nuisance."

He backed out of his parking spot. "It makes a lot of people's jobs harder."

Harvey's house wasn't far, but the quickest route involved a short stint on Congress Street. As soon as Eddie turned onto it, he groaned.

"What?" Leeanne asked.

"I should have taken a detour."

The traffic was thick, and so was the snow. They crept along to the next stoplight. Three guys were trying to push out an SUV that was stuck near the curb.

"Bad night," Leeanne said.

"Yeah, I've seen better. I'll turn off on the side street down there if I can."

They got moving again, and they'd almost made it to where he could turn onto a less busy street when a light-colored GTO going the other way crossed the center line, skidded, and slammed into the minivan in front of them.

Chapter 13

Leeanne gasped and flailed a hand in Eddie's direction, then pushed on the dashboard, bracing too late. Eddie pumped the brakes and managed not to plow into the van, but stopped after barely tapping it.

"You okay?" he asked.

"I think so. The shoulder belt caught me." Her eyes were huge in her tight face.

"Stay put." He undid his seatbelt and checked his side view mirror to see if it was safe to open the door. The car behind them slid into his rear bumper, jostling them.

Eddie swore and caught himself, stifling the next word. "Sorry. Are you still okay?"

Leeanne swallowed hard. "So far."

The car that had started the chain reaction had crumpled the quarter panel on the minivan and buried its nose in the driver's side of the van. Eddie yanked out his phone and pushed 911.

"What is your emergency?"

"This is Eddie Thibodeau. Is that you, Tammy?"

"Yeah, Eddie," the dispatcher said. "You got an emergency?"

"Yes. Pileup on Congress Street. Send a bus and as many beat cops as you can." He told her which block they were on and handed his phone to Leeanne. "Here. Talk to Tammy at the com center while I check things out."

He looked again, then jumped out. They were in the far left lane going south, and all the southbound traffic had ground to a halt. The GTO had slid over from the northbound lanes, and now that side was down to one lane, which crept by the wreck. A thousand drivers honked their horns and yelled in frustration.

Looking behind him, Eddie saw that several vehicles had been involved in fender benders, trying to stop in time. The people in the van were the ones he was worried about. He strode toward it and slipped, catching himself on the rear door handle.

A man climbed out of the GTO, swearing a blue streak.

"Hey," Eddie yelled, "I'm a cop. Just get out of the way of traffic and don't go anywhere." He'd reached the point where the side of the van was smashed in. It was worse than he'd thought. The GTO had sheared along from the headlight about half the length of the vehicle and come to rest with the end of its bumper embedded in the van's sliding passenger door.

He turned around and scrambled to the other side of the van. He was close to other cars now as they edged by, southbound. Eddie yanked on the front passenger door, but it was locked. He knocked on the window. Inside, he could see someone in the driver's seat. After a few seconds, the lock popped up.

He pulled the door open. The passenger side was empty, but a woman sat behind the wheel, staring at him with a blank expression.

"Are you hurt, ma'am?" he asked.

Before she could say anything, someone in the back seat started yowling. A kid.

"My son," she said.

"I'll get him out. Are you okay?"

"I—no. I don't think I can move."

"Help is coming, ma'am."

"Get Mason!"

Eddie could barely hear her over the kid's screams. He tried to open the back door, but it was locked. He pulled off his gloves and reached in from the front. After some fumbling, he got the door open.

"Mason," he said sternly. "Hey, buddy."

The toddler was sitting on the passenger side of the bench seat—good thing. The other side was caved in. The kid was maybe two or three years old, strapped into a padded toddler seat. He had a really good set of vocal chords.

"Mason, Mason, calm down. I'm going to help you."

The child's meaningless screams morphed into "Mommy! Mommy! Mommy!"

"Take it easy, pal," Eddie said. "Mommy's going to be okay."

"Mommy!"

"Hey!" Eddie couldn't unhook the harness, and his patience trickled away as the little boy screeched in his ear. "Mason, I'm going to get you out of here."

"Eddie?"

He had his head and shoulders in the van, but he backed out. Leeanne stood beside him, holding his phone.

"Tammy wants to know if there are injuries."

"Yeah. This little kid might be hurt, and his mother's pretty bad, I think. She was driving."

A siren wailed.

"I'll go flag them down," Leeanne said.

"No, wait!"

She stopped, skidding a little, and flapped her arms before she steadied.

"Do *not* go out in the street," Eddie said. "Just wait here or get back in the pickup."

"Okay." She had that contrite look.

"Tell Tammy we need at least one ambulance that I know of. The guy from the car that hit them may need to be checked, too, and I have no idea what went on behind us."

He turned his attention back to Screaming Mason. Finally his fingers found the release button for the car-seat harness, and the straps relaxed.

"Come to me, buddy." When Eddie started to lift him out of the seat, Mason's screams hit a new decibel level. "I'm sorry," Eddie yelled. "I've got to get you out of the car. My name is Eddie, and I'm going to help you."

The van had enough damage and was in a bad enough spot that he knew it wouldn't be safe to leave Mason there. He picked up the child's seat with him in it and hauled him out.

"Mommy, Mommy, Mommy!"

"Eddie, the car's on fire," Leeanne yelled.

He looked where she pointed. Smoke poured from around the edges of the van's hood, and flames flickered.

"Take him and get as far away as you can." He put Mason, seat and all, into her arms and ran for his truck. When he reached it, he pushed the driver's seat forward and thrashed amid the stuff behind it for his emergency kit. He had a small fire extinguisher. It took him precious seconds to find it, but his hand closed on the cylinder, and he ran to the front of the van. He tried to open the hood, but the release had to be triggered, so he sprayed foam on the cracks. He needed to get that hood up or he'd waste all his ammunition. He went back to the front passenger door.

"Ma'am? Ma'am? Can you hear me?" Eddie crawled halfway onto the seat.

Mason's mother's head had slumped, and she didn't respond to him.

"God, I need some help here." That was probably not a very polite prayer. If Abby had heard him, she'd have called him Rude French Boy again. "I'm sorry," he said out loud, reaching across the woman's body and straining to feel beneath the dash.

"I need your help," he yelled at God. The woman didn't move or speak. "Our Father, which art in heaven, hallowed—"

He found a lever and pulled it, praying it wasn't for a vent or something. He heard a little pop, and something moved.

The sirens were deafening when he climbed out of the van.

"Thank you," he breathed and hurried to the front. The flames meant business now, and the hood was hot. Black smoke roiled out, and the smell of hot oil was almost overpowering.

He pulled a glove out of his pocket and put it on, then threw the hood up. The fire leaped up with a *whoosh*. Eddie let loose with the extinguisher, and the blaze went down pretty fast. He kept spraying until the cylinder was empty. He thought the fire was out, but he wasn't sure.

He looked around. Leeanne stood between cars about thirty feet away. She had gotten Mason free of the car seat and was jouncing him up and down. She saw him and walked toward him.

"There's an ambulance," she yelled, pointing across the lanes of northbound traffic.

"Okay, you *stay here*." Eddie pulled Mason away from her. The toddler started wailing again.

Eddie walked cautiously around the front of the van and the back of the GTO. The vanity plate on the car said "CROOZR." The driver stood a few feet away, hugging himself and shivering.

"Stand away from the vehicles," Eddie yelled at him.

Mason continued to scream. A couple of cops hurried over on foot.

"Hey, I'm Detective Thibodeau. This kid's mother's in the van, and she needs medical help bad. She was conscious, but she's out now. I'll take the boy to the ambulance." He jerked his head at the GTO's driver. "That guy started it. Slid over into oncoming traffic."

One of the two cops was already using his shoulder mic. The other one hurried toward the van as Eddie set out with Mason. He realized the little guy had quit yelling and was sobbing.

"It's okay, Mason." Eddie patted his back. "We're going to get you to a nice doctor. Those cops will get your mommy out."

Mason's stubby little arms came up around Eddie's neck, and he hung on tight.

People were getting out of their cars. Some walked toward the crashed vehicles, but most just stared and got in the way. The ambulance was now in the center northbound lane and had come to a stop. Eddie worked his way toward it, lugging Mason, and the driver rolled his window down.

"I'm a cop," Eddie said. "I pulled this kid out of that silver minivan over there. His mother's trapped inside. She's hurt bad."

"Eddie?"

He bent down and saw Mark Johnson, Jeff's friend, in the passenger seat. He'd been an usher at Jeff's wedding the week before.

"Hey, Mark. Can you guys get to the mother?"

"Yeah. Let Liam have a look at the kid. I'll go help the mom. There's another bus on the way."

While Mark threaded his way toward the crash carrying his kit, Eddie stood back so Liam could get out.

"Bring him around to the back." Liam opened the rear doors on the ambulance and climbed up, then reached for the little boy. A patrol officer appeared and began waving traffic around the ambulance.

"His name's Mason," Eddie told Liam.

Mason didn't want to let go. Eddie held him for a second with his face close to the toddler's, wishing he could fix his mother and heal any pain Mason felt.

"It's okay, buddy." Gently, he peeled Mason's arms away and lifted him. Liam took the child and sat him on a stretcher. Eddie climbed into the ambulance, too.

"Mason, I'm Liam," the EMT said. "Do you hurt?"

Mason nodded. Tears streamed down his face, and his nose was running.

"What hurts?" Liam asked.

Mason put a hand to his stomach.

"Oh, your tummy hurts?" Liam looked at Eddie. "Probably from the harness." He unzipped the kid's jacket and did a quick visual inspection. "I don't see anything obvious. He could have some internal problems."

"I need to get back there." Eddie wrote the license tag number of the minivan on the back of a business card and handed it to Liam. "That's his mom's plate number. I don't know her name yet. Can I just leave Mason with you?"

"Yeah. I'll check him out thoroughly, but I think we're safe to wait for his mom to join him. Do you think your people can clear the street for us?"

"We'll try."

"Good. We'll take them to Mercy."

It was the closest hospital, but not the one where Abby worked. Eddie bent down to Mason's level.

"Hey, buddy, I'm going back and see if your mommy needs help. You're going to be okay."

Mason stared up at him with watery eyes. Poor kid. Eddie stroked his head like he would a puppy's. "It's okay." He wondered how Leeanne was doing. She'd better still be at the spot where he'd left her.

He climbed down, and another officer hurried over.

"You guys need help?"

"Yeah, talk to Liam." Eddie nodded toward the EMT. "He'll need to get out of here once they load their patient."

By the time he got back to the crash site, several more officers had arrived. They worked on getting the northbound traffic moving first, since the wreck didn't impact those lanes much. Liam should be able to edge the ambulance over closer to the scene soon, if one of the patrol officers watched Mason.

Mark and two cops were at work at the van. Another one was talking to the GTO's driver, and Eddie glimpsed a fourth officer weaving among the stopped vehicles behind his, probably checking for more injuries.

He halted by the GTO's driver and said to the officer, "Hi. I'm Detective Thibodeau, and I witnessed the crash."

She nodded at him. "Alicia Peterson."

"I'm off duty, and I have a passenger I need to take home," Eddie said.

"Can you file a report tomorrow?"

"You bet I can." Eddie left her and went around the far side of the still-connected vehicles. Mark was inside the van, tending Mason's mother, and the two officers helping him stood outside the open passenger side doors, barking at each other and into their radios, asking for tow trucks and Jaws of Life.

"Anything I can do here?" Eddie asked.

One of them said, "I don't think there's room for more help, unless you're a doctor."

"No. Sorry."

Eddie turned toward his truck. Leeanne rolled down the passenger window. "Eddie, is the little boy okay?"

"The EMT thinks his tummy's just bruised from the seat belt, but they'll know more later. I guess the mom's pretty bad, huh?"

"Sounds like it. I just got out of the way." She handed him his phone through the window. "Oh, Tammy said for you to call in when you were free."

"Okay." His hands were freezing, and he walked around and got into the truck and put one hand over the heater vent for a minute. Leeanne looked as though she was dying to say something. "What?" he asked.

She shook her head.

"Tammy is a fifty-year-old grandma who's been dispatching since before you were born," Eddie said.

Her eyes got even bigger.

"You weren't thinking that, were you?"

"What?" She looked truly baffled.

"I'm sorry. Come here." Eddie pulled her over into a hug and sat there for a few seconds, holding her. "Thanks for helping. Are you sure you're okay?"

"Yes."

"Your neck didn't snap when they hit us from behind?"

"No."

"Maybe you should get it checked anyway." He knew of cases where people thought they were all right after a wreck, then started having pain a couple of days later.

"Really, I'm fine."

"Okay." He sat up and keyed in the com center's non-emergency number and asked for Tammy.

A moment later she came on the line.

"That you, Eddie?"

"Yes, ma'am." In the background, he could hear other dispatchers talking to callers. It was their worst night of the year, too.

"You all set?" Tammy asked.

"Yeah. I passed the kid off to EMTs, and people are working on his mother now. As soon as I can move my truck, I'm going home."

"Thanks for checking in."

"No prob." After he'd warmed up, he got out and walked around to assess the situation. The on-duty officers seemed to have enough manpower to deal with things. He inspected the rear end of his truck and decided he'd gotten off easy. The driver behind had a broken headlight and gave Eddie his contact information.

"It wasn't your fault," Eddie assured him. "I'm blaming the jerk in the GTO." But he gave him his insurance information anyway.

"Was that car ahead of you on fire?" the man asked. "Because I couldn't move an inch. We were sitting ducks."

"Yeah. God was good to us."

He gave Eddie a funny look.

Leeanne was quiet when he got back into his warm seat. He got her talking about the ice show after a while and decided she would be okay. When she suggested they pray for Mason and his mom, Eddie knew she had her head on straight.

Several more minutes passed before the traffic on their side was unsnarled enough for him to back his truck away from the minivan and ease into the next lane. During that time, they kept talking about inconsequential stuff, and Leeanne called Jennifer and told her they'd been involved in an accident but were all right.

"Jeff and Beth are there," she wailed to Eddie when she'd signed off. "I hope they don't leave before we get there."

"I'm glad they got back safe," Eddie said.

When they finally got to the house, he stopped the truck in the driveway, behind Beth's car. Leeanne hopped out before he could say anything and ran inside.

Harvey, Jennifer, Abby, Jeff, and Beth were sitting in the sunroom.

"Hey, Jeff!" Eddie shook his hand. He was tanned, and his hair had bleached out a little. Beth had darker hair, but she was tanned, too. She stood up and kissed Leeanne and Eddie.

She put a couple of plastic leis over their heads. "Aloha."

"Wow, thanks," Leeanne said, inspecting the fake flowers.

"Don't you know too much sun isn't good for you?" Eddie asked.

Beth grinned at him. "We had the best time, and it was beautiful!"

"We went surfing," said Jeff.

"You went surfing?" Jennifer asked Beth.

"Well, I tried it. I was sort of a wipeout. Jeff was terrific, though."

"Always wanted to try it," Jeff said with a shrug.

"So, when do you go back to work?" Eddie asked.

Jeff smiled. "We both have another week off."

"Great! Let's do something," Harvey said.

Jennifer frowned. "Harvey, they're still on their honeymoon."

"That's okay," said Beth, "We can still do stuff."

The house phone rang, and Harvey looked at

Abby. "Would you get that, please, Abs? It's got to be for either you or me."

She disappeared into the kitchen and didn't come back, but they could hear her talking happily.

"Gotta be Greg," Jennifer said with a frown. Eddie thought maybe Peter was winning out on Jennifer's scorecard.

"I like Greg," said Harvey.

"Oh, I do, too," Jennifer assured him.

Jeff looked over at Eddie. "So, you two were in an accident?"

"Barely, but we couldn't get out of traffic," Eddie said.

Leeanne grabbed Jeff's arm. "He helped rescue a kid."

Eddie shrugged. "There was a little boy in the vehicle ahead of us, and I got him to the EMTs. His mother was badly injured. Your friend Mark was working on her when I left."

"I'll have to call him tomorrow and get the full report," Jeff said.

Abby came back from the kitchen. "That was Josh Wright." Josh was one of Abby's hangers-on at church. "He said you were on the eleven o'clock news, Eddie."

He frowned at her. "What for?"

"He said you rescued a baby from a car wreck, and they showed you carrying him. He said it was very dramatic."

Eddie couldn't remember seeing a camera crew at the scene. It must have been someone with a cell phone or a dash cam, or some kid with a GoPro.

Beth said, "If the late news is over, it's past my bedtime. We'd better get going."

"Don't you want to ring in the new year with us?" Jennifer asked.

It was nearly midnight. She brought out wine glasses and poured ginger ale. Leeanne handed Eddie a glass.

"Happy new year, everybody," Jennifer said.

Abby came around with oatmeal cookies. "Happy new year, friend."

"Thanks." Eddie took a cookie. "How's Greg?"

"Great. He's coming up next weekend."

"So, you have a normal schedule now?"

"Pretty much. Friday and Saturday off, at least for now."

"Thought you'd be out at some fancy party tonight."

"No," Abby said. "Peter's taking me out tomorrow night. We didn't want to drive the same roads as all of Portland's drunks."

"It's their first date without the boys," Leeanne said. "Jennifer and Harvey are babysitting."

Abby took the plate back to the kitchen, and Eddie said to Leeanne, "Do you think she's actually going to marry one of these guys?"

"I don't know." Leeanne smiled. "She likes

them both. One of them's got to come up with some superior drawing card."

"Or make a huge mistake," he said.

Harvey stood up. "Do you want to take your wedding presents tonight, Jeff?"

"Let's get them tomorrow."

Beth nodded. "Tomorrow for sure." She turned to Leeanne. "How long are you here for?"

"Just until Sunday. Harvey's taking me home."

"We could take you," Jeff said. "We were thinking of running up to see the folks."

"Really?" Harvey sounded hopeful. "Not that I wouldn't love to see them myself, but I might get called in this weekend. We've got a case that's kind of all over the place. You never know when something will turn up."

"Sure, we'll take her." Jeff drained his glass of ginger ale.

Beth smiled. "That will be nice, Leeanne. We'd better get going, but we'll come by tomorrow afternoon and get the gifts and show you our pictures from Hawaii, okay?"

They talked for a few more minutes, but Eddie wasn't listening. Leeanne was leaving Sunday, and he probably wouldn't see her again for a while.

The next morning, the priest came to see Eddie. Of the ten people he least wanted to see that day, Father Claude was second, with the first being Abby's coworker Delaney Marshall.

Eddie was scraping the windshield of his truck, figuring maybe he'd go by Mercy Hospital and ask about Mason and his mom, then go to Harvey's and hang around with Leeanne. Father Claude came walking along the sidewalk, bundled up against the cold like normal people, but all in black. He saw Eddie and waved, then came over and stood on the curb, watching him.

"Good morning." Eddie lifted one windshield wiper to scrape underneath.

"Happy new year, Eddie. I haven't seen you for a while, at least not outside news reports."

"Nope."

"You haven't been to Mass for six months." Father Claude sounded a bit aggrieved.

"Nope." Eddie started feeling nervous.

"Your mother's concerned about you."

He kept scraping.

"I am, too," the priest added.

"Well, Maman must have told you I'm going to a different church, sir." Eddie didn't want to call him 'Father,' but it seemed rude not to address him directly.

"Yes. A Protestant church."

Eddie shrugged and moved to the other side of the truck. He prayed in his heart to God, asking whether he should open his mouth or not. He really didn't want to argue with a priest.

"You shouldn't listen to them," Father Claude said. "Your friend is wrong."

So. His mother had been talking to the priest about Harvey. "It's not my friend I'm listening to," Eddie said. "It's the Bible. I go to a church where they teach me what the Bible says."

"Eddie, Eddie. You were in catechism as a little boy. The sisters taught you what the scripture says."

Eddie hesitated. "When I read the Bible, things are different from what I was taught."

Father Claude frowned. "In what way?"

Eddie gulped. "Well, you know it says that Jesus died on the cross for us."

"Of course. The Church has taught you that."

"But I was always told that I had to do all kinds of things, or I wouldn't go to heaven."

"The Bible teaches obedience, Eddie."

"Yes, but that comes after. I'm trying to obey what God says to do, but I know I'm saved and Jesus did everything to save me."

"That's dangerous. To think you can be absolved without obedience . . ."

Eddie's stomach churned. He certainly wasn't getting across what he meant. He wished Pastor Rowland was there, or Harvey.

"I'm not saying we shouldn't obey, or we don't *have* to obey. I'm saying that isn't what makes us pure in God's eyes. We believe. It says it in

Acts, 'Believe in the Lord Jesus, and you will be saved.' That's all we have to do. Jesus did the rest." It was one of the first verses he had memorized, because he was so shaky on that teaching. He hoped he'd said it right. He was sweating like he did when he wore his Kevlar vest in August.

"I should have come sooner," Father Claude said.

Eddie flicked the ice off the blade, opened the driver's door, and tossed the scraper in. "I'm going someplace."

"You can come back anytime."

Eddie thought about that. "What would happen if I did?"

"The Church would welcome you. Your family would rejoice."

"What would God do?"

Father Claude's eyebrows shot up. "He would accept you, of course."

"So, what would I have to do?"

"Just come back."

"What, I wouldn't have to confess?"

"Well, of course. I would give you penance. But if you were truly repentant, it wouldn't be too heavy. Prayers to the Virgin—"

Eddie shook his head. "No, sir. I won't do that. I confess my sins to God now. The Bible says there's one mediator, Jesus Christ. I talk to Him." Where had that come from? Wednesday night

Bible study, he guessed, but he had no idea what part of the Bible it was in.

"May God show you the error of your ways." Father Claude turned away slowly and walked down the sidewalk. He could tell Eddie's mother he had tried.

Eddie got in the truck and turned the key, his hand shaking. He sat there a minute before he put the transmission in gear.

Chapter 14

Saturday, January 1

Eddie got to Harvey's house about nine o'clock. He sat down with Harvey, Leeanne, and the coffeepot and gave them a report on Mason and his mother.

"Mason checked out okay, and his father picked him up at the hospital. The mom needed surgery on her leg, and her pelvis is broken."

"Ouch," Harvey said.

"Yeah. She lost a lot of blood and had serious internal bruising. I keep wondering if I should have tried to pull her out of the van."

"You did plenty," Leeanne said. "The van could have exploded if you hadn't put the fire out. Harvey said so."

Abby came tearing into the kitchen carrying a laptop. "Oh, good, you're here. It's all over Facebook, Eddie."

"What is?" He didn't mess with social media much these days. He'd accepted online friend requests from all the Wainthrop sisters and their three brothers, but he didn't spend much time on there.

"You," Abby said. She plopped down in the chair between Eddie and Harvey and set the laptop on the table. "Look here. I think it's the one that was on the news last night."

The video was grainy and dark, but it was Eddie all right, with Mason hugged up tight against his cheek and his little baby arms hugging Eddie for all he was worth, with his mom's wrecked van just behind them. Emergency lights flickered red and blue over what could have been a junkyard full of cars but was actually Congress Street on New Year's Eve. It lasted all of eight seconds, and the camera panned to follow them. The clip ended as they passed whoever held the camera and headed toward a parked ambulance.

"That must have been taken right after you put the fire out," Leeanne said.

Harvey smiled. "Put it to music and you're the next Audie Murphy."

Eddie looked over at him. "Who's Audie Murphy?"

Harvey shook his head, and Eddie figured it was some old guy he'd never heard of.

Leeanne pulled the laptop over and started the video again. She smiled as she watched him rescue Mason again.

"And that's not all," Abby said.

"What, there's more?" Eddie asked.

Abby grinned. "Yeah. Someone at the TV station put it on YouTube. You've gone viral."

"Maybe I need some medication."

"Funny, funny, French Boy."

Eddie scowled at her. "Hey, that's really annoying."

"Not to mention politically incorrect," Harvey added.

Leeanne glared at her. "Yeah, do you want him calling you Anglo Girl?"

"I don't care. Eddie and I are buds."

They all looked murderously at Abby.

"Okay, okay, I'll find another nickname for you."

"Eddie is fine," he said.

"Or Detective Thibodeau," Harvey murmured and sipped his coffee.

"Hey! Don't be mean," Abby cried.

Harvey laughed.

Her face flushed. She wrestled the laptop from Leeanne and clicked away on the keyboard. "Look at that!"

"Do I want to?" Eddie asked.

"Delaney Marshall shared the post, and look what she wrote."

Eddie leaned in and squinted at the print below the video box. "If you've cried over this guy, raise your hand. *What?*"

Leeanne leaned over on his shoulder and peered at it. "She's already got twenty-one comments, and she only posted it fifteen minutes ago."

Eddie pushed back his chair. "Okay, that's it. I'm going upstairs and lug down a few wedding gifts. Anyone want to help me?"

"I will," Harvey said.

They went up the stairs together.

"Where's Jennifer, anyway?" Eddie asked.

"I told her to sleep in. Babies take a lot of extra rest to grow properly."

"Okay." Harvey was the baby expert now, and Eddie trusted him on things like that.

Wrapped packages were piled all over the spare room bed, dresser, and part of the floor.

"Just grab a few and carry them down to the study," Harvey said. "When Jeff comes, we'll put them in his truck."

They each made five or six trips. As they piled up the last presents downstairs, Eddie said, "It feels like we should be working on the case."

"Mike's new budget doesn't allow much overtime."

"Aren't you worried that Hawkins and Mel Tucker will get away?"

"Not really. This is their turf. But if it makes you feel better, I asked Joey to watch for flags for us."

Joey Bolduc was in the detective squad, and he had taken advanced computer training. He was one of the few officers outside the Priority Unit who had Jennifer's program on his computer.

"I really should go out and clean up the driveway," Harvey said. "The plow guy came this morning, but it's kind of messy."

"I'll help you." They rigged up and told the girls where they'd be.

"You know, more heart attacks happen when people are shoveling after the holidays," Abby called down the hall after them. "Rich food and unaccustomed exercise."

Harvey ignored her, and they went out to shovel for half an hour. It looked pretty good when they'd finished, and they had one giant snowbank at the corner of the yard and the driveway. Eddie wondered how Leeanne felt about digging igloos.

When they went inside, Abby and Leeanne had disappeared, but Jennifer was in the kitchen. Harvey went over and kissed her. "How you doing, gorgeous?"

"Good. The baby's really active this morning."

He patted her tummy, and Eddie pretended he didn't notice.

"Eddie, want some coffee?" she asked.

"Oh, we had some before, but thanks."

Harvey said, "I haven't checked my stocks for days. Excuse me for a few minutes?"

"Sure," she said, and Eddie nodded. Harvey went into the study.

Eddie went over and leaned on the counter near the sink. "Am I here too much?"

Jennifer smiled. "No, Eddie, you're always welcome."

"Thanks."

She was rolling out dough, and something that smelled good was in the oven.

"Do you remember Jane Morrow, from Coastal?" she asked.

"Yeah." How could Eddie forget her ditsy coworker? Jane had ideas about him, but he'd managed to escape unscathed.

"She sent me a link this morning to that video of you carrying the little boy. She said it's had half a million hits on YouTube."

Eddie stared at her. "That's bad, right?"

She laughed. "Depends on how you look at it. I wouldn't be surprised if some national news broadcasts picked it up."

"Why? It was a routine thing. I mean, there were some flames, but I got it out real fast. It's not like the car blew up or anything."

"But you're both so cute, you and Mason."

"Oh." He frowned.

"What's the matter?"

"I'm sick of being cute. And Abby's friend . . . Did you see what she put on Facebook?"

"Yeah. So far fifty-four women have cried over you, and counting."

Eddie let out a little moan. "I'd just like to do my job and be left alone."

"Now you sound like my husband." Jennifer picked up a round cutter and started cutting out biscuits. "I never know how many people I'm feeding anymore, so I just make extra."

"Abby and Leeanne should help you."

"Oh, they do. I'm enjoying this."

He studied her profile as she worked. "Jennifer, does Leeanne have to leave?"

"I think she needs some time at home before school starts again. Mom will go over her clothes with her, and things like that."

"I'm going to miss her. Couldn't she just—" He stopped. Leeanne had said she couldn't.

"What?" Jennifer opened the oven and took out a tray of cookies and put another in. She started taking the baked cookies off the pan with a spatula.

"Nothing. I wish she lived down here, but I know that's not going to happen."

She removed a couple more cookies, then looked at him. "Nowadays it's important for women to be educated and be able to get good jobs. It's not like it was a hundred years ago."

"I guess not."

"What are you talking about?" Leeanne stood in the doorway. Eddie wanted to fix the image in his mind forever, because he felt he was losing her all over again. Her hair gleamed, and her blue eyes were serious. She was dressed in black pants and a green sweatshirt with cardinals on the front. She came in and sat at the table.

"You, going back to school," said Jennifer. She set the cookie sheet in the sink and went back to her biscuits.

Leeanne sat down. "I wish I didn't have to, but I do."

"Do you like it at Farmington?" Eddie asked.

"It's okay. I kind of wish now that I'd gone to a private school, not the state university. The atmosphere is . . . well, there's a lot of drinking and stuff. And the language is awful. Even the professors . . . But private colleges are expensive."

"A lot of them aren't much better as far as the social atmosphere goes," Jennifer said. "Of course, there are Christian colleges, but most of them are outside New England."

Eddie felt pangs of panic. Why did Jennifer have to get Leeanne thinking about schools that were farther away? He'd been thinking of the one across town.

"I've only got one year left after this," Leeanne said. "If I transferred now, I'd probably lose some credits."

"You don't want to add more time to it," Eddie said, watching her anxiously.

"No, I don't."

"Want some cookies?" Jennifer asked.

"Sure. I'll get the milk." Leeanne rose and went to the refrigerator.

Eddie would never turn down cookies, but that wasn't what he really wanted.

Harvey came in from the study, holding a newspaper.

"Are your stocks doing okay?" Jennifer asked.

"The market's off a little. Not bad." He kissed her. She extended her arms to him, and he kissed her again, while Leeanne poured the milk.

"Want some, Harvey?"

"Yeah, thanks."

"Can I talk to you, Harvey?" Eddie asked.

"Sure. Talk." He picked up two cookies.

"I mean alone."

Harvey raised his eyebrows. "Okay. Come in here." Eddie followed him into the living room, and they sat down. "What's up?"

"You're not trying to get Leeanne to go to a Christian college, are you?" Eddie asked.

Harvey smiled. "Wouldn't that be great? Is she thinking about it?"

"No, I guess not. It was just something Jennifer said."

"That would be a wonderful opportunity for her. Think about it. She'd have the chance we never had. To study God's word while she's young, and to be under a Christian influence. It would be terrific."

"Not for me," Eddie said glumly.

"Oh, Ed, she's young. Now is the time for her to do things, go places."

"I was hoping she'd move down here."

Harvey sighed. "You're not ready to make a lifetime commitment."

"Yes, I am."

"Well, she's not. Don't you want her to see what's out there before she settles down? I'd help her out if she wanted to go to a Christian school."

Eddie scowled. "Man, this is a rotten day."

"How rotten?"

"It's Leeanne's last day here, and the priest came to lecture me, and you just wrecked my life."

"Oh, come on. I said I'd help my sister-in-law get a Christian education if she wanted it. I think it would be money well spent." He took a bite of a cookie and chewed. "You're not taking this well, Ed. What's the real problem?"

Eddie looked over his shoulder to make sure nobody else was within earshot. "I love her. I was reconciled to driving two hours each way to see her. But now you want to send her off to—who knows where. And she just said if she transferred to another college, she'd probably lose some credit and have to take extra classes."

"That's probably true," Harvey said. "If she transfers, she may change her major, too. She'd probably need two years after this one—"

"Two years," Eddie almost yelled. "Stop! I can't take this." He put one hand to his forehead and stared at the Murillo print on the opposite wall. *The Divine Shepherd*, Jesus as a little boy, with his hand on a fat, fluffy sheep. He looked a little like Mason.

"The priest, huh?" said Harvey.

"Yup. Father Claude. He says I can come back any time I want to."

"What did you tell him?"

"That we don't have to do stuff. We just have to believe." Eddie looked at him. "He thinks I'm apostate now. That's the word, right?"

"Sounds like you did all right. Talking to Catholics about the Lord is tough."

Eddie gave him a wry smile. "You sound like you speak from experience."

"Yeah. Hey, I'm sorry, Eddie."

"Are you thinking up these college things to get Leeanne away from me? You knew my feelings."

"I didn't think it up. And I did know how you felt. I didn't mean to hurt you. Just try to think of what would be best for Leeanne in the long run. If I had that chance now . . ."

"You're not going to quit the P.D. and go back to school, are you?" Eddie asked.

"No, I've got a family to feed. I don't think God is leading me that way. But Leeanne is in the ideal time for it. God can use her in so many ways, and if she had training—"

"If she had training, she'd probably go off to Mongolia or someplace to preach to the heathen," Eddie said. "Or she'd wind up married to some guy who's a pastor in some little church in Idaho, and have to work to support him because his congregation couldn't."

Harvey just sat there, looking at him. "I wasn't

thinking that way at all," he said at last. "Just give her some space and pray about it."

"I upset Eddie again." Leeanne sat down on the settee and watched Jennifer arranging the Noah's ark set on top of a bookcase.

"How's that?" Jennifer asked.

"He freaked when you mentioned Christian colleges. I'd need an extra semester at least if I transferred now."

"Oh, honey, he just hadn't thought about that sort of thing." Jennifer threw her a smile. "I'm sure if he did, he'd realize you would be in a much better atmosphere. I went to state university, too, don't forget. I know exactly what you're talking about."

"He did, too."

"Yes, but Eddie's background is a lot different from ours."

Leeanne watched her for a moment. "You had some rough times at school, didn't you?"

"Why do you say that?"

"I heard about that guy you dated. Neil What's-His-Name. The one Eddie arrested last fall."

Jennifer grimaced. "Yeah, well, that's something we try not to talk about much around here. And the truth is, those things can happen anywhere."

"I suppose. But Eddie seemed shocked by the idea of me going away. And things were going really well last night. Other than the wreck, I mean. But we worked together, and I thought, wow, we can get through hard things, the two of us."

"I think you can." Jennifer put the two kangaroos in place and stood back to study the effect. "There." She came over and sat down beside Leeanne. "You and Eddie are both smart people. And you've got lots of years ahead of you."

"You and Harvey keep saying that. We're young. Well, we are, but I think Eddie's feeling the big 3-0 coming at him."

"He turned twenty-eight not long ago."

"Yeah, but he sees all his friends getting married and having babies . . . He doesn't want to miss that."

Jennifer frowned. "I did read someplace that when a man's ready to settle down, he's ready. Period."

"I keep asking myself, if I never went anyplace else or did anything huge, but I had a happy life with Eddie, would that be so bad? Would I really miss anything important?"

Jennifer squeezed her hand. "Until you can answer that, you should keep your options open."

Leeanne hugged her stomach. "Sometimes I just ache, thinking about him. Is that what love feels like?"

"No."

"Really?" She stared at Jennifer. "Then why do I feel this way?"

"Okay, let's rewind," Jennifer said. "I did agonize over Harvey, because I knew committing to him would be dangerous in some ways."

"The bombs and stuff?"

"Well, yes, but I also knew the biggest danger was that I could lose him. Suddenly. Violently. Any day I could get that call from Mike."

"Yeah. I've thought about that, too. You're five months along. What if Harvey got killed on the job now?"

"That would be hard. But I made up my mind last spring that it would be worth whatever time I had with him."

"Because you loved him so much."

"Yes, and because he loved *me* so much."

Leeanne studied the lines of Jennifer's dear face. "He's really good to you."

Jennifer nodded. "More than I deserve."

"We don't any of us deserve anything, do we?"

"I suppose not. But I realized one day how important I was to him, and how crushed he would be if I turned him down."

"That's not a reason to marry a man."

"Not in itself, no. But it was part of what made me love him enough to take the chance. If Harvey died tomorrow, I wouldn't regret marrying him. And I know he feels the same."

"Okay, but that's kind of morbid," Leeanne

said. "Realistically, Eddie and I could have sixty or seventy years together."

"That would be quite an adventure."

"Yeah." Leeanne thought about what it would be like to be retired and spending the winter in Florida with a gray-haired Eddie. "I do want to be a reporter."

"I know, and I think that's a good fit for you. But you've got to realize that journalism is changing. In another five years, we might not have newspapers anymore."

Leeanne sighed. "But we'll always need to get the news out. And we'll always need cops."

"Yeah. Unfortunately, that's true." Jennifer smiled. "I think you *should* be a writer. You're so . . . verbal. I know you'll be great at it. And I don't think Eddie wants to get in the way of your aspirations."

"I guess not."

"He's been through a lot lately," Jennifer said. "He feels like his family's abandoned him. He's looking to us as his new family. Us and the Priority Unit. We're the ones he knows he can depend on."

Leeanne nodded. "I don't want to let him down."

"I know. But you shouldn't let that be the reason to commit your life to him, either. Do you love him?"

"I don't know. Part of me says, 'Of course!

How could anyone not love Eddie?' You know?"

"Yeah, I know." Jennifer smiled. "He's very sweet, very lovable. And he's matured tremendously this year. He's also very transparent. When he's sad, you know it, and you want to cry for him. When he's happy, the world is happy."

Leeanne chuckled. "You're right. Harvey keeps things inside. Eddie doesn't."

"I think that's why they're so good for each other." Jennifer stirred as footsteps sounded in the kitchen. "Speaking of the Invincible Duo . . ." She stood as Harvey came to the sunroom doorway. "Hey, sweetie. What's up?"

"Jeff and Beth are here to get the gifts."

Leeanne watched Eddie through the rest of the day. He was mostly upbeat and helpful. But now and then when their gaze met across the room, his sad eyes made her rethink all her plans and hopes. Her emotions swirled, and she knew she had to stay noncommittal for now.

After Beth and Jeff left, Harvey and Jennifer drove to Saco to see Everett Bailey, their house's former owner, and make the second payment on their house. Abby played Risk with Eddie and Leeanne while they were gone. Leeanne didn't want to make Abby uncomfortable, so she kept the tone light and playful. Eddie seemed okay with that.

At four, the Larsons came home with a book on the history of Portland, a gift from Mr. Bailey.

"Don't forget, you're babysitting tonight," Abby told Jennifer.

"We haven't forgotten." Jennifer looked at Eddie. "Can you stay and help us entertain Peter's boys?"

"I guess, if you don't mind," Eddie said.

"I told you, you're welcome anytime, and I think you'd be an asset tonight."

Eddie stayed, and Leeanne was glad.

Peter Hobart dropped Andy and Gary off at five o'clock and took Abby away for the evening. Abby looked especially pretty, Leeanne thought, and she seemed to sparkle when Peter was around. She had thought Abby favored Greg Prescott slightly over Peter, but maybe she was wrong. Maybe Peter was the right man for her, after all.

After supper, she and Eddie played a protracted game of I Spy with the boys, where Eddie would hide one of the Noah's Ark animals and the boys and Leeanne had to find it. Then Harvey and Jennifer sat Gary and Andy down in the sunroom for a game of Parcheesi. Leeanne watched and egged them all on, but didn't get involved in the game.

"Can we talk?" Eddie asked her.

"Okay." She glanced at Jennifer, but her sister was deep into the board game. Leeanne followed Eddie into the living room. They sat down together on the couch.

"I don't want you to leave," Eddie said.

She smiled. "I have to go back tomorrow. Jeff is—"

"Can I come up next weekend?"

"Okay. I'll ask Mom when I get home, to make sure."

"Good. But I really meant that I don't want you to leave Maine."

She caught her breath. "I wasn't really thinking about it. Don't let that upset you."

He reached for both her hands, and she looked directly at him. His eyes brimmed with longing. "Leeanne, I love you." He stopped short and gave a little laugh.

"What?" His reaction confused her.

"I don't think I said that to a girl in English before."

"You're joking."

"No. I haven't said it much anyway, but . . . well, somehow it always seemed . . . I don't know . . . easier in French."

"Less binding?" Her studies had taught her that "*je t'aime*" could mean I love you or I like you. She supposed that might blur the lines in some cases. She could feel a flush creeping into her cheeks.

"I do love you," Eddie said quietly, staring into her eyes. "If I have to wait two or three years, I will, but I want you to know I'm serious about this."

She pulled in a shaky breath, uncertain what to say.

His gaze fell. "I guess it's not fair to ask you to sign your life away without knowing what the alternatives are."

"Oh, Eddie." Tears threatened, and she blinked them back. Already, he was talking about a lifetime together.

"If you take two more years of school, I'll be thirty." He looked embarrassed, as if he hadn't meant to say it out loud. He shook his head. "I don't want to start over at thirty. If you go away, how do I know you'll come back?"

"I . . . guess you don't." She put her hand up to his rumpled collar and turned it down. "How do I know, when I go back home, that you'll still feel this way when I come back?"

They locked eyes.

"I will," he said. She had the feeling he had never meant anything so much in his life. He pulled her in close and kissed her, and she kissed him back, even though something inside told her to be cautious. He was so warm, so loving, so endearing. She could have this for the rest of her life. Maybe. Was Jennifer right, that it was worth the risk? Until she was sure, she wouldn't be doing Eddie any favors if she let him think her heart was settled.

Chapter 15

Little Andy Hobart was sleeping on the couch at half past ten, and Gary stared glassy-eyed at a *Dumbo* tape. Leeanne and Eddie had talked some more with Harvey and Jennifer, and Eddie wasn't hurting quite so much. They'd eaten popcorn and discussed Lamaze class, Leeanne's upcoming course in broadcast journalism, and baby names.

"George for Daddy," said Leeanne.

Jennifer shook her head. "I like Caleb."

"How about Michael?" Eddie asked.

It went on for some time. They'd had this conversation before, and Eddie suspected they'd had it many times. Harvey had a book that told what names meant. Edward was 'rich,' which seemed ironic. Jennifer was 'the fair lady,' and Eddie thought that fit her. Leeanne was a combination of Lea for meadow and Anne, for grace. Harvey supposedly meant something like "worthy in battle."

Harvey sat with his arm around Jennifer all the time, and he smiled every time she looked at him. He was so happy, Eddie couldn't be mad at him. He'd known him when he was miserable, and he'd wanted Harvey to have this contentment and peace.

Harvey hadn't intended to cause any distress,

of that Eddie was sure. He was faithful to Eddie, but he had extended his good will to the whole Wainthrop family now, and Eddie had to accept that sometimes his feelings wouldn't come first.

Peter and Abby returned, and Peter lugged Andy out to his car. Gary went under his own power, and Peter said goodnight to Abby in the entry. Eddie wondered if he was making any progress.

He knew he should leave, too. It was almost eleven, but it was also the last night Leeanne would be there, and he put it off.

Harvey yawned and stretched, bringing his arm up over Jennifer's head.

"Tired?" Eddie asked.

"Kind of."

"Guess I'd better go." He glanced at Leeanne. She looked thoughtful.

Harvey's phone rang, and he went into the study to take the call. Jennifer frowned, but kept the conversation going. When he came back to the living room, he looked at Eddie.

"That was Joey. Melanie Tucker's flag came up."

"Yeah?"

"She got stopped at a routine sobriety check-point last night."

"She was OUI?"

"No," Harvey said. "Perfectly sober, or it would have showed up sooner. One of the patrol officers just dumped their whole list of people they checked into the system this afternoon."

"Weird."

"Yes, but it got us an address and a license plate number for her."

Eddie stood up. "You want to go out now?"

Harvey shook his head. "Let's meet early tomorrow."

"Okay. Seven?"

"How about eight? It's getting late."

Jennifer sighed, then smiled. "My husband, the captain. I wouldn't trade him for anyone."

"If you want him to have a decent night's sleep you'd better haul him off to bed," Eddie said and headed for the kitchen.

Abby was out there getting herself a bowl of ice cream. "Hey," she said, "seventy-one sobbin' women now. They're all weeping over you."

"You're hysterical." Eddie looked back into the living room. Leeanne was standing by her chair, looking after him.

"Come here," he said softly.

Leeanne came through the kitchen to the entry. Eddie got his coat out of the closet and put it on, but he didn't zip it. He stepped up close to her and put his hands on her shoulders. The light in the entry wasn't very strong, but he could see her blue eyes, and they weren't as happy as he'd have liked. He kissed the tip of her nose.

"I'll see you at church, if we don't get hung up on the case tomorrow morning."

"Okay."

"When are you leaving?" he asked.

"I think Jeff and Beth will eat lunch here, then we'll go."

"If it's at all possible, I'll be here." She nodded, and he said, "But just in case I don't see you . . ." She was avidly waiting for whatever he was going to say. It felt good to have her concentrating all her energy on him. "Leeanne, I love you."

She put her hands on his chest, where his sweatshirt said, "*Je me souviens*," and when he kissed her, she moved them slowly, cautiously in under his jacket and around him. He held her close. He loved her so intensely that he wanted to stay with her always. "*Je t'aime*," he whispered into her hair.

"You love me in two languages?" She was whispering, too.

"Yes. *Oui. Avec tout mon coeur.*"

She took a deep breath. "I . . . I need some time."

"I'll wait. *J'attendrai.*"

She said, "I want to be sure. I've—I've never said it to anyone before. In any language."

She raised her gaze to meet Eddie's, and he couldn't help kissing her again, she looked so sweet and, yes, ready for it. He thought her kiss was more definite now, more decided somehow.

He considered taking her off somewhere and

proposing marriage and pleading his cause, but he knew she'd say no then. And she was leaving.

She said softly, *"Bonsoir,"* and he said, *"A demain,"* which was, "until tomorrow," and pulled himself away.

Eddie got to the office first, and he made coffee. Harvey walked in on the dot of eight. They went over what little information Joey Bolduc had left for them. The license plate turned out to be one off a car reported stolen several weeks earlier. They decided to go to the address listed on Melanie's driver's license.

The people who lived in the small wood-frame house were not happy when the detectives woke them up at eight-thirty Sunday morning. They claimed they'd never heard of Melanie Tucker. Discouraged, Harvey and Eddie left their neighborhood.

"What do you think?" Eddie asked Harvey.

"She had a fake driver's license."

"Mm. If she works for a drug dealer, it's probably a perk of the job. So, what now?"

"I don't know."

Eddie frowned. "Maybe Melanie Tucker isn't even her real name."

"Let's go check it out," Harvey said. "We should be able to find out if a real person by that name has a Social Security number."

"On Sunday?"

"I've got some computer sites that should do it."

Harvey had super-high clearance to government sites very few people could access. He actually found a lot of Melanie Tuckers, but only four in Maine, and only one of those lived in Portland. In about twenty minutes, he had not only her Social Security number, but her childhood medical record and a detailed criminal record. A social services file that began when she was a child was sealed, but they did learn she was adopted at the age of two. After that, he found an original birth record and a court record of her name being changed to Melanie Tucker by her adoptive parents.

The one piece of information missing was where she lived now. Harvey collected three possible address, two within the city limits, one in South Portland.

He looked at his watch. "I think I'll save these for tomorrow."

"What now?" Eddie asked.

"Church. Let's go thank the Lord for his mercy and ask him to help us crack this case."

They drove separately, and when they reached the church parking lot, Eddie noted Jennifer's car and Beth's. Mike's was at the far end of the lot, beside a black-and-white.

He looked toward the church door. A uniformed officer stood to one side in the portico.

"Harvey," he said uneasily.

"It's the protective detail." Harvey walked up

the steps. "Good morning, Officer Needham. Any problems here?"

"No, sir, Captain. The chief wanted to come to church is all."

Harvey nodded. "Stay alert."

Sunday school was half over, and Eddie figured they were so late there was no sense disrupting the singles class. He went into the auditorium with Harvey. The first thing he noticed was another patrol officer sitting alone in a pew behind Mike and Sharon. He thought from the color of her hair and the way she wore it that it was Officer Allison Crocker.

"Looks like the chief brought guests," Harvey whispered to him.

Beyond Mike and Sharon in their row sat the deputy chief and a woman Eddie took to be his wife.

"What do you know," he said.

They walked down the side aisle and sat on the end of the row where Jennifer and Jeff were sitting. When the lesson was over, Harvey caught Mike's eye, and Mike came over and shook hands.

"Didn't get a chance to tell you. Jack and I had a talk Friday. He's a Christian. He was hoping they could find a good church down here, so I brought him and his wife along. Come say hello after the service."

"Bring them to our house for lunch," said Jennifer.

"Well, we're going to take them out," Mike said. "Maybe next week."

"Hey, does Crocker want to stay in the service?" Harvey asked. "Because you probably don't need her in the same room with you while Eddie and I are here."

Mike smiled. "You know, they've driven me crazy all weekend. This morning I was a little grouchy. I said to Sharon, 'Can't I even go to church without my shadows?' But then Allison asked if we'd mind if she sat in. She said she normally goes to her own church when she's not on duty, and she would love to be able to worship while she was guarding me. How could I be upset after that?"

"That's great, as long as she keeps her eyes open during prayer," Harvey said.

Mike chuckled. "Good one. Was Needham outside when you came in?"

"Yes, he was. I'd say you're well protected for the next hour."

Beth came from the girls' class she taught, and Abby and Leeanne returned from the singles' lesson with a total of three young men escorting them. Charlie Emery and Josh Wright were standard in Abby's retinue, but the third guy surprised Eddie. He didn't recognize Mr. Tall, Dark and Semi-Handsome, and he was chatting up Leeanne like crazy.

Eddie stood up by the end of the pew and

smiled at Leeanne. She came right to him, like a paper clip to a magnet, and Mr. New Guy got the message and faded away. Abby disengaged from Charlie and Josh and squeezed into the row, too, but Peter Hobart came at the last second and said something to her, and she got up and went with him. Everybody shuffled a little, and the service began.

The pastor was up to his usual form, and Eddie knew he needed to pay attention and learn, but with Leeanne's shoulder touching his, it was hard to concentrate. The minutes ticked away. He wanted to hold her hand, but she had her notebook out, so Eddie pulled his out, too. At least if he took a few notes, he could look at it later and not totally lose the point.

After the service, he and Harvey met Mrs. Stewart and welcomed her and the deputy chief. Mike had a few words with Harvey, and he and Sharon headed out with the Stewarts and the security detail.

When Allison Crocker passed Eddie, she smiled. "I didn't realize this was your church, Eddie."

"Yeah. Mine and Harvey's. And the chief's."

"Nice. I enjoyed it. Oh, and I saw you on YouTube." She hurried off after the Brownings.

Lunch at Harvey's went too fast. Before Eddie knew it, Leeanne was upstairs changing her clothes, and Jeff was loading her big suitcase into Beth's car.

"Mike says he wants to arrange more first aid training for us," Harvey said.

Eddie shrugged. "We had it at the Academy, but I guess a refresher wouldn't hurt."

"Well, one of the patrolmen was stabbed last night. His partner controlled the bleeding. Seems like we have more and more injuries on the job. Mike wants us all to have advanced training, maybe even the EMT course."

"Guess it might be good. Who got hurt?"

"McFarland. You know him?"

Eddie shook his head. "Not really. I know who he is. Do we get paid for the training?"

"I'm not sure yet. But Mike's also thinking about a body armor rule."

"What, make us wear our vests all the time?"

"Well, the patrol officers, anyway."

"Man, what a pain. Remember last summer, how hot it was?" Eddie asked.

"Do I ever."

"Where's all this coming from?"

Harvey shrugged. "Stewart, maybe."

Ah. The new deputy chief was trying to make his mark.

Leeanne came downstairs in jeans and a plum-colored blouse, carrying a small duffel bag and her purse.

"Let me get those," Harvey said. He took the bags from her and went out.

Eddie stood looking at Leeanne. Her hair fell

softly on her shoulders. She walked toward him, smiling ruefully.

"Guess this is it until Saturday."

He held out his arms, and she walked into them. He held her very gently.

"Do you think in English?" she asked.

"Yes. I'm as American as you."

"I'm sorry. It's just that my professor said that's how you know you're proficient in a language, if you start thinking in it. I don't believe I could ever think in French."

"Maybe when I was little," Eddie said. "It was kind of a mix, I guess. We always talked English at home, except to my grandparents. Well, not always . . . hey, do we have to talk about this now?"

"No."

He kissed her and tightened his hold on her. She nestled her head in against his chest. Eddie let his cheek rest on top of her head.

"Guess I've got to leave." She touched the leather strap on his shoulder and followed it down to his holster. "You take care."

"I will." He could tell she was thinking about the hazards of his job. Maybe Harvey had said something about the body armor. He said, "We don't get shot at much."

"How often?"

Eddie shrugged.

"Once a month?" she asked.

"Less." He tipped her head up and looked into her eyes. "I'll miss you."

She let him kiss her again, and he took his time, but when he was done she pushed away, smoothing her hair, her cheeks flushed. He took her hand and walked out into the kitchen with her. Everybody was standing around talking, waiting for them. Leeanne blushed more when they looked at her.

"Come back when you can," Harvey said to her.

"I'd like to."

Jennifer and Abby hugged her, and she got her coat and walked toward the door with Jeff and Beth. Five thousand things rushed into Eddie's mind, things he should have said. He walked outside. It was warm, and everything was dripping. She waved before she got in the car. Harvey came and stood beside him. The car disappeared at the corner of the street.

"She'll be back," Harvey said.

"I'm going up Saturday, if I don't have to chase pushers."

They went inside, and Harvey went to his computer. Eddie leaned in the study doorway, waiting for him to finish.

When he sat back, Eddie said, "You want to work?"

"No. Well, yes, but I'm not going to. Mike says I've got to learn to let it go when I'm off duty, and Jennifer feels that way, too."

"I guess I should go see my folks." Father Claude's visit still churned in the back of Eddie's mind. "What would you say to a mother who sics a priest on you?"

Harvey thought for a minute. "I guess I'd say, 'I love you, Mom. Thanks for caring about me.'"

"Thanks. I needed you to say that. It wasn't at all what I was thinking of saying."

"Be grateful for your mother, Eddie."

He nodded. Harvey had lost both his parents when he was eighteen. Where would Eddie have been for the last ten years, if not for Pop and Maman?

He drove over to his neighborhood feeling a little nostalgic and, thanks to Harvey, thankful. He parked at the curb because Pop was blowing the driveway. He shut the machine off when Eddie walked over.

"Hey, Pop."

"Oh, so finally we get a visit. Where you been all week?"

"Working."

"Hmm." He turned the engine on again.

Eddie yelled, "Why don't you let me finish this after I say hello to Maman?"

"Yeah, I just might."

"Good," Eddie said. "Leave it right here. I'll come finish it."

He shut it off. "You can't go to confession to make your mother happy?"

Eddie raised a hand, remembering why he'd made himself scarce the last few months, but his father had turned away, toward the garage.

Eddie walked to the side door and went into the kitchen. His mother was loading the dishwasher.

"*Sacré bleu*, it's my only son."

Eddie laughed. "Hello, Maman." He kissed her cheek.

"Oh, sweet boy." She stepped back abruptly and scowled at him. "What do you mean, being sassy to the priest?"

Eddie pulled in a deep breath. "I wasn't trying to be rude to him."

"Don't lie to me, Edouard Jean!"

"*C'est vrai.*" But she wasn't buying it.

"And what in heaven's name is this vulgar thing online about all these women whose hearts you've broken?"

"Uh . . ." He didn't have a good answer for that one.

"Lisa showed me," she said. "A hundred and thirty-seven women are saying you made them cry. What's *that* all about?"

Eddie had deliberately avoided checking the numbers. He should have known other people would. He spread his hands, trying to find words.

"But the video of you toting the little boy is sweet." Maman grabbed him and kissed him on the cheek. "*That's* my son, the good one. The one saving little children, not the one making women cry."

"Okay. I'm going to go out and finish the driveway for Pop."

"Why didn't you come an hour ago, before he started?"

Eddie almost swore, but then he remembered Harvey's advice. It came from his boss, but he thought God was responsible for the reminder. He pointed a finger at his mother.

"I love you, Maman. Thank you for caring about me."

Her face softened.

He went out and spent the next half hour blowing snow and shoveling the walks. Pop was nowhere in sight.

Chapter 16

Sunday, January 2

Eddie almost didn't go back to church that night, but he knew that came from laziness, fatigue, and loneliness. He made himself get ready and go.

Officers Emily Rood and Aaron O'Heir were standing near the church steps.

"Don't tell me," Eddie said. "The chief's here."

"Yep," Emily said. "He told us we didn't need to go in, since Captain Larson and Deputy Chief Stewart are here, and now you."

"Well, if you want to hear a good sermon, or if you just want to swap off and get warm, this is the place."

"Thanks, Eddie," Emily said.

He went inside. Abby was at work, but Harvey and Jennifer were already there. Eddie dropped onto the pew beside Harvey.

"How are your folks?" Harvey asked.

"Same as usual. I cleared some snow for Pop, but it's so warm out now, it probably would have melted anyway. And I took your advice with my mother."

Jeff and Beth came in after a record trip to Skowhegan and back. Beth assured him Leeanne was safely home.

After the service, Jennifer talked to Jeff about her parents. He and Beth had stayed only an hour at their house, but they had messages from Mrs. Wainthrop, and late Christmas gifts for the Larsons.

Rachel Trueworthy walked past in the aisle, and Eddie said, "Hi."

She looked at him in surprise. "Didn't think you were speaking to me."

"No, I—"

"It's okay, Eddie." She walked away. She was a nice girl, and Eddie did like her, but when he thought about Leeanne, he knew his feelings for Rachel were in a totally different category. He hoped she wasn't Weepy Woman Number 138.

"It's raining," Jennifer said when they went out to the parking lot.

Eddie didn't like that. A thaw in January was not necessarily a good thing in Maine. In some ways, it was better if it stayed cold until it was done being cold.

The temperature dropped again in the night, and when Eddie went outside on Monday morning, the driveway was slippery with frozen rain. He had to scrape the ice off the windshield before he could go anywhere. Power lines and tree branches glittered like Christmas garlands as the first rays of dawn hit them.

It was too dangerous to run outside, where

everything was coated with ice. He drove to the campus in a glistening, eerie landscape where trucks crept along, spewing sand and salt on the slick pavement. Tree limbs were bowed down. Some had cracked under the weight of the ice. Harvey was already inside the track house.

"So, today we try to run down Melanie Tucker?" Eddie asked while taking off his jacket.

"Her and Al Hawkins," Harvey said.

If they could find either one of them that day, Eddie would be happy.

They did their three miles, and Eddie's thoughts drifted off to Skowhegan while he ran. He wondered if Leeanne was awake yet, and if she was looking online at far distant colleges. Probably she was out in the barn, feeding her goats. Her dad would be glad she was back, so he didn't have to do it.

At the station, the dispatcher called in reserve officers to help with all the collisions. Power lines started snapping, and some companies put the word out for their employees to stay home. The rural areas were hit hardest, with trees going down on the wires. To the north of the city, thousands were without power.

Nate couldn't get to work because a tree had fallen across his road. Harvey told him to take his time and come in when he could. The rest of them set to work on Melanie Tucker's possible location. Harvey didn't want anyone to go out looking for her until the temps climbed above freezing again. The roads were slicker than a greased eel.

A half hour into the shift, Paula came to Eddie's desk with a handful of phone message sheets.

"What's this?" he asked.

"You had a few calls. I didn't put them through—thought you'd want to screen them first."

He looked at the first one. It had a phone number and "Celeste" on it. He frowned, not recognizing the name. The other five were similar, but with different women's names and numbers. Eddie looked over at Paula.

"Do any of these have to do with the case we're working on?"

"No, those are ones where the caller said it was personal." Paula gave him a sweet smile.

Eddie threw them in his trashcan.

He made a few calls to confidential informants and people he knew who lived in bad neighborhoods. Between him and Harvey, they knew just about every felon in the city, but most of them didn't want to talk about Al Hawkins, and they all claimed they'd never heard of Melanie Tucker.

Harvey was glued to his desk, too. They both put everything they had into finding the man who wanted to kill Mike. Harvey did a lot of scowling and staring at his screen. Eddie knew what that meant. He would go over and over the information he had until either something jumped out at him or he went berserk.

About nine o'clock, he closed a phone call, got up, and walked over to Eddie's desk.

"Mike wants us both upstairs."

Eddie tried to read his face. "New case?"

"I don't know yet. He just told me to make sure I brought you."

Eddie didn't like the sound of that. "I hope nothing happened at his house last night."

"I think we'd have heard."

They took the stairs. Mike's secretary, Judith, eyed them solemnly when Harvey opened the security door. She was sixtyish and gray-haired, Mike's legacy from the former chief.

"Good morning, Captain. Detective." She buzzed Mike on the phone. "Captain Larson and his gendarme are here."

Eddie was startled. Had Judith actually made a joke? He'd never seen her smile, and she was always polite and professional. He couldn't believe it.

Harvey looked amused, but he didn't say anything.

"Go right in, gentlemen." Judith turned to her computer and ignored them, typing rapidly.

Jack Stewart was in Mike's office with him.

"Hope you fellows don't mind if Jack sits in," Mike said.

"Not at all." Harvey nodded to Jack and took

251

a seat, leaving the most comfortable chair for Eddie. That was just Harvey.

"Good," Mike said. "I've discussed this new matter with him."

"A new case?" Harvey asked.

"More like a new opportunity. At least, that's what Jack's trying to tell me. Coffee?"

The bosses were both drinking coffee, and Harvey said, "Sure."

"I'll get it." Eddie jumped up and went over to the table where Mike had his coffee setup. He had a new coffeemaker. Maybe a Christmas gift? It was one of those ones where you made the individual cup. Eddie didn't want to interrupt them, so he picked a container marked Original Medium Roast for Harvey, because it sounded impossible to hate, and decided to try one called Mocha Fudge himself.

"This involves an interview for one of your detectives," Mike said to Harvey.

"About the Quinlan case?"

"No, something else. Jack thinks it would be good P.R. for the department. It would mean half a day off his regular routine—paid, of course— for Eddie."

Eddie was just about to carry Harvey's Original Medium Roast to him, and he almost dropped the mug. He got a grip on it and stared at the chief. Mike was watching him.

"Me?" he said.

"Yeah, you, Eddie."

"I don't know if I can spare him right now," Harvey said. "We're really pushing on the Quinlan case, Mike. None of us wants to do a P.R. stunt while your life is in danger."

Mike made a face. "Well, nothing's happened since Kyle Quinlan died. I'm thinking we got all wound up over nothing."

"No, it's not nothing," Harvey said. "The guy who made the deal with Kyle still wants you dead."

Jack Stewart cleared his throat. "They wouldn't send the camera crew until Wednesday."

"Camera crew?" Eddie asked.

Mike grinned. "Yeah. Whether I survive this thing or not, *Morning Nation* wants to interview you. They're going to show the clip of you that's apparently taken the cyber world by storm, and—"

"Hold it," Harvey said. "This is about that kid he pulled out of the wreck Friday night?"

"Yeah. I never go to YouTube, but apparently at least a million other people do."

"A million?" Harvey swiveled around and gaped at Eddie.

"And that doesn't even count the two hundred women whose hearts you've broken," Mike said, with a nod of respect—or fake respect—Eddie's way.

Eddie managed to put the coffee mug in Harvey's hands. He completely forgot about the Mocha Fudge and staggered to his chair. He knew about YouTube, but he'd never seen *Morning Nation*. He had a vague impression it was a morning news show, but it was always on when he was at work. He looked over at Harvey, who calmly sipped the coffee.

Jack leaned toward Eddie and smiled. "You could be an ambassador for the Portland Police Department on national television, Detective Thibodeau. Everyone will see you committing a heroic act, and then the hosts will have a little fun at your expense, mentioning how this video sparked a poll of women who've lost their hearts to you."

Eddie swallowed hard. "Okay, two things. First, it wasn't that heroic. The kid wasn't in danger anymore, unless it would be another car slamming into their van. They ought to be interviewing Mark Johnson, the EMT who kept his mother alive until they could get her out of there. Second, the kid has nothing to do with that blasted Delaney Marshall or any other woman I've dated."

"Language, Eddie," Harvey murmured.

"Sorry."

"Who's Delaney Marshall?" Mike asked.

"I believe she's the one who started the thing about women who've cried over Eddie," Harvey said. "She's a nurse at Maine Medical, and she posted it on Facebook with a link to the video of him rescuing the child." He made it sound so normal, Eddie almost calmed down. Almost.

"You know—" Eddie looked at Mike and tried to forget that Mike was his boss's boss and held his career in his hands. "Sir. The alleged fact that a woman—quote—shed tears over me—unquote—doesn't mean I did anything to her."

"That's a good line," Jack said. "You should use it in the interview."

Harvey said, "He's right. Some of them might be women who wished Eddie would look their way twice, but he never did, so they cried about it—whether literally or figuratively, I can't say."

"Hmm." Mike clicked a few keys on his keyboard. Eddie always thought of Mike as being a little out of the loop where computers were concerned, but a moment later, he turned the monitor to face them. "Is this the Delaney Marshall you know?"

It was the same Facebook page Abby had showed them Friday night.

"Yeah."

"She's got more than a thousand comments on her post about you."

Eddie stared at him. Probably not safe to utter one word.

"That's a lot," Harvey said, unnecessarily. "Could be she started it to drive traffic to her page."

"She's not selling anything," Mike said.

Harvey shrugged. "Then I have no explanation for it."

Eddie scowled. "She wants attention." At that moment, he was gladder than ever that he hadn't called her again after their one outing. Definitely not his kind of woman, even if he'd thought she was a fun date at the time.

Mike leveled his gaze at Eddie. "So, how well do you know Ms. Marshall?"

Eddie hesitated. "Do I have to answer that?"

Mike looked away for a second, and his mouth twitched like he was trying not to say something. Then he looked back at Eddie. "Is this something that could blow up in our faces and be an embarrassment to the P.D.?"

"Uh . . ." Eddie looked at Harvey.

"Answer the question," he said softly.

"Well, uh, let's see, I only took her out once. Possibly twice, but—no, no, it was only once. I'm sure. And it was about five years ago."

Mike blinked. "That long?"

"At least."

"You must have made an impression," Jack said.

"I . . ." This wasn't something where Eddie could beg off and tell them to let somebody else do the interview.

Harvey set down his mug. "I don't know, Chief. This could get messy. What if they looked her up and put her on the show?"

"Hmm." Mike tapped his chin. "They say they want to film here and take him to the hospital to be reunited with the kid and his parents in the mother's hospital room."

"That sounds okay," Harvey said.

"The hospital?" Eddie squeaked out.

"Didn't you say they took her to Mercy Hospital?" Harvey asked. "That's not where Delaney works."

Eddie breathed. "Right."

Mike looked at him expectantly.

"I . . . guess it would be okay. I wouldn't mind seeing Mason again. But what if a bunch of angry women picket outside, or something like that?"

"I just had a thought," Mike said. "Let me see what I can do to counteract any negative comments. And don't you talk to anyone about this, you hear?"

Eddie nodded.

"Right. Be ready when you come in Wednesday morning."

Eddie opened his mouth and closed it again. When the chief spoke, you didn't talk back.

"If you're sure, Mike," Harvey said.

"Yeah, I'm sure." Mike turned to Jack with a grin. "I love these guys. These are the two men I know are praying for me every day."

Jack nodded. "I was really glad to hear we had a couple of Christians in the department." He smiled at them. "Wasn't sure what I was getting into when I moved down here."

"Funny," Mike said, "we sweated for months over who to hire. Harvey knows. We interviewed a ton of people. Of course, I wasn't a praying man then, but I guess Harvey was praying about it."

"I was," said Harvey. "Not that I had any say in it, but I sat in on most of the interviews." He looked at Jack. "I missed yours, sir. Anyway, I was praying hard for the right person to take this position."

Mike nodded. "These guys have regular prayer times. Maybe we can get in on it with them sometime."

Harvey said, "Anytime you want, Chief. Mr. Stewart."

"Okay. I'll let you boys get back to work." Mike stood. "You got any leads on Hawkins yet?"

"Maybe," Harvey said. "The roads should be better this afternoon. We'll be out in the West End, looking for him."

"Keep me posted."

Eddie and Harvey left the office and went back to Priority. Just outside the door, Eddie stopped. "Harvey, Mike wouldn't do anything dishonest to slant the interview, would he?"

"No, Mike wouldn't—" Harvey stopped with his hand on the door handle. He got a funny look on his face.

"I know he's a Christian now," Eddie said, "but it hasn't been for long, and you gotta admit he has some screwy logic sometimes."

"Yeah." Harvey's chin jerked up. "Don't you ever say that to anyone else."

"I won't. Just an observation."

Harvey glanced at him. "Our Sunday school class has started a series on Genesis. You know—creation and all that."

Eddie nodded. In the singles class, they were doing a different study, but he'd caught half of Harvey's the day before.

Harvey said, "Mike called me yesterday to ask me how God could create plants before he created the sun."

Eddie thought about that for a second. "Plants need sunlight, don't they?"

"Yeah. For photosynthesis."

"Let there be light." Eddie frowned. "He created light before he created the sun, too. So, there must have been some for the plants."

"Yeah. I suppose there was light in heaven before that. But none of it gets to the earth."

They looked at each other.

Harvey said, "I wish he wouldn't ask me these questions when I'm in the middle of a case."

"You're always in the middle of a case."

"Come on. Maybe I'll have time to do some reading tonight." Harvey opened the door.

Chapter 17

Nate Miller jumped up as soon as he saw Harvey. "Captain, I think we've got a solid lead on Melanie Tucker."

Harvey looked out the window. "The roads?"

"All the main arteries are good. They're working on the side streets."

"Okay, let's do it. Body armor. I'll ask for some backup."

The men swarmed the locker room to get ready.

"What happened to the tree on your road?" Eddie asked Nate.

"My neighbor has a chainsaw and a tractor."

When Eddie came out of the locker room, Harvey was talking to Jennifer. Eddie only knew because he heard his final, "I'll be there, gorgeous."

Eddie wished for a moment that he could call Leeanne, but she would only worry. Then he saw a pile of square message memos on his desk. He picked them up and turned to scowl at Paula.

"All personal," she said. "Sorry."

Eddie shook his head and tossed the lot in the trash.

They usually drove their own cars for this type of work. Tony had a vintage Mustang he loved, but he hadn't brought it that day. Too risky with all the ice. They took Harvey's SUV and Eddie's truck, because both had four-wheel drive if needed. The backup officers followed them in a squad car.

When they got to the address Nate's informant had provided, Eddie said, "What is this, a crack house?"

The run-down duplex looked neglected. All the blinds were drawn, and an old Chevy was parked out front.

"Either that or a meth lab," Nate said. "Dusty didn't want to be too specific."

"Oh, yeah, Dusty. I've met him. It probably *is* a meth lab."

Eddie got out, and so did Nate. Harvey had pulled in behind them, a couple of lots down from the targeted house. The squad car rolled around a corner and parked out of sight. Nate and Eddie walked back to meet the others.

Harvey gave them their assignments, making sure all the doors and windows would be covered, and they got into position. Jimmy and one of the uniformed cops, Chuck Norton, went with Eddie to the back of the house.

"Hey, Eddie, did you send up a prayer for us?" Jimmy asked.

Chuck shot him a curious glance.

"Yeah." Scanning the windows, Eddie saw a flicker of movement at the small one that was probably a bathroom window. "They know we're here." Harvey signaled him on his earpiece, and Eddie nodded at Chuck. "Go." He tried not to think about how meth labs can blow on you.

Chuck kicked the door, and they heard yelling and a couple of shots fired at the front. Eddie's heart raced as he and Jimmy jumped into position, but it was already over. Harvey and Tony had two men and a woman lying face down on the floor. One of the men was bleeding, and Harvey was calling for an ambulance. Nate and another patrolman came in behind them. Together they checked all the rooms of the house, including the closets and attic, but the three people in the room with the setup for making crack cocaine were the only ones there.

"Melanie Tucker?" Nate asked the woman.

"Yeah?"

"Put your hands behind your back." Nate met Eddie's gaze above the sprawled prisoners, and Eddie nodded.

When she stood up, he was surprised at her appearance. Her hair was brown with gray roots, and she had serious wrinkles around her mouth. Eddie pegged her at fifty to sixty years old. If she'd been a book, he'd have said she was pulp fiction and showing some shelf wear. He was dying to question her, but the plan was to get them all secured in custody first and talk later.

Harvey knelt and put pressure on the injured man's wound, but that didn't stop him from having the officers frisk all three prisoners. Eddie asked Tony who the shooter was.

"Me." The hotshot looked a little shaky.

Eddie said, "You better sit down, Tony."

"I'm okay."

Chuck went to bring up the squad car. The two patrolmen would take Melanie back to the station and book her, so that she would be through processing when the detectives got there. Harvey asked for transport for the uninjured male prisoner.

The ambulance came first. While the EMTs tended to the injured guy, Tony and Eddie bagged up the improvised lab equipment, supplies, and finished product. Nate and Jimmy's thorough search turned up four thousand dollars in the kitchen and another twelve hundred in a bedroom.

The second patrol car came for the other prisoner, whose driver's license said he was Bruce Leare. Eddie didn't remember him specifically, but he thought Leare had crossed his radar before.

Finally a team of techs came to clean up after them, and the EMTs put the wounded man in the bus and drove off. The detectives headed back to the station. A soft mist was falling.

In the police garage, the first thing Harvey said was, "Okay, Winfield, put your gear away and go home. You've got a couple of days off, maybe more. Enjoy it."

"Aw, Cap'n, can't I just hang around and watch?"

"Better not, Tony." Harvey was probably thinking of his last suspension after a shooting. He, of all people, knew it was best to stay out of it until the administrative hearing came up.

"We'll keep you posted, Tony," Eddie said.

"Man, I really wanted to be in on this."

Harvey said, "I'll push things through as quick as I can, but trust me, it's good to take a little time off after a shooting."

Tony dragged up the stairs with Eddie and stuck his vest in his locker, swearing under his breath.

"Who are you mad at?" Eddie asked.

"Myself, I guess. If I hadn't shot that guy . . ."

"If you hadn't shot that guy, he'd have blown your head off," Eddie said. "Go on. We'll miss you."

"Yeah, because I won't be there to edit your reports, Shakespeare."

"Touché."

Eddie did a quick rundown on Bruce Leare and the guy Tony had shot. As he had thought, Leare had quite a rap sheet. The injured man had some smalltime infractions.

Harvey called Tony over and talked to him quietly for a couple of minutes. Tony seemed attentive and nodded a lot. Eddie guessed Harvey was telling him what to expect for the hearing. He'd have to see the department's head shrinker, too. Tony wouldn't like talking to the psychologist.

Paula came over to Eddie smiling. "Glad you guys all came back in one piece."

"Thanks," Eddie said.

"The desk sergeant just called to tell you the prisoner is ready for you."

"Okay."

She slipped more messages into his hand. "Highly personal, all of these."

Eddie glanced down at them. Heather. Did he know a Heather? He threw them away without looking at the rest.

As soon as Tony left, Eddie told Harvey the news. They brought Melanie up to their interview room.

Harvey wanted Jimmy and Nate to get some experience, so he had Nate stand guard in there while Eddie questioned Melanie, and he took Jimmy into the observation room to give him the annotated version and answer any questions Jimmy might have.

The first thing Eddie asked her was what she was thinking, getting involved in a drug ring.

"What? You think I should get a job at a classier place?" she said.

Eddie let that pass. "Tell me about Al Hawkins."

"Never heard of him."

"Wrong answer. Try again."

"Oh, buzz off, you bozo."

Eddie sat back and looked her in the eye. "I've got all day, Melanie. Start telling me about Al Hawkins. That's who you were making the crack for, wasn't it?"

"I wasn't making it."

"Who was?"

"Those two imbeciles."

"And your job was . . ."

"I was just there to do laundry."

Eddie frowned. "Launder the drug money, maybe."

"Ha, ha."

"Okay, Mel, this is how it works: You tell me about Al, and I tell the D.A. not to set your bail too high."

She scowled. "You're that guy on the news, aren't you?"

Eddie tried not to miss a beat. "I don't know, am I?"

"Yeah. All the girls have been talking about how hot you are."

"All what girls, Mel?"

"Oh, you'd like to know, wouldn't you?"

"You got some girls working for you, or are they working for Al?"

"Go easy on me, handsome, and I'll set you up with a couple."

"No, thanks." Just what he needed, on top of YouTube and *Morning Nation*. "Just tell me about Al. He's the only thing I'm interested in right now."

She tried to stare him down, but Eddie had a lot of practice.

"Can I use the can?"

Eddie sighed. "We'll get a female officer to escort you."

"I can go by myself, hot stuff."

It was ludicrous, coming out of her mouth when she was so patently unattractive.

With Harvey in the observation room, Eddie knew he would already have put the call in, so he just waited. After about half a minute, Melanie said, "I really gotta go."

"I'm sure you do. Any minute now."

A knock came on the door, and Nate opened it.

"Ta-da," Eddie said.

Allison Crocker came in. She glanced at him, then at Melanie. "Let's go."

Melanie got up and shuffled out into the office.

"Use our locker room," Eddie said. Behind Melanie's back, he gave Allison the "watching" signal, pointing at his eyes, then the prisoner, meaning keep your eyes on her.

"Oh boy, the locker room," Melanie simpered.

Eddie looked at Nate. "Wait outside for them."

Nate followed them down the short hallway. Harvey and Jimmy came out of Observation.

"She's tough," Harvey said.

"Yeah. Why haven't we arrested her before?"

"Maybe she's good at hiding. Want me to take a crack at her?"

"Sure. Maybe she'll like your blue eyes better than my brown ones."

"I doubt it. She seemed pretty taken with you."

Jimmy laughed. "I heard you're big stuff right now, Eddie, since that news clip ran of you carrying a baby."

"It wasn't a baby, it was a kid." Eddie shook his head. He didn't want to get into that again.

"Why don't you take Jimmy down and have a few words with Mr. Leare," Harvey said. "Nate and I will take on Ms. Tucker."

"Yeah, thanks."

Bruce Leare at first seemed surprisingly eager to talk. Maybe Tony shooting his buddy scared him. He admitted he'd been making crack cocaine for the man they were looking for, since Hawkins got out of jail.

"Who did you work for before that?" Eddie asked.

"Nobody."

"Sure." Like Eddie would believe this was the first time he ever manufactured crack and sold it. "You were in jail in New Hampshire a month ago."

"Yeah. I did my time."

"Why did you go to work for Hawkins? You could have made a fresh start. Now you're going back in the slammer."

Leare bit his lip and made faces, and then he said, "I need a lawyer, and I can't pay for one."

Eddie didn't like it, but he had to stop questioning him.

When he and Jimmy got up to the office, Harvey was sitting at his desk and Nate ambled over.

"Did Melanie spill, or did you get tired of flirting with her?" Eddie asked.

"She's about as cooperative as a rock," Harvey said. "I sent her back downstairs. How did you make out?"

"I'd say I got about as much information from him as you did from Mel."

"What, you couldn't read his mind?"

Eddie folded his hands and gave him the Altar Boy persona. "I don't even pretend to know what guys like that are thinking, Captain."

Nate grinned at him. "Sure you do, sweet stuff."

Eddie frowned. "Watch it."

"I think it's 'hot stuff,' Nate," Jimmy said.

Nate laughed. "Oh, yeah, that's it."

"Gentlemen," Harvey said, "let's get back to work, shall we?"

Chapter 18

Tuesday, January 4

The two prisoners were arraigned Tuesday morning. Melanie made bail. At least they knew where to find her. At any rate, she promised not to elude them if they went looking for her again. Leare was held over.

They worked all morning on what they knew about Hawkins, but at lunchtime they were no closer to finding him.

Around two, Eddie took a call from the sergeant on the main desk.

"Bruce Leare wants to talk to you."

"Is he still here? I thought he went to the county jail."

"He did. You'll have to go over there."

Eddie told Harvey about the call.

"Let's pray before you go," Harvey said. "Mike is really chafing about this. We need something solid, and soon."

They went into the breakroom and shut the door. They didn't usually take time out for prayer during work, but this case was different. The fact that an armed killer had planned to go into Mike's house festered. The chief was doing his job on the fourth floor, as usual, but he wanted results. Eddie couldn't blame him. They prayed briefly but sincerely.

"Get going," Harvey said when they'd finished. "Don't promise Leare anything, but try to find out if he has a vulnerable spot."

Eddie drove over to the jail, passing by the exact spot on Congress Street where the accident had occurred Friday night. Traffic moved along smoothly today.

An officer brought Leare into the visitors' room. It was outside regular visiting hours, so no one else was in there. Leare shuffled to his spot and sat down across from Eddie.

"Hey," he said.

"You asked for me?"

"Yeah. I can't stay in here, man."

"That's not up to me," Eddie said.

"You can help me."

"What makes you think that?"

He sat there for a long time, fidgeting.

"Let's not waste time, Bruce," Eddie said.

"Okay. What do you want to know?"

"Everything about Al Hawkins."

Leare huffed out a breath. "He said if I didn't do what he wanted, he'd have me snuffed, like he had Kyle."

"Hawkins told you he killed Kyle Quinlan?"

"Yeah."

Eddie wondered what Hawkins's game was, claiming a murder that he'd had no part in.

Probably he was using Kyle's death to scare Leare, and it was working.

"So, tell me about the operation."

Leare told him where and when he handed money off to Hawkins and who came to get the product at the house where they'd arrested him. He named four runners Hawkins used to distribute for him, and then he looked at Eddie.

"Is Rog going to die?" Rog, Eddie took it, was Roger Tasker, the man Tony had shot.

"I don't think so."

"Good." Leare squinted at him. "But the kid died."

"What kid?"

"Kyle. He was one of Al's dealers. I heard that he told Kyle if he didn't take out the cop that nailed him, he'd kill him. And now Kyle's dead."

"Oh, that kid," Eddie said.

"It wasn't you he was after, was it?" Leare asked.

"No, not me."

"So who killed him? I know Al wouldn't do it himself."

Eddie wasn't about to tell him, so he said, "Odd things happen when you mix it up with guys like Hawkins."

"Yeah." Leare frowned. "If he was out to get you, I was going to tell you who Al tapped to do the hit when Kyle messed up."

"Oh yeah? I'd be interested in that."

"You know who they're gunning for?"

"I find it hard to believe you don't."

Leare sat there for a few seconds with a calculating look. "I heard it was a big-time cop."

"Then you know it wasn't me. Tell me who the new triggerman is."

"You gotta get me a deal."

Eddie wasn't really allowed to deal, but he thought that for this information, Mike might be able to pull some strings. Once they knew who now held the contract, they could protect Mike from him.

"Who's your lawyer?"

He told Eddie the attorney's name.

"Did he talk to the D.A.?"

"Yeah."

"I probably can't do anything for you, but I'll give it my best shot. Now, who's Al's new shooter?"

"Skinny guy they call Rooster. Real name's Bentley. Is he really after the chief of police?"

So he did know. Eddie eyed him keenly. "That's the scuttlebutt."

Leare grinned. "I knew it!"

Eddie left and went back to the office.

"Well?" Harvey asked.

Eddie smiled and handed him the tape from the interview. "He was ready to talk. Listen and rejoice, my friend."

Harvey put on his headset and listened. Eddie

went to his desk to start looking for intel on Rooster Bentley. Three more messages had appeared like magic. The top one read, "Let's reconnect. Dani," and a phone number. He swiveled and looked across the room at Paula. She smiled and waved.

Harvey came over, frowning. Eddie said, "What?"

"Leare was awfully eager to dump on Hawkins when he talked to you."

"Yeah. But remember, he just got out of jail in New Hampshire. I think he's scared to do another stint, and I know he's afraid of Hawkins."

"How long was he in jail?"

"Nine months," Eddie said.

"Hmm. When did he land back in Maine? Because his rap sheet says he's a native."

"About three weeks ago."

Harvey's forehead wrinkled. "Maybe he wants to see Hawkins put away for a long time and figures he can take over part of his turf while he's in prison."

"Maybe, but I think he's just plain scared."

Now that they had some good information on Hawkins's drug operation, they had a strong possibility of finding him. Nobody wanted to wait, but they had to do some work first.

Harvey, Nate, and Jimmy started in on the new data on Hawkins and his runners. Eddie focused on locating Rooster Bentley. By quitting time, he had some leads he hoped would pan out.

It was Lamaze night, and they all knocked off at five o'clock.

"I think we're going to tour the delivery suite and the neonatal nursery tonight," Harvey told Eddie.

"Maybe you'll see Abby."

"Yeah. I'm hoping that if I see the delivery room ahead of time, I'll stay conscious when we go there for business."

He reminded Eddie to come in early on Wednesday and be ready to work with the TV crew. They seemed to have managed to keep the TV taping a secret, but Paula had continued to deliver phone messages, which got more provocative as the day went on. Eddie ignored them.

He went home and called Leeanne. She sounded glad to hear from him.

"My folks saw you on the news with Mason," she said.

"Really? Way up there?" Eddie tried to make it sound insignificant.

"Yeah. And I showed the YouTube thing to Travis and Randy. They think it's cool."

"Well, uh, I might get to see Mason again tomorrow."

"For real? That's exciting."

"Yeah, I, uh . . . I'm doing a news interview about it. They're doing this reunion thing."

"Wow, I am so impressed. Will it be on the Portland station?"

"Uh . . ."

"Eddie?" she said.

"Yeah, I'm here. I think it's going to run in the morning."

"Morning news?"

"Do you, uh, know what *Morning Nation* is?"

"Holy smoke! Oops, is that a bad word?"

"I don't know."

Leeanne laughed. "You're not kidding, are you?"

"I wish I was."

"Why? This is awesome."

Eddie sighed. "I'm afraid they'll ask me about the other thing."

"What other thing? Oh, you mean the Sobbin' Women, as Abby calls them?"

"Yeah. You're not mad about that, are you?"

"No. I've been getting some reflected notoriety because of it. I told one of my friends that I was with you New Year's Eve when you rescued Mason, and she's been telling everyone she knows and asking me if I've cried over you yet."

"Have you?"

"Yes, but I didn't tell her."

Eddie wasn't sure what to say. Somehow, Leeanne sounded more confident now, and less fragile where their relationship was concerned.

"Leeanne, if they make me look like a heel—"

"It's okay, Eddie. I know you, and television is television. I won't buy into anything they say to make you look bad."

"Promise?"

"Absolutely."

"Thanks." He wished he totally believed that.

"You saved two lives. Why would they want to smear you?"

"For ratings."

"Maybe they don't know about the crying poll."

"Maybe." But he knew they did.

Eddie got to the station at seven-thirty on Wednesday morning with a churning stomach. He and Harvey had agreed to skip the run that day, but they prayed in the garage before they went in. Paula had been warned and also arrived early. The television reporter, Mia Hennessey, and her makeup artist and cameraman were waiting. Paula introduced them to Eddie.

"You're the hero?" Mia said.

He gulped, and Harvey said, "He's your man."

"My, you're beautiful." She looked Eddie up and down.

"Harvey," Eddie said, eyeing him without hope.

"Relax. You can do this."

"Let's sit you down and get you made up for the show," Mia said.

"Do I have to wear makeup?" Eddie asked.

"Trust me, you want to look good. Not that you

don't, but Leeza can play up those Gallic eyes and the planes of your cheekbones. There won't be a woman in America who isn't in love with you after our show airs."

Eddie looked desperately toward Harvey, but he'd gone to his desk and was opening his briefcase.

"We're going to the hospital, right?" Eddie asked.

"Yes, after we do some shots here," Mia replied.

"Oh, man. People will see me wearing makeup."

"It will make you look better," Leeza said. "Where can I set up? Is that your desk?" She pointed.

"Not out here!" Jimmy came in from the stairway. "Can't we go someplace else?" Eddie pleaded.

Harvey came over, smiling a little. "Why don't you take Leeza to the interview room?"

"So the other guys can watch?"

"All right, the breakroom."

"Okay." To Leeza, Eddie said, "It's small, but it's more private."

"Lead the way."

The next hour was sheer torture. First the makeup, and Leeza trimmed the back of his hair a little. Even though he insisted she take it easy on the makeup, that took at least twenty minutes. Then the cameraman taped him working at his desk, handing Harvey a report, and taking his Kevlar vest out of his locker. Mia had him take off his sport jacket so his shoulder holster showed.

She did a little introduction to the interview standing in front of the door that said PRIORITY UNIT.

Finally, they settled down for some questions, with Rudy, the cameraman, in Eddie's face. Mia prompted him to tell about the accident. Eddie didn't tell her Leeanne's name, but that he had a friend with him that night. He told her about the crash, Mason and his mom, the fire, getting the extinguisher, spraying the engine, and going back for Mason.

"That's great," Mia said. "We'll use the video clip that's been posted to YouTube, and we located another person who caught the fire on her phone."

"You have footage of the fire?"

"Yes. So, how did it feel when you pulled Mason out of that burning van?"

Eddie glanced at Rudy. The red RECORD light still glowed. "Well, I was glad, but I wished I could have helped his mother, too. She was hurt pretty bad. But before she passed out, she told me to get Mason out, and I did."

"Did you try to get Mrs. McInnes out, too?"

"By the time I got Mason free, we could

see flames under the hood, so I ran for my fire extinguisher."

"Do you always carry a fire extinguisher?" Mia asked.

"It's part of my emergency gear."

Mia grinned. "Detective Thibodeau, is rescuing people your superpower?"

Eddie eyed her warily. "Not really. I don't get to do it very often."

"Oh, so what *is* your superpower?" She didn't bat her eyelashes, but Eddie recognized the flirty tone in her voice.

Our Father, which art in heaven, help me not to make a fool of myself.

"I don't think I have one, but I have a supernatural person helping me."

Her eyes widened, and before she could stop him, he said, "I'm pretty sure God helped me and the EMTs that night."

She barely skipped a beat, but her smile tightened. "Have you seen Mason since the accident?"

"No, I haven't. I checked on his mom once at the hospital."

"Would you like to go with us over to the hospital now? I'm told he's there, visiting his mother, whom you also helped save when you put out that terrifying fire."

"I would like to do that, yes."

She smiled at the camera. "Let's go."

On the way out of the building, she had Rudy take some shots of the front of the police station. Eddie took his truck and followed Mia and her crew to Mercy. As they walked into the lobby, people stared at them. Eddie kept walking, hoping no women out of his past would pop out at him. They took the elevator to what they called a med-surg floor.

Mason's mother looked terrible. She had purple bruising all over one side of her face, and she was strapped up in bed and had a cast on her left leg, up to her waist. A machine had wires going to her to take her pulse and monitor her breathing, and an IV pole stood near the head of the bed.

Even with all that, she smiled at Eddie and said, "I remember you. Thanks for all you did."

"Hey, it was nothing. I'm just glad you're going to be okay." Eddie tried to forget about the camera and talk to her like he normally would have.

Her husband was holding Mason.

"I'm Bill McInnes. Thank you so much."

"You're welcome. I really didn't do that much."

"Oh, we've thanked the EMTs, too, but if you hadn't been on the spot and put that fire out . . ." Bill shook his head. "We're all grateful. Right, Mason?" He looked at the little boy, who eyed Eddie soberly with big, blue eyes.

Eddie stepped toward them. "Hi, Mason. I'm Eddie. Do you remember me?"

Mason cringed against his father for just a second, then reached toward Eddie and leaned out away from his dad. Eddie caught him in his arms.

"Hey, buddy." He chuckled as Mason almost choked him with his hug.

"Eddie." Mason burrowed his face into Eddie's shirt.

His parents laughed, and Eddie thought they were a little relieved. If Mason had screamed, that would have ruined their moment.

Mia stepped up with her microphone. "Mason, do you remember when Eddie took you to the ambulance?"

He wouldn't look at her, but he nodded up and down vigorously against Eddie's shirt.

"Did you know Eddie was a policeman?"

"P'wiceman."

Eddie reached into his jacket pocket. He'd popped into the mall the night before for a keepsake. "I brought you something, Mason. If your daddy doesn't mind."

Bill McInnes looked at the plastic ambulance in his hand and nodded.

"Here you go," Eddie said. "You got to ride in one of these with your mom."

Mason clutched the toy and dug in again on his chest. Eddie hugged him and patted his back. "You feeling okay now?"

Mason nodded. Rudy weaved a little, looking for the best shot of Mason's face.

Mia said, "What a great moment for our hero and little Mason McInnes. Now, Detective Thibodeau, may I show you something else?"

"I guess." Reluctantly, Eddie handed Mason off to his dad. What was she pulling now?

Leeza handed Mia an iPad. She lowered her voice and stage-whispered to Eddie, "We'll show this full screen when the segment airs."

Oh, great. He didn't get a chance to preview it. She turned the iPad toward him and hit a button. A video started.

Eddie's mouth went dry.

Sarah!

Chapter 19

Eddie's jaw just about hit the floor. Sarah looked great. He supposed they did makeup on her, too, but she looked absolutely terrific. She wasn't wearing her uniform, but a very girlie-looking pink blouse and matching lipstick. He was suddenly very conscious of Rudy taping his reaction.

"Sarah Benoit," Mia said off-screen, "You're a police officer with the Portland Police Department. Do you know Detective Thibodeau?"

"Sure, I know him pretty well."

"Are you one of those women who admit to crying over this man?"

Sarah gave a little smile. "I didn't put my name on the list, but, yeah, I've shed a few tears for Eddie."

"Recently?"

Eddie's heart pounded like a jackhammer. How did they find Sarah? She could bust his chops royally if she wanted to.

"We dated for two or three months last summer, and he's the sweetest man I've ever met."

Eddie breathed.

"What sort of dates did you have?"

"We went to the lighthouse, a concert—lots of places. He was always a fun date, and always considerate."

"Ms. Benoit, more than two hundred women have admitted to crying over this man."

"I'm not surprised. Who wouldn't want to marry him?" That was the smile Eddie used to watch for. Sarah had a fantastic smile.

"But the two of you broke up a few months ago," the reporter said. "Who broke it off?"

"It was mutual," Sarah said, as if it was no big deal. She didn't look mad or bereaved. "We were headed down different paths."

"So, why did you cry?"

"It was a difficult decision—for both of us. We came to the conclusion that we weren't right for each other. But, yeah, I was sad about it."

"You still work for the same police department. Do you ever see Detective Thibodeau anymore?"

"Of course," Sarah said. "Several times a week. We're still friends. But I'll say this: Whoever takes Eddie Thibodeau to the altar is one lucky woman."

Mia passed the iPad to a minion and stuck the microphone in Eddie's face. "Did you know we were going to interview your ex-girlfriend Sarah?"

"No, I had no idea."

"She speaks well of you, even though she cried over you."

Eddie managed a strained smile. "Yeah, well, I probably cried a little, too, but that's part of life, you know?"

The reporter turned to face the camera and said brightly, "There you have it! Our heart-breaking hero has a heart himself."

All the guys were waiting when Eddie got back to the office. It was no secret the TV crew had been there, or that he'd gone with them to see Mason.

"How'd it go?" Harvey asked.

"Could have been worse. They're going to show it tomorrow morning."

"Way to go," Nate said.

Jimmy grinned at him. "Cool, Eddie."

He looked at Harvey. "Did you know about Sarah?"

"Sarah?" Harvey's face went blank. "Sarah Benoit?"

"Yeah, they interviewed her. My token ex-girlfriend, I guess."

"What did she say?" Harvey asked. They all waited, probably wondering if Sarah had put his head on a figurative pike.

"She was nice."

"Were you surprised?" Nate asked.

"Well, I think it could have gone either way."

Harvey laughed. "You'll have to send her flowers."

"No, I don't want her to get any ideas. I will say thank you, though."

"Why do you suppose they picked her?" Harvey asked.

"I don't—" Eddie stopped. "Mike. Remember what he said?"

Harvey got this oh-no-he-wouldn't look. "I remember."

"You don't think he'd comp Sarah for not dumping on me, do you?"

"What, like give her a bonus?" Jimmy said.

"Yeah," Eddie said slowly. "Or recommend her for a promotion or something."

"No," Harvey said firmly. "Absolutely not. Mike wouldn't do anything like that."

"Are you sure?" Eddie asked.

Harvey said, "Ninety-nine-point-nine-nine-nine-nine percent sure. Excuse me."

He went over to his desk. Jimmy and Nate updated Eddie on what they'd learned about Hawkins's henchmen. They weren't ready yet to go after Hawkins himself, but they were compiling files on each of the drug runners they knew had worked for him.

Harvey came to his side. "I'm going to run upstairs for a minute. After these guys bring you up to speed, see what you can do about Rooster Bentley, hmm?"

"*D'accord,*" Eddie said.

"Yeah. *Merci.*"

Eddie tracked him with his eyes as he went to the stairway. Maybe he was going to find out what lay behind Sarah's interview.

Part of him wanted to call Leeanne, and part of

287

him said that would be a bad idea right now. He held off. He wasn't getting anywhere by phone or computer to find Rooster, and he teetered on the edge of frustration. Jimmy and Nate went out to get lunch.

"Did you eat?" Harvey asked Eddie when he returned.

"Not yet."

"Come home with me. I told Jennifer I might bring you."

Eddie put on his jacket and went down to the garage with him. On the way he said, "I've tapped every source I can without some leg-work. I think I should go out in the field this afternoon. We need to get Rooster before he gets to Mike."

"If he's really the one gunning for him now," Harvey said.

"Well, yeah. I've got informants who'll only talk to me in person."

"Get a few twenties from Paula, from the petty cash."

"Right."

"And don't go alone."

"I'll be okay."

"I said, don't go alone."

"Who should I take?" Eddie asked. "Tony's on the bench."

"See if Ron can loan us one of his detectives."

"Okay."

Harvey drove in silence for a minute then said, "I asked Mike about Sarah."

"Yeah?"

"He's not comping her, but he suggested her to Mia."

"Did he coach Sarah?"

Harvey shook his head. "Mike says he just asked her if she'd be willing to help *him* out by telling a reporter how she honestly feels about you."

"Come on, Harv, you don't know what she said."

"Yes, I do. They let Mike have a copy of Sarah's interview."

"Wow. She made it sound like we were both okay with the breakup, and like we're best buds now."

"Yeah, she went really easy on you. Do you think she had an ulterior motive?"

"I don't know what. She could have pulverized me."

"How? By telling the world you believe in Jesus Christ now, and you no longer date women who don't believe in him?"

"When you put it like that . . ."

"It might sound a little snooty, but I don't think people could hate you for that."

"Maybe not."

"Mike said he and Jack prayed about it before he approached Sarah to do it, and he swears he didn't put words in her mouth. He's thanking God for the outcome. Maybe you should do the same and not fret over it."

"Yeah, I'll do that. Thanks, Harv."

Jennifer and Abby welcomed Eddie and put an extra plate on the table. While they ate turkey pie, Harvey told Jennifer how boring things were at the office. She could see through him. She knew he liked nothing better than untangling the knots in a tough case.

"Did you have your big interview, Eddie?" she asked.

"Yeah."

"They're showing it on *Morning Nation* tomorrow," Harvey said.

Jennifer smiled at Eddie. "That's great."

Abby grinned. "We'll tape it. Was it scary?"

"Kind of."

"So, the new deputy turned out to be a keeper," said Jennifer. Eddie felt like she was changing the subject to put him at ease.

"Yeah," Harvey said. "I prayed so hard about getting the right man in there, but I never presumed to ask for a Christian."

"His wife seemed nice." Jennifer reached for the water pitcher. "They're eating here Sunday, right?"

"Yes, and Mike and Sharon."

Jennifer nodded. "You can come, too, Eddie."

"Thanks," he said.

When they'd finished, Harvey stood. "Excuse us if we eat and run."

"Can't you please sit down with me for ten minutes?" Jennifer pleaded. "I hardly see you these days."

Harvey looked at his watch. "Five, but you sit on my lap." They disappeared through the study door.

"Think he'll be back in five minutes?" asked Abby.

"Yup. Harvey's very punctual."

She started putting the food away. "Have you talked to Leeanne since she left?"

"Yeah, last night." Eddie hesitated. Abby was a friend who still thought in terms of singlehood. "I'm sort of afraid to, since the interview."

"Why?"

"I dunno. She hasn't seen it yet."

"You're really serious about her, aren't you?" Abby carried dishes to the sink.

"I'm dead serious. I'd marry her tomorrow."

"Wow." She turned the water on and looked at him. "When did this hit you?"

"End of October, I think, when she came down here. I'm done looking."

"Whew. I don't know, Eddie. She hasn't really had many serious boyfriends."

"I know. That's okay. Don't you think the first one can be the right one?"

Abby frowned as she squeezed out the dish-cloth. She went over to wipe the table. "I never really had a serious boyfriend, either."

"Oh, come on, you've got two now." Eddie had heard something about a doctor up in Waterville, too, when Abby worked at the hospital there, but that relationship seemed to be history.

"No. If either one of them was serious—for me, I mean—then I'd send the other one packing."

Eddie eyed her in disbelief. "You don't take either one of these guys seriously, but you keep them both around? I don't get it." He used to go out with a lot of different girls, but it was mostly for fun. If they started talking commitment, he said goodbye. But he was over that. And he knew Peter, at least, was in dead earnest.

"It's not that way," Abby said. "I like them both. I think I could be serious about either one of them. But how do I choose? How do I know which one is really the one for me? It's for life." She shook her head. "I've been praying about it. I don't want to hurt either one of them. But every time I think Peter's the one, Greg calls and I get this feeling . . . and every time I think Greg's the one, Peter does something that makes me reevaluate."

"Has either one said anything? About marriage, I mean?"

She laughed. "Peter proposed on our second

date. I told him I couldn't answer then. I need to marry a man I can love forever, not just two adorable boys I'd love to mother."

"You don't feel that way about Peter?"

"Well, sometimes . . . but if I really loved him God's way, I wouldn't get all giddy whenever Greg calls, would I?"

"They might not hang around forever."

"I know," she said miserably. "Maybe, subconsciously, I'm waiting for one of them to throw in the towel."

"Marry the other by default?"

"Well, persistence is a good quality."

Eddie said, "I hope in a year or two, you and I can sit down and laugh over this conversation."

"We'll probably both still be single," Abby said.

"I hope not. I'm tired of being a bachelor."

"Well, if both my guys give up, I'll let you know."

"Forget it," Eddie said. "We tested those waters. It's your sister I'm after."

She smiled. "You're a good friend, Eddie. I'll tell you something."

"What?"

She pushed her long, blonde braid back over her shoulder. "When Leeanne puts her mind to something, she stays with it. She's had those stupid goats for ten years. Ten years! She was in 4-H for six, but she kept those animals afterward.

She could have just sold them, but no, she has a commitment. You see what I'm driving at?"

"If she loves me, she'll stick with me, even if she outgrows me?"

Abby laughed. "Not so long ago you were taking a different girl out every weekend. And you're suddenly ready to give up your freedom?"

"Yes."

She looked at him with eyes somewhere between Jennifer's gray-blue and Harvey's ultra-blue. "Maybe that's what's wrong with me. Maybe I'm just not ready."

"Then don't do anything drastic," Eddie said.

Harvey came out through the study. "Time to go, Ed."

Eddie saw Abby check the clock.

The full autopsy report on Kyle Quinlan was waiting when they got back to the station. Harvey sent Eddie a copy, and he dove into it. After Harvey had read it thoroughly, he sat all of the men down in the interview room to discuss it.

"Everything lines up with what the medical examiner told us last week," he said, "but the amount of cocaine in Kyle's system was surprisingly high. And they found residue in his nostrils and on his fingers."

"Do you think he was using on the way over to Mike's?" Eddie asked.

"Maybe. Or shortly before he left the apartment. Misty wouldn't know how much was in his system."

"How did she get him to take all those sleeping pills, anyway?" Nate asked.

"Three pills, according to the M.E. It's more than is safe, but it's really not that many. They think it was the cocaine—or the combination—that stopped his heart."

"So, did Misty kill him or not?" Eddie asked.

"I guess that's for a court to decide. I'm going to see if I can get in to have another talk with Misty this afternoon, and Jordan, too, if they'll let me. Meanwhile, preserving the chief's life is still our main goal. You guys get to work on Hawkins's crew."

Eddie went over his leads on Rooster, put on a ragged sweatshirt and a beat-up lumberman jacket from his locker, got the petty cash from Paula, and went down to the second floor where the detective squad was housed. Sergeant Legere listened to his explanation and grudgingly told Joey Bolduc to go with Eddie.

"I got a case I'm working on, boss," Joey said.

"I know, but this is more urgent. It's the chief's life we're talking about."

Joey swore but took off his tie and sport jacket and went with Eddie.

They scoured the worst neighborhood in Portland. Eddie caught up with a couple of his informants. One guy, who went by the name of Silver, had sworn to give him straight intel whenever Eddie came to him. A pornographer had lured his thirteen-year-old sister away from home, and Eddie had tracked them down and brought her home. Silver considered he still owed Eddie, two years later. He tried not to call in favors too often, so Silver wouldn't get sick of him. Silver had given some good tips in the past, and he hadn't burned Eddie yet.

Eddie took Joey into a dive he knew Silver liked and spotted him shooting eight-ball with another dude. They watched until the black ball sank. Silver lost a fiver.

"Tough luck, Silver," Eddie said, and the informant looked full at him for the first time.

"Eddie, my man."

"Yeah, let me buy your next drink."

Silver handed off his pool cue and followed Eddie and Joey to the bar. Before Eddie could tell the bartender to give him a draft, Silver said, "We better take it outside."

Eddie arched his eyebrows. Silver jerked his head toward the door.

"Okay." Maybe somebody was watching Silver. Outside, Eddie asked, "What's up?"

Silver scowled at him. "Your mug is all over the tube these days, that's what."

Eddie swore and was hit by a jolt of guilt. "Sorry."

"Sorry? You gone soft, Eddie?"

"No."

"He got religion," Joey said.

Silver scowled at him. "Do I know you?"

"He's with me," Eddie said.

"Looks familiar."

"Well, don't tell the world."

"Right." Silver walked around the corner of the building, and they followed. "Awright, what do you need?" he asked.

"Two things. Rooster Bentley . . ."

"Hmm. Maybe."

"And Al Hawkins."

"Can't do that."

"Can't get the data, or can't give him up?" Eddie stuck a twenty in his hand.

Silver looked down at it. "My life's worth more than a twenty, man."

Eddie took another from a different pocket.

Silver nodded. "Okay, this Rooster guy, he's tight with Al."

"Tight how?"

"He's one of his top men. What do you like him for?"

Eddie glanced at Joey. "You heard about the hit on Chief Browning?"

Silver nodded. "Heard the kid who was supposed to do it wimped out, and Al had him skewered."

"That's not quite accurate," Eddie said.

"What happened, then?"

"Who's paying who here?" Joey said.

Silver glared at him. "Whom."

"Why, you punk." Joey drew back his fist, and Eddie grabbed his arm.

"Easy, Bolduc. Silver and I understand each other, right, pal?"

"Sure, Eddie." Silver shrugged and shivered.

"Hey, man, you don't have a coat." Eddie started to take off his plaid jacket.

"Left it inside," Silver said.

"You sure?"

He lifted his chin, like Eddie had offended him.

"Okay," Eddie said. "Is Rooster on tap for that job?"

"What, rubbing out the chief? Maybe. Yeah, probably. You understand, I ain't privy to Al's business, but things I've heard, yeah. The word is they'll be looking for a new chief before MLK Day."

"Martin Luther King Day?" Joey said.

Silver gave him a withering look.

"Where can I find Rooster?" Eddie asked.

"I seen him come out of a place on the water-front." He gave Eddie the street and described the building.

"Okay, good. What about Al?" Eddie asked.

"I can't say."

"Sure you can," Joey said and started to step forward again, but Eddie shoved him in the chest.

"Back off, would ya?" He looked at Silver. "How's your little sister?"

"Good. Still in school."

"Great. Look, you know it would be a good thing if we put Al back behind bars."

"I don't know, Eddie. I don't want to end up in the bay."

"What do you think will happen if Rooster gets a shot at Chief Browning? I'll tell you. This town will be turned upside down and set on fire. Every man, woman, and child that looks sideways at us will get hauled in, and half of you won't see daylight again."

"You wouldn't take me in, Eddie."

"You bet I would."

"Aw, come on. You're the guy that saves kiddies' lives."

"I'm also a guy who respects Browning. You get me?"

"Sure. He's not a bad chief. He put Al away, didn't he?"

"Yeah, he did. And we'll do it again, with or without your help. It'll be much better for you if you're on our side."

"I don't know."

"Yes, you do," Eddie said. "Come on."

Silver sighed. "I'm freezing."

"Take the jacket."

"No, man."

"Tell me where to find Al."

"You get Rooster, he's your best bet. He can lead you to Al."

"I can't wait that long," Eddie said. "Look, I'll stand you another twenty."

Joey made a little sound in his throat, and Eddie held up a hand, watching Silver.

"I heard he's got a lady friend in Bayside."

"Pretty swanky neighborhood," Eddie said.

Silver shrugged. "Al don't sleep with the swine."

"You got an address?"

"Nope. Woman name of Cynthia, though."

"Last name?"

He shook his head.

"Okay." Eddie put his last twenty in his hand. "Get out of here."

"Don't come around again if you're going to be a TV star." Silver pointed a finger at him. "And watch your back." He slid around the corner and was gone.

Joey stood there staring at Eddie.

"What?"

"You gave him sixty bucks."

"Silver's been good to me."

"More like, you've been good to him. For what? The address of a flophouse where your pal Rooster might or might not be crashing, and a woman named Cynthia."

"His intel's never come up bogus." Eddie started walking back to his truck.

Joey fell in beside him. "Well, he's right about one thing."

"What?"

"You can't do undercover with your face all over the news."

Eddie wanted to say, "If you think it's bad now, just wait until tomorrow," but he decided discretion was the better part of undercover work. He was *so* glad Harvey hadn't picked Joey for the Priority Unit.

Chapter 20

The shift was over, but Eddie reported in to Harvey, and they hashed over his interview with Silver. Harvey decided Silver was right—Eddie shouldn't show his face tomorrow, especially with *Morning Nation* scheduled to show it for him. His visit to Misty hadn't helped much. She'd said she got Kyle to take the pills shortly after Jordy left, and she hadn't seen him do the cocaine.

"Tomorrow I'll send Nate and Jimmy to check out the address Silver gave you for Rooster Bentley."

"Really, Harv? They don't have a lot of training yet, and they could make a mistake and ruin it."

He sighed. "Okay, I'll go with Jimmy. You and Nate stay here and try to get a line on this Cynthia."

Eddie didn't like it, but he guessed it made sense.

He went home and nuked a frozen dinner, then decided he had time to call Leeanne before going to the midweek service at the church.

"How was the interview?" was her first question.

"I think it will be okay," Eddie said. "Unless they add in something I don't know about. And, uh, they did interview one woman about the, uh—"

"The crying thing?" she asked.

"Yeah. They talked to Sarah."

Leeanne was quiet for a moment. "You mean the Sarah you were dating last summer?"

"Yeah."

"Did she bash on you?"

"No, she didn't. She could have."

"Oh, Eddie, I don't believe you treated all those women badly. I went and read some of the comments on Delaney's page, and a lot of them said they'd cried just because you were so sweet and handsome, and you're out of their reach. Women who've been looking for Mr. Right and not finding him. I'll bet at least half of them are women you've never even met."

Eddie's lungs got that giant-squeezed feeling. "I hope you're right. I don't want people to hate me. I mean, I always thought a lot of people liked me."

"They do."

He could think of several who didn't, and not only people he'd arrested. Joey Bolduc, for instance. But women? He couldn't think of any who had said they hated him, at least not to his face. Maybe she was right.

"Abby said she's going to poll all the women in your Sunday school class and see how many of them adore you and post it on her Facebook page."

"What? No! Tell her not to do that."

"I can't wait to see the interview."

Eddie swallowed hard. "I'd better get going. Don't want to miss church."

They hung up, and he felt like he should have said more. Like I love you. He wanted to kill Blabby Abby.

Eddie went in to work at the normal time on Thursday. The Priority Unit office was full of cops. Absolutely full. At least thirty people were in there, including the chief and the deputy chief, and a flat screen TV was set up on Tony's desk, facing the room.

"Twenty minutes, people," Nate yelled as Eddie walked in the door.

Mike spotted him. "There he is, the man of the hour."

"Hey, Eddie!" Everyone started crowding around and slapping him on the back and shaking his hand. He edged through the crowd to find Harvey.

"Is this your idea?"

"Mike's," Harvey said. "He thought it would be good for morale. He even had me call Tony last night and tell him to come in and watch it with the rest of us, even though his hearing isn't until Monday."

"Do I have to stay in here?"

"I don't think it will kill you."

"It might."

Harvey shook his head.

"Hey, Shakespeare."

Eddie whirled around to find his erstwhile partner behind him, grinning like a jack-o-lantern.

"Tony! Hey, how you doing?"

"Okay. Went skiing at Sugarloaf yesterday with Uncle Bill."

Uncle Bill was the governor. Eddie said, "Oh, hobnobbing with the rich and famous."

"You ought to talk," Tony said. "National TV."

"If I could have let you do the gig, I woulda."

All too soon, the interview came on. Eddie tried to fade to the back of the crowd, but he bumped into someone.

"Sarah. I'm sorry."

"No problem."

She had her uniform on, and no makeup, but she still looked pretty good.

Eddie said, "I—uh—thanks for—you know."

Joey Bolduc looked at them and said, "Shh!"

On screen, Mia introduced the segment.

"I'm not sure I can watch this," Eddie whispered to Sarah.

"Let us be proud of you, Eddie."

Was she kidding? He frowned at her, but he stayed.

You could have heard a foam rubber pin drop as the video of the fiery van played. Eddie had never seen that one, but there he was, throwing the hood open. Backlit by the flames, he doused the fire with his extinguisher. It looked scarier than it had in real life. They switched to the video that had been on YouTube—Eddie weaving between the vehicles with Mason in his arms, heading for an ambulance two lanes over.

Next was the hospital part. They had cut it down to about fifteen seconds, the highlights being Mason saying "P'wiceman" and hugging him, and Eddie giving him the plastic ambulance. The final shot was of Mason and Eddie, cheek to cheek and smiling. Everybody cheered. Eddie felt pretty good.

Then came Sarah's spot. The room went quiet.

"Wow, is that you, Benoit," Brad Lyons, the day sergeant called.

Sarah's color deepened, but she hiked her chin up and watched the TV. Eddie caught a vibe for a second, but he wasn't sure what it was. Did she have something against Brad?

When Sarah said in the video, "whoever takes Eddie Thibodeau to the altar is one lucky woman," the place erupted with laughs, whistles, and shouts. Mia gave her punchline, and they faded to commercial.

They had cut the question about superpowers. Eddie was disappointed. That was the part he wanted the world to hear.

"Th-that's all, folks," Mike said and clicked

the TV off. "Go to work, and watch out for each other."

Everybody wanted to touch Eddie—shake his hand, slug his shoulder, rumple his hair. He felt like a punching bag by the time most of them were gone.

Sarah touched his arm for a second. "Good job, friend."

"You, too. Thanks."

"I enjoyed it, and I meant every word." She headed for the stairs.

Tony stood three feet away. He gave a soft wolf whistle. "I gotta say, she was some classy looking on the tube. Maybe I can convince her to sob over me the next time."

"Grow up."

Before Eddie could make a dive for the locker room, Harvey called, "Eddie! Can you come over here for a minute, please?"

The chief and deputy chief were grinning at him.

"First class work, detective," Jack Stewart said.

"Thank you, sir." Eddie let him shake his hand.

Mike winked and stuck out his hand. "I never doubted you, kid."

"Sure. That's why you sent in the big guns."

"Wasn't she terrific? I call that a decisive victory for the P.D. Don't you, Harvey?"

"I didn't know it was a war," Harvey said.

Mike laughed.

Harvey shook his head. "I agree it was a success, but now Eddie's ruined for undercover work, at least for a while."

"No, seriously." Mike laid his paw on Eddie's shoulder. "You got some intel on Hawkins?"

"Maybe. We heard the new shooter is a guy named Rooster Bentley."

"Sounds familiar. Have you checked his record?"

"Yeah, I'll send you his file and his DMV photo, so you can be on the lookout. We're going to try to run him to ground today."

"Good luck. I'm getting tired of the bodyguards. Sharon and I went to the movies last night, and two uniforms went with us."

"I hope they enjoyed the picture," Eddie said.

"Eh, it was a chick flick. Sharon's pick."

After the brass and Tony left, Nate wheeled the TV into the breakroom and they got down to work. Eddie had some contacts in Bayside—rich people whose art had been stolen a few months earlier. They felt indebted to him and Harvey for getting it back. He started calling and reminding them who he was. The art wouldn't have mattered, as it turned out. They'd all watched him on TV and recognized him.

Once they got past the pleasantries, or in Eddie's case the mortification, he asked them if they knew a woman named Cynthia who lived in the area. On his third call, to a doctor who'd had some good prints stolen off his office walls, Eddie got a hit.

"Do you mean Cynthia Sheridan?" Dr. Eldred asked.

"I don't know," Eddie said. "Tell me about her."

"Her father's an attorney. She was married to a dentist, but they got divorced. I think she got a pretty good settlement. She's got a condo in an upscale development."

"How old is she?" Eddie asked.

"Maybe forty."

"Good looking?"

"Oh, yeah, she takes care of herself now," Dr. Eldred said.

"What do you mean, *now?*"

"Well, I don't know as I should say. I wasn't her physician, but . . ."

"Hey, Doc, this is between you and me, and it has to do with a felony case."

"Hmm. Well, my understanding is that she was into drugs as a youngster. Dropped out of college, and her parents put her in rehab."

"No drugs nowadays?" Eddie asked.

"I don't really know. I rarely see her, but she doesn't live far from me. Once in a while she drives by, and I wave. Her father is more in my social circle."

"Might she have a live-in boyfriend?"

"I wouldn't know."

He gave Eddie the approximate address, and he easily found her on the computer, without even dipping into their special law enforcement databases.

Harvey was elated at this and started planning a raid. He talked to Mike, and it turned out the chief knew a city councilman who lived in the same gated community as Cynthia Sheridan. The councilman agreed to tell the gatekeeper to let in a couple of detectives. Harvey sent Nate and Jimmy out that afternoon to do some reconnaissance on the condo.

"No offense, Eddie," he said, "but these people in the leisure class are ones who might stay home and watch morning TV shows."

Jimmy and Nate returned after talking to several residents.

"There's been a man staying with Cynthia for a few weeks," Nate told them. He gave them the descriptions they'd gotten. They all agreed, it could be Hawkins without the beard on his six-year-old driver's license.

"Why would a rich woman like that take up with a criminal?" Jimmy asked.

"Maybe she doesn't know he's an ex-con," Nate said.

"And maybe she likes his product," Harvey added. "Don't forget, she was in rehab fifteen years ago."

He had gotten into her medical records and

found the rehab sessions—two of them, one when she was twenty-one and one five years later.

"The chances are pretty high that she's relapsed," Nate said, frowning.

Jimmy didn't think anyone was in Cynthia's condo at the time they observed it, but they had no way to be sure. A neighbor had seen Cynthia drive out around eleven that morning. Al could be inside sleeping or supervising his business by phone or computer.

"Our best bet is to catch him at night," Harvey said. He'd gotten a blueprint of the condominium complex from the city planning office, and they worked over it for an hour, planning their nocturnal visit. At two o'clock, he told the men to go home and come back at ten.

"We'll focus on Hawkins and hope that Bentley gives up his mission when we get his boss," Harvey said.

Eddie hung around his apartment and tried to take a nap, but it was no good. He felt like an animal was pacing inside him, and it was hard to sit still. Finally, he called Leeanne. When he heard her voice, the critter inside him settled down.

"We saw you on TV," she said.

"Oh, yeah?"

"Yeah. My mom was swooning. She adores you now."

"I hope that's a good thing."

"For sure."

She didn't say anything about Sarah. Eddie was afraid to say any more about the interview.

"You did great," Leeanne said after a pause. "Are you on a break?"

"No, I got sent home early."

"Did something happen?"

"No. We're going to work tonight."

"Oh." Neither of them spoke for a moment. He wasn't sure if she understood or not. Jennifer would know immediately what was up when they worked a split shift, but Leeanne wasn't used to the way detectives worked. Best to change the subject.

"You going back to school Monday?"

"Yeah. I'll probably go back to the dorm Sunday. I miss your church down there. I really like it."

"It's a good church," Eddie said. They talked for a few more minutes, but he had so many off-limits things to not talk about, the conversation started to stress him. "Hey, I'll see you Saturday, all right?"

"Yeah."

"Okay. Leeanne . . ."

"Yeah?"

He took a breath and felt like he was only getting half the air he should. "I love you."

After they hung up, he felt all twitchy. Maybe he should have just told her about tonight's plans. Was it better for her to be prepared, or for Harvey to call and tell her something happened to him? He remembered the day Mike went and got Jennifer and drove her to the hospital for Harvey. *Lord, don't let that happen.*

Rain pattered on the window. Terrific. They were in for another icy night.

His phone rang. He looked at the screen but didn't recognize the number.

"Hello?" he said cautiously.

"Eddie Thibodeau?" a woman said.

"Who wants to know?" He had a sudden vision of Al Hawkins diverting him with a phone call while his henchman got into position to kill him.

"This is Stacy Plourde. Do you remember me?"

"Uh . . ."

"Stacy. From the nightclub."

Nightclub. Which one? Eddie didn't want to know.

"Sorry, I guess not. Gotta go." He clicked off, feeling guilty for being rude, but he certainly didn't want to talk to any Stacy he'd met in a nightclub. How did she get his cell number, anyway?

His phone rang again. He almost threw it across the room, but fortunately he looked at the screen first. Leeanne. He pushed the button and held the phone to his ear.

"*Ma chérie?*"

"Eddie, I told Randy what you said. He's really smart, you know."

"What do you mean?"

"He said you're probably going on a raid tonight. Is that true?"

He hesitated. Her youngest brother wanted to be a cop. And she was right—Randy was smart.

"Yeah. I wasn't sure I should tell you, but I needed to hear your voice."

"Oh, Eddie!"

He was afraid she was going to cry and become Woman-Two-Hundred-and-Whatever, but her next words surprised him.

"I'm so proud of you."

He swallowed the lump. "Pray for us."

"I will. You be careful."

"Yeah. And I'll have Harvey at my back, and Nate and Jimmy."

"And Tony?"

"No, he can't work tonight."

She didn't ask why. "Well, I'll be praying for all of you."

"Thanks." His phone beeped.

Leeanne said, "Is that on your phone or mine?"

"Mine, I think."

"Someone's trying to call you. You'd better take it."

He didn't want to hang up on Leeanne for another Weepy Woman, but the thought that it might be Harvey made him say, "Okay. *Je t'aime*," and click to the new caller.

"Hello?"

Without any preliminaries, his father said, "Where did you leave the shovel?"

"I hung it up in the garage, Pop."

He swore, and Eddie could tell he'd been drinking.

"Pop, you don't have to shovel any today, do you?"

His father hung up on him. Eddie sat down in his favorite chair and tried to string together a prayer for his pop.

By five o'clock, Eddie was going crazy from the waiting and from Pop's phone call. He decided to drive by his folks' house and see what they were up to. It was raining hard. He put on all his gear in case he didn't come home again and dashed out to his truck.

He drove past their house slowly. Everything looked normal. Light spilled out the front windows. He pulled over and sat there trying to decide whether to go in. They were probably eating supper. He prayed for them. He'd been doing that for six months, but it was hard. He didn't know what to ask for.

Finally the rain slacked off, and he got out and walked to the door. He knocked, and after a minute, Maman opened it.

"Why are you standing in the rain? Come in."

He walked in and wiped his feet on the rag rug inside the door.

"Did you eat?" she asked.

"No."

"We were just sitting down. Have some spaghetti."

"I just came by to see how you and Pop are doing."

"*Bien.* Now come eat."

"I really didn't come looking for a meal."

She shook her head. "Boys."

He walked into the kitchen. Pop was sitting at the table, piling spaghetti on his plate. "I heard you were on TV this morning."

"Yeah."

"We didn't see it," Maman said bleakly. "Why didn't you tell us?"

Eddie shrugged.

"Sit down," she said.

"You only come when you're hungry," Pop said, which wasn't true.

His mother went to get him a plate. "Mrs. Pelletier saw it."

"Yeah?"

"She said you grew into the most handsome man in Cumberland County, and some girl cop said you made her cry."

Eddie sighed. "First of all, it was Sarah. You know Sarah."

Maman nodded, eyeing him curiously. "You're dating Sarah again? What happened to Leeanne?"

"No, I'm not dating Sarah again. She was just on the show. And second of all, she did *not* say I made her cry. She said she cried a little when we broke up. That's all."

"It's the same thing," Pop said.

"Didn't Mrs. Pelletier say anything about the little boy?"

"Yeah," Maman said. "She told me you gave him a toy."

"I did. He's a cute kid." Eddie looked at Pop. He was shaking Parmesan cheese on his spaghetti. "Did you find the shovel, Pop?"

"What do I need the shovel for? I just wanted to be sure you put it away."

"Four days later?"

Pop forked a huge bite of spaghetti into his mouth and chewed.

Maman held out the dish of meat sauce. "Eat."

The overhead lights flickered and went out, and the furnace fan stopped rumbling.

Chapter 21

At the police station, everything was running on generators—computers, minimal lights, the com switchboard, security monitors, everything. Harvey and Jimmy were already in the office when Eddie arrived.

The office had big windows on two walls, but it was dark outside, and none of the streetlights were working, so they sat in eerie twilight.

"Got power at your house?" Eddie asked.

"Nope. It went out around six. I left Jennifer with a flashlight and a fire in the fireplace. Abby should be home in a couple of hours." Harvey frowned. "But the alarm system went out."

"She'll be okay," Eddie said.

"Yeah. But I don't like leaving her alone in a blackout."

"Is the power out at your place?" Jimmy asked Eddie.

"Yeah. I was over at my folks' house, and theirs went off, too."

Nate came in.

"Okay," Harvey said. "I sure wish we had Tony tonight, but we don't."

They went over the plan again. Harvey had picked up the warrants and set it up for them to get into the gated community.

They trooped to the locker room to get their Kevlar vests. Harvey grabbed his and went out to his desk. Eddie followed him.

"Time for a quick prayer?" Eddie asked.

"Of course." They stepped into the interview room and prayed for wisdom and safety.

Harvey's desk phone was ringing when they came out. He picked it up, and Eddie could tell it was Mike. Harvey told him briefly about their plans to find Hawkins through Cynthia Sheridan.

"I'm going to have Sergeant Miles send two more patrolmen to your street." Harvey paused. "I think it's indicated with the power outage. Yes, really." Mike must be giving him a hard time about extra security.

"This will be a bad night for wrecks and burglaries," Nate muttered.

"Yeah." Harvey was right, as far as Eddie was concerned. Someone might think it was the perfect time to get to the chief.

When Harvey hung up, he called the night sergeant and requested another unit at Mike's house, just to be on the safe side. When he signed off, he said, "Dan says they're already spread too thin."

"But there are two uniforms over there now, right?" Eddie asked.

"Yeah."

"I'll go over after we wrap this up, Captain," Jimmy said.

"We'll see."

They went to the garage, and Eddie rode in Harvey's SUV. Nate and Jimmy took Nate's car. While Harvey drove, Eddie talked to the dispatcher on the radio and told him they were going out on a high-risk duty. The dispatchers would track them electronically, and if they didn't check in after twenty minutes, they would call the men to check on them.

"All set," he told Harvey.

Harvey grunted, his mind obviously elsewhere.

"We'll find him," Eddie said.

As they drove toward Bayside, they came into an area with streetlights blazing.

"Hey! How come the ritzy neighborhood didn't lose their power?" Eddie asked.

Harvey looked in his mirror to make sure Nate had made the turn behind him. "Call your congressman and complain."

"I haven't met the new one we got after we arrested Murphy," Eddie said. "He probably wouldn't listen to me."

"Especially not if you ever dated his daughter."

"Ha, ha. I am pretty sure I never dated any of his relatives."

Harvey chuckled. "Seriously, Eddie, you did a good job on the interview. I always sweat bullets when I have to do a press conference. That performance was above and beyond."

"Maybe I'll get a medal or something."

They parked at the corner of the condo complex's lot, pointing out. Cynthia's unit had three levels. The units were staggered, which looked nice but made it easier for criminals to take cover. They had Cynthia's license plate number, and Eddie spotted her white Lexus out front.

He and Harvey went up to the door while Jimmy and Nate went around to the back. When Nate radioed they were in place, Harvey rang the bell.

Cynthia opened the door. Eddie recognized her from pictures they'd seen online and on her motor vehicle record. She had some crow's feet but was still pretty. She looked appraisingly at Harvey.

"I'm Captain Larson with the Portland P.D. This is Detective Thibodeau. May we come in?"

As he said Eddie's name, her eyes snapped over to his face. Eddie had his badge on his coat, but she wasn't looking at that. Her gaze narrowed.

"To what do I owe the honor?"

"We'd like to ask you a few questions," Harvey said.

She lingered a second, watching Eddie. "I guess so." She stepped aside.

In her foyer, Eddie could see that this wasn't just an upscale place, it was top of the line, millionaire swank.

"We wondered if you're acquainted with this man?" Harvey held out a photo of Alfred Hawkins.

Her eyebrows arched delicately. She took the photo and studied it for a moment.

"I don't believe I am. Who is he?"

"He's a known drug dealer, and he was recently released from the Maine State Prison," Harvey said.

Her lips pressed together, and she passed it back to him. "Are you asking all the residents about him?"

"We've asked some others. A few thought they'd seen him in the building."

"This building? *My* condo?"

Harvey shrugged. "We're just inquiring."

"The answer is no."

Harvey reached into his jacket and brought out the warrant. "We'd like to search your dwelling."

"You must be kidding."

"No, ma'am."

She spread her hands. "Well, you have a warrant, so I guess I can't say no."

"That's right." Harvey nodded to Eddie. By their plan, he found the back door and let Nate and Jimmy in.

"Nobody left here," Nate whispered.

"Okay. You two take the second floor," Eddie told them.

Harvey had asked Ms. Sheridan to sit on the

sofa. He went into the kitchen while Eddie started combing over the foyer and living room.

As he opened the drawer in an end table, she leaned toward him. "You're as cute in person as you are on television."

Eddie swallowed hard and kept working.

"I'm holding a party tomorrow night. Would you be interested in coming?"

"No thank you, ma'am."

"Pity," she said. "I'd love to show you off to some friends. We could have some fun."

The way she said it sent a shiver down his spine. He shook his head and moved to the entertainment center.

They found a small amount of marijuana—small, but more than allowed for one person under the current law. She wouldn't admit to sharing it with another person. Jimmy found about two thousand dollars in her bedroom, but Cynthia said there was nothing wrong with keeping a little cash on hand, was there?

The biggest point against her was the male clothing and accessories in the bedroom. Someone besides Cynthia was using the closet and one of the walnut dressers.

"Care to tell us who your housemate is?" Harvey asked.

"Do I have to answer that question?"

"No."

"If I don't, what will happen?"

"We'll arrest you for obstructing an investigation."

She gave a scornful grunt. "My father would have me out within an hour."

"Fine, if that's the way you want it." Harvey turned to Eddie. "Arrest Ms. Sheridan and take her to the station and book her."

"Happy to," Eddie said.

She smiled at him. "I think I'll almost enjoy this."

Eddie threw Harvey a glance that he must have interpreted as panic.

"Detective Cook, you take over that detail," Harvey said. "I need Detective Thibodeau for a minute."

Jimmy stepped forward, pulling his handcuffs out of the case. Harvey nodded to Nate, and he stayed with Jimmy while Harvey and Eddie slipped into the kitchen.

"Okay, what was that about?" Harvey asked.

"She, uh, made a pass at me before."

Harvey's eyebrows morphed. "What, you can't reject a woman's advances? Not the Eddie Thibodeau I know."

"I'm sorry. She brought up the TV interview, and it distracted me."

"Distracted you?" Harvey looked toward the living room and back at Eddie. "I'm not even going to ask you what that means, but I'll have Miller and Cook take her in."

"Thanks, boss."

"No thanks necessary. I don't want her in my vehicle. It's Nate's, or ask for a transport unit, and I'm already taking flak about the extra hours for guarding Mike."

"Who's giving you grief about that? Mike's the only one above you now. Not Stewart?"

"No, but don't forget the city council."

"You can't tell me they begrudge the chief a protection detail?"

"It's been almost two weeks. They hoped we'd settle it by now."

"The mayor too?"

Harvey shrugged. Mayor Jill Weymouth was usually on their side. "She hasn't weighed in, for which I'm grateful. Come on, let's get out of here."

On their way out, Harvey stopped for a chat with the gatekeeper. He admitted to seeing Hawkins go in and out several times over the past few weeks. Harvey emphasized the wisdom of calling him if Hawkins came back.

The police station was still on generators. Nate booked Cynthia Sheridan and made sure every technicality was followed, but she still bailed out in two hours, almost unheard of at that time of night, with her father, the high-powered lawyer, at her side. She refused to talk to Harvey or Eddie, and she wouldn't even look at more pictures of Al Hawkins.

"Her father doesn't look happy," Eddie noted

as he and Harvey watched the two of them leave the station.

"His little girl is forty, and she's still getting into scrapes," Harvey said.

"Yeah, and he's still coming to her rescue."

Harvey led the way to the stairs. "Even when I told him she's abetting Alfred Hawkins."

Eddie opened the door to the office, which was still dimly lit. "I'll bet he's got something to say to her in the car about letting an ex-con live with her."

They hashed over the evening with Nate and Jimmy.

"Okay," Harvey said. "Let's all go home and get some rest. We'll regroup tomorrow. Everybody drive carefully. I hope you have electricity at home."

Nate and Jimmy headed for the locker room. Harvey looked at Eddie.

"You got heat at your place?"

"I got a little kerosene heater after the big ice storm last year."

"If you get home and it's freezing cold, come over to the house. We've got the fireplace in the living room and a little woodstove in the garage. I can set it up in the sunroom if we need it. There's a chimney flue there."

"I'll be okay."

"I'd worry about you dying of carbon monoxide poisoning."

"I can go to my folks'. They've got a wood-stove."

"If you want," Harvey said, "but we'd be happy if you came to our house."

"Thanks. To be honest, I don't want to wake them up now."

Eddie drove home and took his flashlight out of the glove compartment. It seemed extra dark, without any street lamps or lights from any apartment windows. He trudged up to his apartment and went in. It was nearly as cold in there as it was outside.

It took him a while to get the heater going. When it was burning in the kitchen, he used Poland Spring water from a jug and made himself a glass of Tang, then sat in front of the heater, warming his hands. When they were warm enough, he made a sandwich and ate it.

He wanted to call Leeanne, but it was after two o'clock. He sent her a text. "We're ok." He hesitated, then sent a duplicate to his mother. The heater sputtered and went out.

He double checked to make sure it was turned off and called Harvey.

"Hi. Sorry. I'm out of fuel. Is it too late to come?"

"Nope."

"Okay, ten minutes."

He grabbed his sleeping bag, pillow, and a few clothes and drove to Harvey's house. The rain was freezing on the roads.

The power was still out in the neighborhood. Harvey met him at the door and took him into the living room, where a couple of candles burned on the mantel.

"You can sleep on the couch. You'll be warmer down here by the fireplace than in the guest room upstairs." Candles burned in the kitchen, sunroom, and living room. Harvey had the woodstove in the sunroom, and he had built the fires up.

"Jennifer's in bed, but I'll get you some sheets."

"You don't need to. I brought my sleeping bag."

"Okay."

"What about Abby?" Eddie asked.

"She's upstairs. She got home a couple of hours ago."

The living room was comfortably warm. Harvey went into the sunroom and checked the stove, then opened the door to their bedroom. Jennifer came out in sweatpants and a gray sweatshirt with "Maine Criminal Justice Academy" on the front.

"Cold in there?" Eddie asked.

"It will warm up soon if we leave the door open," she said.

"Well, I could have stayed home. I don't think I'd freeze to death."

She looked embarrassed. "Eddie, we want you here."

"Okay. Thanks."

Harvey helped him open out the couch, and he laid out his sleeping bag and pillow. Harvey went around blowing out candles, and he and Jennifer went into their room.

Eddie put his flashlight on the floor beside him and lay looking up at the ceiling, watching the flickering light of the fire. He wished it was his castle hall, and that the chatelaine was there to keep him warm. He thought about reading his Bible by flashlight, but he was so tired, he nodded off while he was thinking about it.

He awoke to the house phone ringing. After two rings, it stopped. He heard Jennifer's faint voice.

The gray light of a rainy morning shone through the windows. The electronics had no blinking lights, so Eddie figured the power was still out.

He got up and pulled on his jeans and rolled up the sleeping bag. His head ached slightly from lack of sleep. He went through the study to the bathroom near the entry. When he came out, he went to the kitchen.

Jennifer was still on the phone there. She said, "No, I'm trying to put together something for breakfast. Are the boys going to school? Really. Yes, they're working day and night. I'm okay. Is Leeanne there?" She threw a glance at Eddie. "Hi, hon. How are the goats? How you doing? Thought so. Eddie's here. Want to talk to him?"

She held the receiver out to him, and he walked over and took it. "Thanks, Jennifer."

"Don't mention it." She went out into the sunroom, and Eddie sat down on a chair.

"Hi."

"Hello," said Leeanne. "I got your message. I guess everything went all right last night?"

"Yeah. We made one arrest, but not the one we really wanted."

"I'm sorry. You're at Jennifer's awfully early."

"I slept here after our late shift."

"I miss you."

He took a deep breath. "I miss you, too. I still want to come up Saturday. Is it okay?"

"Yes, I asked Mom and Dad."

"I'll come as early as I can and leave that night."

"All right. What do you want to do?"

"Anything."

She gave the contented little laugh that caught at him.

"Leeanne, come back down."

"Oh, Eddie."

"Please?"

"I can't right now."

"Sorry. I shouldn't have asked you to. I just wish you were here."

"Are you reading in the Bible?" she asked.

"Yes. I try to every day, if I don't forget. I usually read at night after I get home."

"Where are you reading?" she asked.

He was glad he could answer without having to think too hard. "I'm up to II Corinthians 5. It's really interesting. How we'll be with the Lord as soon as we leave this body. When we die, you know. And we'll go to the judgment seat of Christ and get rewarded for what we've done."

"Mom and I were talking about that," she said. "A woman in our neighborhood died last week, and Mom and Dad went to the funeral. I guess the pastor used that verse. Absent from the body, present with the Lord. Mom is really close to salvation, I think."

"I pray for your folks every day," Eddie said.

"I'm praying for your family, too."

"Thanks. Pray hard, because every time I try to talk to them, they get upset."

"God can soften their hearts."

"I don't know. My mother wants me to come over all the time, but when I do, she gets really uptight."

"God changes people."

"I guess so. Oh, I know he does. He's changed me and Harvey and Mike. I can see that. But my folks . . . I would never in a million years think they would leave the Church."

"Did you think you would?"

"Hmm. Know what? You're too logical."

She laughed. "You want me to be scatter-brained?"

"No. Why do you want to be a journalist?"

"I just . . . I love writing, and I think it's important to get the news out to everyone in a clear, accurate way."

"Why do you need a degree?"

"Most employers want it," she said.

"I guess so. I just can't help wishing you were closer."

"We'll be together Saturday."

"I want to be with you all the time."

"That's sweet. I guess I should get moving. I have to pump water and haul it to the goats."

"Okay. I still love you, Leeanne. I want to be able to look you in the eyes every day and tell you that."

"Maybe . . . someday. I'll see you soon, Eddie."

He hung up the phone, lonelier than before, and wandered out to the sunroom. Three pans of ice and snow were melting on the woodstove. Harvey and Jennifer were sitting on the wicker settee, drinking bottled water and eating Pop-Tarts off china plates.

"Morning," Harvey said.

"Want some?" Jennifer asked, starting to get up.

"I can get it myself." Eddie went to the kitchen and found the Pop-Tart box on the counter in the twilight. He took one and went back in where they were, by the stove. Harvey had finished his, and he was unbraiding Jennifer's hair. She was eating placidly. Eddie sat down and ate.

"How's Leeanne?" Harvey asked.

"Good. Hauling water to the goats."

Harvey fluffed Jennifer's long hair out over her shoulders and put his arms around her. "Maybe we'll get a break today."

"We're not running, are we?" Eddie asked.

"I don't think so. If we go to the station early, we can have showers in the locker room, before the shift changes and the generators are put to peak use."

"Great." Eddie stood and picked up his empty bottle and took Jennifer's from her. He went to the kitchen and put them in the sink. No water for dish washing. There were a few dirty dishes, but not many, mostly silverware.

Abby hadn't shown her face. Eddie packed up his stuff and said goodbye to Jennifer. He and Harvey went out and drove to work separately, passing two fender benders on the way. All the stoplights on their route were out, which made it tricky, especially with the ice-covered pavement. People were in the park, chopping ice with hatchets and filling buckets. They would take it home and melt it to wash with. Eddie hoped they wouldn't drink it unless they boiled it.

Harvey brought two gallons of bottled water to the office.

"Jennifer stocked up when she heard we might get iced up again," he said. "She bought twelve gallons of water and a pile of flashlight batteries and candles and protein bars." He handed Eddie one. "That's in case you don't get lunch."

They hit the showers.

Nate and Jimmy were at their desks when Eddie had dressed and went out into the office. Harvey allowed they could use enough electricity to make a pot of coffee, since it was a critical service for cops, so Eddie made it.

"Hey, guys, get over here," Harvey called ten minutes later. They all crowded around his desk.

"A license plate reader just picked up Cynthia Sheridan's car on Market Street. I called the gatehouse at the condos, and the morning watchman said she left about fifteen minutes ago."

"Was she alone?" Tony asked.

"As far as I know."

"Where's she headed?" Nate asked. "She doesn't hold down a job."

"I have no idea, but you guys get out there, and I'll let you know if we get another hit."

The three detectives scrambled to get to their vehicles. Harvey stayed at the office to use all the available tracking software. The men cruised around the main arteries of the peninsula, looking for Cynthia's car, without success. Eddie even drove to the condos and had a talk with the gateman. He said the car hadn't returned. Eddie showed him Hawkins's picture, and he said he hadn't seen him for a couple of days.

After about an hour, Harvey called him.

"Eddie, do you know where Peter Hobart's dealership is?"

"Yeah, I'm about a mile out. What's up?"

"I've got Peter on the phone. Let me patch him through to you."

Eddie pulled to the curb.

"Eddie? Harvey said to give you the scoop," Peter said. "There's a woman here who wants to buy a vehicle for cash. A used Blazer with a twelve-thousand-dollar price tag. When I asked her how she wanted to finance it, she opened her purse and took out a stack of hundred-dollar bills. I'm supposed to report this, right?"

"Yup, any purchase over ten grand in cash. Does she have a name?"

"She didn't want to give it, and she's putting the title in some scruffy-looking man's name."

"What?" That didn't sound right.

"Yeah, she wants to pay and give him the Blazer."

"Weird. Why didn't she just give him the money outside and have him buy it?"

"I get the feeling she doesn't trust him completely."

"Stall her. I'm there in five minutes."

Peter said, "I guess I can offer her a rebate on that Blazer. She ought to be willing to wait for a discount."

"There you go." Eddie put his strobe on and

moved into the street. He hit his shoulder mic. Charlie Doran answered his call.

"Tell Captain Larson to send any other unit from Priority to back me up."

"Will do."

When he was within a couple of blocks of Peter's dealership, he cut the light.

"Eddie, I'm on your six," Nate said in his ear.

"Good." He could see Nate's car in his mirror, four lengths back.

He nosed the truck cautiously into the lot. Peter was putting a bearded, fortyish man into a five-year-old Blazer and handing him the keys. Eddie parked beside a van so they wouldn't have a good view of him, but he'd be able to get out to the street quickly.

"I see Ms. Sheridan's Lexus," Nate said.

"Where?" Eddie looked around, but couldn't see Cynthia's car in the parking lot.

"She's heading back toward her condo."

Eddie made a quick decision. "Stick with her. Charlie, you there?"

Charlie, in the com center, said, "Affirmative."

"Send me another unit. Tell the captain."

"I'm here," Jimmy Cook said. "Almost to the dealership. What do you want me to do, Eddie?"

"Cruise through the lot and block the far exit. There's a black Chevy Blazer I don't want leaving here." Eddie reeled off the dealer plate number.

The Blazer was moving. Eddie eased his truck

out of his spot and got into position right behind it. Eddie passed Peter, who stood there watching, and waved.

Jimmy drove in at the exit and turned his car sideways. The Blazer's driver slammed on his brakes and leaned on the horn. Jimmy got out of his car and approached the vehicle. Eddie stopped a few yards behind the Blazer, drew his gun, and walked up on the driver's side.

The bearded man jumped out swearing. He roared at Jimmy, "What are you doing, idiot?"

"Take it easy," Jimmy said.

The other man's hands swung up, and Jimmy's eyes widened.

"There's no need for that." Jimmy reached toward his holster.

"Police," Eddie barked. "Drop the weapon." He couldn't see it, but from Jimmy's reaction, he was pretty sure the driver had a pistol. He stood still for a second. They always had a brief moment of decision, and Eddie took advantage of it. He really didn't want to shoot him.

"Don't do it. Just drop the gun."

The man still stood there, his back to Eddie. Jimmy reached slowly inside his jacket and brought out his .45. "You heard the officer. Put down the weapon now, Mr. Bentley."

Eddie had figured it was Rooster Bentley, but he hadn't clearly seen his face yet. Slowly, Rooster stooped and laid his pistol on the pavement.

Eddie exhaled and sent up a mental prayer of thanks.

They ordered transport, and after the car arrived, they drove back to the station. Nate reported in that Cynthia had returned to her condo.

By the time they had finished the booking and paperwork, Eddie was exhausted.

"We ought to be able to charge Cynthia with something," Nate said.

"I'll fill in the D.A.," Harvey told him. "If they think they can make aiding and abetting stick, we'll arrest her."

"She bought him a getaway car," Eddie said.

"Yeah."

"And his license is suspended."

Harvey shrugged. "We have no evidence that Bentley committed or intended to commit a crime, other than the fake driver's license he handed Peter. Be glad we had one civilian out there on the ball, or we might not have caught him."

"Peter really is sharp," Eddie agreed. "Abby doesn't know a good thing when she sees it."

Nate said, "Does this mean we don't have to keep guarding the chief?"

Harvey shook his head. "When Kyle died, Hawkins just hired another shooter."

"You're right," Eddie said. "We have to get Hawkins."

Chapter 22

The lights came on full strength, and all of the married men called home to see if their wives had electricity. Eddie called Leeanne.

"I miss you," he said, as soon as he heard her voice.

They'd been through that before, but this time, she said, "Come up tonight."

Eddie thought about it. Maybe he could. "I'll try. If we're not too busy at work, I will. Your folks won't mind?"

"No, it will be fine."

"Do you have power?" he asked.

"Not yet, but they've got it downtown. We're supposed to get it anytime."

"Can I bring anything to help out?"

"No, we're okay."

"Leeanne, you know I won't be able to keep from telling you I love you."

"Why would you want to?"

He took a deep breath. "No reason at all." His resolve to wait for her was renewed.

Harvey came to his desk as he put away his phone.

"Jennifer says we've got power. How about your neighborhood?"

"I don't know. I can call Maman and ask."

"If it's still out, come stay with us again," Harvey said.

"Leeanne just told me to drive up there tonight."

"Oh. Well, that's progress."

Eddie grinned. "Yes, it is."

Harvey huddled with an assistant district attorney for a half hour, but Bentley wouldn't talk to them without his lawyer. Eddie tied up his paperwork as tightly as he could.

Nate said, "Jackie tells me our street is still dark."

"Bummer," Eddie said.

"There are a few pockets still out, but the power company's on it," Harvey told them. "You should have power by this evening."

Nate sighed. "I'll bet there have been a lot of thefts."

"Yeah," Harvey replied. "Generators. And quite a few business break-ins." On the dot of five, he said, "Get out of here, everyone. I'll see you Monday, unless something breaks on this case."

Eddie drove straight to his apartment. The heat was on, and the microwave and DVD player flashed the wrong time at him. He packed his duffel bag for the trip to Skowhegan. There was no time to do laundry. He decided to make do with what was hanging in the closet.

He called his mother before he left the house. His parents were still in darkness, which made him feel a little guilty. "It shouldn't be long," he told her. "The power's on here."

"I think we're the last," she said.

"Well, I'm going up to see Leeanne, but if you want to, you can come over here and take showers or whatever." Pop and Maman had had the key to his place since the day he moved in.

"*Merci*," she said. "I think we'll be okay, and your father's tired."

"Did he work today?" Eddie asked.

"Yes. They can't afford to get behind on this job."

Eddie wished he could help somehow. "I'll call you Sunday, okay?"

"Sure," said his mother.

He threw away a few things from the refrigerator and headed out.

Leeanne had left the porch light on for Eddie, and when his truck drove in, she hurried out onto the steps and stood there shivering. Eddie jumped out of the truck carrying his duffel bag and walked quickly toward her.

"Hey, you've got power."

"Yeah." They went in, and he pulled the door shut behind him.

"It's ten below," she said.

"It feels like it out there. Glad I didn't have a flat tire on the way."

She pulled him into the kitchen, over to the line of coat hooks on the wall. He unzipped his coat and took it off, and she hung it up for him.

"Everybody gone to bed?" he asked.

"Mom's still up. Dad and the boys crashed early because they're going ice fishing in the morning. They were hoping you would go."

"I came up here to see you, not spend all day in a freezing little shack on a pond."

"That's what I told them." She was glad, in a way, but she wished he had some chance to get to know her father better.

Eddie put his arms around her. Her pulse ratcheted up at his touch. She wasn't sure what her mom would think if she walked in at that moment. Eddie moved to kiss her, and she stepped away from him. He let her go, but looked a bit disappointed.

Leeanne caught her breath. "Are you hungry?"

"A little."

She brought out leftovers from their supper, lasagna and salad and pie. Eddie sat down, and she brought him the plate of lasagna from the microwave. She sat opposite him, and he started eating, but kept glancing over at her, as though he was self-conscious with her sitting there watching him eat. She hadn't supposed he ever minded anyone looking at him. People must have stared at him all his life.

Her mother came into the kitchen.

"Hello, Eddie. Glad you made it here safely."

He jumped to his feet. "Thanks, Mrs. Wainthrop."

"Oh, sit down and eat."

"Thanks. It's very good."

She smiled and went into the laundry room off the kitchen. The dryer door opened.

"Tell me what you've been up to," Eddie said.

Leeanne shrugged. "After the power came on, we did laundry and opened the freezer to see if we lost any food, and Travis and I cleaned out the barn. Do you want a cup of coffee?"

"Not unless it's decaf."

"Milk?"

"Sure."

She got a glass and took the stoneware pitcher from the refrigerator. Eddie watched her pour it.

"Goat's milk?" he asked.

"Yes. Geneva had twins in the middle of the ice storm. It's early, but what can I say?" She handed him the glass of milk.

"I thought you had a scientific breeding program."

"So did I, but I forgot to tell them. Lucerne will wait until March, I hope."

Eddie laughed and sipped the milk. His mouth twitched a little. She was used to the aftertaste, but people who didn't drink goat's milk regularly found it odd.

"Here, have some apple pie."

"Thanks." He took a big bite and grinned at her. "Did you make that?"

She shook her head. "Mom did."

"It's great."

She sat down again. Finally, Eddie laid down his fork and just looked at her.

"I'm glad you came," she said.

"Me, too."

Her mother came back through with a basket of clean laundry.

"Thanks for letting me come up tonight," Eddie said.

"You're welcome. Leeanne said you had a little excitement last night?"

"Nothing dangerous, really. We went to search a condo where we thought a felon might be hiding out. Today was better. The woman who owned the condo tried to buy a getaway car for a criminal, and we caught him."

"What about the woman?" Leeanne asked.

"So far she's still loose, but Harvey's trying to get the D.A. to charge her with abetting."

"Sounds like you've had a long day," Marilyn said. She disappeared with the laundry.

Leeanne and Eddie talked quietly for another half hour, but her mother didn't make a return appearance. He caught Leeanne up on all the happenings at church and with Harvey, Jennifer, Abby, and Jeff, and she told him that her younger brothers had had two snow days off from school that week and outlined the classes she would start on Monday.

Finally she asked, "Do you want a shower tonight?"

"That would be great." Eddie stood and picked up his bag.

"Use the bathroom down here." She took him to the doorway and turned the light on. "You won't wake anybody up that way. You're sleeping in Abby's room. Want me to show you?"

"The room Harvey and Jennifer had last time we were here?"

"Yes. I'll turn the light on when I go up, so you can find it."

"Okay."

"Just turn out all the lights when you go up."

He put his duffel bag on the floor in the doorway to the bathroom and reached out for her. She hesitated then moved into the circle of his arms and laid her head on his shoulder.

"*Je t'adore*, Leeanne."

A wave of warmth swept over her. She soaked up the moment, enjoying the feel of him against her and the strength of his arms around her.

"We'll talk in the morning." She squeezed him a little, and Eddie squeezed her a lot.

She pulled gently away, and he stroked her hair, looking into her eyes. She rubbed her hand along his scratchy jaw. She'd never dared to touch a man that way before—never wanted to. He bent and brushed his lips against her cheek. She stepped back, her heart pounding.

"Good night, Eddie."

"*Bonsoir, ma chérie.*"

She smiled and went silently up the stairs, her pulse tripping.

Marilyn was ironing in the dining room when Eddie got up the next morning. He'd shaved and dressed for farm life—black jeans and a plaid flannel shirt.

"Good morning," she said when he went downstairs. "Leeanne is feeding the goats. She'll be right in."

"Did George and the boys get off on their fishing trip?"

"Yes, they left about six. We'll see them at suppertime."

She turned the iron off and hung up the shirt she'd been pressing. Eddie never ironed.

"Let's get you some breakfast." Marilyn bustled ahead of him into the kitchen.

Leeanne came through the back door, from the ell attached to the barn.

"Good morning!" Her cheeks were red, and her eyes glittered. She pulled off her mittens and coat, sat on the bench under the hooks, and pulled off her boots.

"Eggs and bacon?" Marilyn asked, moving a

cast iron frying pan onto the cooktop over the stove's wood-burning firebox.

"I can do it," said Leeanne.

"Okay." Her mom went back to the dining room.

Leeanne opened the refrigerator for the bacon and eggs and started peeling off slices of bacon.

"I usually eat cold cereal," Eddie said.

"So, live a little." She covered the pan and turned toward him.

He stepped toward her and she smiled, raising a hand to his cheek.

"You're frozen." He pulled away from her icy fingers. She chuckled and held her hands over the stovetop.

"Can you come down next week?" Eddie asked.

"I think so. I'll let you know after I get my classes squared away."

He put out his arms, and she came to him. He breathed in her scent of hay and goat feed and the light floral tinge of her shampoo. Not a bad mix.

"Come down to Portland this summer. You could get a job there and be with . . . Harvey and Jennifer." He wanted to say, "with me," but that might be a little too strong.

She turned back to the stove and tended the bacon.

Eddie stepped back a little, away from the splatters. "So, what are we doing today?"

"I thought we might go ice skating, but it is really cold out. I think we'd better stay in."

"I hope your father has a heater in his ice shack."

"Oh, he does. Don't worry about them." She took the bacon out of the pan and put it on a plate covered with paper towels and cracked three eggs into the grease. Stepping sideways to the counter, she got bread from a cupboard and put two slices in the toaster.

Eddie watched her work. She had a tomboy quality, but without striving for femininity, she achieved it. She stood in her stocking feet on the spotless linoleum. Brown corduroy pants, a navy zippered sweatshirt over a dark green shirt. Her hair was in a ponytail, and her sculpted ears showed. She poured a coffee mug half full of milk and put it in the microwave.

"Warm milk?" Eddie asked.

"*Café au lait*," she said.

"I'm not as French as you think I am," he protested.

"I know you like milk in your coffee."

He smiled and let her do it. When the milk was hot, she filled the cup with coffee from the pot that Marilyn had left keeping warm.

They finally sat down to breakfast, and it was really good, so filling Eddie probably wouldn't want lunch. When they finished, Leeanne washed up the breakfast things. He grabbed a dish towel off the rack and started drying them.

"You don't have to do that," she said.

"I want to. I do dishes with Abby all the time at Harvey's house."

When the kitchen was clean, they went through the dining room, where Marilyn was folding up the ironing board, to the living room.

Leeanne brought out the textbooks for her new classes, and they browsed through them. Eddie was glad he had finished school.

He set aside the one he'd been looking at. Leeanne was still absorbed in the psychology book she'd chosen. He sat in the corner of the couch, watching her profile. Her lips were pursed slightly, and her eyelashes fluttered a little when she blinked. She had an almost Irish look, dark hair, blue eyes. His gaze was drawn to her ear again. He leaned over slowly and kissed the perfect earlobe. She jumped a little, smiled, and pulled away, dropping the book in her lap.

"So, what do you think?" She nodded toward the ethics textbook he'd examined.

Eddie slid his arm around her waist. "I think you have a lot of work ahead of you this semester."

"Thanks. I'm pretty sure I'll find my classes interesting this time."

He edged closer to her and kissed the side of her neck.

She stood and unzipped her sweatshirt. "I think we'd better do something. Do you want to play a game?"

"Can we talk?"

"Well, yeah, if you really want to talk."

He realized she was fending him off, so he stood up and looked her full in the face. "Okay, sure, let me sit over here." He moved to her mother's rocking chair.

She seemed a little surprised, but she took off her sweatshirt and sat down again on the couch.

"What do you want to talk about?" she asked.

"Lots of things. Tell me why you picked journalism."

He'd asked her that before, but she took a moment to collect her thoughts this time. "Journalism seems kind of noble. Getting the word out about what's going on. I think we need truthful people telling us the news, don't you?"

"Yeah, but sometimes I think the reporters are telling us what they think, not what's really going on."

She nodded. "It carries responsibility. And it's a little scary, but it's exciting. Interviewing was my worst class last semester. It's hard for me to just start talking to a stranger, and you have to keep the important points in mind and figure out what question to ask next. I want to be a good reporter."

"Do you like the writing part best?"

"Sure. It's fun, and I don't have to talk to people when I'm writing." She smiled ruefully. "Actually, the best part isn't the writing."

"It isn't? What is?"

"It's after you've written something and somebody else reads it. If they like it, that is. My first article got torn to shreds in class. That was not fun."

"But you've had some better experiences?"

"Yeah, I got some good feedback on the last assignment before vacation."

"If you become a reporter, you won't be able to choose what to write about," Eddie said. "Maybe you'd rather pick your own topics?"

She thought about that. "Well, you don't get to pick your cases, do you? What kind of cases do you like best?"

"Homicide, I guess."

"Really? That's so gruesome. Is it because you enjoy putting away people who did something really awful, or what?"

"Maybe. I like the challenge, but it's frustrating sometimes. You work and work, and you don't feel like you're getting anywhere. Then all of a sudden you get a break, and it feels really good. Like yesterday. We'd been after this guy Bentley for a week or so."

"And you caught him."

"Yeah. Peter gave us a tip."

"Abby's Peter?"

"Yeah. His was the dealership where they tried to buy the getaway car."

"That's awesome. Does Abby know?"

"I'm pretty sure Harvey told her."

"So, was this connected to the dead man you found in the Brownings' yard?" she asked.

"Yeah. But the case isn't closed yet. We still haven't caught the guy behind it all. In some ways, I feel like I should have stayed there, in case they get a break this weekend."

She looked a little worried. "I'm glad you didn't."

"I'm all yours for the day."

She smiled.

Eddie said softly, "Can I come sit over there now?"

She hesitated, and he put up both hands. "It's okay. This is good. Really. I just . . . it's okay."

She looked doubtful, and he wished he hadn't said anything. Maybe he'd just come on too strong this morning. He honestly hadn't meant to pressure her. Did she regret the liberties she'd allowed him the week before? Or maybe she just didn't want to risk him kissing her the moment her mother decided to walk in. At any rate, she was too serious at the moment, so Eddie made a funny story about Cynthia Sheridan trying to vamp him while they searched her apartment.

"Good grief," Leeanne said. "I hope they're going to send that woman to jail."

"What, for inviting me to a party?"

"Not exactly."

He laughed. "Actually, I'm not supposed to tell you all this stuff. Sorry. It's off the record. You know what that means."

"The most misused phrase in journalism. But don't worry. I won't tell anyone about your case. So, what exactly would you do if I said you could come over here?"

The question hadn't ended the way he'd expected, and his heart picked up speed. "Oh, just . . . enjoy the company, I guess." He locked eyes with her. Her knockout smile came very slowly, but it was there, all right.

She made a tiny, beckoning motion. Eddie went quickly, before she changed her mind. She put out her hand and clasped his tightly as he sat down beside her.

"I think that's close enough for now," she said softly.

"I can handle it."

She nodded. "You told me once that if I asked you to back off, you would."

"And I meant it. I'm sorry if I was out of line. I really want to do this right."

"Thanks. So, tell me how you survived the ice storm."

They talked for a long time. When Marilyn came through the room, he thought Leeanne would pull her hand away from his, but she didn't. Not touching her, other than holding her hand and giving it a squeeze now and then, was an exercise in discipline for Eddie. They made a lot of eye contact, and they laughed a lot. He didn't think he'd ever talked to a girl he really liked for that long without kissing her, but he didn't lose interest.

Finally, she excused herself to help her mother get lunch. Eddie called Harvey on his cell phone.

"Hey, Eddie! How you doing up there?" He sounded happy.

"Great," Eddie said. "It's cold. What's up in Portland?"

"I'm at home. Jennifer is about to put lunch on the table."

"Good. I was afraid you were working, and Jennifer wouldn't see you all day."

"No, I went to the county jail this morning, but that didn't take too long."

"Find out anything?"

"Bentley insists he didn't do anything for Hawkins, but he did admit Hawkins wanted him to."

"So he didn't give you anything that will help us get Hawkins?"

"Not yet."

"What about the protective detail for Mike?"

"He's chafing," Harvey said. "Sharon is very grateful, but the city council chairman is making 'over budget' noises again."

"They'd better not stop the guard detail."

"I don't think they will. Mayor Weymouth won't let them. She knows how important Mike's safety is."

"Well, I hope you get some R and R this weekend."

"Oh, Jenny has plans for me this afternoon." Harvey sounded content.

"Going somewhere?" Eddie asked.

"Nope. She got a new sonagram video from Margaret yesterday. We're going to watch it about seventeen times. She tells me our son is sucking his thumb. After that, well, you never know."

"What about Abby?" Eddie asked.

"Greg's in town. Abby is gone for the day. I don't expect to see her again until midnight."

"Enjoy," Eddie said.

"I plan to."

Chapter 23

Eddie and Leeanne played Scrabble that afternoon, and Marilyn sat nearby in the rocking chair for a while with her mending. When she went to tend the kitchen fire, Eddie carried more wood in from the shed and filled the woodbox beside the kitchen range. Marilyn started baking, and he went back to finish the game with Leeanne.

After she beat him soundly, she showed him a picture of her dormitory and the catalog descriptions of the classes she would take that semester. Broadcast journalism, psychology, computer applications, reporting, Article Writing II, and Ethics and Libel.

"Sounds pretty stiff," Eddie said.

"It's a lot of credits, but I want to get things out of the way, so I won't have to take so much in the fall. I think it will be okay."

"The last year looks a lot lighter," he said, looking at the list for fourth-year courses as he sat carefully, three inches from her, on the couch.

"It is. I've already taken this one, too," she said, pointing to Oral Communications for Professionals. "I'll fill in the credits I need with electives. Maybe I'll take another semester of French."

"You don't have to for me," he said.

"Would you rather I didn't?"

"Well, I guess I like it that you want to master the language. But it's not like it's my first language or anything."

"I know, but it would be more of a bond between us, don't you think?"

He shrugged. *"Tu l'aimes quand je parle français. Si tu es heureuse, je suis heureux."* You like it when I speak French. If you're happy, I'm happy.

She smiled and said, *"Je suis très heureuse maintenant. Je suis joyeuse."*

Eddie smiled. He could hear Marilyn somewhere kitchenward, probably putting something in the oven. He moved a little closer and said, *"Peut-être je peux t'embrasser maintenant."* Maybe I can kiss you now.

She hesitated, and he wondered if she was untangling his syntax, or if he'd been *trop aggresif encore.* After a few seconds, she said very seriously, *très serieusement,* *"Je le voudrais."*

His stomach jumped. She would like it.

He heard wheels crunching on snow in the driveway, and a car door slammed. Eddie tried not to rush it, but he knew George and the boys would descend on them in seconds. His timing was lousy. Oh, well.

Leeanne heard it, too, and she moved a little, as if she would jump up, but Eddie put his hand on her arm, and she swung around and looked into his eyes. He slid his arms around her and kissed her slowly, deliberately. This might be the only chance he got all day.

George and the boys stormed in the front door, but they were still a room away, and they talked excitedly to Marilyn. Eddie lingered a couple more seconds, then released Leeanne, smiling into her solemn eyes, and stood up just as Randy and Travis came, half running, through the doorway.

"Eddie! You should have gone! We caught four togue and seven brook trout and two pickerel," Randy said.

"Wow! Did you bring them all home?"

"Only the three biggest brook trout," said Travis.

"Did you go on a raid Thursday night?" Randy asked.

"Not exactly," Eddie said. "We did arrest someone, and we picked up another guy for questioning yesterday afternoon."

"Will it be on the news tonight?" Travis wanted to know.

"I doubt it, but maybe."

Marilyn called to the boys to wash for supper, and they went noisily up the stairs. George sauntered in, holding out his hand.

"Well, Eddie, good to see you."

Eddie shook hands with him. "Thank you, sir.

Sorry I missed you this morning. The boys said you had a good day on the lake."

"Not bad." He picked up the newspaper off the coffee table. "It was cold."

Leeanne went to help her mother, and Eddie wondered if he should try to make conversation, but George seemed engrossed in his paper. "Construction accident in Newport," he said, shaking his head. "They shouldn't try to build things in January in this part of the country."

They had a huge supper for the starved fishermen, and as always in the Wainthrop house, the food was excellent. Eddie offered to help with the dishes after, but Marilyn shooed him and the boys out of the kitchen.

George turned on the news, and Eddie didn't see any footage from Portland. When Leeanne had finished doing dishes, she sat with him for a while, talking quietly.

Randy and Travis came in and organized a game of Risk that lasted about two hours. When Randy finally won, Eddie said, "Guess I'd better hit the road soon." He went up and packed his things and brought his bag downstairs.

"I'm late feeding the goats," Leeanne said. "You can help me, can't you?"

Eddie was happy to go with her, out through the woodshed and a long hallway to the main part of the barn, where there were stalls and pens and a haymow. The barn wasn't exactly warm, but it was less frigid than outside. The goats bleated for their supper. Leeanne shook out flakes of hay into the pens. The barn had a faucet, and she drew bucket after bucket of water. Eddie carried them for her, wherever she directed him.

"If it gets below zero again tonight, the pipe will probably freeze again," she said. "Then I have to carry it from the house."

The goats must have been extra thirsty. Eddie counted eleven buckets. Geneva bleated proudly over her twin kids, and they were pretty cute.

Leeanne leaned over the low wall surrounding Geneva's stall, looking at the babies. "I'm thinking of selling them."

"The two kids?"

"No, all of the goats."

Eddie hadn't expected that. "You've had them a long time."

"I know, but they're a lot of work. I think maybe it's time. There's a boy in Canaan who's interested in buying the herd for a 4-H project. I'd give him a good deal, and all my records."

"Do you really want to do that?"

She shrugged, watching the kids suckle. "I don't know yet. Maybe I'd keep one or two for pets."

Eddie put his arms around her, and it felt strange with all the layers of coats between them. She suddenly burrowed her head into his shoulder. "You're leaving when we go in, aren't you?"

"Yes." He thought maybe she would tell him to stay the night and go home the next day, but she didn't. He held her against him, rubbing her back and looking at the goats. It was harder to leave her this time. "Seems like we haven't had time to get reacquainted today."

"Oh, I don't know." She choked a little on it, then was quiet.

"I like talking to you and learning how you think about things," he said.

"Yeah."

Eddie just held her. After half a minute, she straightened up and took her gloves off, stuffing them into her pockets. Her eyes very large, she reached out and unzipped his parka. Slowly, she put her hands in underneath his jacket, on his flannel shirt, and around him. He pulled her in, close and warm.

"I love you," he whispered. "I'll always love you."

He felt the enormity of his words, but he didn't regret them. The smell of her hair overcame the hay and goat smells, and he soaked it up to remember. "Everything I learned about you today made me more certain."

She didn't move, but kept her cheek against the front of his shirt. Her hands were warm on his back, through the flannel and the cotton T-shirt.

Her wool coat was thick and was definitely a barrier, but he decided she wanted it that way. He would hold her as long as she would let him.

After about a minute, she stepped away. "I'll be down on Friday."

"Great. Should I go to Harvey's after work?"

"Yes."

"Could I kiss you now?"

She brought one hand out from under his coat and up around his neck. Her fingers went into his hair, and he bent down to kiss her. Her lips were warm. He stood holding her after, with her cheek against his, prolonging the moment, but knowing he needed to hit the road.

"Eddie." It was the barest whisper.

"What?" He tried to match her tone.

"I've been reading all week in the Bible, trying to find out what love really means. Not the way people talk about it, but real, lasting, honorable love."

"What did you find out?"

"It's wanting God's best for the other person, not being selfish, putting them first all the time. Doing whatever you need to do to make them happy and keep your relationship true and holy."

He thought about that. "I think I have that for you," he said at last. "It's a lot, but . . . I do feel that way. If God is telling you somehow to wait, it's okay."

"Thank you."

"And I wouldn't want to think about anyone else."

"Not even the rich woman with the condo and the fancy car?"

He laughed.

She pulled his head down and put her lips close to his ear, as if she didn't want the goats to hear what she would tell him. "I do love you, Eddie. I know that now."

He held her close against his pounding heart as he savored the gift she'd given him. When his breathing was steady again, he tipped her face up and kissed her once again, a kiss full of desire, yet at the same time restrained.

They went into the house together, leaving the goats in companionable darkness. Eddie thanked Mr. and Mrs. Wainthrop, said good-bye to the boys, and picked up his duffel bag. Leeanne stepped onto the porch with him, and her eyes looked almost luminous in the starlight.

Eddie touched her cheek. "I'll call you tomorrow."

Chapter 24

On Sunday morning, Eddie tried to readjust to his weekly routine. Laundry was becoming critical, so he took a load to the basement to wash while he ate breakfast. He called Harvey at eight for an update, so he wouldn't have to monopolize him at church. Things were status quo with the case—Rooster still in jail, Cynthia still loose, and Hawkins nowhere to be found.

"Maybe Cynthia already bought Hawkins a car or a plane ticket, and he skipped town," Eddie said.

"Nah, I think he wants to finish the job."

Eddie didn't like that, but Harvey was probably right. Hawkins wouldn't give up until Mike was dead, or at least hurting badly.

"Our unit volunteered to take some of the security shifts for Mike and Sharon without pay," Harvey said. "It's strictly voluntary, but we figured it would keep the city council off Mike's back."

"Count me in," Eddie said. "What shifts are open?"

"You want to do a four a.m. Tuesday, until he goes to the station? You can follow him in."

"Sure, why not?"

"I'll put you down."

"Okay. I've got to go switch my wet laundry to the dryer, but I'll see you at church."

Greg, the airline navigator, was with Abby at Sunday school, but he left before church to catch his flight out. Eddie did like Greg, but Peter Hobart's droopy eyes were starting to earn his sympathy. Eddie felt like shaking Abby.

Harvey lined up their lunch guests: Mike and Sharon Browning, Jack and Rachel Stewart, Beth and Jeff, and Eddie. Once they all arrived at the Larsons' house, Harvey gave the two officers guarding Mike some money and told them to go get some lunch and come back in an hour or two.

Eddie was glad to sit in on the session after lunch, when Harvey went over Friday's events with Mike and Jack.

"I really want to see some action," Mike said. "How about you, Jack?"

"Sure," Stewart said. "I've been itching for some field work ever since I came on board. But I think you should keep your head down until this case is closed."

"That's right," Harvey told Mike. "We'll get you in on a case as soon as it's safe. You too, Jack."

Eddie said, "Do you think you should go into action together? Isn't that a little like flying the President and the V.P. on the same plane?"

"I agree," Harvey said. "Separate situations, definitely."

Mike frowned at him. "You worry too much, Harv."

Harvey shrugged. "Right now, part of my job is to make sure you stay alive."

Sharon, Jennifer, and Mrs. Stewart came into the living room. That left Abby somewhere. Eddie wandered out to the sunroom and found her sitting on the wicker settee, perusing a thick book.

"Heavy reading?"

She looked up. "Yeah. I've got a maternity patient with borderline toxemia, and I'm refreshing my memory on that before I go in."

He sat down in a chair opposite her. "When do you go?"

"I have to be there at three." She put a book-mark in her place and shut the tome. "So, you survived the fifteen minutes of fame."

"Fifteen and a half." He told her about Cynthia.

Abby laughed. "People will forget eventually."

"Yeah, as soon as somebody does something more newsworthy, which you'd think would be every day."

"I heard what Chief Browning said about field work." She glanced toward the doorway and frowned. "Wouldn't that be weird, working with your boss and his boss and his boss?"

"Jack's not Harvey's boss," Eddie said.

Abby made a face. "Oh, get technical."

"Yeah, well I can't believe you're parading

Greg like a trophy in front of Peter. Peter is a good guy. You're causing him a lot of hurt."

"Peter understands."

"Understands what?"

"I haven't made up my mind yet."

"Well, he's a fool if he keeps hanging around you," Eddie said.

She looked pained. "Eddie, I thought we were friends."

"We were."

"Does that mean we aren't anymore?"

"No," he said slowly. "It means I'm disappointed in you. I understand if you're not ready to settle down. I've been there. But when I was dating around, all the girls knew I wasn't getting serious. You don't keep stressing people over it. Tell Peter you won't see him anymore. Even if you're not sure about Greg, it's the only decent thing to do if you're going to keep seeing Greg."

"Really?" She eyed him soberly.

"Yes, really. Or if by some chance I'm wrong, and you want to continue your relationship with Peter, tell Greg to buzz off. Consider them one at a time. You're driving us all insane. I can't imagine how those guys feel."

"I thought you were the expert at juggling multiple girls at the same time."

"It's not as fun as it's cracked up to be, trust me."

Harvey came to the doorway. "Eddie, Mike and Sharon and the Stewarts are all planning to attend a city council meeting Wednesday night. They'll need extra security. I wondered—"

"I'll do it."

"Great. We've got two uniforms scheduled, but I'll put you and Miller on it."

After the brass left a half hour later, with Mike's watchdogs in tow, Harvey went into his room to change and came out wearing jeans, sneakers, and a sweatshirt.

"Eddie, ride with me," he said.

"Sure." Eddie never questioned Harvey. "Have a good evening at work," he told Abby.

In his Explorer, Harvey said, "I didn't get a chance to ask you how things went in Skowhegan."

"Good."

Harvey threw a glance sideways at him and pulled out onto the street. "Leeanne is coming down Friday night?"

"Yes."

"Anything new on the college front?"

"She's planning to finish her degree at Farmington, so she won't lose any credit."

"I can't say as I blame her."

"We talked about love," Eddie said tentatively.

"In general, or specifics?"

"Both. What it means, the real, biblical kind, and . . . you know, I had told her before, when she was down here. Well, she says she loves me, Harv."

Harvey pulled into the parking garage at the station. He killed the engine and looked at Eddie, long and deep. Then he stuck out his hand and they shook.

Harvey smiled. "Just don't rush things."

"Yeah. You know, whenever I spend time with Leeanne, I learn new things about her. She's a really deep thinker."

"Is she?" He was still smiling.

"Yeah. She's *smart*. She showed me some of the papers she wrote for class last semester. Really good stuff. And she wants to do things God's way."

"I'm glad. Do your part."

They checked in with the com center and went up to the office.

"I want to check my flag program and see if anything's come up, and make sure we've got Mike covered for the next few days," Harvey said.

"Are you losing sleep over this?"

"Maybe a little. Mike Junior called me last night to ask if I really thought his parents were safe. He said they should leave Portland for a few days. I told him he could suggest it, but I doubt Mike would go for it."

"Besides," Eddie said, "we couldn't let them leave town without security."

"I agree, but I didn't say that. I knew Mike would nix the idea if his kids brought it up."

They spent a half hour at the office. Eddie went over the updates for the weekend while Harvey fine-tuned the schedule for Mike's protective detail. When they got back to the house, Eddie said, "Guess I'll head home for a little while."

Jennifer put a zipper bag of cookies in his hand. "Take these. Oh, and Abby had to go to work, but she asked me to give you a message. She says she's been thinking about what you said to her before you left."

"Oh, about Greg and Peter."

"What did you tell her?" asked Harvey.

"That she'd better put them out of their misery. Peter looks awful."

"We've been praying about that situation," said Jennifer. "I don't think she realizes how badly one of them is going to be hurt."

Eddie drove to his apartment and called Leeanne.

"*Comment ça va, ma belle?*" he asked.

"*Bien.* I'm packing my clothes for school, but I don't know how to say it in French."

Whenever he heard that lilt in her voice, Eddie felt like little fireworks were going off inside him.

He got the impression there were other people in the room with her, so he didn't press her on sensitive topics. He gave her a quick rundown on church, lunch at Jennifer's, and Harvey's, and his run to the office.

"Is Harvey working seven days a week now?" she asked.

"Just about. When a case is breaking, some things just won't wait. We need to find this Hawkins guy."

"Be safe," she said a little plaintively.

"I will. Keep praying for us."

When they'd signed off, it struck him how many names he'd swiped through to get to Leeanne's number. He sat down and put hers on speed dial. Then he started culling his list of contacts. He didn't count, but he thought he'd removed at least twenty women's phone numbers. For some of the names, he couldn't remember the face. Maybe Abby was right, and he was a heel. He didn't really have the right to get after her.

He sent her a text: SORRY ABS, U R RIGHT DON'T LISTEN 2 ME.

He stuck the phone in his pocket and headed for the basement laundry. As he was pulling his clothes from the dryer, it pinged with an incoming text. He looked at it. NO, F.B., U R RIGHT, 2 IS 2 MANY.

He smiled, even though she was still digging at him with an abbreviated "French Boy"—or so he thought. Seconds later it pinged again: PS THAT STANDS FOR FRENCH BROTHER.

He grinned and texted her back, "KK, GABBY

SIS." He picked up his laundry basket and headed upstairs.

Harvey went to Eddie's place for breakfast after their run Monday morning, and Eddie fixed instant oatmeal and coffee.

"This is kind of shabby next to a Wainthrop breakfast," Eddie admitted. He told Harvey what Leeanne had fixed at her house.

"I don't let Jennifer feed me like that," Harvey said. "I'd be fat as a hog if I ate that way all the time."

"I'm planning on marrying Leeanne, Harv."

"I figured. Does she know it yet?"

"I haven't said it in so many words."

"Don't rush things."

Eddie nodded. "She gets a little nervous if I move too quickly."

"So don't. There's time."

"I'm trying."

Harvey eyed him seriously. "Don't try to take it at Leeanne's pace, Eddie. Take it at God's pace."

Eddie sipped his coffee and thought about that. "Right. She worries about our field work, too. Afraid I'll get hurt."

"Well, it could happen. I'll ask Jennifer to talk to her sometime. A woman just has to come to terms with that if she's going to marry a cop." He smiled. "I'm happy for you, Ed. We've come through a lot, haven't we?"

"Yup. I think God is in this."

Their workday was so normal Eddie was bored silly. They kept plugging at what leads they had left, but nothing was coming together. Harvey went to attend Tony's hearing on the shooting after lunch.

Nate, Jimmy, and Eddie gave it all they had, but none of their informants would hazard a guess as to who Al Hawkins would turn to for a new shooter, now that Rooster was out of circulation. Eddie went across town alone to touch base with Silver.

"Eddie, you're making things hot for me. Leave me alone for a while," Silver said.

"Come on, all I need is one good break."

"I told you about that Cynthia woman." Silver didn't actually say *woman,* but it was what Tony would call a synonym.

"She wasn't any help," Eddie said.

"Oh, yeah? I heard you tossed her condo, and he's been hiding out ever since."

"Yeah?" So maybe their little jaunt to Cynthia's had done some good after all, if it had Hawkins scrambling. "You know where he's hiding?"

"Me? No."

He said it so quickly, Eddie had his doubts.

"You also told me Rooster would give me some intel, but he hasn't lived up to that stellar recommendation."

"Sorry about that, but I don't blame him."

Silver shook his head. "You get more information with a little cash than with handcuffs."

"Is that a hint?"

"Hey, I got nothing for you, Eddie. I'm giving it to you straight."

Eddie sighed. "You call me if you hear anything about Hawkins."

Silver nodded.

"Anything," Eddie said.

"Yeah, yeah. Now, go away."

Eddie went back to the office. As he emerged from the stairway, Harvey stood up, his desk phone's receiver clapped to his ear.

"Eddie just came in. We'll get right over there."

Eddie checked his stride.

Harvey hung up. "Come with me."

"What's up?" Eddie U-turned, and they went quickly down the stairway.

"Sharon Browning found a note on her car's windshield at the grocery store. That was Mike on the phone. I told him we'd handle it."

Eddie's heart pounded. Harvey's vehicle was closer to the garage door than his, and they jumped into it. Harvey headed for a Shop 'n Save a mile away.

"Didn't she have the protective detail with her?" Eddie asked.

"Yeah. Ted Marston's with her. He's the one who called the chief. They've only kept one officer with Sharon after Mike came to work."

"Probably enough," Eddie said.

"Let's see that note before we pass judgment." Harvey paused at a traffic light and looked over at him. "It was all I could do to keep Mike from racing over there."

"You think that's what Hawkins wanted?"

"It wouldn't surprise me. Mike said he told Marston to get Sharon inside, out of sight."

Eddie's chest was tight as they drove into the shopping center's parking lot and cruised toward the grocery's front door. He hopped out of the vehicle and strode inside while Harvey parked.

Ted Marston and Sharon were waiting near the service desk, and Eddie hurried over.

"Hey. You all right, Mrs. B.?"

"Yes, I'm fine, Eddie. Thanks for coming."

He nodded. "Harvey's outside." He looked at Marston. "You got the note?"

Ted held out a small slip of paper. Hand printed on one side were the words, "Watch your back Browning." The paper appeared to have been torn from an envelope. "Where was it?"

"Under the wiper on the driver's side of Mrs. Browning's car. I was driving, and I spotted it when we left the store, before I started the engine."

"Okay. Where's the car, exactly?"

They stepped with him to the door, and Ted pointed out Sharon's parked sedan. Harvey walked in to join them. They all stepped to one side, out of the path of shoppers, and Eddie quickly updated Harvey.

He nodded. "Sharon, I'd like you and Ted to stay inside while Eddie and I check your vehicle. If it looks okay, we'll escort you out. Ted can take you home, and we'll follow, to make sure you get there safely." He smiled at her. "We'll even lug your groceries in for you, after we clear the house."

Sharon clutched his sleeve. "Thank you, Harvey. You don't think this is a real threat against me, do you? It seemed like a message to Mike."

"Hard to say. But we'll get that note right to the lab and see if they can tell us anything. Ted, take Mrs. Browning over near the service desk, and stay alert. We'll only be five or ten minutes, but we want to do a thorough check."

Ted handed Harvey the keys to Sharon's car and led her away from the entry. Eddie and Harvey went out to the car.

Harvey brought a movers' blanket and a flashlight from his vehicle, and Eddie went down on his back to do a complete check of the car's underside. When he was sure nothing odd had been added, Harvey cautiously opened the driver's door. He popped the hood and did a painstaking examination of the engine compartment. Then they did the same for the trunk, which already held Sharon's groceries, and the passenger compartment, just to be sure.

"Looks okay," Eddie said as he shut the trunk.

"Yeah." Harvey took out his phone and called Mike. "The car's clear, Chief. We'll see Sharon home."

He signed off and turned to Eddie. "You watch the car, and I'll go get Sharon and Ted." He handed Eddie the flashlight and went inside.

Eddie surveyed the lot and every person moving. Harvey brought Sharon out and put her in the passenger seat. Ted got behind the wheel. Eddie and Harvey got in the Explorer and followed them to Bingley Lane. As promised, they searched the house and carried in the groceries. A second patrolman arrived to help with the vigil, and the two detectives finally went back to the station.

"Start the report, okay?" Harvey said. "I'll go straight up to Mike and try to scrape him off the ceiling."

When Eddie got up to the office, Tony was sitting on his desk wearing a suit, drinking Pepsi, and recounting the details of his hearing to Jimmy and Nate.

"Hey, are you cleared?" Eddie asked.

"Yup. I'll be back to work in the morning."

"Good." Eddie wouldn't have believed it a week earlier, but he'd actually missed the guy.

Tony started pushing buttons on his phone.

"What are you doing?" Eddie asked.

"Ordering pizza. Want some?"

"Sure, I'll go halves if you'll proof my report. Mine and the captain's, that is."

"You writing for two, Shakespeare?"

"Yeah, Harvey's holding the chief's hand. You heard about the note on Sharon's car?" Briefly, he told Tony, Nate, and Jimmy what had happened. He couldn't be flippant about it. "Sharon's really shook up," he said. "I think she'll be okay, but this was a big scare. Which is what Hawkins intended. He was hoping Mike would tear out of here with no guards."

"Okay," Tony said, "you write that up, and I'll edit. We've got one large pepperoni on the way."

Eddie got the report done in record time, since he didn't have to agonize over grammar. He emailed it to Tony.

"Holy Hamlet, Shakespeare, didn't you ever learn what commas are for?"

"Grammar is not my superpower, Mr. White."

"Well, I'm sure Clark Kent writes better than this," Tony said.

"Are you guys living in Metropolis or Elizabethan England?" Nate asked.

"We'll let you know if we figure it out," Eddie said.

Paula called across the room, "Detective Winfield, there's a delivery for you downstairs."

"I'll get it," Eddie said. He figured it was the least he could do, since Tony was correcting his extra-sloppy report, and he wasn't even on the clock. He hurried downstairs.

"You Winfield?" the delivery girl asked. She looked about sixteen in her uniform and cap, with auburn hair in pigtails.

"No, I'm Thibodeau, but I'll pay you for the pizza."

"You're not grabbing his—" She stared at him. "You're the rescue guy that everyone cries over, aren't you?"

Eddie handed her a twenty. "Keep the change."

The elevator opened, and the deputy chief got out. Eddie grabbed the pizza. Even though he never used the elevator, he zipped into it before the door could close.

Chapter 25

As Eddie got out of his truck in front of his apartment building that evening, his phone rang.

"Hey! I have some news," Leeanne said. "I couldn't wait to tell you."

"What kind of news?" His pulse picked up, and flashes of apprehension tore through his brain, although she sounded happy.

"I saw my academic counselor today. If I take my internship this summer, I'll have enough credits to graduate at Christmas. That's if I stay in the UMaine system and don't change majors."

"Next Christmas? You can knock off a whole semester?"

"Yes. Can you believe it? Because I'm taking so many credits now, I can finish early. It will save a ton of money, and I'll have my degree."

"That's fantastic." Eddie leaned against the door of the truck. They had prayed for a resolution, but this was better than the best scenario he'd imagined. "Thank you. I know you're not doing this for me exactly, but I feel like God did it for me personally."

"Maybe he did," she said. "I'm not looking forward to another year of campus life, but having this goal should make it bearable."

"Do you have to live in the dorm?" he asked.

"Well, it's pretty hard driving down to the early classes in winter."

"Next fall, you could—don't they offer the classes you need down here?"

"I asked the counselor," Leeanne said. "She thinks I could do it."

"Finish at USM, you mean?" His pulse leaped.

"Yes. If we still want to do that when the time comes, I could take my last semester in Portland."

"Why wouldn't we?" She was talking about the future in the plural. The future in Portland in the plural.

"Well, if for some reason it became awkward. I mean, Harvey is your best friend, and he's your boss now. I wouldn't want to be right in your face all the time—at church and everything—if things didn't go well between us."

"Don't even think like that," Eddie said. "This is long term." He wanted to say forever, but he wanted to be in the same county with her when he said that.

"I'm selling the goats," she said.

"Really? It's definite?"

"Yes, I've decided to let them all go. The boy and his father are bringing a cattle truck to get them tomorrow. The next time I go home, the barn will be empty."

"You okay with that? You've had them a long time."

"It will be a relief to the family," she said.

"They have to take care of them while I'm at school. And it will be a relief to me, too. I'll miss them a little, especially the babies."

"Come down here at the end of the school year, and you can play with Jennifer's kid," he quipped.

Leeanne laughed. "I just might do that. We'll have to talk this weekend, you and Harvey and Jennifer and me. And Abby. She's in the mix, too."

"Yeah. I think Abby and I understand each other now."

Eddie told her about the pizza girl and was able to laugh about it with her. He told her again that he loved her, and she said softly, "I love you, too." It was a pretty good ending for a chaotic day.

Eddie got up very early Tuesday—three-thirty in the morning—and drove to Mike's. Aaron O'Heir and Allison Crocker had been on watch since midnight. Jimmy Cook joined him, and they took turns sitting in the truck out front and checking the perimeter. Jimmy had brought a thermos of coffee, and it wasn't too bad.

Mike was up by six and offered them breakfast. Jimmy went in first and ate eggs and toast while Eddie kept his eyes open for people who didn't belong. Then Jimmy came out, and Eddie had breakfast while Mike got dressed for work.

Sharon brought the coffeepot over to the table. "Refill, Eddie?"

"No, thanks, I've had enough to keep me awake all week."

She smiled. "We really appreciate you guys doing this on your own time."

"No more notes?" he asked.

"Nothing."

"Well, that's good. The lab couldn't get anything off the one from your car, though."

Bill Theriault and Sarah showed up at seven-thirty. They stayed at the house, and Jimmy and Eddie drove to the station, keeping an eye on Mike's vehicle. They walked into the building with him and separated on the stairway. That was the most excitement they had all day, except that Tony returned to work.

They tried to drum up something substantial in the case, but every lead seemed to peter out. Things were calm at five o'clock, but all the men were frustrated by the lack of progress.

"Time to go home, Eddie," Harvey said, packing up his briefcase.

"It's your baby night, isn't it?"

"Yes, we get the hospital tour tonight. They postponed it." Harvey actually sounded eager.

"Guess it's sort of like a date for you and Jennifer."

He laughed. "Oh, yeah. Dating. Don't remind me."

Eddie followed him to the locker room. "Leeanne gave me some news last night," he told Harvey as they opened their lockers.

"What's that?"

"She can graduate from the University of Maine next Christmas with her journalism degree."

"No kidding?" Harvey asked. "I'm impressed. She's a bright girl."

"She'll need to do her internship this summer, and she could finish down here in the fall."

"That so? Might be good for Jennifer."

"How do you mean?"

"You never know—we might lose Abby by then."

Eddie frowned at him. "Do you really think so?"

"She's still unsettled. I wish she'd take a page out of your book and come up with a goal."

"I have goals?" Eddie asked.

"Well, Leeanne."

"Oh, absolutely."

Harvey looked at him with speculation. "Where do you see yourself in five years, Eddie?"

"What is this, my evaluation?"

"No, I'm just curious, man to man."

"Right here, I guess. I like this unit. I intend to stay with Priority as long as the city will fund it."

"And?"

"And married, I hope. Maybe going to Lamaze classes, like you."

Harvey laughed and cuffed him on the shoulder.

Eddie stopped at the Burger King for supper, then went home and called Leeanne. She was at the dormitory.

"Can't keep myself from calling you," he said.

"That's okay."

"Do you like your classes?"

"So far," she said. "My counselor's going to try to help me get an internship for the summer."

"I was hoping you'd be down here, but I guess it's good to get that out of the way."

"Yeah. She said I might be able to get on in Waterville, Augusta, Lewiston, or Portland. Or Bangor, but that's farther north."

"Any of those other towns would be closer than you are now."

"Yeah, but if I can't get on this summer, I'll have to wait and do it in the fall. I put down Portland as my first choice, but if that's out of the question, then I guess I'll take it wherever I can."

"Harvey knows John Russell, the managing editor at the *Press Herald*," Eddie said. "Maybe he'd put a word in for you."

"Wouldn't hurt, I guess."

The more Eddie thought about it, the more he liked the idea. "Call him."

"Okay."

"Oh, wait until nine o'clock or so. He and Jennifer have their baby lesson tonight."

"You're so funny."

"Well, I guess I've got to get over this," Eddie said. "My sister Lisa's expecting again, too. I should be used to being around . . . pregnant women. Okay, I can say the word."

She laughed. "It will be different when it's yours."

"That's what Harvey says." Eddie didn't voice his own thought, that he hoped she'd be the one in Lamaze class with him. "*Je te manque?*" he asked. Miss me?

"*Oui, tu me manques beaucoup*, but . . . I know I'll see you soon. That makes it easier."

Harvey and Eddie ran in the frosty air Wednesday morning. It was barely twenty degrees, but they opted for nature, not the track. Harvey was gasping when they finished at the park.

"I dunno about this," he said. "My lungs are old."

"You okay?" Eddie had forgotten Harvey's partially collapsed lung the summer before.

"I will be. Let's pray at my house. Go change and come for breakfast." Harvey got in his Explorer and drove off.

When Eddie got there, Jennifer was making coffee and toast.

"You look nice, Eddie," she said when he took off his jacket.

"Thanks. Court today."

"Leeanne called last night when we got home from the hospital."

"Yeah?"

"She asked Harvey to speak to John Russell about an internship for her next summer. I guess you knew about that."

Eddie smiled. "Yup."

She smiled, too. "We think it would be terrific."

"I'm glad." He doctored his coffee and took a sip. "Was Harvey okay when he got home this morning?"

"I think so, why?" Jennifer arched her eyebrows at him.

"It was pretty cold out. I thought maybe he had a twinge in his lung."

She stood with a plate of toast in midair, staring at him.

"He'll be fine," Eddie said.

She set the plate down. "Do you think he should see Carl?"

"No, it's nothing, I'm sure. We should have gone to the track, is all."

Harvey came in from the sunroom dressed for work. His hair was wet and curly. Jennifer kissed him and put coffee and toast in front of him. "I'll make you some oatmeal," she told him.

"No, just give me the Wheaties," he said.

"It's cold today. You need a hot breakfast." She didn't look at Eddie while she made the quick oatmeal and brought orange juice and a bottle of vitamins.

She watched Harvey while he got the vitamin out and swallowed it.

"What?" he said.

"Nothing. I'm just trying to keep you healthy. You'll need to get up in the middle of the night and change diapers soon."

He pushed his chair out and tugged her toward him. She put her arms around his neck and let him pull her onto his lap.

"If I gain any more weight, you won't be able to do this," she said.

He smiled and pulled her closer. He'd been that way since they got married. Rather cuddle with Jennifer than eat. After a few seconds, she wised up, though, and stood.

"Eat the oatmeal," she said.

"You better eat some, too," he told her. "Feed that baby."

She got herself a dish and sat down with them.

"So, how was the hospital?" Eddie asked.

"I didn't pass out."

Jennifer laughed. "We saw Abby, and we saw the delivery rooms and labor rooms, and the newborn nursery."

Harvey sipped his coffee. "They've got three sets of twins in there right now."

"Think you might have twins?" Eddie asked Jennifer.

"Me? No. We've got movies of the baby, and there's only one."

"You want to see it?" Harvey had an eager look.

"No, thanks. I might pass out."

"Oh, Eddie, it's just a baby. And it's in black and white," Harvey said.

"I think I'll wait until it's my own progeny."

Eddie spent most of the morning at the courthouse on a previous case, taking Tony with him. When they got back to the office, Harvey told him Rooster Bentley's lawyer had contacted him. Rooster would talk to the district attorney the next day, and Harvey was welcome to sit in.

Jennifer called and asked Harvey to bring Eddie home with him for lunch, so Eddie went. Jennifer and Abby had the food ready, knowing the men had a limited amount of time.

"Can I talk to you, Eddie?" Abby asked, as they were finishing their chocolate pudding.

"Sure. You mean now?"

She looked around the table. "Actually, I should probably talk to all of you. It concerns you all. I know I've been acting rather adolescent, and you've all been praying for me."

"Does this have anything to do with the phone call last night after you got home?" Jennifer asked.

"Yes." Abby scraped the bottom of her pudding dish. "It was Greg."

"Surprise, surprise," Eddie said.

"Yes, well, he's going to California."

They all just sat there, waiting for the rest of it. After a few seconds, Harvey said, "When will he be back?"

"He won't."

"What?" cried Jennifer. "You mean he's moving?"

"Yes. He's switching to Western Airlines. He's going to fly out of SFO, starting in two weeks."

"San Francisco?" Eddie said. "How come?"

"They offered it to him, and he accepted."

"But why?" asked Jennifer. "And did you know about the offer, and will he come back to see you, and what does it mean?"

"One question at a time, gorgeous," Harvey said. Jennifer reached for his hand.

Abby said, "Well, it's more money, for one thing."

"That's not important, or it shouldn't be," said Jennifer. "He makes plenty now, doesn't he?"

Abby shrugged. "I did know about it. He told me last weekend he was thinking about it." Two bright red spots had formed high on her cheeks. "He wanted me to go with him."

"As in marriage, I hope?" Harvey asked.

"Yes. He—proposed Saturday night. I guess I should have told you all, but I was pretty mixed up. It was kind of a funny proposal, I thought."

"In what way?" Harvey sounded like an irate father who didn't want his baby girl hurt.

"He wanted to get married right away if he went to California. Before he left."

"And if he stayed?" asked Harvey.

"Then I could pick the date."

Jennifer shook her head. "Just like that? Get married and move to San Francisco? That's like jumping off the edge of the world."

"Not for Greg. He doesn't have a tight family, and he's used to flying all over."

"So, what did you tell him?" Eddie asked.

"I hadn't told him anything until last night." She looked into her coffee cup, but it was empty.

"But he accepted the position before you accepted his proposal?" Jennifer asked. "Unbelievable!"

Abby shook her head. "I don't completely understand it, either. I thought he would give me a few days to think about it."

"Sort of an ultimatum?" Eddie asked.

"I didn't think it was. I thought he was open to staying here. In New York, I mean. But I told him Saturday I wasn't sure I'd want to move so far away from everyone I love."

"Except him," said Jennifer.

"Well, yeah. But then I got to thinking maybe even Brooklyn was too far." Tears welled up in her eyes, and she looked pleadingly at her sister. "It's not like I can't cut the apron strings, but to move to a strange city where I don't know *anyone,* and my husband would be away for days at a time . . . I kept thinking about friends of mine whose marriages didn't last. I think airline personnel have a poor track record."

"Every profession has its drawbacks," Jennifer said.

"I know." Abby's smile quavered. "Your husband has an easy eight-to-five office job, and he comes home for lunch. Ha, ha."

Harvey reached out and squeezed her hand. "Abby, it's okay to say no to a guy when you're not sure. That's the only safe thing to say."

"I think he was worried about Peter," she said. "San Francisco was like a test. If I said I'd marry him in a week and leave Maine and all of you behind, it would mean leaving Peter and the boys behind, too. He wanted to make a clean, three-thousand-mile break."

"Can't blame him," Eddie said.

"You can't?" she faltered.

"No. I mean, if Leeanne had an old boyfriend hanging around, I'd want to get her as far away from him as I could. Right, Harv?"

Harvey said gravely, "I guess you're right, Ed. I didn't want a certain man to even look at Jennifer's picture."

Jennifer ignored that and focused on Abby. "So, you turned him down."

"Yes. I told him I couldn't do that. I prayed about it. I really did. In some ways, it seemed exciting and—and—I do feel strongly for him. I'm not saying he should be willing to come live in Maine and change careers or anything. I just think it's too drastic a change for me. But I thought he'd wait to give them an answer until I gave him one."

"He took the job for sure?" Eddie asked.

She nodded miserably. "He's going."

"Did he say he loves you?" Jennifer asked. Eddie thought that was a little personal, but Abby nodded and sobbed.

"He said he loves me, and if I really loved him I'd go."

"Hoo, boy," Harvey said. "I thought Greg was more mature than that."

"I think—" Jennifer handed Abby a tissue, and she paused to wipe her face with it. "I think maybe I just pushed him too far with non-commitment. Is that a word? I mean, I had told him way back that I was seeing Peter, and I never told either of them I wouldn't see anyone else. But Greg wanted an exclusive relationship. Right away."

"But you do want to get married?" Eddie asked, trying to grasp what she really felt.

"Yes, someday, but not next week. And maybe not to him."

"I guess the courtship period was too protracted

for him," Harvey said. "I can sort of understand it. He's thirty-six years old. He didn't want to dangle after you for two or three years and then have you break up with him. He wants a family."

"I know." Abby sobbed, and reached for another tissue. "I feel like I've done something awful, to him *and* Peter."

"Peter doesn't know about this, does he?" Jennifer asked.

"No, not yet. Do you think I should tell him?"

"When the opportunity arises," said Harvey.

"I think I need to apologize to him and tell him to start looking for someone who knows what she wants." Abby wiped her eyes.

Harvey sneaked a look at his watch, which made Eddie look at his.

"We're going to be late getting back," Eddie said.

"Right." Harvey eyed Abby. "Let's take a minute to pray about this and let God handle it."

They all held hands, and Harvey asked the Lord to help Abby and Greg. Then Harvey and Eddie both hugged Abby.

"We support you, Gabby Sis," Eddie said.

"Thanks, guys."

In the truck, Harvey said, "I hope she learns something from this and just stays out of circulation for a while."

"You think that's what she needs?" Eddie asked.

"I don't know what she needs. Thank God, I'm not the one who has to know that."

Eddie nodded, aching for Abby.

Chapter 26

They hadn't been back in the office long before Mike called Harvey upstairs. Eddie figured he wanted an update on Hawkins. While Harvey was gone, he did some computer checks on everyone involved in the case, from Kyle Quinlan to Rooster Bentley. He even checked on Misty Carney, hoping for something. Anything. And got nothing.

When Harvey came back, Nate and Jimmy were out of the office. Harvey said, "Eddie, Tony, come here a second," and sat down heavily in his desk chair.

Tony and Eddie walked over to his desk.

"Sit down."

Eddie's inner radar blipped. He took his desk chair over, and Tony sat in Harvey's visitor chair.

"Chief Leavitt died." Harvey looked a little gray.

"That's too bad," Eddie said. "You okay, Harv?"

"Yeah, it's just . . . I wasn't expecting it." Dwight Leavitt was the previous police chief, and he had been critically injured in a car accident the summer before. Mike had been promoted as a result. Leavitt had been in the hospital for three months, then transferred to an intensive nursing facility.

Eddie said, "I knew he wasn't recovering well, but I didn't think he was going to die."

"His heart finally gave out, I guess," Harvey said. "The funeral will be at two o'clock Saturday."

"And we'll all be there," Eddie added.

"Us and every other cop in Portland who's not on duty. Lots of dignitaries, too." Harvey smiled faintly at Tony. "Including your uncle."

"Where is it?" asked Tony.

"Don't know yet. They've got to have a pretty big hall. Other police departments will send contingents."

"It's not like he died in the line of duty," Eddie said. "He was trying to miss a raccoon."

Harvey frowned. "It's a show of respect for his position."

"I know." Eddie felt guilty because he had been selfishly thinking it would ruin his Saturday with Leeanne. He sent up a silent prayer of confession for that. Maybe Leeanne would see it as a unique date.

"Mike will be expected to show support to Patsy Leavitt at the funeral," Harvey said. "He and Sharon, and Jack and Rachel Stewart, will go to the visiting hours at the funeral home Thursday evening, and probably Friday as well. Mike will introduce all the officers that go to Mrs. Leavitt and her children."

"That will be a huge security risk for Mike," Eddie said.

"Yeah. I'm going to work on the schedule. It'll be rough, but we need to be extra vigilant."

Eddie worked all afternoon with nothing to show for it on the Quinlan case. At ten to five, Harvey told him, "Don't forget your security detail tonight."

"Yeah, I thought I'd get something to eat. I go on at six, right?"

"That's right. The two patrolmen can keep an eye on the house while you and Nate escort the chief to the city council meeting."

Eddie had just time to grab a burger and call Leeanne. He and Nate were at the chief's house on Bingley Lane right on schedule.

"You want one of us to play chauffeur, Chief?" Eddie asked, since downtown parking was at a premium.

"No, I'll drive," Mike said.

He and Sharon got in Sharon's car, and Eddie's pickup led the way, with Nate bringing up the rear in his Stratus.

Eddie drove into the parking lot beside city hall, and a patrol officer directed him to two vacant spots they'd kept for him and the chief. Nate parked on the street.

Eddie got out and walked over to the Brownings'

car. Mike didn't climb out until he got close and took a good look around. Eddie was glad he wasn't showing his impetuous side tonight. Maybe the note on Sharon's car, or the somber mood since Chief Leavitt died, had something to do with it. Nate came jogging up the sidewalk, and he nodded at Eddie.

"All set, Chief," Eddie said.

Mike walked around the car and opened Sharon's door. Man, they were beautiful. Eddie couldn't help a quick comparison to his folks, who were about the same age. It wasn't that Mike and Sharon were extraordinarily good-looking, either one of them, though both were attractive and had taken care of themselves. It was more that they were a happy couple who enjoyed being together and performing a service for others. Next to Harvey, Mike was Eddie's hero. Okay, so he asked nutty questions and drank Moxie all the time. Everyone had their quirks.

They had decided Nate would go into the council chambers with them, and Eddie would patrol the lobby and check the parking lot now and then. If the meeting lasted more than an hour, they would swap off.

About a hundred people went in, and Jack Stewart and his wife paused to say hello to Eddie. He saw a few other people he knew—Ryan Toothaker from the *Press Herald*, a councilwoman he'd met in an official capacity, and the owner of a bakery downtown who had been a witness in one of his cases.

Once the chairman called order, the meeting got quiet. Eddie did a thorough check of the lobby for loiterers, located every exit just for drill, and had a look in the men's room.

He went outside and did a survey of the parking area and street, then went back into the lobby. Repeat. After an hour, the council showed no sign of winding down. Nate sneaked out to trade with him.

"Grizzly's fine," Nate said. It was their illogical code name for the chief.

Eddie went in and located Mike and Sharon. Jack and Rachel were sitting next to the them in the second row. He did a quick visual sweep of the crowd. Nothing odd there. He stood against the wall in the back, where he had a clear view of Mike.

Ten minutes later, Mike was asked to say a few words. The chairman remarked that he was glad to see the chief in good health. Mike told them that he and Sharon were very thankful for the security detail, and he hoped they wouldn't need it much longer. Jack got up and gave the council a very persuasive talk on why they needed to hire several new patrolmen and send them to the next class at the Academy. He was starting a plug for refresher training for all the officers who hadn't had a first aid course within the last five years when Charlie Doran contacted him on his earpiece.

"Heads-up, Eddie. Miller asked me to tell you he's got a situation in the parking lot."

Eddie took one step outside the chamber, into the foyer. "What's up?"

"A loiterer who might be watching the grizzly's car. Miller's handling it. Just stay alert."

"Copy."

Eddie went back in and took up a post where he could see both doors and Mike clearly. He leaned against the wall and crossed his arms, with the fingers of his right hand inside his jacket, touching the butt of his service revolver.

He prayed Jack Stewart wouldn't talk too long. When the deputy chief wound down his spiel, a couple of council members asked questions. The chairman thanked Jack, and finally the meeting closed.

Eddie strode to the front as Mike and Sharon were putting on their coats.

"I need you to stay in this room for a minute, while Miller checks out something."

Mike raised his eyebrows. "Okay. All right if I have a word with the mayor?"

"Yes, but it would be good if you and Sharon stay close together."

Less than a minute later, Nate assured him that all was well outside. Eddie informed Mike.

"Stay close to me when we go out," he told

the chief. Eddie walked out just ahead of the Brownings, on high alert.

Nate waited for them beside Mike's car.

"Everything okay?" Eddie asked.

"Yeah, there was a guy sitting in his car with the engine running, just across from the chief's car. I asked what he was doing, and he said he was waiting for someone in the meeting. I asked him to leave, and then I ran the plate and checked out the Browning's vehicle, to make sure there wasn't any funny business. Seems all right."

"Okay. Best to be careful." Eddie turned to Mike and Sharon. "Sounds like it's okay to get in the car and go home."

They did the mini motorcade in reverse, with Nate leading, Mike in the middle, and Eddie trailing.

When they got to the Brownings' house, they checked with the patrol officers who had stayed to watch the house. Nothing odd had occurred while they were gone. Just to be sure, Eddie went inside and searched every room before Mike and Sharon went in. Then he and Nate headed home.

Harvey met with Rooster Bentley, his lawyer, and the assistant district attorney Thursday morning. Rooster didn't give them the definitive information they'd hoped for, but he told Harvey three places he'd gone to meet with Hawkins in the last month, one of them being Melanie

Tucker's apartment. The others were a bar and a pub with pool tables.

Harvey split up the unit to check out the three locations. He sent Eddie and Tony to the pub. Eddie put on his wool buffalo plaid, and Tony produced a camouflage jacket that looked like it came from army surplus. They parked Eddie's truck a block away and walked to the pub.

Tony went to watch the pool players while casing the place for Hawkins, and Eddie sidled up to the bar. The bartender lifted his chin in Eddie's direction.

"Hey, I'm looking for Al Hawkins," Eddie said.

The bartender looked hard at him, and Eddie wished he'd let Tony do the asking. Maybe his undercover days really were over.

The bartender leaned toward him and said in a low tone, "You're a cop."

"So?"

He shrugged. "You're bad for business."

"Tell me if Hawkins is here, and I'm out of your hair."

"He ain't here."

Eddie nodded. "He come in here much?"

The bartender looked around and stepped closer. "What's it worth to you?"

"Five." Eddie hadn't asked for any petty cash, but he had a couple of bills in his wallet.

"He don't come here much."

"But you know him. When was the last time?"

"Maybe a week ago."

"Yeah? You sure you haven't seen him since then?"

"I'm sure."

Eddie took out the fiver and laid it on the bar, but kept his hand on it. "Is he still in town?"

The bartender's eyes narrowed. "I ain't heard otherwise. Now, have a drink or get lost."

Eddie let go of the bill, and the bartender palmed it and turned away. A cheer went up from near the pool table. Eddie looked over and caught Tony's eye. He nodded toward the door.

Outside, he told Tony, "He says Hawkins hasn't been in here for a week."

"What if he's lying?"

"He might be." Eddie shook his head. "A week ago, we arrested Cynthia."

"Yeah. He's been hiding out since then."

They ambled back toward the pickup. Eddie's phone vibrated, and he eased it out of his pocket. He didn't recognize the number.

"Yeah?"

"Eddie?"

He stopped walking. "That you, Silver?"

"Yeah. I heard Hawkins is making his move soon."

"You mean—"

"You know what I mean, but you didn't hear it from me."

"Gotcha. Do you think he'll try tonight?"

"Could be, but I'm not certain. Very sketchy."

"Thanks, pal," Eddie said. "I owe you one." He clicked to end the call and looked at Tony. "Get in the truck." Once they had the doors closed, he said, "That was one of my informants. He says Hawkins is making his move soon, maybe tonight."

"We gotta tell the captain."

Eddie started the truck and made a U-turn.

At the station, Harvey heard him out, authorized Paula to replace Eddie's five-dollar bill, and went up to the chief's office. Nate and Jimmy came in from their foray to the bar with nothing they could use.

"That leaves Mel Tucker's place," Tony said.

A few minutes later, Harvey returned, and they all went to his desk.

"It's no good," he told them. "Mike refuses to lay low until this is over."

"What's his plan for tonight?" Nate asked.

"After supper, he and Sharon are going to the visiting hours at the funeral home."

"Who's scheduled to go with him?" Eddie asked.

"Cheryl Yeaton and Joe Clifford have the six-to-ten shift. Nate and Jimmy are taking the ten to two at the house."

Nate nodded to confirm the assignment.

"I told Jimmy and Nate to come in late tomorrow," Harvey said. "I know you guys are doing it on your own nickel, but I want you alert when you come back on duty."

"Sure, Captain," Jimmy said.

"Sleep late if you can, and come in at ten tomorrow." Harvey frowned. "I don't like having the chief go out again tonight, and he plans to do it again tomorrow night and Saturday."

"Why does he have to go to the funeral parlor both nights?" Tony asked.

"To support Mrs. Leavitt, and to make his presence felt."

Tony looked at Eddie. "What do you say, Shakespeare?"

Eddie nodded. "Put us on in the evening. Yeaton and Clifford can stay and watch the house, and we'll go with the chief to the funeral home."

"Are you sure?" Harvey asked. "You did a stint last night."

Eddie nodded. "It's for the chief."

Harvey frowned for a moment then nodded. "Go home now and take a nap. I don't want you yawning when you're guarding him. I'll go with Nate and Jimmy to see if we can find Melanie this afternoon."

"We're not supposed to take time off," Eddie said.

"That's an order."

"Okay."

It was only two o'clock, and Eddie doubted he could sleep. He drove to his parents' house, but no one was home. He remembered that his pop was working on a new wing on a bank downtown. He thought he knew which bank. He'd seen the scaffolding on the addition.

Two trucks with the company logo on the doors sat in the bank's parking lot. Eddie left his pickup and sauntered over to the new wing. No workers were outside, but he could hear pounding and the whir of a power tool from within.

He went to the front door of the bank and walked into the lobby. One of the tellers was free, and he walked up to her station and smiled. "Hi. I'm detective Thibodeau. My father's working on the new addition. I wondered if I could see him."

"I recognize you, Detective," the fiftyish woman said coyly.

"Oh, well, thanks. Is it okay if I go see my pop?"

"We don't really have anything to do with that." She grinned at him. "But I think if you walk around to the back of the construction site, you can get inside. And thanks for your good work, Detective."

"You're welcome." Eddie winked at her and walked out. He'd decided it did no good to try to explain things or act embarrassed. Best to leave them happy with the local police, even if he felt like burnt toast.

He moseyed around the new part of the building. The sounds of the workmen grew louder. At the back of the new wing, a section wasn't closed in yet, but had thick sheets of plastic hanging over what would be a doorway. He pushed the plastic aside and went in.

It didn't take him long to spot his father on a ladder, mounting wallboard with a cordless screwdriver. Three other men were working on other parts of the project.

Eddie walked over to the ladder and stood to the side, looking up about eight feet, and waited for the whirring to pause.

"Hey, Pop."

His father looked down.

"What are you doing here?"

"Just saying hi. I'm working a split today, so I had a minute."

His father grunted and set another screw. Eddie waited. Pop put in three more screws, descended a rung, and put in two more. Finally he came down the ladder.

When he reached the floor, he set the screwdriver on one of the ladder steps and put his hands to his lower back and stretched.

"You okay?" Eddie asked.

"Yeah, yeah. Just sick of this sheetrock."

Eddie looked around the large, high-ceilinged room. "Looks like you're almost done."

"Then we gotta tape it."

"Oh, right." Eddie shrugged. "Got time for a coffee?"

"No, the boss wouldn't like it."

"Okay. Well, I'll see you."

"Sure." His father turned away, muttering.

Eddie sighed and found his way out through the plastic sheeting. He went home and lay down but couldn't sleep. He didn't know if Leeanne had classes on Thursday afternoon or not. He sent a text asking for her schedule but didn't get a reply until it was time to meet Tony.

He pulled up at the chief's house right behind Tony. The squad car was already there. Joe Clifford waved to them, and Eddie and Tony walked up to the house. Cheryl Yeaton was talking to Mike and Sharon just inside the door.

"Oh, so it's you two pulling the extra detail," Cheryl said.

"Yep." Tony nodded at Mike. "Evening, Chief."

"Hey, Winfield. Eddie, don't you ever sleep?" Mike asked.

"I caught a few winks this afternoon," Eddie said.

"If you want to stay here, Joe and I can tag team the Brownings to the funeral home," Cheryl said.

Tony gritted his teeth. "Please don't make me sit still for four hours."

Cheryl laughed.

"It won't be that long," Mike said. "The visiting hours are from seven to nine tonight. We should be home by 9:30. Tell you what, Cheryl, you and

409

Clifford sit on the house, and you can leave when we get home."

"Yeah, we'll stay with the chief until the next unit gets here," Eddie said.

Cheryl scrunched up her face. "Up to you, Chief."

Mike scratched his chin. "No offense, but I happen to know this guy is one of our best marksmen." He clapped Eddie on the shoulder. "If someone's coming after me, I'd rather have the sharpshooter with me and Sharon than sitting here defending an empty house."

Cheryl sighed. "Guess I'd better spend some more time at the shooting range."

Mike grinned. "Oh, your record's not bad, either, Cheryl. But Tony, here, that's another story."

"I qualified," Tony protested.

"Yeah." Mike didn't say any more, he just smiled.

Tony looked a little disgruntled, but Eddie had seen Tony's score from the last qualification round, too. He'd passed, but he was in about the thirtieth percentile among the officers who did, while Eddie was near the top.

"Okay, we'll see you later." Cheryl went out.

"We're not quite ready to go," Mike said. "You guys make yourselves at home."

They didn't take him literally, but sat uneasily in the living room. Tony talked about the Red Sox lineup for spring and whether or not he'd have to take the first aid update. Sharon and Mike came down the stairs twenty minutes later.

"Well, hello." Sharon smiled at them. "Eddie, this is getting to be a regular thing."

"Yes, ma'am," Eddie said.

"Good of you to come, too, Tony."

Eddie let Tony take the lead on the first lap. He followed Mike's car close enough that no other vehicles got between them. They had no problems parking at the funeral home. Two officers were directing traffic, and the funeral home had stationed two employees outside to assist with parking.

Eddie went in with Mike and Sharon, keeping back while they offered condolences to Mrs. Leavitt, but always within reach of Mike if he needed anything. Tony stayed outside.

The Brownings sat with Mrs. Leavitt and her children and introduced police officers and P.D. employees who came to pay their respects. After an hour, Eddie went out and sent Tony in. He called to check in with Cheryl. All was quiet at the house. At nine, Tony came out with the Brownings.

The patrolman directing traffic made the oncoming cars wait so that Eddie, then Mike, then Tony could drive out smoothly and stay together. Eddie kept watch for anything out of the ordinary, but the drive seemed pretty tame.

He caught himself yawning and remembered Harvey's words. He should have rested longer, instead of going by to see Pop.

A half mile from the Brownings' house, a dark sedan roared out of a side street. Eddie hit the gas and watched his side mirror. It looked like the car clipped Mike's rear bumper, but Mike stuck with him. In the mirror, he caught a mess of red lights behind them before rounding a curve.

Chapter 27

Tony came on the radio, calling dispatch for help.

"You okay, Winfield?" Eddie asked.

"Yeah, but the driver's getting away. I'll try to get him."

"Stick with the grizzly," Eddie said.

Charlie Doran came on, calm as ever. "What's up, Detectives?"

"Interloper vehicle," Eddie replied.

"He nicked the grizzly and slammed into me," Tony said. "I'm turning around."

"No, stay with your detail," Charlie said. "I'm sending units. What's your 20?"

Eddie gave him the exact location of the crash. "We're continuing to the bear's den." The code was silly, because obviously the people trying to get Mike knew who they were protecting and where he lived.

"Was that collision intentional?" Charlie asked.

Eddie said, "Probably," but at the same time, Tony said, "Definitely."

"You really okay, Tony?" Eddie asked.

"Yeah." He sounded close to losing it, and Eddie was betting he wished he hadn't driven the Mustang that night.

He put on his blinker and pulled to the curb in front of the Brownings' house. Mike's car entered the driveway, and Eddie hopped out and hurried to his window. Mike lowered it six inches.

"What was that?" Mike asked.

"Hawkins's people," Eddie said, drawing his gun. "Put the garage door up, and I'll check it."

Cheryl and Joe hurried over.

"Everything okay?" Cheryl asked.

"Talk to Tony," Eddie said. "And make sure he's not injured."

Tony parked at the end of the driveway, and Eddie glimpsed the two patrol officers examining his crumpled fender. He faced the garage warily, but it was clear. Mike drove in, and Tony came trotting up the driveway.

"Charlie's sent the two patrolmen that were going to relieve Yeaton and Clifford to chase that guy," he reported.

"Okay," Mike said.

Eddie shook his head. "I don't like it."

"You stay with Mr. and Mrs. Browning, and I'll check out the house," Tony said.

Eddie still didn't like it, but he didn't like holding Mike and Sharon in the garage any longer than necessary, either.

"Okay."

Mike told Sharon to stay in the car. He got out and looked at his dented rear bumper. It wasn't too bad. Shaking his head, he put down the overhead door and then gave Tony the house key and the security alarm code. Eddie stood in the open main door while Tony entered the house. Lights came on as he went through the rooms and then upstairs.

"Not the way I hoped to end the evening," Mike said.

"Sorry, Chief."

"It's not your fault, Eddie. And Winfield's car is going to cost the department some cred with the insurance company."

After about five minutes, Tony came out.

"All clear."

Mike went to Sharon's side of the car and helped her out.

"Thanks, boys," she said. "Would you like to come in for coffee?"

"No thanks, we're good," Eddie said. "Let me just escort you in."

He followed Mike and Sharon into their kitchen. Mike reset the alarm then went right to the wall phone and called the com center.

"This is Chief Browning. What's going on?"

Sharon and Eddie waited while he listened.

"Got it. Keep me posted." He hung up. "Sounds like they lost the suspect. They should have let Winfield go after him."

"Your safety's more important, Chief."

Mike sighed. "Well, we're in for the night now. Send Yeaton and Clifford home. One of you guys wait outside until the relief unit gets back here, okay?"

"I think we should all stay," Eddie said.

"Nah, they won't come back here now. They'll disappear for another week or two."

Eddie didn't like it. Mike was probably right, but if anything did happen, he'd never forgive himself. "I really think we should stay. No disrespect."

Mike frowned. "At least send Yeaton and Clifford home."

"I think my husband is right," Sharon said. "We don't need four of you here now. What we need is someone finding the man who's responsible for all this."

Eddie blew out a big breath. "Okay. Good night, Mrs. Browning."

"Good night, Eddie, and thanks again."

"You're welcome." He went outside. Tony was down at the curb, looking at his fender and swearing. Cheryl and Joe waited in the drive-way.

"The chief says for you two to split. Winfield and I will stay until the relief unit gets here."

"You sure?" Cheryl asked.

"No, but the chief is."

"Okay," Joe said. "Take it easy, Eddie."

They headed for their squad car, and Eddie ambled over to Tony.

"We're staying until the relief arrives. You see anything out here?"

"Uh, no." Tony looked a bit guilty, and Eddie

figured he'd been focused on the car, not the house.

"Let me walk around back," Eddie said.

"Yeah, okay."

"Keep your eyes open."

"I will." Tony leaned on the Mustang's hood and folded his arms, staring at Mike's house.

The relief would be there any minute, and they had put Hawkins, or whoever was in the sedan, on the run, but Eddie felt uneasy as he walked back up the driveway. He let himself through the gate into the back yard. The snow was all messed up, and he couldn't tell if anyone had been there that day or not, even with his flashlight. He walked along the back of the house to where the fence ran out toward the street. He completed the circuit at the sidewalk and strolled back to Tony's car.

"I didn't see anything. We should keep making the rounds, though."

"Okay," Tony said.

Eddie shone his flashlight on the smashed fender. "Call the insurance agent first thing."

"Don't worry, I will."

Eddie walked over to his truck. His ears were getting cold. He was tempted to sit in the cab, but Mike and Sharon were both in the house. He and Tony had better both stay outside, where they could see and hear things clearly.

He thought about calling Leeanne. It would be

too late by the time he got home, and he could make Tony watch while he did it. He stuffed the thought in his mental reject bin immediately. This detail was too important. He rummaged for his gloves and knit hat and put them on. That was a little better, but the wind off the bay had picked up.

The kitchen went dark, and a light came on upstairs. Eddie sent Tony to circle the house again. He came back a couple of minutes later.

"Everything's quiet."

"Okay." Eddie paced in the driveway, then walked around the garage and peered for a minute along the length of the house's back wall. The relief should be here. With the breeze blowing and tree limbs cracking, it was hard to hear softer sounds. He walked to the front.

After five minutes, he reached to his shoulder mic to check with Charlie on the relief's ETA. As he pushed the call button, a soft light came on behind the living room drapes, probably a table lamp. Eddie squinted at it.

A muffled scream came from inside the house. He stood stock still.

"Yeah, Detective?" Charlie said over the radio.

"Trouble. In the chief's house." Eddie pulled his pistol and shouted, "Tony!"

Winfield had been slumped against the side of his car, but he straightened. Eddie ran for the kitchen door.

It was locked, of course. He stepped back and executed his best door kick ever. It jarred his leg all the way to his spine. The alarm base unit beeped obnoxiously.

"Chief?" he yelled.

Another scream drew him into the kitchen, leading with his gun.

"Charlie, get me backup, *now!*"

"It's on the way."

Eddie cautiously crossed the dim kitchen toward the lamp-lit living room.

Mike stood halfway down the stairs, wearing his suit pants and T-shirt, hunched like he was ready to spring.

Beyond him, near the patio door, a man held Sharon with a gun at her temple.

Mike had his service pistol in his hand. He watched the intruder like a hungry cat eyeing a mouse with one foot caught in a trap.

Eddie stepped forward. "Let her go."

It was Hawkins with a week's growth of graying beard. Sharon tried to pull away from him, but he squeezed her hard around her waist, pinning one of her arms. Mike came down a step.

"Chief, I got this," Eddie said. "Hawkins, let her go."

Hatred gleamed in the cold, gray eyes. Hawkins had come for one reason, and Eddie couldn't stop him.

"Mike, get back," he yelled.

He wasn't sure he could get Hawkins without hitting Sharon, but he had to try. Hawkins's hand barely stirred, but the gun's muzzle moved away from Sharon and trained on Mike's chest.

Mike dropped down on the stairs, and Sharon rammed backward with her elbows, into Hawkins's kidneys.

A shot let loose, and Eddie fired at almost the same instant. Hawkins went down. Sharon sprang away from the gunman and sprawled on her hands and knees. She scrambled up and hurried toward the staircase.

"Michael!" Her voice was raw with panic.

Eddie couldn't pay attention to them. He stepped closer to Hawkins. In his fall, he'd hung on to the pistol. He lay on his side, breathing raggedly. A puddle of blood formed near his shoulder on Sharon's spotless ivory carpet.

"Drop the gun," Eddie said, pointing his .45 at him.

Tony charged into the kitchen behind him and yelled, "Police."

Eddie held up his left hand. Tony halted behind him.

"Drop it," Eddie said.

Hawkins's arm shook. With a big sigh, he let his hand thump to the rug, gun and all. Eddie walked over cautiously and nudged the gun away from Hawkins's hand. He picked it up and turned around.

"Chief?"

Mike sat up awkwardly on the stairs. "I'm good, Eddie." Sharon flung herself at him.

Eddie handed Hawkins's gun to Tony. "Hey, hotshot. I told you to stay alert."

Tony gave him a cockeyed smile. "When do I listen to you, Shakespeare?"

Eddie watched the EMTs put Al Hawkins in the ambulance. His bullet had gone through the gunman's collarbone and come out above his shoulder blade. Eddie didn't know how bad it was, but he'd heard one of the EMTs call in and tell the hospital to have the O.R. ready.

Harvey had come, and he talked to Mike for a long time in the house, while Mike held Sharon in his arms, and then Mike came out and stood beside Eddie on the steps. The air had warmed, and the icicles on his porch roof were dripping.

"Good work, Eddie."

"Thanks, Chief." Eddie looked over at him. "Does this mean I'll be suspended again?"

Mike almost smiled. "Kid, I was in the same room when it happened. Barring any wild flap in the press, I think I can move this one along pretty quickly."

"You think the press will make a fuss?"

Mike shrugged. "Hero cop shoots lowlife drug dealer? I doubt it."

Eddie thought about that for a sec. If he knew Ryan, and he thought he did, he'd love that headline.

"So, what happened?" he asked. "We cleared the house."

"I think he came in that back door, after you'd checked it." Mike shook his head. "I'd just started getting undressed, and Sharon remembered she'd left her purse downstairs, and her glasses were in it. She went down to get it, and next thing I knew the alarm went off, and she screamed."

"I heard her," Eddie said sadly. He and Tony should have kept a better watch.

"He coulda got me," Mike said, "but he grabbed Sharon, and she kept him busy until I got partway down there. I couldn't get a good shot, and he didn't want to let go of her long enough to be sure he'd got me. I guess when you came in, he didn't have much choice."

"Yeah." Eddie studied Mike's face. "I really thought you were done."

"Thanks for doing your target practice, kid."

The ambulance pulled out of the yard.

"How's Sharon?" Eddie asked.

Mike shrugged and let out a slow breath. "She'll be okay. She wanted a shower, but I told her to get dressed and we'll go to a hotel."

"I'll bet she wants you to retire ASAP."

"She knows I can't."

"Right. I'm sorry, Chief. You should be retired, playing with the grandkids and going off to fish anytime you feel like it."

After a long moment, Mike said, "I used to think that, too." He turned his head and looked at Eddie. "I don't know why, but God didn't let me retire."

"Yeah." They stood there a little while. "He didn't let Al Hawkins get you, either."

Mike smiled at him as Harvey came out the door. "Must have been all the people praying for me."

The next morning, Eddie couldn't sleep late. Leeanne had emailed her schedule, and he sent a note back explaining why he'd been unable to call her the evening before. The temperature was still above freezing, and he went to the park to meet Harvey and Jeff for their run.

"You're not supposed to be here," Harvey said. "I told you to sleep in."

Eddie shrugged. "I laid awake most of the night thinking what if I'd missed, and what if Hawkins hadn't?"

"You can't keep brooding on it."

"I know. But it stays with you."

"Yeah."

Jeff gave Eddie a sympathetic half smile. "Harvey told me what happened. You going to be okay?"

"Yeah, after a while. Mike took a dive at just the right time, or . . ."

"He's pretty good at elusive diving," Harvey said.

Eddie stared at him blankly for a moment, then laughed. "Right. Let's run."

They headed out on a circuit of the park. The physical activity and routine soothed Eddie. He watched Harvey when they got into their third mile, to see if his breathing was labored, but he seemed fine.

"You all right?" he asked as they slowed to a walk.

"I'm fine," Harvey said. "I wish Jennifer thought so."

"What's up?"

"She made me an appointment with Carl this afternoon. I'll have to leave work early."

"Okay," Eddie said. "Just tell me what to do when you go."

"If my prayers are answered, I'll be telling you to go to Al Hawkins's arraignment."

Harvey took them back to his place for breakfast. Abby wasn't up yet, but Beth was there, helping Jennifer with the French toast and bacon. Eddie asked Jennifer how Abby was doing.

"Pretty solemn," Jennifer said. "She cried some. She really likes Greg, maybe even loves him a little."

"She said she seriously thought about marrying him."

"Yes, she did," said Jennifer. "I'm not saying she's rational right now, Eddie. But she does feel guilty. Like she should have known sooner this wouldn't work." She handed him five plates, and Eddie put them on the table.

"Can't believe he's giving up," Jeff said. "He seemed to be crazy about her."

"He was." Harvey poured himself a mug of coffee. "Maybe that's why he gave her the ultimatum. He was scared she was going to break up with him, and he couldn't take it again."

"Again?" Jeff asked.

"He has a broken engagement in his past. Pray for both of them."

They all helped get breakfast on the table, and Harvey asked the blessing.

"Beth, how's school?" he asked.

"Good. I've got a really sweet bunch of kids this year."

Jennifer smiled at her. "You love teaching, don't you?"

"Yes, but . . ."

"But she's not going to do it forever," Jeff said.

Beth nodded. "This is my last year."

Jennifer eyed her for a moment. "Won't you be bored?"

"I'll make sure she doesn't have time to be bored," said Jeff.

"Are you going to live with your crazy schedule at the fire department forever?" Eddie asked him. "How can you do that?"

Beth poured maple syrup over her French toast. "Not forever. He's going to do what Harvey did and work his way up to management. Someday he'll be the fire chief, and then he'll have decent hours."

"Dream on," Jeff said. He sat contentedly with his arm around Beth's shoulders. They were the first to leave, and when they'd gone, Eddie asked Harvey about Abby again.

"Last night she seemed to be coping," Harvey replied. "Jennifer thinks Abby will grow up because of this. I don't know. I hope so."

Jennifer carried their coffee mugs to the dishwasher. "We love them both, Eddie. Of course, we'll support Abby, but there was wrong on both sides."

Eddie frowned. "There's got to be a better way to find a mate. This dating thing is too painful."

Harvey nodded. "You're right. You don't see dating in the Bible."

"What did they do then?" Eddie asked.

Jennifer smiled at him across the kitchen. "Arranged marriages."

"I guess the guy just picked out the girl, then his parents went to visit her parents and took them a string of camels," Harvey said.

"Not quite like that." Jennifer made a face at

him. "But I know the girl wasn't given her choice of a whole lineup of men."

Eddie looked at Harvey. "Maybe you two could arrange a marriage for Abby."

"No way. After this fiasco? I don't want to have anything to do with it."

"There's Peter," Eddie said.

Jennifer wiped out the sink with a sponge. "Peter will probably be discouraged when he hears about this."

"I don't think so," Harvey said. "I think Peter is in this for the long haul."

Eddie stood up. "Well, if you see him coming up the driveway with a string of camels . . ."

Chapter 28

The arraignment was postponed until Hawkins left the hospital, which might not be for a week or two. His condition was rated serious after the surgery. In the meantime, the unit had plenty to work on.

Mike came into the office around nine Friday morning, and the detectives crowded around him.

"You okay, Chief?" Nate asked.

"I'm fine, boys, thanks to Eddie."

"How's Mrs. Browning?" Eddie asked.

"She's okay, too. She was a little shook up last night, but Sharon is one tough cookie. We'll be going to the funeral home again tonight and sit with Mrs. Leavitt for a while."

"Do you still need an escort?" Jimmy asked.

"I don't believe we do, but I'll be wearing my sidearm, just in case."

Tony grinned at him. "Don't leave home without it."

"Sorry to disappoint you," Harvey said, "but I think we'd better keep eyes on you until Hawkins is out of the hospital and in jail."

"We'll talk about it. I just came down to thank all of you," Mike said. "Thanks for running point on this one, Captain."

Harvey nodded. "I'm glad it turned out okay."

Mike looked at Eddie. "Thibodeau, I'll see you next Wednesday at three in the conference room."

His hearing. "Thank you, sir. Should I stay home until then?"

"Hawkins's wound isn't critical. I don't see any need for you to stay out of the office, and Deputy Chief Stewart agrees with me. Unless you'd like a couple of days off?"

"I'd just as soon keep working," Eddie said.

Mike slapped him lightly on the shoulder. "Good. Let's just not have you out on field work until the hearing, huh?"

"You got it."

"Thanks, Chief," Harvey said.

After Mike had left, they all got to work. Eddie made several calls, checking in on some of their witnesses and uncovering more information about Hawkins's drug operation. Harvey ate lunch with the Priority detectives at the diner so they could compare notes.

After lunch, Jimmy and Nate went out and rounded up three of Hawkins's runners. Harvey took Tony with him to the hospital to see if they could talk to Hawkins. They came back happy about the interview.

"Tony, you transcribe the tape, please." Harvey checked his watch. "I've got to get over to Carl's. Jennifer's meeting me there, so I can't be late. Eddie, you're in charge."

He left, and Eddie went back to work. He and Tony were down to documenting the evidence from Mike's house and paperwork on the Quinlan case. Jimmy and Nate spent an hour down in booking and then questioned the prisoners they'd brought in.

A little after four, the day patrol sergeant called.

"Thibodeau, you've got a visitor."

"He got a name?"

"A Miss Wainthrop," said Brad.

"All right! I'll see her anytime."

"You coming down, or should I escort her up there? It's no trouble."

"Calm down, Brad. I'll be right there."

Eddie ran down the stairs and into the lobby. Leeanne stood near the window at Brad's desk, where she had asked for him, and Brad was out from behind it, standing with her, trying to charm her up close. She turned as Eddie came through the doorway and smiled broadly.

"Leeanne!" Eddie kissed her on the cheek. "Thanks, Brad."

"The men in the Priority Unit seem to have a knack for finding beautiful women," he said.

Leeanne rolled her eyes at Eddie, and he took her to the elevator and keyed in the code.

"What's with that guy?" she whispered.

"Don't mind Brad."

They got in the elevator. Eddie knew there was a security camera rolling, and that Brad was probably watching the monitor, so he didn't try to get too friendly.

"I hope you don't mind me coming here," Leeanne said.

"No, I'm glad."

"I got away earlier than I expected, but when I went to Jennifer's no one was home."

"Oh, she went to the doctor's office to meet Harvey. Sorry about that. They should have given you a key."

"Harvey meant to, but I think he forgot. I hoped Abby would be there, but she wasn't."

"If you want, you can just stay here for about"—He checked his watch—"fifty minutes, and I'll go over there with you."

They stepped out into the office, and Eddie said, "Paula, Tony, this is Leeanne. You remember Nate?" Jimmy was out of the office.

Leeanne smiled. "Yeah. Hi, everybody."

"Want some coffee, or a soda?"

"I don't need anything." Leeanne unbuttoned her coat.

"It's no bother. I haven't had a break this afternoon. Come on." Eddie guided her to the breakroom and prompted her to choose something to drink. He got her a Pepsi from the machine and poured himself a cup of coffee, which he set carefully on the table.

"*Viens, ma belle.*" He held out his arms.

She looked a little flustered. "Jennifer told me

she never let Harvey kiss her at the police station because there were cameras everywhere."

Eddie smiled. "That is an exaggeration. I know where the cameras are, and there aren't any in here."

"Hey, Eddie," said Jimmy from the doorway. "Any coffee left? Oh, hello." He smiled at Leeanne and moved to the coffeemaker.

"Hi," she said. "You're the only one I haven't met, so you must be the one who got shot last spring when Harvey did."

Eddie made the introduction, and they all took their drinks out into the office.

"So, you're okay now, Detective Cook?" Leeanne asked.

He grinned. "My leg still bothers me a little sometimes, but I was back to ninety-five percent on my last physical. And you can call me Jimmy."

"Thanks. And I'm glad for you."

Eddie sipped his coffee and asked Leeanne about her folks and school.

After a while she said, "You're supposed to be working. Just do what you need to do. I'll keep quiet."

Paula transferred a call to Eddie from the patrol sergeant. When he hung up and turned back toward Leeanne, Tony was leaning against the end of his desk, smiling down at her.

"So, you're Mrs. Larson's sister?"

"That's right."

"We've met once or twice, I guess," Tony said.

"Yes, I think so. I'm here to visit Jennifer and Harvey, but Jennifer's out this afternoon, so I came here to wait." Leeanne was looking her most incredible. Her dark, glossy hair fell over her shoulders, and her blue eyes were big and bright. She wore lip gloss, and her lips looked luscious. Her blue shirt looked soft and touchable. Tony was taking it all in.

"My name's Tony Winfield."

"I remember."

"Do you? That's encouraging." He smiled again. His light hair stuck up a little in the back, in a cowlick, but he was cute. Like a kid.

"So, Tony, have you filed your reports yet?" Eddie asked.

"Well, not yet."

Eddie reached up to the shelf over his desk and straightened the frame with the picture of Leeanne.

"But I guess I'd better go do it," Tony said.

"Good idea," Eddie told him. "I'd like to be out of here at five to take Miss Wainthrop to her sister's."

The next half hour was torture, to have Leeanne within arm's reach and not be able to do anything about it. Part of being an adult. Eddie made a meticulous report for Harvey. He asked Leeanne to look it over instead of Tony, and she only found one mistake.

On the dot of five o'clock, he and Leeanne got on the elevator. She had parked on the street. Eddie kissed her on the cheek and put her in the car, then went to get his truck. She pulled out ahead of him, and he followed her to Harvey's house.

Jennifer and Harvey were just getting home. The garage door was still up when they drove in. Jennifer got out of her car and ran to embrace Leeanne. Harvey followed a little slower and kissed his sister-in-law.

Eddie grabbed Leeanne's suitcase, and they went in. Jennifer said, "Eddie, you'll stay for supper, of course."

"If you don't mind."

"I was planning on it." She took a covered dish out of the refrigerator and put it in the oven.

"Where's Abby?" Leeanne asked, taking off her gloves and scarf.

"Peter came around two o'clock and carried her off," said Jennifer.

"Where to?" Eddie asked.

"No clue."

"Does he have employees to run his business while he's gone?" Leeanne asked.

"Several," Harvey said as he fiddled with the thermostat.

Eddie cleared his throat. "So, Harv, how did the checkup go?"

"Fine. I'm fine."

Jennifer looked at Harvey, then at Eddie, but said nothing. Leeanne offered to help her set the table, and Eddie followed him into the sunroom.

"Harv, are you really okay?"

"Yes, really. Carl thinks my blood pressure could be better, but I told him I was tense because everybody seems to think there's something wrong with me." He sounded a little testy.

"I'm sorry. I just wanted to make sure."

Harvey pulled off his necktie. "Oh, they're making me take a blood sugar test. It's stupid. I'm fine."

"He thinks you're diabetic or something?"

"The opposite. Low blood sugar. Hypoglycemia."

"So, when do you take this test?"

"Tomorrow morning."

"I'm sorry, Harv, but if there *is* something like that, it's better if you know it."

"Why? So I can have you and Jennifer fretting about it all the time?" He shook his head. "I'm healthy. I'm not as young as I used to be, but I'm in pretty good shape. Aren't I?" He suddenly looked doubtful.

"Yes, you are. No question. If you don't eat, you get a little shaky sometimes, but anybody would, I guess."

Harvey sighed and turned toward his bedroom, trailing the necktie on the floor. "I'll be right out."

Eddie went back to the kitchen, and Jennifer looked at him anxiously.

"Did he tell you?"

"He's taking a blood sugar test tomorrow," Eddie said.

"Yes."

"That doesn't sound too serious."

"Well, it could be."

Eddie frowned. "I think we both need to quit showing him how much we worry about him."

"You're probably right. He was a terrible patient when he got shot. If we treat him like he's sick, he'll be awful to live with." She turned to Leeanne. "So, Baby Sister, you're going to do an internship this summer?"

Leeanne smiled. "I hope so. Harvey probably hasn't had time to talk to Mr. Russell, has he?"

"I think he called him. You'll have to ask him when he comes out."

Jennifer served Jell-O salad and broccoli and a chicken casserole. It was good, and Eddie was with three of his favorite people. He couldn't ask for more. He and Leeanne loaded the dishwasher afterward, while Jennifer put away the food.

They landed in the living room a few minutes later, and Harvey had a blaze crackling in the fireplace. Jennifer sat down beside him on the hearth and began kneading his shoulder muscles. He tossed a last stick onto the fire and sat watching it while she rubbed his back. Eddie sat down on the couch beside Leeanne and reached for her hand.

"I've got to go to the funeral home tonight," Harvey said.

Jennifer kissed the back of his neck. "Stay home."

"I really ought to go."

She kept on rubbing his back, and after a few minutes he slid off the hearth and lay on his stomach on the rug, his head on his arms. Leeanne got up and took a pillow over and put it near his head. Harvey reached out and stuffed it under his head, murmuring, "Thanks."

Eddie felt like they were intruding. He looked at Leeanne, and she raised her eyebrows at him. He shrugged. Harvey drove himself during an active case, forgetting his physical needs, and by the time it was over, he was exhausted.

After a few minutes, Harvey rolled over and said sleepily, "Come here, gorgeous," reaching for Jennifer.

Eddie jumped to his feet. "Leeanne and I were thinking of . . . riding down to the store for . . ."

"Ice cream," said Leeanne.

"Right, ice cream."

Jennifer smiled. "You don't have to. I'll keep him in line."

Harvey sat up and focused on Eddie. "Sorry. I'm a little tired."

"You never slow down all day, Harv," Eddie said.

He sighed. "Seems like I sit at a desk all day. I shouldn't be tired."

"You don't. Well, you do some, but you drive around, and you walk, and you talk to people, and when nothing's happening, you pace. You never sit still long, and when you do, you're pouring energy into something."

"Then I go home and collapse."

Jennifer frowned at him. "You just had a good supper. Give it some time to digest, and you'll feel better." A car drove in, and she got up and went to the window. "It's Abby and Peter."

"No boys tonight?" Eddie asked.

"I don't see them. He must have gotten a sitter."

They came in through the kitchen, and Jennifer went out to meet them. Everyone sounded happy. They all came into the living room, and Harvey stood and shook Peter's hand.

"Peter! Good to see you."

"Thanks. You got that woman who bought the Blazer?"

"Actually, we let her go, but we got the man we really wanted."

"Did she buy that vehicle with drug money?" Peter asked. Harvey had sent the bills to be checked, to see if any of them were traceable.

"I don't think so, but we're not positive yet," Harvey said. "She does have money of her own.

We're still checking on it. I think you'll either keep the Blazer or get the money back."

"I'd rather have the money."

Leeanne and Abby were hugging, and Abby was getting the scoop on the Wainthrop family.

"I really ought to go to the funeral home for a few minutes," Harvey said.

Jennifer frowned. "Let's not."

"You don't have to, gorgeous, but I do. He was the chief."

"If you're going, I'm going," she said. "Just let me get changed. I'll be right back."

Peter excused himself and said to Abby, "We'll see you in the morning." He left, and Harvey went to his bedroom.

"So, you're going out with Peter tomorrow?" Leeanne asked.

"Peter and Andy and Gary." Abby grimaced. "I guess Jennifer told you about Greg?"

"Some of it, at least."

"Well, I don't know why, but Peter still wants to see me. And you know what? I want to see him."

"Where did you go today?" Eddie asked.

"To his mother's. He left the boys there tonight, but we're picking them up in the morning and going to the skating rink. I'm going up to change." She climbed the stairs.

Eddie was alone with Leeanne. Finally.

He went over to her and drew her in against

439

his chest. Her shirt felt as fuzzy and soft as he'd thought it would.

"I'm so happy to be here," she said. She stayed contentedly in his arms until a door opened, then she sat down on the couch. Eddie sat beside her and draped his arm along the back of the sofa.

Harvey came in, wearing his suit again, or maybe it was a different one. He dressed a lot better since he made captain.

"We'll just be gone a few minutes. Well, maybe an hour." He was wide awake now, and in the efficient mode. Eddie didn't know how he did it. He'd seemed totally out of it, but now he was refreshed and ready to face anything, including viewing the corpse of his former boss. Eddie, on the other hand, could tell his own lack of sleep was catching up with him.

Jennifer came into the room looking sweet and maternal in a dark red dress with black trim. Her hair hung loose over her shoulders and down past her hips in the back. She didn't wear it that way often in public, and Eddie thought she might be trying to make Harvey feel less depressed.

Harvey's smile broke out and he opened his arms to her. Jennifer went to him, and he gave her a squeeze, then looked at Eddie and Leeanne. "All right, gang, we'll be back in an hour."

" 'Bye," Leeanne called.

Abby came down the stairs as the front door closed. "Any ice cream left?"

"I'm not sure," Leeanne said.

Abby went into the kitchen, and Eddie looked at Leeanne.

"*Ma chérie*, one kiss?"

Abby chose that moment to come to the doorway and ask if they wanted some mint chocolate chip, and they decided to join her. They sat decorously at the kitchen table, eating it.

"What are you guys doing this weekend?" Abby asked.

"I have a command performance at the old chief's funeral tomorrow." Eddie turned without much hope to Leeanne. "I don't suppose you'd want to go with me?"

"Man, you're as weird as Harvey," Abby hooted. "He used to say he'd go anywhere on a date with Jennifer, but a funeral for some man you hardly knew and Leeanne never saw? That is totally gross."

"Well, I have to be there, and I don't want to miss out on a couple of hours I could spend with your sister." He looked at Leeanne. "If you think it's too morbid, that's okay, but we could hold hands under the hymnbook or something."

She laughed. "I'll go."

"Great. Did you and Peter talk things out?" he asked Abby.

"Yes, we did. I told him that if I want to start dating someone else I'll tell him, and that's it for us. I'm not going to date two men at once again."

"But you're still leaving it open," Leeanne said.

"Well, I'm really not sure Peter's the husband God has planned for me," Abby said soberly. "I don't want to give him false hope."

Eddie considered how he'd feel if he were on the receiving end of that declaration. "I guess that's fair to Peter."

Abby smiled ruefully. "I told him he should just forget about me. I'm too fickle."

"What did he say?" asked Leeanne.

"He said . . . he'll never forget about me."

Eddie smiled. "Didn't know he was such a romantic."

"Yeah, he has a really romantic streak."

"So, tell me again," Eddie ventured. "The reason you don't want to marry this man is, what?"

Abby sighed and leaned back in her chair frowning a little. The doorbell rang, and she sprang up and went to the entry.

Eddie pulled Leeanne over against his shoulder. He was getting his TLC in small doses.

Abby came slowly back to the table carrying a large bouquet of flowers.

"Wow, beautiful," cried Leeanne.

"Yes." Abby set down the container. It held gorgeous gold and brown and orange flowers, and little cattails and ferns.

"What are those?" Eddie asked.

"Chrysanthemums." Abby pulled a card from

the arrangement, opened the envelope, and smiled. "From Peter."

"Now, that's classy," Eddie said.

"I feel like baking." Abby went to the cupboard and took out a mixing bowl.

"Bet she's making pie," Eddie whispered. "Peter and the boys need nurturing."

"What do you need?" Leeanne asked.

He smiled. "Just you. Just knowing you love me."

"I do, Eddie." She finally let him kiss her, and it was worth the wait.

Chapter 29

When Eddie got to the Larsons' house late the next morning, dressed in jeans and carrying his funeral duds, the three sisters were eating blueberry muffins and drinking tea. Jennifer started to get up and get him some, but Leeanne told her to sit down, and she waited on him instead.

"Did Harvey go to the hospital?" Eddie asked.

"Yes. He wouldn't let me go." Jennifer didn't look happy about that, but it made perfect sense to Eddie. She held Harvey as her hero, and he didn't want her to see him in a moment of weakness.

"Jennifer, when he comes back you have to be smiling for him."

"Thanks, Eddie. I will be. He won't find out anything today, anyway, so nobody ask him what the results were, okay?"

They all nodded.

"Good. Carl will tell him Monday."

Harvey pulled in about a quarter to eleven. Jennifer met him in the entry and kissed him. "You must be hungry, honey."

He shrugged. "I could eat."

"Come on. They didn't let you eat anything before the test."

He took off his jacket and sat at the table. Jennifer got the muffins and poured him a glass of milk.

"Butter?" she asked.

"Sure. Whatever."

She smiled a little sadly and brought the butter and a knife.

When Harvey was into his second muffin, Eddie noticed a definite change. He was perkier and looked at Jennifer with more animation.

"So, gorgeous, whatcha wearing to the funeral?" he asked.

"Oh, I don't know. Maybe your Bar Harbor shirt and sweatpants?"

Harvey laughed. "Okay. You'll still be the prettiest woman there."

She smiled. "How about the plaid dress?"

"The new one?" he asked.

"Yes, the new as in I-can't-fit-into-any-of-my-old-clothes dress."

"No, the new it's-a-baby-and-we're-ecstatic dress."

Eddie looked at Leeanne. He could tell she felt the same relief he did. Harvey was acting like his normal self. Jennifer stood behind his chair and put her arms around his neck.

The doorbell rang, and Abby ran to let Peter in. He came into the kitchen with her and said hi to everyone.

"I love the flowers," Abby said, showing him

the bouquet, and he nodded with approval.

"This is for today." He pulled a pair of red pom-poms from his pocket. "For your skates."

"They match your jacket," Jennifer said.

Abby got her ice skates from the closet in the entry. She sat at the table and tied one pom-pom to a shoelace. Jennifer did the other one. Abby held them up, eyeing the pair critically.

"All set," she declared. "Thanks."

"Do you skate much, Peter?" Leeanne asked.

"Not a lot. I can usually stay upright."

Eddie had the feeling he was being modest.

"Want to come back here for lunch?" Jennifer asked.

"Thanks, but I promised the boys pizza," Peter said. "I'm not sure when I'll bring Abigail back."

"That's okay," said Harvey. "If she's not home by midnight, I'll send out a detective or two."

Abby put on her red jacket. " 'Bye! Have fun at the funeral." She grinned and went out the door with Peter.

"What do you think?" asked Harvey.

"I think maybe," Jennifer said. "We'll have to wait and see."

The four of them ate lunch together, then Harvey, Jennifer, and Leeanne went to dress for the funeral. Eddie took his stuff into the hall bathroom.

He wasn't sure what to expect from the women. He knew it wasn't cool to wear all black

446

anymore. He and Harvey had it easy—they put on their dress uniforms, which they rarely wore anymore unless a police officer died. For the ex-chief, everyone would turn out looking spiffy and official. Even Mike would be in uniform.

Leeanne came downstairs wearing a dark green skirt and a matching sweater with an ivory blouse.

"You look good," Eddie said.

"You look absolutely gorgeous." She eyed him from head to toe. "I had no idea."

Eddie smiled. "Wait until you see the captain."

She shook her head. "All those women are going to be staring at you, aren't they?"

"All what women?"

"The ones at the funeral."

"I hope not." The fact that she thought of it made Eddie uncomfortable. There were times when he'd wanted every woman to look at him, but not anymore. He wished he could skip the funeral, or maybe wear a mask or something. He also wished—not for the first time—that he'd refused to do the TV interview.

Since parking would be at a premium, they decided to go in one vehicle—Harvey's. The funeral was being held in the biggest church in the city, and they had some serious parking area, but experience from other VIP funerals had taught the men a few things. They went half an hour early, but already dozens of people were

447

walking into the church. Uniformed cops were everywhere, directing traffic, standing honor guard at the entrance, and heading inside.

"I wonder if Mike's here yet," Eddie said as they walked toward the steps.

"Doubt it," Harvey replied. "He'll probably come in at the last minute. At least, I hope so."

They've still got a guard on him?" Jennifer asked.

"Yes, until Hawkins is out of the hospital and actually behind bars. And the governor's Executive Protection Unit will be with him, too." Harvey shook his head. "I'm glad I'm not in charge of security today."

As they went up the steps, Harvey's phone rang. He and Jennifer stopped walking, so Leeanne and Eddie did, too. People behind them dodged around them and kept going. They all squeezed off to the side on the steps and waited while Harvey checked the screen and put the phone to his ear. "Yeah, Charlie?"

Charlie Doran calling him on a Saturday couldn't be good.

Harvey said a word Eddie hadn't heard him say in almost a year. Jennifer's eyes widened. He said, "Okay. Right. Eddie's with me. Thanks." He looked at Eddie. "Al Hawkins got past the guard and left the hospital on his own."

Eddie clenched his fists. "What do we do?"

"You're off duty," Leeanne said.

"All the on-duty units are out on details or here, and he can't call anyone else in unless it's an emergency." Harvey pushed two buttons on his phone, speed dialing.

"Hey, Mike, what's your 20? Okay, did you leave anyone at Bingley? Copy that. Hawkins is loose. Yeah. Got it."

He clicked off. Eddie had seen that look before.

"What?" he asked.

"The chief's ten minutes out. He's got four officers with him, and there are a hundred more here to keep him safe. Charlie's informing all the sergeants and lieutenants."

"So, we go in?" Eddie asked.

Harvey shook his head. "Hawkins would be stupid to go after him here. But there's no one left at Mike's house."

"Let's go," Eddie said.

"Do you want us to stay here?" Jennifer asked.

"No. If Eddie and I aren't there, no one will notice, but if you show up without me, it will be pointedly obvious I'm not there. Come on, we'll drop you and Leeanne at our house."

"We can take a cab, Harvey." Jennifer walked briskly beside him, back across the acres of parking lot.

"I'll feel better if I see you home." He opened the door of the Explorer for her. Leeanne and Eddie got in the back.

As he started the engine, Harvey looked at

Eddie in the rearview mirror. "Déjà vu, Eddie?"

"Yeah. Just like your wedding."

"Exactly."

"I don't get it," Leeanne said.

"All the cops were in the church," Eddie said. "Just like today—they'll be at the funeral. The perfect time for Hawkins to make his move."

"Eddie—"

He put his arm around her and pulled her close. He kissed her temple and whispered, "We'll take care of each other. We always do. But we need to get this guy. Please don't worry."

"I'll try."

"Good. You stay with Jennifer and pray for us, but don't cry, and don't brood."

"Okay."

He kissed her then, the kiss he'd been wanting to give her, long and meaningful. If Harvey looked in the mirror, he didn't say anything. Ten minutes later, they pulled in at his house. Eddie squeezed Leeanne and then pulled away.

"Go on in," he told her. "I need to get some gear out of my truck."

Harvey hurried inside, and Eddie figured he was going for his Kevlar vest. Jennifer lingered for a moment.

Eddie said, "We'll be okay, Jennifer."

She smiled tremulously. "I believe that. Just watch his back, Eddie. The baby—I don't think I could stand it now."

"I know." He walked over and squeezed her arm lightly. "I'll bring him home safe. I promise."

"You really think Hawkins will go after Mike again?" she asked.

"Yeah. He's determined to finish the job." Eddie frowned. If he'd finished the job himself Thursday night, they wouldn't be doing this. He'd taken the best shot he could without possibly hitting Sharon. He almost wished Hawkins had raised the gun again after he fell, giving Eddie a perfect excuse to nail him.

Leeanne still stood there. "Get inside before we go, and lock the door," Eddie told her. "*Je t'aime*."

She pulled him down for one more quick kiss, then hurried inside with Jennifer.

Eddie had kept his vest in the truck since the first time he'd joined Mike's protective detail. He grabbed it and a couple of extra clips, peeled off his uniform jacket and pulled on the vest. Harvey came out, and Eddie met him by the Explorer.

"Want me to drive?"

"Sure." He gave Eddie the keys. When they pulled out of the driveway, Harvey was already on the phone.

"Charlie, track us. Detective Thibodeau and I will be in my vehicle to the location. No, not until I ask for it."

"No backup?" Eddie said.

"I can be wrong."

"You're never wrong, Harvey. Not about stuff like this."

Harvey grimaced, but he made another call. A minute later, he told Eddie, "Sergeant Miles is pulling Benoit and her partner. They'll come out to Bingley in an unmarked car, ETA thirty minutes. They'll park down the street."

"Girls?" Eddie said. "We get two girls?"

"Can't be helped," Harvey said. "Everyone's going to the chief's funeral. And they're women, not girls."

"But Sarah's new partner is as green as your St. Patrick's Day tie."

"I told Miles to make sure they wear body armor. You heard me."

"Yeah, yeah." Eddie turned in on Bingley Lane. "Where do you want me to park?"

"Around the corner."

Eddie frowned at him. "We won't be able to see the house."

"We're going in. Mike gave me a key and his new security code Thursday night after the shooting incident."

"Why didn't I know this?"

"You didn't need to."

They strolled down the street and into the driveway. Harvey took out his key ring.

"Check around the back of the house."

Cautiously, Eddie opened the gate and peeked into the back yard. Nothing. He went in and shut the gate. He couldn't see anything unusual. No fresh footprints leading up to the patio door Hawkins had breached two nights ago.

He rounded the house, even though he was wearing dress shoes and sank in three inches of snow. He looked around the corner at the front of the building, then went back the way he'd come.

Harvey had the door unlocked and was standing just inside. The alarm panel wasn't beeping, so he must have shut it off. He nodded toward the bathroom, and Eddie checked it while Harvey headed into the kitchen. They went through the downstairs quietly but thoroughly. Nothing. They went up the stairs with Eddie leading and checked everything up there. Nothing.

Harvey holstered his gun in the upstairs hall-way. "I'll check the attic. You get the basement."

"Really?"

"Eddie, it's not clear if we haven't checked everything."

"Okay, but we beat him here. You know we did."

"Basement." Harvey reached for the pull cord for the attic stairs.

"Yeah." Eddie hurried down the stairway, his eyes darting from side to side. He went to the kitchen, where the cellar door opened between the refrigerator and a pantry cupboard. Mike's basement was all concrete and had small windows at the top of the foundation, two on each side. He had a workbench down there, and an oil furnace. Jars of preserves glistened on a shelf unit. Sharon had made jam that year and canned some green beans. Eddie looked behind the furnace and headed back upstairs.

Harvey met him in the living room. The drapes were closed. The carpet had been removed on that side of the room.

"Is Sarah here yet?" Eddie asked.

"Nope. Twenty more minutes."

"So, what now?"

"We wait." Harvey sat down on the couch and picked up Mike's newspaper.

It was better than sitting outside in a vehicle in the middle of winter. Eddie pulled his gun and sat down in an armchair facing the kitchen and the stairway. He did the check-in with dispatch and told them everything was quiet.

"I forgot to tell Leeanne I talked to John Russell." Harvey glanced at the headlines on the front of the paper. "He'll be at the office tonight if she wants to go over there."

"Great," Eddie said. They sat for five minutes in silence. "I wonder how the funeral's going." He got up and went to the kitchen and looked out the window in the front door and the one over the sink, facing the back yard, then went back to the living room.

Harvey stood by the patio door, peeking out

between the slats of the built-in blind. "Maybe I should call home."

"Do it," Eddie said. "Tell Leeanne I'll take her to see Mr. Russell after we get home."

Harvey took out his phone and called his house. "Hey, gorgeous." He always smiled when he talked to Jennifer, and it made Eddie feel confident just to look at him.

While Harvey talked, Eddie walked to the front window and lifted the edge of the drape with one finger. He couldn't see the unmarked unit, but he might not be able to, depending on where Sarah parked. Probably still too early for it.

Harvey ambled a few steps as he talked. "I have a message for Leeanne. Forgot to tell her I spoke to John Russell. He'll see her tonight around six, if she wants to go over there. Eddie says he'll take her."

Eddie went to the other window and peeked out through the slit where the drapes met.

"Hey, I've got an idea," Harvey said to Jennifer. "Put her on my computer and tell her to start writing up this little adventure. She can take John a sample of her work tonight. I'll brief her when I get home, and she can present the *Press Herald* with an exclusive. Tell her everything I've told you about this case. I'll read it before she takes it in."

He started getting mushy then, and Eddie tried not to listen, but half of him was curious. Harvey was telling her pretty much the same things Eddie had told Leeanne. I love you, we'll come home safe, don't worry. Harvey's eyes were crinkled up at the corners, and he looked happy.

Eddie walked into the kitchen and looked out into the back yard. He jumped back from the window, his adrenaline surging.

He stepped back into the living room, taking great care to stay out of the line of vision from the patio door.

"Harvey," he whispered.

Chapter 30

Harvey was just putting away his phone. Eddie pointed toward the back wall of the house. Harvey took out his gun.

"How many?"

"Just one. I think it's him, but I didn't get a good look."

"I'll call dispatch. Did he see you?"

Eddie shook his head.

Harvey flattened himself against the wall beside a bookcase while he made a very quiet call. Eddie crouched down at the side of the stairs, below where Hawkins's bullet had hit the wall a couple of nights ago.

Eddie's phone vibrated, and he took it out. As he looked at the screen and read "SARAH," he heard a faint noise from the kitchen. He looked at Harvey.

Harvey nodded. He'd heard it too.

Eddie clicked twice to hang up on Sarah and sent her a frantic text. "AH at back door." He hoped she and the rookie were within striking distance and she hadn't called to say they'd be late. He pocketed the phone as he heard the back kitchen door swing open.

The alarm didn't ring. Eddie looked at Harvey.

He gave a thumbs-up. So, he hadn't rearmed it. Okay.

Eddie's heart pounded. He made himself take a slow breath. He and Harvey both aimed their weapons toward the kitchen.

Before Eddie got a visual, Harvey tensed and aimed his weapon. At the same moment, the front door crashed open and a gun fired.

Eddie jumped up behind Harvey, aiming toward the kitchen. Hawkins had left the back door open, and the rookie officer charged in through it. Hawkins was in the middle of the kitchen, aiming at the figure in the front doorway. He fired again. Sarah flew backward onto the steps, her arms splayed.

Harvey was one step ahead, blocking Eddie's line of fire, but two more shots crashed out almost together.

Eddie stepped around Harvey. His ears rang. Al Hawkins lay on the kitchen floor. Blood had splattered everywhere.

Harvey looked at Sarah's partner, the rookie. "You okay, Officer?"

The young woman nodded, her face white. Harvey had his phone out.

Eddie ran past the fallen intruder. Sarah lay on the steps, both hands to her chest, gasping. Her pistol lay beside her, where she'd dropped it.

"Sarah! You hit?"

"It's okay," she puffed out.

She had her vest on, and Eddie took a deep breath. He holstered his gun and sat down beside her. "Breathe, *mon amie*." He knew it could be serious. Harvey had suffered a similar injury the previous year, when he'd landed hard and cracked some ribs.

Eddie put his hands on Sarah's shoulders and looked into her brown eyes. "*Ça va*? You all right?"

She nodded, still pulling in fast, shallow breaths.

"Do you hurt?" Eddie asked.

She shook her head. She reached up and cupped her hand to his cheek for a moment. "I'm good. Go do your job."

Eddie rose slowly. Harvey came to the doorway. "Everything okay? Sarah, do you need medical?"

"No, Captain. Just had the wind knocked out of me. Thanks."

Harvey eyed her critically and nodded. "Okay. I asked for an ambulance, but Hawkins won't need it. We'll have the EMTs take a look at you."

"How's Debbie?" Sarah asked.

"Officer Higgins is fine."

Harvey went back inside, and Eddie followed him. What Harvey hadn't told Sarah was that the rookie was losing her lunch in the kitchen sink. Eddie looked down at the corpse.

"You both hit him?"

Harvey gritted his teeth. "Afraid so. I think my bullet got him in the chest."

"Natch." Harvey wouldn't blow half a guy's head off. That had to be Higgins's shot.

Eddie wished they could clean up the kitchen for Sharon, but they had to leave everything the way it was.

He went over to stand beside Higgins.

"Hey, you gonna be all right?"

She snatched a paper towel from the rack beside the sink and blotted her face. "Yeah. Thanks."

Within minutes, a dozen more cops arrived.

Harvey took a call from Charlie Doran, then one from Mike.

"What did the chief say?" Eddie asked when he'd hung up.

"He wanted to know what you were up to, when he told you to stay off field work until your hearing."

Eddie's jaw dropped. "We couldn't help it."

Harvey smiled and clapped him on the shoulder. "He knows that. Just be glad you didn't have to shoot Hawkins again."

Eddie went outside and found Sarah sitting on the back of the ambulance. Jeff Wainthrop was inside, handing a bottle of water down to his partner. Mark Johnson, stethoscope in hand, gave it to Sarah.

"Okay, rest up tonight," Mark said to her. "You've got some bruises, and you'll probably feel like garbage in the morning. Take some ibuprofen as needed. Are you on duty tomorrow?"

Sarah shook her head.

"Okay. Take it easy."

Sarah glanced up and saw Eddie. She reached to fasten the top two buttons of her uniform.

"Stand up slow," Mark said. "You might be a little wobbly."

Sarah stood and smiled. "I'm fine now."

"Her partner is the one who's probably wobbly," Eddie said.

"Debbie shot the creep, didn't she?" Sarah asked.

Eddie made a face. "Yeah, she and Harvey both. A bit of overkill. She tossed her cookies after."

"I did too, my first time. I'd better go find her," Sarah said.

"Why don't you stay out here? I'll bring her outside. You don't need to go back in there."

Sarah hesitated then nodded. "Thanks, Eddie. Guess we should protect the scene."

"Right." He went to the front door and met Harvey coming out with his hand on Debbie Higgins's arm.

"Okay?" Harvey asked her. "Just hold the railing and go slow down the steps."

"Hey," Eddie said. "Mark and Jeff will take a look at her."

"Good." Harvey gave Debbie a reassuring

smile. "Let's have the EMTs give you a quick check, Officer."

"I—I'm okay, Captain."

"I know you are, but people can have a delayed reaction the first time. I don't want you folding up on me when the chief gets here."

"He's coming now?" Debbie's eyes darted about in panic.

"Well, this is his house," Eddie said.

Harvey patted her shoulder. "I asked the sergeant to have the protective detail keep Mr. and Mrs. Browning away for a couple of hours, but I know the chief pretty well, and I'll be surprised if they can keep him caged that long."

They were nearly to the ambulance. Harvey nodded at his brother-in-law. "Hi, Jeff. This is officer Higgins. She's just gone through her first shooting, and I thought maybe you guys could give her a place to sit and some juice or something."

"Sure," Jeff said.

Sarah came to her. "You did good, Debbie. Isn't that right, Captain Larson?"

Harvey nodded. "She sure did."

Jeff and Sarah led Debbie toward the ambulance.

"Did she really?" Eddie asked softly.

"Yeah."

"She could have hit you."

"No, I wasn't in her line of fire," Harvey said.

"She didn't exactly hit the central body mass."

"No, but everything was moving pretty fast, and she saw Hawkins let one off on Sarah."

Eddie nodded, wondering what he'd have done in Debbie's place. His shot would have been cleaner, but just as sure.

"Poor Sharon."

Harvey pulled in a deep breath. "Yeah, it's a mess. And it looks like we both get to chat with Dr. Slidell next week. Us and Debbie Higgins."

Eddie drove to the police station while Harvey talked on the phone. After telling Jennifer they were safe and that he loved her immensely, he talked to Leeanne almost the whole trip, giving her details to work into her story about the take-down of Al Hawkins. He gave most of the credit to Higgins.

When they got to the office, Harvey went into overdrive. Briefing, evidence, paperwork. He hardly took a breath for over an hour, but went from one task to another, seemingly by instinct, knowing what had to be done next.

At four o'clock Eddie told him, "You need to read Leeanne's story before I take her to the paper."

"Have her upload it to me here."

Eddie called the Larsons' house, and Jennifer answered.

"You guys going to be here for supper?" she asked.

"Harvey might be late. I'll pick Leeanne up at 5:30 and take her to the *Press Herald*. Harv wants her to upload her article so he can read it here."

"Okay, I think she's got a couple more questions."

Leeanne came on the phone and asked Eddie for some background information. He filled her in, and she said she would email the story to Harvey.

Eddie went to the breakroom and got a candy bar for Harvey. When he reached his friend's desk, Harvey was laughing.

"Just brought in my e-mail," he said.

Eddie looked at his monitor. On the screen, a cartoon baby was waving his arms and saying, "Goo-goo! Thanks for eating lunch and catching the bad guys, Daddy!"

"Jennifer's project this afternoon," he said.

"Well, at least she wasn't sitting home crying her eyes out and biting her nails." Eddie held out the candy bar.

"What's this?"

"If you're going to be late for supper, you need something to keep you going in between."

He ate it as he read quickly through Leeanne's story, making a few minor changes and adding a line or two to the background section. Then he printed it out.

"Better go get her and take her to her appointment." He handed Eddie the pages.

"Jennifer's hoping you'll be home for supper," Eddie said.

Harvey looked at his watch. "Could you tell her I'll be home at six?"

"This is official?"

"You got it. Tell her I expect candlelight and soft music."

"Does that mean I should keep Leeanne out for the evening?"

"Oh, you two are coming back?" Harvey laughed. "Take her someplace fancy." He pulled out his wallet and handed Eddie four twenties.

"You don't need to—"

"I know," Harvey said peevishly. "This is a personal favor you're doing me. Don't come home until at least ten o'clock, okay?"

"What if Peter brings Abby home?"

"I'll bribe him, too, and tell him to take her back out."

"Okay." Eddie picked up his jacket.

"Tomorrow's Jennifer's birthday," Harvey said.

"Is it? I knew it was coming right up."

"Well, it's here, and tomorrow is Sunday, so I won't get a chance to romance her in private."

Eddie smiled. As always, he had Harvey's back.

Leeanne was ready. She had borrowed a tailored trouser suit from Jennifer, very businesslike. Her hair brushed her shoulders in soft waves. No matter how she felt inside, she looked confident.

He handed her the folder with her article, and she glanced through it.

"Oh, good, he fixed that," she murmured.

"Harvey will be here by six, and we'll be back at ten or so," Eddie told Jennifer.

"Terrific." She smiled.

"Oh, and he wants candles and soft music."

"Spectacular." Her smile was even bigger.

"He loved your e-mail, and he was purring when I left him," Eddie said. "Load him up with carbohydrates when he walks in the door."

In the truck he told Leeanne, "We're supposed to go out to dinner after. Harvey's orders."

"Really? What's the occasion?"

"Jennifer's birthday tomorrow. He wants the evening alone with her."

She laughed. "He's quite a guy."

"Yup. I thought we'd stop by the mall, too. I don't have a present for Jennifer yet."

At the newspaper building, Eddie sat in a chair in the third-floor hallway while Leeanne talked to John Russell for forty minutes in his glassed-in office. Eddie fought the urge to get up and pace. He figured the protracted interview was a good sign.

Finally she emerged smiling, without the folder.

"How'd it go?" Eddie asked.

"Tell you in a minute." She pushed the button for the elevator.

She waited until the elevator door closed, then

threw her arms around him. "I got it, Eddie! He says I can start the Monday after school lets out. The internship is eight weeks, but he says I can work full time all summer if I want it. And he'll probably hire me after I graduate, if I do well this summer."

"Wow!" Eddie kissed her, and she kissed him back. The elevator door opened and she jumped away from him. A middle-aged man waited while they stepped out into the lobby, then entered the elevator, shaking his head.

"Can't do that around here if I'm going to be an employee," Leeanne whispered. Eddie held her coat for her, grinning, and they went out to his truck.

"So, did he like your story?" he asked, backing out of the parking spot.

"He loved it. I told him Captain Larson had approved it for publication, and his jaw about hit the floor. He asked if I minded if he called Harvey, and I said, 'Please do.' It was so funny! Only I didn't laugh, of course."

"Of course." Eddie smiled. His woman. He put the truck in gear and reached for her hand.

Snowflakes were falling when he took her home at 10:15. Peter and Abby were standing in the breezeway.

"Cold out here," Eddie said. "You two had better come in."

"I didn't know if we were allowed to yet," said Abby. "We came home at seven-thirty, and Harvey made us leave again. We took the boys to their Grandma Hobart's and went to a piano recital at the college. Can you believe it? He kicked us out."

"I believe it," Eddie said. Leeanne opened the door and the four went in, stomping their boots noisily.

Peter and Abby lingered in the entry, but Leeanne took Eddie's hand and forged ahead, through the kitchen and the sunroom. The bedroom door was wide open, so she bypassed that and went into the living room. Harvey was holding Jennifer on the couch, and they looked very cozy. A blaze crackled in the fireplace, and empty glasses sat on the coffee table. Jennifer was wearing her robe, but Harvey had on jeans and a green T-shirt. No shoes on anybody. Jennifer's hair was quite disheveled. Harvey looked positively replete.

"He gave me the internship, no problem." Leeanne rushed over to kiss him on the cheek.

"He sounded quite impressed when he called me," Harvey said.

Jennifer reached out to her. "I'm so glad." She got a kiss, too.

Leeanne grinned. "He thought it was fiction at first, I think."

"It will be on page one tomorrow, in the Sunday

paper." Harvey stretched a little and settled again with his arms around Jennifer.

"Yes, with a *byline*." Leeanne bounced up and down on her toes. "He told me they'll put 'special to the *Sunday Telegram*, by Leeanne Wainthrop.' "

"Your first published credit?" asked Harvey.

"Except for school newspapers."

"Going to be a real reporter," he said. "You'll be good at it. Your article was great."

"Well, it feels pretty good right now. But I didn't have to interview a lot of strangers."

Eddie laughed. "Just the captain of the Priority Unit. If he doesn't intimidate you, nobody should."

"Did you have a nice evening?" Jennifer asked Eddie.

"Yes, very nice, thank you. How about you?"

"Fantastic."

Harvey kissed her hair. "Did I hear Peter?" he asked.

"Yeah, he brought Abby home," Leeanne said.

"I'd better go speak to him." Harvey got up and went into the sunroom calling, "Hey, Peter, about that Blazer . . ."

Eddie said, "Well, I'd better go home. I'll see you all in the morning."

"Goodnight," said Jennifer.

Leeanne went with him to the sunroom. Harvey was talking to Peter and Abby in the kitchen.

Eddie pulled Leeanne toward the patio door, where the others couldn't see them.

"*A demain, ma chérie*." He kissed her tenderly.

Beth brought a huge cake for Jennifer's birthday party, with teddy bears on top and "26" in fancy frosting. Harvey had invited about a million people from church—well, thirty or forty—and Jennifer's family.

Mike and Sharon insisted they were fine despite the previous day's ordeal and showed up bringing a big package wrapped in silver foil paper. Sharon pretended at first to be angry at Harvey for messing up her house again.

"I'm really, truly sorry, Sharon," Harvey said.

Mike arched his eyebrows at him and grimaced. "Next time, you guys do your shooting outside, huh? I don't blame the rookie, but *you, Harvey*—"

Sharon pulled Harvey into a hug. "Don't you worry about it. I'm getting a new living room carpet and new paint in the kitchen. And we stayed at the Hilton last night, so you can't beat that, can you?" She pulled away from him. "Again, we owe our lives to some courageous officers. This city has the best of the best."

"How's Higgins doing today?" Harvey looked to Mike. "Have you spoken to her?"

"Yeah, I gave her a call when we came out

of the service. She'd been to her own church this morning. She sounded very thankful, but subdued."

Abby's gift for her sister was a maternity dress in Jennifer's best color, royal blue. Leeanne and Eddie gave her the book they'd bought the night before—a fat new mystery by her favorite author—and a T-shirt for the baby they'd had imprinted with "Someone in the Priority Unit loves me." Size six months, blue. Mike and Sharon's package held a bread machine. Jennifer's parents had brought her a new coat. Travis and Randy gave her a mobile for the baby's room. Pastor and Mrs. Rowland brought a new game that was the hit of the afternoon. Others from the church gave her baby clothes and small personal items.

Jennifer sparkled while everyone waited on her. Abby and Leeanne served the meal and made her sit chatting with her guests while they cleaned up the kitchen. Jeff came in just as the cake and ice cream were served.

"I'm only here for half an hour," he said. "If my beeper goes off, I'm outta here! Give me some cake."

He kissed Jennifer and gave her a sterling silver chain he and Beth had chosen and then sat happily beside Beth, eating his cake.

No one had said anything about Harvey's gift to his wife, but everyone knew he would present it sooner or later. He read the directions to the new game and declared that he and Jennifer would take on the whole crowd. It was a word game, and Eddie figured they would win, although Leeanne was pretty good with words, and Pastor Rowland was quite a scholar.

The teams were battling it out when the doorbell rang. Leeanne looked out the window.

"It's Peter."

"Oh, he must be here to see Abby," said Jennifer.

Harvey stood and reached for her hand. "No, actually, he's here to see you, gorgeous."

"Me?"

"He's delivering your birthday present."

He helped her up, and they went to the kitchen. The others trailed along to watch. Abby was already opening the door to Peter.

"Happy birthday, Jennifer," Peter said. "It makes me very happy to give you this." He held out a key fob.

Jennifer stared at him. "A car?" She turned to Harvey. "I didn't think you were serious about that."

"Of course I was," said Harvey. "Come on, we'll take it for a test drive."

"Did you kick the tires and check the lights for me?"

"You bet I did."

Abby brought Jennifer's new coat, and Harvey

got his jacket. He took her outside to the new minivan.

"It's got the built-in baby seat and voice-activated GPS." Harvey sounded almost like a kid.

Jennifer looked long and hard at the brand new, red van then threw her arms around his neck.

"You know you shouldn't have." She was crying a little.

"Shh. Yes, I should. Come on." He opened the driver's door for her.

"No, you drive. I can't right now, not with all these people watching."

He took her around to the passenger side and put her in, then went to the driver's door. "We'll be back," he yelled, and they rode away down Van Cleeve Lane.

The party kept on, with Beth refilling punch cups and Abby feeding Peter cake and ice cream. In twenty minutes they were back, and Jennifer looked nearly overwhelmed.

Abby declared she had to leave for work early, as she was dropping Peter off first, and Jeff had to leave, too. The church crowd and Jennifer's parents and brothers all left, and finally it was just Jennifer, Harvey, Leeanne, and Eddie.

Eddie sat on the couch with Leeanne, and Harvey plunked down in a big armchair. Jennifer seemed content to sit on his lap.

"I really should head north," Leeanne said.

473

"Can't you stay tonight?" Jennifer pleaded.

Leeanne shook her head. "My first class is at 7:45 a.m. It's Ethics and Libel, and I need to keep my grades up if I want to keep on impressing John Russell."

"You going to the dorm tonight?" Harvey asked.

"I think so. If I go home, I'll have to get up really early."

"When will I see you again?" Eddie asked. "Can you come down again next week?"

"Maybe. But Mom and Dad will want me to go home sometime. Can you come up?"

Jennifer shifted her weight, making a face.

"You okay?" asked Harvey.

"Your son is kicking the stuffing out of me," she said.

Harvey rubbed her stomach. "Settle down, Connor."

"So it's Connor?" Eddie asked.

"Or Caleb," said Harvey. "What do you think?"

Eddie said, "Connor," but at the same time Leeanne said, "Caleb."

Harvey and Jennifer laughed.

"Need a nap before church, gorgeous?" Harvey asked.

"Only if you'll nap with me," Jennifer said, and he smiled.

Leeanne stood. "I'll say good-bye, so you two can retire." She kissed Jennifer and Harvey.

"Eddie can carry my suitcase out. Thanks for everything this weekend."

"What color do you want your room to be for next summer?" asked Harvey.

"The same room I used this weekend?" she asked.

"Yup."

"It's great the way it is."

"Okay," Harvey said. "I guess you'll want a computer in there, and maybe a file cabinet."

"No, it's great. Don't spend money! I don't think I'll need that stuff at home."

"We'll see," said Harvey. Eddie could tell he was already planning what fun he and Jennifer would have setting up Leeanne's home office. It wasn't that Harvey had such a huge salary, but he'd been single a long time and had invested his savings well. Now he enjoyed using it to make people he loved happy.

Leeanne went upstairs for her luggage, and Eddie carried it to the car while she got her coat, hat, and boots out of the closet. When he went back in, and she was putting on her gloves. He kissed her and held her close. "Drive safely. I need to see you next weekend."

"Come up if you can." They left it at that.

Chapter 31

Eddie wore a suit to work Monday and Tuesday. He was in and out of court, and he spent a lot of time at the district attorney's office, going over the evidence with one of the assistant DA's. By all indications, they would make charges stick on at least five of Hawkins's drug dealers and runners.

He called Leeanne Monday night and emailed or texted her every chance he got. Short, happy messages came back to him, boosting him in the middle of his workdays.

On Tuesday afternoon, his phone vibrated as he left the courthouse from Jordan Quinlan's hearing. He had paused at the bottom of the courthouse steps and put it to his ear.

"Detective Thibodeau."

"Eddie?"

"Yes?"

"It's Lisa."

He hadn't recognized his sister's voice at first.

"What's wrong?" he asked.

"It's Pop."

Eddie's pulse skipped and then raced. "What?"

"His heart, they think. He collapsed at work."

"Where is he? Which hospital?"

476

"No, Eddie. He's dead."

He stood very still, staring at the street without seeing the passing traffic.

"Eddie?"

"Yeah, I'm here. What should I do?"

"Can you come home? I'm here with Maman."

"Yeah, I'll be right there."

He called Harvey, and his friend answered immediately.

"What's up?"

"It's my father. Lisa just called me. He had a heart attack. Just keeled over. Harv, he didn't make it."

"Oh, Eddie, I'm so sorry. Go on. Don't even think about coming back to work today."

"Thanks."

"Take tomorrow if you need it, too," Harvey said. "Just call me later."

Eddie drove across town. It was trash day in the neighborhood, and all the plastic garbage cans stood in a row along the edge of the street. He pulled into the driveway and wondered where Pop's truck was. Probably still at the construction site at the bank.

Lisa met him at the door, red-eyed. Eddie folded her into his arms, and she dissolved in sobs. Eddie patted her back feeling helpless, with tears streaming down his cheeks.

After a couple of minutes, Lisa pulled away, rubbing away tears with her sleeve.

"Sorry."

"No, it's okay." Eddie took out his evidence handkerchief and held it out to her. She took it and wiped her face.

"Where is he?" he asked.

"They took him to the funeral home. Eddie, Maman was here alone. They called and dropped it on her like an anvil and asked her where she wanted him to go."

Fresh tears spilled over Eddie's eyelids. He sniffed. "So, Pelletier's?"

"Where else?"

Of course Maman would use the only French undertaker in the city.

"Did she see him?" he asked.

"No. She called me, and I came right over."

"Where is she?"

"In the bedroom."

Eddie walked through the kitchen and living room with heavy steps. His parents' bedroom door was ajar, and he tapped on the panel then walked in. His mother lay curled up on top of the bedspread, facing the far wall and his father's empty side of the bed. Eddie trudged around the bed and sat down on the edge.

"Maman."

She looked at him with red-rimmed eyes but didn't sit up.

"Edouard."

"Yeah." He touched her hand, and she curled it around his.

"Lisa told you." Her voice quivered.

"Yeah."

She pulled in a ragged breath. "I don't know what to do."

Eddie swallowed hard. "Have you talked to the funeral home?"

"Not yet."

He nodded. "I can call them if you want."

"Thanks."

A painful lump had formed in his throat. "Whatever you need."

"Your Mémé."

"She doesn't know?"

"I couldn't," Maman said. "Her son, Eddie."

He nodded, thinking how his mother would feel if Al Hawkins had killed him last week. She wasn't always happy with him, but she would be desolate if he was ripped away.

"I'll go see her," he said. "She needs to hear it in person, from someone who loves her."

"Yes."

His mother had heard it from a stranger, over the phone. She rolled over and reached for the tissue box on her night stand. She wiped her eyes and blew her nose and then stood cautiously.

Eddie jumped up and strode around the bed, fearful for a few seconds that she might crumple up on him, but she didn't.

"So," she said. "If you'll fix it with Pelletier's, and tell your grandmother."

"Yeah. Does Monique know?"

"Lisa called her. She's coming as soon as she can get a babysitter."

"Okay." Eddie held out his arms to her. "I'm sorry."

She hugged him fiercely for a moment then pulled away. "You're a good boy. Now, go. I need to change. People will come."

He went out into the kitchen. Lisa was texting.

"Who are you telling?"

"My friend Paulette."

"Mémé doesn't know yet, so don't tell too many people."

Lisa scowled at him, and he grabbed the telephone book from the counter. He looked up the funeral home's number and took a deep breath. While he was talking to the owner and assuring him that the family wanted him to take care of his father, Lisa left the room. Eddie gave the barest information and made an appointment for his mother the next morning, when she could settle what she wanted for the casket, the viewing hours, and all the other awful details.

"I'll bring her in at ten o'clock." He hung up the receiver and stood with his hand on the wall phone for about fifteen seconds. His pop was gone.

Trash filled the open kitchen wastebasket to the

brim. Eddie got a clean bag out of the drawer and pulled the full one out of the basket.

"What are you doing?" Lisa stood in the doorway, glaring at him.

"Taking out the trash."

"Our father is dead, and you want to take out the garbage?"

"It's Tuesday. You have to take out the trash. The truck will be here any minute."

"You should be in there holding Maman's hand," Lisa said.

Eddie shook his head. "A lot of people will be coming to the house. You know she'd be embarrassed if the garbage was overflowing and they saw it."

"Fine. Have it your way."

"Thanks. I will."

Lisa's scowl deepened. She looked like she had fifteen years ago, when bickering was one of their daily pastimes. "*Tu es bête.*"

"*Tais-toi,*" Eddie snapped.

"What are you two arguing about?" Maman stood behind Lisa, looking in at him.

"Nothing." Eddie felt guilty to his toes. "I was just going to take out the trash on my way to see Mémé."

"Good. Lisa, you can make a cake."

"What?" Lisa stared at her.

"We'll need cake. And lots of coffee."

Eddie picked up the bag of trash and went out.

The garbage truck was coming down the street, and he hurried to put the Thibodeaus' green trash can out at the curb.

He got in his pickup and started the engine. His thoughts were all over the place, and he wondered if he ought to drive. He felt disoriented, as though he'd been drinking all day, but without the headache.

God, help me with my Mémé. And help me to get there in one piece. I don't know how to tell her. Please, can you show me what to say?

He breathed out slowly and put the truck in gear.

When he got to the retirement home, he walked past the front desk and headed for her hallway, but he glanced into the lounge on his way past. His grandmother sat in there with three other oldsters, sipping wine and talking in French. Eddie stood in the doorway for a moment, gathering his courage.

She looked up and saw him. A huge smile burst across her face.

"Edouard Jean! Look, Estelle, it's my grand-son."

"Oh, what a handsome young man," her friend said.

Eddie stepped forward, still uncertain.

Mémé's smile faded. "What? Why are you here? You never come on a weekday. *Mignon,*

482

what?" She looked terrified by the time he reached her.

Eddie went to his knees beside her. "*Je le regrette, Mémé. C'est Papa.*"

"*Non!*" She peered at him with glistening eyes. "*Il est . . . mort?*"

Eddie nodded.

"*Non, non!*" She sagged against him, and Eddie held her in his arms. "*Mon Paul. Mon enfant.*"

Her friends made sympathetic sounds and rose slowly. They shuffled out of the room. Estelle patted Eddie's shoulder as she passed him. They were alone, and his grandmother continued to weep.

Eddie called the house, and Monique answered the phone.

"Hey," he said softly. "Mémé wants to come. What should I do?"

"Well, yeah, she should probably be here," Monique said.

"She wants to stay over."

"No," Monique said firmly. "Maman can't take care of her overnight. You can bring her, but one of us will have to take her back after supper."

"Okay." He hung up, his heart heavy. "Come on, Mémé. Do you need to get anything from your room?"

"My nightdress—"

"No," Eddie said gently. "I'll bring you back

here later. Maman can't have you stay. I'm sorry."

Mémé sat still for a moment. "My purse, then."

"Of course. *Allons.*" He helped her up.

On the way to the house, she was quiet, but as they turned onto the family's street, she looked over at him.

"Did he have last rites?"

"I don't know," Eddie said. But he knew. At least, he was pretty sure there hadn't been time.

A black Lincoln was parked at the curb outside the house. When they walked in, Lisa met them in the kitchen. The air smelled of fresh-baked cake. Lisa hugged her grandmother and took her coat.

"Come on in, Mémé. Father Claude is here. He's talking to Maman about the funeral."

Mémé walked with tiny steps beside Lisa into the living room.

Eddie didn't think he could face the priest at that moment. He hesitated and went outside. All the trash cans were empty, with the lids hanging down to the side. He went and got his parents' and took it to the garage. Then he leaned against his truck and called Leeanne.

"Hi," she said, bright and a little breathless.

"Are you in class?"

"No, I just got out. I'm walking back to the dorm."

"Okay."

"What's going on?" she asked. "Have you been to court?"

"Uh, yeah." Eddie blinked. Court seemed years ago. "I . . . *Chérie* . . ."

"What?" Her voice took on a wary, urgent tone.

"It's my Pop. He . . . he had a heart attack." Eddie's head ached as the tears swelled once more.

"Oh, baby, no." She said it so tenderly, he closed his eyes and imagined she was beside him. "I'm so sorry. Tell me."

"He's gone. Just like that."

"Oh, sweetheart. I'll come down."

Relief washed over him. "Would you?"

"Yes. Yes, of course."

"You should stay in school."

"Not if you need me."

He pulled in a deep breath. "Wait until I find out when the funeral is, okay? I'm taking Maman to talk to them tomorrow. I'll call you then."

"All right," Leeanne said. "But I could come tonight."

"No. Do your homework and go to class in the morning. What time are you free?"

"My last class ends at 2:15 tomorrow."

"I'll call you then."

"Yes. I love you, and I'll pray for you. All of you." Her tenderness made him feel worse.

"*Merci, ma belle. Je t'aime.*" He closed the

485

connection and took a couple of deep breaths then called Harvey.

"How's it going, buddy?" Harvey asked.

"It's hard."

"Yeah." Harvey paused. "I'm praying for you. I hope you don't mind, but I told Mike and Jack."

"No, that's okay."

"They're praying, too."

"Thanks." Eddie swallowed hard. "I had to call the undertaker and go tell my Mémé."

"I'm sorry."

"Oldest son, you know?" It came with duties.

"Yeah," Harvey said. "And only son at that. I understand."

Eddie blew out a big breath. "The priest is here."

"What, at your mother's house?"

Already, it was his mother's house, not his parents'. Eddie's chest tightened. "Yeah. Father Claude. The one who . . ."

"I remember."

"He's in there now with my mother and my grandmother, and he's probably telling them my pop didn't get the last rites, and he's probably . . . Oh, man. I don't think I can go in there while he's here. Maman's going to want him to do the funeral."

"You can't do anything about it, Eddie," Harvey said. "You don't want to upset your family now.

God knows what you're going through. Don't let the priest upset you."

"Okay. You pray."

"I will. Do you want me to come over?"

"No. You've got so much to do. I mean, Maman thinks a lot of you, but I don't think it's the best time right now."

"Sure."

"And Leeanne's coming down. Maybe tomorrow. I've got to tell her when we set the funeral time, and she'll at least be here for that."

"I'm glad," Harvey said. "Hang in there, Eddie."

"Yeah."

"You'll probably want to stay with your mother tonight, but come over to our place any time, any hour, if you just need to get away from it. I know families can be . . ."

"Yeah," Eddie said. "They can."

Father Claude came out of the house as Eddie put his phone in his pocket.

"Edouard."

Eddie nodded, not trusting himself to speak.

The priest eyed him for a moment. "I guess you will come to the church this time. I'm very sorry about your father."

Eddie opened his mouth and closed it. Father Claude walked past him, got in the black car, and drove slowly away. Eddie took a few deep breaths and turned to the house.

Lisa was in the kitchen. Eddie shut the door and unzipped his jacket.

"Hey."

"Hey," she said.

"I'm sorry I told you to shut up."

Her face scrunched up like a squeezed-out sponge. "I shouldn't have called you stupid."

Eddie took the first step, and she met him in front of the refrigerator.

"Aw, Eddie what are we going to do without Pop?" Her words were muffled against his chest. She was probably crying all over his best courthouse necktie, but he held her and let her sob.

He went the next morning to Harvey's, arriving a little earlier than their running time. Harvey didn't have his shoes on when he opened the door, and Eddie waited while he put them on. They stretched a little in the house and went out and ran in the crisp January air. As he sucked it into his lungs, Eddie thought what a fragile thing life was.

After two miles, he slowed to a walk. His nose was running, and all the crying he'd done made it so he couldn't breathe as well as he normally did. Harvey walked beside him back to his house, and they went in and sat in the kitchen. Jennifer had made coffee, and the three of them prayed together.

It was nearly seven o'clock.

"I should go home and shower and get ready to take Maman to the funeral parlor. Are you sure you don't need me today?" Eddie half hoped Harvey would tell him to go to work.

"No. Do what you need to. Oh, and Mike said they'll postpone your hearing until next week."

That hurt. "It was supposed to be today."

"Yeah."

"You mean, I'll be suspended longer?"

Harvey shook his head. "I don't think so. Take the rest of the week if you want to, and whenever you feel like it, come to the office. I'll give you some computer work until Mike or the board or whoever needs to signs off on you."

"Are you working?"

"Yeah. Mike said he couldn't get by without me this week, but it's desk work only."

"What about Higgins?" Eddie asked.

"She's on administrative leave, but they're going to try to meet tomorrow, on her case and mine. If Mike can get them to push yours through at the same time, he will."

"Without me there?"

"Extenuating circumstances, pal."

Eddie nodded. If he didn't have to face the inquiry panel, that would make his life a smidgen easier.

Jennifer reached over and squeezed his hand. "Is there anything we can do for you, Eddie?"

He shook his head.

"You tell us when the visiting hours will be."

"I will. Maman would probably like it if you both come. Mémé, too. They're fans of Harvey's, you know."

"They're not still mad at me?" he asked.

"I don't think so." Eddie's family had blamed Harvey when Eddie left their church, but they still liked him.

Jennifer said softly, "Harvey told me that the priest came around."

"Yeah." Eddie grimaced. "He's doing the funeral Mass. I was hoping it would be at the funeral home, but my mother wants it at the church."

"Well, I'm not sure this will help," Jennifer said, "but there's something I read yesterday that made me think of you, Eddie."

"I need all the help I can get."

Jennifer smiled. "I don't know if I'm taking it right, but it's in the Old Testament, telling about one of the prophets. Have you heard of a man called Naaman?"

Eddie shook his head.

"Well, he went to the prophet to get healed from his leprosy. And after he was healed, he asked a question. Hold on a sec."

She dashed into the sunroom.

Eddie looked at Harvey.

"I have no idea what she's talking about," Harvey said.

"If Jennifer says it, she probably thinks it's important."

"Yeah."

She came back carrying her rose-colored Bible. "Here it is. Elisha was the prophet, and when Naaman was healed, he went back to thank Elisha, and he told him he wouldn't worship any idols from then on. But then he said when his master, who was the king of Syria, went to the idol temple, Naaman had to go with him. He was expected to, I guess." She looked down at the Bible. "And Naaman said, 'When I bow myself in the house of Rimmon, the Lord pardon your servant in this matter.' And Elisha told him, 'Go in peace.' You see?"

Eddie shook his head.

"I think it means God would forgive him for going to the idol temple with his master, because God knew his heart. It's not the same as what you're going through, but . . . Well, it's saying God knows your heart."

Eddie thought about that. "Okay." He smiled and leaned down to kiss her cheek. "Thank you. I'll remember that when my mother starts in about the funeral."

Chapter 32

Eddie went to the office the next morning. Harvey stood when he saw him and met him between the stairway door and his desk.

"How are you doing?"

"Okay. Better, in fact."

"Good. Visiting hours are tonight?"

Eddie nodded. "And Leeanne is coming after her last class today."

"She called us. I'm glad."

"Yeah. She said she could take cuts tomorrow and stay until Sunday. So the funeral is Friday at one, and they can't do the graveyard until May." Spring burials were standard in the land of long winters with frozen ground.

"The other guys and I will be there tonight and at the service," Harvey said. "And let us know when they do the burial, and we'll try to come for that, too."

"Thanks." Eddie blinked hard. "Man, every time I think I'm okay, something hits me, you know?"

"Yeah, I do."

Eddie nodded. Harvey would know.

"Can I stay here today?"

"Are you sure you want to?" Harvey asked.

"Yeah. Yesterday was . . . well, it wasn't fun,

but you know, I had to do that stuff. Help my mother."

"Sure."

"She wanted to see him."

"How was that?"

Eddie hesitated and glanced at Harvey. "I thought I was going to pass out."

"I'm sorry."

"It didn't look like him."

Harvey squeezed his shoulder. "I'll find you something to do. They're letting Jordan Quinlan off, and Misty, too, unless the D.A. can make a drug charge stick on her."

Eddie was glad he'd changed the subject. "I think it's right that they're letting Jordan walk. Those sleeping pills didn't kill his brother, and he wasn't even the one who gave them to him."

"No. Kyle made the decision to take a whopping dose of cocaine on top of it."

Eddie nodded. "Jordan still should've told Mike."

"Yeah."

Eddie and Harvey walked to the coffeemaker while they talked. Nate was fixing himself a mugful.

"Eddie, welcome back. Sorry about your dad."

"Thanks. Hey, they're keeping Rooster Bentley, aren't they?"

"Oh, yeah," Nate said. "He's staying put for a long time."

"Melanie Tucker, too," Harvey said. "Turns out she was one of Hawkins's main distributers. We squeezed the others from the crack house, and they started talking."

"Good. How's the chief?"

"He's okay. Sharon asked if they could see Dr. Slidell together."

"She volunteered to see the shrink?" Eddie frowned at him. "Who *wants* to do that?"

"She thought it would help them both," Harvey said. "Of course, Mike didn't want to, but she told him she needs it, so they're going to have a few sessions."

"Wow. Next time I want to do the impossible, I'm calling Sharon."

Harvey laughed. "Bring your coffee. I've got a computer case you can work on."

Leeanne was a little nervous when she walked into the funeral home with Harvey and Jennifer that evening. At least fifty people milled around in the large outer room. A line had formed for those wanting to sign the guest book and go in to view the body and greet the family.

Jennifer signed for herself and Harvey and handed Leeanne the pen.

"Do you want us to go in and tell Eddie you're here?"

"Would you?"

"Of course." Jennifer hugged her. While

Leeanne bent over the guest book, her sister and Harvey moved on with the line. After she signed, Leeanne squeezed between people and found a spot where she could stand out of the way.

Eddie surprised her by coming from a different direction.

"Hey."

She turned toward him and took in his careworn features, still handsome enough to turn heads, his impeccable charcoal suit, and his gleaming brown eyes. She held out both hands, and he took them and pulled her toward him. He stood there in front of all those people, many of whom had known him since he was in diapers, clinging to her. She desperately hoped she wouldn't embarrass him in any way.

"Yo, Eddie!"

"Dave." Eddie let go of Leeanne and shook a man's hand. He looked sort of familiar, and a lot like Eddie.

"My cousin," Eddie said in an aside.

"Oh, right."

Eddie greeted Dave's wife and a couple more people then whispered in her ear, "There's another room. Let's go in there."

He pulled her by the hand down a hallway and into a large room full of chairs that were empty at the moment. At the other end, a casket was set up.

"Who's that?" Leeanne asked, her breath a little labored. "That's not—"

"No, that's some other guy whose service is later. I figured nobody would bother us in here right now."

He bent to kiss her, and Leeanne felt a bit odd, knowing there was a corpse in the room. She shivered.

Eddie pulled away and looked at her. "Okay, this is creepy, I guess."

"A little."

"Come on, we can go in the back way to where Maman and my sisters are. But I'll warn you, they're sitting up close to my pop."

"I think I can handle it," Leeanne said.

"Good, because every time I look at him, I get kinda wobbly."

"Oh, *cheri*." She hugged him close.

"It's stupid," he said. "I've seen all kinds of mangled bodies. Last week we had a really bad one at Mike's, and it didn't bother me as much as this. I mean, Pop hasn't got a mark on him."

"But he's your pop."

"Yeah." He held her a while longer and then took a deep breath. "Okay, you ready?"

"Yes. Are you?"

"Yeah, let's do it." He led her around to the lesser-used door to the viewing room, and they came in between the first row of chairs and the casket. Leeanne concentrated on his mother, who sat in the chair nearest the center aisle with Eddie's grandmother beside her.

"Leeanne, dear," said his mother, rising to embrace her.

"I'm so sorry, Marie." Leeanne looked into her haggard face. No makeup could hide the ravages of grief.

"I'm so glad you could come down. Such a comfort to Eddie, I'm sure."

"Thank you," Leeanne choked out.

His Mémé held out her wrinkled hand. "Thank you for coming."

Leeanne nodded. *"Ce n'est rien.* I'm so sorry about Paul."

"Have you looked at him?"

"Not really," Leeanne confessed.

"Go and look," Mémé said. "They did a nice job."

Leeanne looked up at Eddie.

He took her hand. "It's okay."

He led her over to the casket. Harvey and Jennifer were standing nearby, talking quietly with Eddie's cousin Rene and his wife and one of the police sergeants. Leeanne swallowed hard and looked down at Mr. Thibodeau's face. Eddie was right. It didn't look like his father. Not really. All the cantankerous life was drained out of his features.

Eddie squeezed her hand and whispered, "Tell her he looks good, if you can."

She nodded.

They went back to Mémé's chair.

"He looks very handsome," Leeanne said.

"Eh, not bad. But Eddie got his looks from his mother."

Leeanne smiled. "Or maybe from you?"

Mémé waved a hand, but she smiled. "You like his tie?"

"Oh, yes," Leeanne glanced back at the body to see what color it was.

"Marie picked it out."

Next to her, Monique stood and reached toward Leeanne.

"Thanks for coming, Leeanne. I know it means a lot to Eddie to have you here."

"Thank you." She shook hands with Monique's husband, Wyatt Fortier. Lisa pulled her in for a kiss on each cheek, the French way. Leeanne quickly overcame her surprise and gave Lisa a little squeeze. Eddie had told her on the phone that he and Lisa had fought rather bitterly the day their father died, but had made up later on.

"I'm glad you're here," Lisa said. "You make my brother happy. Anyone can see that."

"Thank you." Leeanne decided to take a chance. "He told me about the trashcan."

"Oh." Lisa's eyes widened.

"And that you made a really good cake that day."

"He said that?"

Leeanne nodded.

Lisa gave a little laugh and then darted a self-conscious glance around her. Her eyes brimmed with tears. "I made Pop's favorite."

Leeanne hugged her again. "It's going to get better."

"Yeah. Nowhere to go but up from where I'm sitting."

Eddie's arm slid around Leeanne's waist. He winked at Lisa and led Leeanne over to where Jennifer and Harvey stood.

"Hey," Jennifer said softly, giving her a quick appraisal. "Are you okay?"

"Yeah."

"Then get ready to meet about a hundred cousins." Jennifer smiled up at Eddie. "I know you're dying to show off Leeanne."

"A party would have been better, but this will do," Eddie said.

Leeanne took a deep breath. He was going to be all right. "Which is the one who crashed Jennifer's wedding?" she asked.

Eddie and his mother got to the church early on Friday. Maman had insisted on having the funeral at the church, even though Pop had attended only when he couldn't get away with skipping. Eddie wished he could have gone to fetch Leeanne, but some things had to be done a certain way today to please Maman. His job was to drive her and

Mémé, and Leeanne would come with her own family.

The funeral director and the priest talked to his mother about details. Leeanne was one of the first to arrive, and Eddie walked down the aisle to meet her and her sisters.

"Come see Maman?"

"Sure." She walked with him toward his mother.

"Leeanne, you sit with us," Marie said firmly.

Leeanne looked back at Abby and Jennifer, and they nodded and found seats several rows back.

"Thank you." She took Marie's hand. Eddie breathed, realizing he'd feared she would refuse.

His mother smiled wearily. "I think you'll be around for a long time. Someday I'll tell you how much we all appreciate that."

"Not today," Leeanne said. "Just think about Paul today."

Marie squeezed her hand. "You're a good girl."

Eddie led her to the front row. His mother had fully accepted Leeanne. He couldn't think about that now, but his pain was lighter.

Monique and Lisa and their husbands came in, with all the children scrubbed clean and dressed up special. They filled the second row. Leeanne stood up with Eddie and turned around to talk to them. She hugged his sisters over the back of her chair. Although Leeanne appeared to be poised, Eddie knew she was nervous. She greeted Lisa in flawless French and Monique in sincere English.

Harvey came in a few minutes later with Tony, Nate, and Jimmy. To Eddie's surprise, Mike and Sharon followed and sat halfway back, with the detectives.

As the church filled, he swiveled once to look at all the people who had come to honor his father. Seeing Pastor Rowland seated near Harvey and Jennifer shocked Eddie.

"The pastor came," he whispered to Leeanne.

"That's nice of him," she said.

Eddie nodded, the weight lifting even more.

"You're surprised?" Leeanne whispered.

"Yeah. I didn't think he would come here."

"He's here for you, Eddie."

He felt tears starting again and fumbled for his handkerchief.

They sat through the service, and it was short and sad. When Father Claude got up, Eddie kept thinking about the man with leprosy whose heart God knew. Go in peace.

He hardly heard the priest's words, but when people got up and told stories about his pop, he listened and held Leeanne's hand tight. Monique read a poem, and Lisa got up and choked out a story about when Pop had worked overtime to buy her a bike. There was no way Eddie could get up and say anything.

Then the people came forward from the back, row by row, to take a last look at the body and say how sorry they were. Eddie was surprised

at how many cops turned out. All of the construction crew was there, and a contingent of
Pop's drinking buddies. A scattered few people
came from the Baptist church.

Afterward, Eddie had to go to his mother's
house. There was no getting around it. All of
the cousins and their wives, the aunts, and the
neighbors, had brought food. The cops and the
Baptists stayed away from that gathering, but
Harvey, Jennifer, and Abby came.

People talked and caught up on old times. Once
in a while, laughter would break out, then be
quickly stifled as the laugher remembered it was
a sad occasion.

Leeanne stayed at his side, and everyone came
to meet her. Eddie's large extended family filled
the kitchen, the dining room, the living room, and
even the little entry hallway. Leeanne was kissed
dozens of times and asked the same questions
over and over. Where did she live, how long had
she known Eddie, what was she studying, and
were they getting married? Amazing how brazen
his cousins could be.

She blushed scarlet the first time anyone asked
her if they were engaged, and Eddie told Cousin
Michel's wife, "Not yet." That seemed to satisfy
her.

Leeanne gave him a sideways look, but after
that, when people asked, she would just say no.

Harvey and Jennifer stayed an hour or so, and

Eddie saw Harvey talking earnestly to his mother and his Mémé. Jennifer and Abby helped serve food with Eddie's sisters, until his mother made Jennifer and Lisa sit down.

"Expectant mothers should not be on their feet so much." Maman drafted two of the girl cousins to take over.

Abby came by with a tray of wine glasses and soft drinks. Eddie grabbed a bottle of Pepsi, and Leeanne took one of water.

"Thanks, Gabby Sis," Eddie said.

Abby scrunched her eyes at him. "BFF, Eddie. You need anything, we gotcha covered."

He looked at Leeanne and smiled. "I'm good."

That night, Eddie took Leeanne back to Harvey's and enjoyed the peace in their home. There were still people at his mother's. He'd made Wyatt promise to take Mémé home.

Harvey and Jennifer sat with them a while, then left them in the living room alone when Harvey's sister Rita called. Rita's family was planning to come up from New Hampshire to visit them soon for a weekend. Harvey went to the bedroom, and Jennifer got on the phone in the kitchen so they could both talk to her.

Eddie put his arms around Leeanne and pulled her against his shoulder. They had already settled that Eddie would go to Skowhegan the next weekend if his mother didn't need him.

"*Je t'aime*," he said.

"*Je t'aime aussi*."

"Leeanne, I can hardly wait until you're down here all the time."

"Soon."

"Yeah. I wish we had some kind of—well, do we have an understanding, as they used to say?"

"Oh, Eddie, I don't know as we're ready for that."

"When will you know?"

"Well, I think, maybe—"

He leaned over and kissed her softly. "Your birthday's in March, isn't it?"

"Yes."

"You'll be twenty-one."

"Yes."

"Will you be ready then?"

"Maybe."

"Well, be prepared," he said. "I want to put a sign on you that says, 'Eddie's girl,' or 'future Mrs. Thibodeau,' or something."

"Eddie—is this a proposal?" Leeanne pushed away, and her eyes flickered.

"No," he said, kicking himself mentally. "You'll know when it is."

He only intended to do it once in his life, and he wanted to do it right. Maybe Harvey would give him some pointers for that.

"Should I . . . have a talk with your father

before your birthday? Or is Harvey the accepted watchdog? Because I've already—"

She looked expectantly at him. "Already what?"

"Oh, you know, told him a few of my thoughts."

Her gaze turned solemn. "I guess Dad deserves a show of respect."

"No big deal."

"Really?"

"Well, not too big," Eddie said. "I might sweat a little, but we're doing things the old-fashioned way."

"And I appreciate that." She smiled, the kind of smile that made him feel the drawbridge was down and they'd soon be over the moat.

Harvey walked into the room with his cell phone in his hand.

"I'm going out. Just got a call, but you stay here, Eddie."

Eddie pulled away from Leeanne and sat up straighter. "What, a new case? I'll go with you."

"No, you're still on leave. Stay put, or you'll get us both in trouble."

"Okay. Is it bad?"

"Bad enough. Nate and Tony are meeting me there."

They heard Jennifer go with him to the door, and then it closed.

"Wow," Leeanne said. "So, that's what it's like."

"Yeah. It's exactly like that." Eddie watched her face.

Jennifer came in and gave them a bleak smile.

"So, you had to cut short the conversation with Rita," Eddie said.

"Yes, but we'd settled the details of the trip."

Leeanne looked to her sister. "Is there anything we can do? I feel kind of—well, useless. Do you feel that way when Harvey gets called in at night?"

Jennifer sat down in the rocking chair. "Sometimes, but you're not useless."

"What can I do?"

"Pray for the guys on the scene, and for the victims and their families."

Leeanne nodded. "That's a good thought."

"It helps me not to focus on me," Jennifer said. "It's a lot easier to keep from being afraid if you think about other people's needs."

"Can we pray right now?" Eddie said.

Jennifer smiled at him. "Sure."

When they finished a few minutes later, Eddie rose.

"It's getting late. I guess I'd better head out."

"Come back tomorrow," Jennifer said.

"Thanks, I will." As if he would stay away when Leeanne was here. But he would check in on his mother and Mémé first.

Leeanne walked with him to the entry, and Eddie put on his coat.

"Call me in the night if you can't sleep," he said.

Leeanne nodded gravely. "Thanks. I'm going to keep in mind what Jennifer said. Still, I feel a little guilty knowing Harvey's out there dealing with bad stuff, and we're comfortably at home."

"It's where God wants him tonight."

She nodded, thinking about that for a moment. "You're a smart guy, you know it?"

Eddie stooped to kiss her. "*Je te verrai demain.*" I'll see you tomorrow.

"*Nous serons ensemble,*" she replied. We'll be together.

He smiled. "Just keep talking about the two of us in the future tense." That earned him another kiss.

Questions for Book 4, *Heartbreaker Hero*

1. Eddie's French-Canadian background and family have a profound influence on him. How is Eddie different because of it? What concessions does he make to his roots?

2. Eddie has had many romantic relationships, but Leeanne Wainthrop throws him for a loop. Eddie is sure he's ready to settle down, but his past reputation as a flirt and a heartbreaker keeps Leeanne on edge. Is his recent conversion enough to counterbalance that? Should he have to prove his intentions?

3. Kyle Quinlan is an acquaintance of the Browning family. When he's found dead, Mike volunteers to go and break the news to his parents. How would you tell a friend horrible news? Is it better coming from a friend or from a stranger in an official capacity?

4. Mike is more worried about his grandchildren's safety than his own. Should the family have moved its holiday celebration to another location? What else might they do to ensure security?

5. Eddie's sister Monique insists her children speak only English. She's seen how speaking French hurt her father, and recent studies have shown that Franco-Americans with French-sounding surnames have historically not advanced as far in career fields as their counterparts with more English-sounding names. What advice would you give her? What about Leeanne, who is somewhat fascinated with Eddie's heritage and might marry a man with a very French-sounding name?

6. Eddie is very tense when Father Claude comes around. He wants to get out of there as fast as possible. Is this something he'll have to deal with for the rest of his life? How can he avoid future confrontations, or should he avoid them? How can he reconcile his upbringing with the new path he's taken?

7. Eddie is thrown into the limelight after his rescue of a child. He tries to ignore the social media posts and throws away phone messages. How could he handle this embarrassing publicity better? What should he say to his mother when she tells him, "*That's* my son, the good one. The one saving little children, not the one making girls cry"?

8. Sarah does Eddie a big favor at Mike's request. Do you think everything she said is genuine? Is she still in love with Eddie? What should Eddie do?

9. Eddie's troubled relationship with his father has deteriorated since Eddie was saved. His pop doesn't even want to talk to him, and Eddie doesn't know how to handle the family tension. Harvey gives him some advice now and then, but what else could Eddie do to build bridges with his parents?

10. Is Eddie really ready to get married, even at 28? What wisdom can you share with him? How about Leeanne? Should she wait a while? Should she accept him as he is and love him, or should she run the other way?

About the Author

Susan Page Davis is the author of more than seventy published novels. She's a two-time winner of the Inspirational Readers' Choice Award and the Will Rogers Medallion, and also a winner of the Carol Award and a finalist in the WILLA Literary Awards. A Maine native, she now lives in Kentucky. Visit her website at: www.susanpagedavis.com, where you can see all her books, sign up for her occasional newsletter, and read a short story on her romance page. If you liked this book, please consider writing a review and posting it on Amazon, Goodreads, or the venue of your choice.

Find Susan at:
Website: www.susanpagedavis.com
Twitter: @SusanPageDavis
Facebook: https://www.facebook
.com/susanpagedavisauthor
Sign up for Susan's occasional newsletter at
https://madmimi.com/signups/118177/join

Books are produced in the United States using U.S.-based materials

Books are printed using a revolutionary new process called THINKtech™ that lowers energy usage by 70% and increases overall quality

Books are durable and flexible because of Smyth-sewing

Paper is sourced using environmentally responsible foresting methods and the paper is acid-free

Center Point Large Print
600 Brooks Road / PO Box 1
Thorndike, ME 04986-0001 USA

(207) 568-3717

US & Canada:
1 800 929-9108
www.centerpointlargeprint.com